REBEL'S RAPTURE

Also by Pamela Windsor
Forsaking All Others
At Passion's Tide

REBEL'S RAPTURE

PAMELA WINDSOR

CUTTING EDGE

ISBN-13: 978-1-957868-09-7

Published by
Cutting Edge Books
PO Box 8212
Calabasas, CA 91372
www.cuttingedgebooks.com

REBEL'S RAPTURE

CHAPTER ONE

M ARINA VALERIAN knew it was wrong. It was wrong to be in the arms of one man while thinking of another. Especially when she had no love for either. Especially when one was merely a device to avenge herself upon the other. But there were times when one was driven to do the wrong things for the right reasons. And it was more than right—it was imperative that she return to the *palazzo* a violated woman.

A half-moon filtered a weak light through the lone, cracked window of the ramshackle hut. She turned her head to look up at the young man who lay next to her on the coarse blankets thrown on the splintered wood floor. Her eyes lingered on Gilbert Tosti's trusting young face. He was the same age as she, nineteen, yet so much younger in every way except the one that had brought her to the hut. He had never been outside his little Neapolitan fishing village of San Angelita and had read little and seen less. The shores of the Tyrrhenian sea had been his boundaries, while she had traveled and studied in half a dozen countries. For all her nineteen years Marina was a woman of the world, save for that one way, and even that ignorance she intended to dispel tonight.

Gilbert Tosti was a young man without guile or pretensions, awed that she lay beside him in the dark of the little shack. It had been easy to convince Gilbert that an attraction between the high-born ward of the all-powerful Count Gamborelli and a simple fisherman's son was one of those rare passions that simply happen. To make him fall in love with her had been as easy as picking grapes from the vines. From the time she was fifteen

1

she had flowered with the lusciousness of the rich olive groves of Terracina and had quickly learned how covetously men stared at her ripe young body. The art of flirtation came naturally to Marina Valerian, just as her striking beauty came without effort, needing neither powder nor wigs, beauty marks nor corsets.

Arousing desire in the men around her had been effortless and amusing. But now, with Gilbert Tosti, from whom she had expected animal lust and covetousness, she'd found the last thing she'd wanted, a kind of reverential awe the peasants called *rispete*—the respect given to the one loved and honored, and Gilbert was overcome with it. How frustratingly wrong and infuriating. She'd often watched the lusty young men of the province, like stallions eager to bed any passing maiden in the nearest haystack. It was in their eyes, their words, and their blood. That was perfectly all right, of course, as long as the girls were not above their own station. That was considered desire, as though desire and respect couldn't go together. Rejecting that foolishness, she pulled Gilbert's face down to her.

She'd worn a loose-bodiced gown which, with but a small wriggle of her shoulders, freed her young, full breasts to rise upward without confinement. She heard Gilbert Tosti's muffled groan of pleasure, his lips soft against her skin, moving and seeking. She felt her own response, purely animal, yet too strong to deny. Maybe this was the moment that would sweep all else away, a time of pure desire to trample all other feelings. She'd not stop now. Lord, no. She'd planned too carefully for this moment. She'd hold him as though she really were a lover and take whatever pleasure the moment would return. Gilbert was not without beauty; his young, supple body felt good to her touch and his spirit was infused with a tenderness for which she was grateful.

She was arching her back, pressing her breasts upward, and summoning up reservoirs of determination when she suddenly felt Gilbert's lips pull away and heard his strangled gasp of anguish. Her eyes opened to focus on his deep, dark gaze.

"It is not right this way," he stammered. "Not for you, Marina Valerian, not for one such as you."

Marina kept her lips from turning down in anger, tightened her hands upon his broad, young shoulders, saw him shake his head in painful emphasis. She reached up, took his face in her hands. "But it *is* right, Gilbert," she whispered.

His unlined face grew serious, a frown pressing down over his brows as he stared at her. "Perhaps," he murmured, "perhaps it is so. But I think perhaps it is different with us."

"No! Let it be as it is, Gilbert," Marina urged.

His arms pulled her to him. "Oh, *mia cara*, you must love me as I do you or you would not be here beside me, not you who have everything," the young fisherman murmured.

Marina let her silence seem like agreement while she tried to force away the bitter wave of guilt that was the price of her determination. Coupling with Gilbert had not burst into her mind that day when she'd first watched him pulling fishing nets from the boat onto the wharf. It had been there, gathering itself gradually, and when she saw the young man it had suddenly taken on direction. The rest had been easy enough. At first flattered by her attention Gilbert had happily entered into the clandestine trysts and nighttime rendezvous and had fallen quickly and deeply in love. He feared her uncle and guardian, Count Gamborelli, as did most everyone in the region, but she had convinced Gilbert that when the time came she'd handle everything smoothly. The time had come and now, once again, she reached up to Gilbert in reassurance with her lips.

The distant sound of a bell drifted into the hut and she felt Gilbert grow tense. "Time already," he said. "You must go." Concern and protectiveness filled his voice. She was glad he could not see the chagrin in her eyes at another meeting wasted.

But she did have to go. The secret meetings had to be timed to the instant, while Buffo, the stableman, was at his cottage for a few hours. The clandestine encounters were surrounded by danger—too much danger to go on indefinitely. "I can't continue like this, Gilbert," she told him. "I go back to my bed burning, too full of wanting. Next time you must have me, my darling. Have me or I can't go on seeing you. It is too much for me this way."

He was no longer surprised at her boldness. She had made him believe it was not boldness at all but a fierce passion she could neither deny nor contain. "I know," he murmured in understanding. "I know. Next time, *mia cara*, I promise. I cannot hold back any longer either. Tomorrow night."

"No, it cannot be tomorrow night, or the night after. My guardian gives a ball for my betrothal, and I must prepare. It must be Friday night," Marina breathed.

"Yes, Friday night," Gilbert Tosti assented. He helped her to her feet and watched as she bent forward to slip her breasts back into the deep bodice of her dress. *Friday night*, she repeated to herself, repressing a smile of satisfaction. He had promised and she knew Gilbert well enough to know he had not done so lightly. It would be fitting in its own way, the night after the grand ball. She would have her own surprise for her guardian.

Picking up the heavy brown muslin cape, she put it on with one quick motion, drawing the hood over her head, then slipped from the shack. She hurried around to the rear of the hut, where Orion, her favorite hunter, waited. The big chestnut gelding tossed his head as she appeared and she rested a hand on his snout to stifle a whinny of greeting. Swinging up into the saddle, she took the horse up the incline into the trees, moving at a slow walk so no sound of hoofbeats disturbed the silent dark.

Marina moved through the cedars away from the shore and threaded her way through the woods. A long sigh escaped her as it did each night she left Gilbert Tosti in the little hut and a certain grimness settled over the patrician beauty of her features. Shame surged through her again and she felt remorse. It was wrong, yet whom was she actually wronging most?

Gilbert? He would get over it in time. It would be a hurt that youth and time would absorb until he looked back at the episode with pride. Her uncle and guardian, the Count Aldo Gamborelli? That esteemed wretch deserved more punishment than she could ever mete out to him. No, it was herself she was wronging most.

"Some choices are not choices at all, old friend," Marina whispered to the gelding and his ears twitched at her voice. She ran her hand along the velvet-smooth fur of his neck and she thought at once of Gilbert's smooth, young flesh. If only it could happen for itself, for the right reasons...

Maybe one day it would, she reflected. Maybe one day she would know arms that were not substitute arms and lips that were not surrogate lips. Too much pulsating desire smoldered inside her to be denied. There would come a time, with the right place and person, when she'd not turn away but give herself completely.

The low cedar branches loomed up, marking the edge of her estate. *Her* estate, she thought with mockery—not if her uncle had his way. Like the magnificent gardens of laurel, rhododendron, and manicured hedges, and like the stables of championship hunters, the kennels of prize mastiffs, greyhounds, and harriers, Marina was but one more part of the estate, to be sold for the best price it could bring. She was heiress and mistress of the great villa in name only, mistress by leave of her guardian, the Count Aldo Gamborelli. Marina Valerian's eyes narrowed as she reined the horse to a halt and slid to the ground. "Guardian" and "owner" were interchangable terms to her uncle, but not to her, as Count Aldo Gamborelli would soon be moved to realize.

Holding the bridle in one hand, Marina moved forward on foot, staying inside the deepest shadows at the edge of the trees, circling around to the rear of the stables. From the kennels, one of the dogs—a mastiff—barked deep and low and the girl hurried the horse into the stable, leading him down to his stall at the far end. A lone lantern hanging on the wall sent a fitful light flickering across the stall as Marina unbuckled the girth and lifted the saddle of fine, hand-tooled Venetian leather. Unbridling the horse, she hung everything in place in the tack room and hurried out of the stables, once again using the rear gate.

Her brown-caped figure moved silently along the hedges, then slipped into the great villa, hurrying up the dark wood stairs and along the thickly carpeted hallway to her room at the head of the corridor. As she entered, a girl as tall as Marina but thinner and flatter of figure rose from one of the rose-colored brocade chairs. Marina removed the brown cape and handed it to her. "Thank you, Felice. I think only one more night—Friday."

The girl's smile was soft. "I don't mind, *signorina*. It is nice to sit here in your room and dream." Despite the protest in Marina's eyes, she curtsied and quietly left.

Felice, who doubled as personal maid and servant girl, was from a family of tenant farmers trying to subsist on the count's land while paying his usurious rents. Since the beginning of Marina's secret trysts with Gilbert, she had worn the girl's plain, brown cape as a disguise. Felice had assumed there was a secret lover but had not dared to pry and Marina had not explained any further.

Marina went to the dresser along one wall. The top was white marble and the rest was polished cherry wood inlaid with ebony that formed a laurel-leaf pattern on each of the three doors. She took the silver-handled hairbrush and drew it vigorously through her full, luxurious, jet-black hair. Unbuttoning the dress, she let it fall to the floor and did the same with her chemise and the small cinch at her waist. Free of clothing, she stretched, drawing a deep breath. Naked, she always felt improperly wanton and sometimes wondered what it would be like to just run out into the summer night and join the wood nymphs of stone in the garden.

The gold-framed circular mirror on the wall reflected a girl with the voluptuous figure of a goddess with hair like an onyx halo framing her face. But it was not the shimmering, vibrant black hair that made Marina Valerian so strikingly beautiful. In this land many young girls had lovely jet tresses. Most, however, had softly olive skin, while Marina had skin of almost alabaster white, in the daylight touched with the glow of rose petals, a heritage, along with her dark-blue eyes, from her English mother. Her aquiline, patrician nose and high cheekbones echoed the Roman handsomeness of her father.

Marina turned to the painting of a woman that hung near the dresser, very much her image, seated beside the standing figure of a handsome, black-haired man with intense, ebony eyes and in the uniform of the Neapolitan cavalry. When Marina was eleven, her beloved mama and papa were killed when their carriage overturned and plunged down the side of a cliff near Amalfi. Aldo Gamborelli had become her legal guardian but her schooling had been provided for from a special fund beyond his reach. She'd been sent to the finest of schools in Florence, Paris, and London and given the best private tutors. She had absorbed everything from mathematics to drawing-room etiquette to awareness that the privileged seemed to possess a natural insensitivity to the plight of the less fortunate.

Thoughts of the privilege of rank brought her back to the present. When it was all finished and she'd outmaneuvered Aldo Gamborelli by making herself unmarriageable, she'd find a way to make it up to Gilbert, as she would to Felice and to all the people Gamborelli was oppressing. Until then, she'd do whatever she had to.

She stepped into the bath chamber where the tub, standing free on short, gold-lacquered feet, had been filled by Felice. She sank down into the water's warm caress and felt herself slowly relax. She stayed in the tub with eyes half closed till the water cooled, then rose and dried herself with the thick blue-and-gold towel, hurried to the enormous bed, and crawled under silken sheets. She knew she was risking all her comforts in refusing to go along with her guardian's plans and she would miss them bitterly. Comfort was an opiate, and all good things were subtle thieves that robbed the will. She closed her eyes, slept, and waited for Friday.

The early summer sun had already flooded the high-ceilinged rooms when Marina came downstairs. She had pulled her jet-black hair back, tied it with a simple ribbon, and put on a simple cotton work smock with a deep V at the neck. The spacious parlor fairly glowed with reflected gold, the tall French windows leading to the *terrazzo,* had been opened, to admit the best of the morning sun. The room and the main reception salon adjoining it had been designed by Ludovic Caracci and frescoed in the grand manner with scenes of the Greek huntress Diana and her court of near-nude, lithe maidens.

Only one thing marred the beauty of the grand parlor this morning and that was the tall, slender figure of Count Aldo Gamborelli standing near the great windows, obviously waiting for her to appear. She made no effort to disguise the contempt in her dark blue eyes, for it was long past time for such minor disguises. Aldo Gamborelli could not help looking covetously at everything that passed before him. He might have been handsome in an elegant, aristocratic fashion if beauty were simply an outer quality. But in the elegance of his features one saw cruelty and his pale blue eyes were as cold as Carrara marble.

"I don't see that you've begun any preparations for the ball tomorrow night," he began icily.

"There's plenty of time. Catherine is waiting for me in the garden," Marina answered off-handedly and saw her guardian's face darken at once.

"Your cousin's been here a month. Her visit is almost over. The ball tomorrow night is far more important. I don't like this waiting till the last minute."

"I don't like any of it," Marina snapped, aware that her dark blue eyes sparkled with the electricity of instant anger. "I don't intend to be on display for His Highness the Duke d'Albatore."

"You know it's the custom for a gentleman of nobility to formally pass upon a young woman before he consents to marry her," Aldo Gamborelli said.

"An obscene custom," Marina snapped. "And as I don't intend to marry that pig in fancy clothes, there's no reason for it at all."

Aldo Gamborelli's anger escalated. "You'll marry him. That's all been arranged. It's the proprieties we must observe."

"Because you say so? Because you've picked him out for me?" Marina flung back.

"Because it's necessary. I've explained that to you," he replied sternly.

"You've explained nothing. All you've done is tell me that the villa, the land, and everything else is in jeopardy and the Duke d'Albatore's wealth is needed," Marina persisted. "I don't know of any bad ventures you've made or of the lands not producing. I've a right to know more about these things."

The count slammed his palm down on the top of a small table. "You've no right to know anything. That's the English in you talking. You're my ward and I can make any marriage arrangements I want to make for you, whether you like it or not."

"We'll see." She spun on her heel and strode past him out of the tall French doors to step outside onto the *terrazzo*. She halted at the low stone wall to let her fury subside, but it was only the flame that subsided—the embers stayed to smolder deep inside her.

Aldo Gamborelli watched Marina as she stalked angrily outside. If her part in his plans weren't so crucial he'd go after her, drag her into a bedroom, and show her something about rights. Her insolent tongue would be tamed soon enough, he consoled himself. The morning had brought yesterday's problems with it. He'd had to eject old Fiduci and his wife from the acreage past the olive grove. The wizened graybeard wasn't up to meeting the new production quotas that had been set, yet he actually expected the count to let him continue living there and working the land. The count shook his head in disgust.

The stupid boy from the Palleses' had interfered with the men sent to turn out Fiduci and his wife. He'd been thoroughly horsewhipped for that, and the entire thing had been an object lesson for all the other tenant farmers. But now it was necessary to find another couple to work the old man's acreage. Aldo Gamborelli sighed.

His glance returned to the girl outside. She'd be one problem less. Marrying her off to d'Albatore had been an inspiration, a solution to all his needs at one stroke. The duke had agreed to the price at once, high as it was, and promised further support. Aldo Gamborelli's lips curled into a tight smile. An inspiration indeed, he reflected. With her marriage, not only would his great plans be set into motion but Marina would also be out of his house. A little longer and he'd have been unable to keep from bedding the sharp-tongued little hoyden, and that, of course, would have destroyed his trump card. It had all worked out for the best. Tomorrow night the formalities would be observed, the Duke d'Albatore would pay homage to tradition, and the agreement would be sealed. Count Aldo Gamborelli tore his eyes from the girl outside and strode from the room.

Marina took a deep breath and stepped from the stones of the terrace toward Catherine's plump figure at the far end of the garden, where she was busy trimming the laurel hedges. Catherine brought her English love of gardening on her yearly visits, though back in Surrey she had nothing to match the formal grandeur of the landscaped gardens of Villa Valerian.

Marina's gaze slowly traveled across the gardens designed a century earlier for her grandfather by the noted landscape architect, Vasanzio, as was the villa itself. They stretched elliptically in carefully pruned rows of laurel and rhododendron hedges backed by cultivated, trimmed cypresses. Openings cut at regular intervals through the hedges allowed light and air to prevent the green walls from overpowering those who strolled in their shadow. It was all as perfectly designed as a cathedral.

But the spot she loved best few knew about, even those who worked and lived at the villa. Beyond the gardens, where the woods rose and weeds and wildflowers sprang up in tangled profusion, a little footpath led through an overgrowth of vines and branches. For those determined enough to follow the almost obscured little path, the woods suddenly fell open to reveal a *giardino segreto*—a tiny, secret garden—in the center of which stood a brass cherub astride a porpoise surrounded by wild carnations. As a little girl Marina had chosen the secret garden as her hiding place and it still served as a private retreat, its existence unknown even to her guardian. She wanted to seek its solace now but she could not, for to walk to it in daylight might lead to its discovery by Gamborelli.

Her thoughts snapped off as she saw her cousin straighten up and wave to her. Marina stepped from the terrace and hurried down steps to the soft carpet of grass. In another two days, Catherine would be on her way back to England, and Marina would miss her. It was good having her cousin for company; it was a distraction that helped pass the tense days.

"Another argument with Aldo?" Catherine asked gently. Marina felt the older girl's gentle, soft consoling touch on her arm. "Maybe you oughtn't to be so against Aldo's ideas," Catherine suggested. "This is too lovely a place for arguments and anger. There's so much beauty here that I envy you for it, Marina. The days are so lush and warm here, especially after the fogs of London. I can't imagine not being content and happy here."

"The mask of Italy." Marina smiled. "But, you know, sometimes I envy *you,* cousin," Marina continued, contemplating Catherine's capacity for acceptance of the status quo.

"Well, I envy you all the time," Catherine's words were wistful. "I repeatedly tell all my English friends about my beautiful

Italian cousin who lives in a *palazzo*. Perhaps you must learn to accept the happiness given to you, Marina."

"I think happiness is something you make for yourself, not something you have to accept," Marina insisted.

Catherine's round-cheeked face retained a hint of persistence. "And you know, Marina, Aldo is under a lot of tension. I heard him only this morning, before you came down, talking heatedly to a visitor."

"What did you overhear that so upset my solicitous guardian?"

The other girl ignored the urgency in her cousin's tone. "One of the tenant farmers, the one with the best horses, was raided again last night."

"The Montevali place?" Marina persisted.

"Yes, that was the name. Fifteen horses were taken. By a band of outlaws in the mountains, I heard Aldo say."

"The Camorrists," Marina murmured. "Led by the one who calls himself the Red Camorra."

"What does the name mean?" Catherine asked.

"A camorra is a loose-sleeved shirt. The Camorrists have taken to wearing these shirts as a kind of uniform," Marina told her.

"Aldo said they were common thieves," Catherine remarked.

"Of course he'd say that. He'd like the explanation to be that simple," Marina snapped.

"Well, then, what are they?" Catherine pressed.

"A secret society who operate not only in Sicily, but in Liguria and as far north as Venezia."

"A secret society for what? For robbery? It's easy to give yourself a daring name to justify common thievery." Catherine sniffed.

"From what I've heard, the Camorrists strike out for ordinary people who've been wronged. They've also set up machinery to settle disputes among the farmers and the village people."

"They make their own laws—above the law of the land? That's treason!" Catherine protested.

"But this is not England, this is Italy, where there's not much law for the ordinary people," Marina pointed out. "When they've a dispute all they can do is take it to the landowner or local lord for him to settle. He charges them for settling it and they usually go away with less than they came with in the first place. I'm told the Camorrists have put an end to that by giving out fair justice to everyone who comes to them."

"You sound as though you're in favor of them," Catherine said, a hint of disapproval in her tone.

Marina thought for a long moment before replying. "I don't know if I am or if I'm not. But it seems to me that the laws oughtn't to be just for the wealthy and powerful. Isn't that what your William Pitt is saying in Parliament right now?" Marina asked.

"Yes, I suppose. But I don't bother with politics," Catherine said, backing from the subject quickly.

Marina linked her arm with the older girl's. "Let's go inside. You can help me start to prepare for tomorrow night," Marina urged her.

"Well, that's better. You do at least intend to do your part in that." Catherine breathed an almost audible sigh of relief.

"Of course," Marina snapped back and then walked on ahead quickly. Her eyes had suddenly flooded with tears of self-pity and she hated herself for the indulgence. Damn her slippery guardian and his blasted betrothal party. And damn the duke, who would examine her closely to see if *she* deserved him! Damn them all, Marina cursed in silent fury. Well, they were going to be greatly surprised when they all found their plans abruptly changed. At long last she'd take their arrogance and hurl it back in their faces.

Halting at the French doors, she looked back and waited for Catherine to catch up to her. "I'm sorry," she apologized to her cousin as Catherine reached her.

"What made you so angry so suddenly? Thinking about tomorrow night?" Catherine queried.

"I suppose so." Marina's abrupt reply cut off further queries. She crossed the parlor and entered the huge salon. The huge room was overembellished in true baroque style with the ceiling ornamented above the great glass chandeliers, the walls covered with stucco, and the lacquered carvings set onto the stones. The ceiling was vaulted and bas-relief columns were spaced along three of the walls, some with doors painted between them on the walls to give the effect of a house within a house. All in all, the salon was a triumph of *trompe l'oeil* architecture. So very Fitting, Marina mused. So much in the Kingdom of Naples deceived the eye.

Marina's dark blue eyes narrowed as she let herself envision the room as it would be filled with the crowd of glittering men and women only a night from now. The count had given her the guest list, which included people he wanted to impress from as far away as Turin and Milan.

"You've all the room in the world here!" Catherine exclaimed.

"Not as much as you'd think. The stone fountain will be brought in and set against the far wall. It always serves as a centerpiece and a punch bowl. It takes up a tremendous amount of space, but it is unique and people love it," Marina said. "Then the tables will take up the sides of the far wall and the musicians will occupy the one corner entirely. There will not be too much space."

"I'm so thrilled about being here for it," Catherine cooed. "My last night here will be marked by a fabulous party. It'll be something to talk about all year back in Surrey."

Marina only nodded. Before she left, Catherine would have a lot more talk to carry back to England.

"Come on, let's start with the china," Marina said to her cousin and led the way to an open-top, carved oak chest. She lifted the top up and backward and Catherine gasped.

"Good heavens, Marina, what a collection," she exclaimed.

"My father's family were connoisseurs."

Marina brought out two round plates, one glazed with a garland of leaves around a pattern of fleur-de-lys. It had a light blue background, gold and deep blue insignia, and dark green leaves. The other majolica plate, in soft yellows, ochers, and blues, depicted a scene from the Bible, that of Joseph and Potiphar's wife. She set it down and took out another plate to put beside it. It was similar in tonality, with a scene of Jesus at Cana painted under the glaze.

Felice entered the room. Marina called to her and gave her the heavy majolica plate. "This set for tomorrow night. If you need more, take the other set from Faenza with the gold borders. Have Carlos take them to the kitchen for you."

The girl nodded and Marina moved to the big wall cupboard nearby. "Now for the crystal," she said, opening the first set of cupboard doors. An array of glasses, goblets, chalices, and decanters greeted her. Some were of sparkling cut glass, some tinted and ornate, others clear and pristine. "What shall it be, the Venetian goblets or the Waterford?" Marina asked.

"It's all so beautiful," Catherine replied helplessly.

"The Venetian crystal is ornate, perhaps too much so for the majolica. They might overwhelm each other. I think the lightness of the Waterford crystal is appropriate," Marina mused aloud. She nodded to Felice standing by and the girl returned the nod. "Now for the linen." Marina pulled open the long, wide drawers at the bottom of the wall cupboard. She chose four matching damask cloths of an uncluttered off-white design.

"You're the floral expert, Catherine." Marina smiled at her cousin. "What flowers shall we have?"

"The red and white carnations in the garden are lovely. Let's have big bunches of them all over," Catherine suggested.

"Have Pietro tend to that," Marina told Felice. The next stop was the kitchen with its heavy black iron kettles hanging from one wall and the brass pots and pans from another. Giacomo, the chef, was there, his hair white but still thick and matched by a full mustache. "Have you prepared a menu, Giacomo?" Marina asked. "I presume the count has told you how many he has invited."

The chef nodded. "*Fritto alla Romana,*" he said.

Marina nodded. "Fried dishes in the Roman style," she translated for Catherine.

"Veal chops *alla paesetto* and *baccalà,*" Giacomo went on. "Salt codfish," Marina explained to Catherine.

"*Carciofini* and *biscotti,*" the chef said.

"Artichoke hearts and cookies," Marina translated. "Enough, with whatever else you prepare to go with it," she said to the chef. "Will you see to the wines? I'd like the Lachrima Christi, the Orvieto, and some Soave for the Tuscans, and, of course, Port, Madeira and Sherry. And don't forget the Armagnac."

"I will see to it," the chef said, and Marina nodded and left the kitchen with Catherine beside her.

"How did you ever learn so much about so many things— the right wines, the china, about balances and good taste? One would think you'd been hostess of a great house for years."

"I spent an entire summer in Paris taking special lessons in those things," Marina replied. "My mother had arranged for that before the accident. She felt it was something one ought to know *before,* not after, marriage." She halted at the side door of the villa. "How about a ride before the afternoon ends?" she suggested.

"Wonderful. I'll change and meet you at the stables," Catherine agreed. Marina watched her go, then sought out Felice for a whispered exchange.

"Same time Friday night," she said, and the girl understood with a motion of her eyes. Marina went to her room, pulled the smock off, and donned her riding habit. She reached the stables first and helped Buffo saddle Orion and the gray mare,

Annabelle. When Catherine arrived Marina was waiting outside with both horses. She led the way on a leisurely canter into the hills, through lemon groves and cool clusters of pine trees. The hills deepened with wildness, tall cypresses standing as though they were sentinels peering down upon the two young women on their mounts. Catherine reined up as they reached a small, rocky protuberance.

"Aren't you afraid, coming up this far?" she wondered apprehensively.

"Of the Camorrists? Maybe I should be, but I'm more curious than afraid. I'd love to see the one they call the Red Camorra," Marina declared.

"Not I," Catherine retorted. "I doubt that he'd show any sympathy to Count Gamborelli's daughter."

"Probably not," Marina conceded. "Perhaps we should start back. It will be getting dark soon. Come, I'll show you another way back past a mountain brook." She patted the hunter and he broke into a trot at once. The wind had suddenly grown chilly and Marina drew her riding coat tighter, glancing back to be sure that her cousin had not fallen too far behind. Catherine was not a natural horsewoman and rode stiffly as though she were on a hobby horse of wood. Catherine was sweet and placid and belonged in a cottage happily sewing samplers, Marina decided. And where did she herself belong? In a few days, she would be with Gilbert in the little fisherman's shack, this time finally to end it. And after that, who could say?

She kicked a heel against the big hunter and sent him into a gallop that would allow the wind to blow thoughts from her mind, as if it were that simple. She halted finally at a clearing and waited for Catherine to catch up to her in the soft gray dusk. It was almost dark when they reached the stables. Buffo took the horses from them and Marina rode to the villa. She found her guardian waiting in the great foyer, which was handsomely tiled in diamonds of red and black.

"I shall not be dining with you this evening," he announced, including Catherine in his statement. "I am joining the sheriff and his men in a hunt for this Red Camorra cutthroat." He paused, but Marina made no comment. His smile was cold as his pale blue eyes found Catherine. "Marina hopes that I do not return from the hunt." He saw the girl start to protest and cut her off. "—If I do not return, the bethrothal will not take place."

He reached out a long arm and took Marina's chin between thumb and forefinger, his expression a caricature of a smile. "But, my dear niece, I *shall* return. You may count on it." His soothing voice was a burlesque of warmth.

Marina struck his fingers away from her face and her eyes blazed. Silently she watched as he went through the big oaken doorway into the new night. She glanced at Catherine and saw her cousin watching her in concern.

"I'm sorry, Catherine, I'm really too angry to eat now," Marina told her. "Giacomo can prepare something just for you, if you don't mind."

Marina brushed cheeks with the older girl, then hurried up to her room, closed the door, and shed the riding habit. She lay down on the bed and let the night air cool her skin, finally pulling the coverlet over herself. She lay still in the darkness of the room and let time tick on. She dozed fitfully, then woke to the sound of the great clock in the foyer below. If only it were Friday night! But it was not, and before she took her proper vengeance she would have much to endure from her guardian and the duke. But the delay was worth waiting for—*well* worth it!

She would be fresh and sparkling, for the ball, at her very best. Once again she vowed to extract her own, private pleasure from showing the Duke d'Albatore what he would not have. Perhaps she would not be there when the moment came, when his own twisted, demeaning standards were flung in his face. Her pleasure had to come in seeing that he would never be able to forget her this night. And she would laugh silently, through tears no one else would see, for the price of victory would be paid out of her own tomorrows. It had to be so. There was always a price.

She slept on her stomach, arms held to her breasts, the silken sheet pulled up over her head as if she were hiding.

Count Aldo Gamborelli poured another glass of Spanish brandy for himself, folded his long frame into a brocaded chair, and allowed a narrow smile of satisfaction to touch his lips. All in all, things were going uncommonly well. Marina would always be a danger until she was a prisoner in the Duke d'Albatore's bed chamber.

She was indeed a luscious package, that one. There was a time when he'd thought about pulling those long, smooth legs around himself, enjoying her screams of protest. As for her infuriating, tempestuous willfulness, the duke was not a man to suffer women with heads full of independent ideas.

It was in her blood, of course—plus too much schooling and too much exposure to the world. Ideas were dangerous things. They could spread like a plague. Consider the news that trickled from France these days. There were all kinds of rumblings. Louis XVI was too damned much of a fool to crack down and too much of a weakling to stand firm against the whims of that sorceress, Marie Antoinette. The secret of power was to crack down hard and fast whenever trouble showed its head. And Marina was trouble.

He sipped on the brandy, scowling as he thought about her. Any other girl would have accepted his explanation entirely, but she kept probing. She seemed to have accepted his story of the villa being lost if money was not found to save it, but she was overly suspicious of how matters had come to such a state and had been furious and demanded an explanation.

How enraged she would be if she knew the real reasons for his bargain with d'Albatore. She'd learn in time, of course, but then it would be too late for her. She'd be the duke's possession and he'd pay her no heed except in the bedroom. It served the little baggage right, the count thought. He had never liked her, not even as a child. She always had that direct, unsettling way of looking at him, as though she knew more about him than she should. He'd watched her grow into the ravishing creature she was now, but that direct, discomforting stare had stayed.

Count Gamborelli's eyes roamed across the great library as he toyed with the brandy snifter, taking in the rich paneling of the walls and the fine carved stone fireplace mantel. The Villa Valerian should be the home of a man of real power and prestige, the head of a new state, he mused idly. It was wrong to leave a house such as this to a slip of a girl, an empty piece of pleasure— to any girl. But this Marina was worse than most. She had her own delusions of power and grandeur, and cleverness was one of them. She'd find out how clever she was. He downed the remaining brandy in the glass and pulled himself to his feet. It was time to go to bed. Tomorrow night would come quickly. It would be a time of concluding arrangements, a most thoroughly enjoyable evening. Perhaps most enjoyable would be watching Marina, knowing how she would be seething inside and, more important, knowing that she could do nothing to destroy his carefully planned arrangements.

The promise of a rare evening of unalloyed pleasure at her pain excited him as he strolled past Marina's doorway to the master bedroom.

CHAPTER TWO

THE GRAND SALON SHIMMERED; it was a sea of color, laughter and, gaiety. The soft sound of the string quintet somehow cut through the hum of voices and the great crystal chandeliers blazed light down upon the men and women who crowded the huge room. Marina, on the lower steps of the stairway, looked across the scene, taking in the resplendent gowns of the ladies and the elegant evening dress of the gentlemen. Extra waiters had been hired, each clothed in deep orange *justaucorps* and black breeches.

The men were colorful enough, many in outfits of gold lamé and brocade with ruffled silk *jabots*. But it was the gowns of the ladies that made the room seem to spin with color. Marina had heard how the "flying shuttle," the new weaving invention by the Englishman John Kay had opened up entirely new material for use by the *marchands des modes,* the dressmaker-designers of France whose products governed fashion throughout the continent and England. Many ladies were wearing the new, printed fabrics by Girtanner of Saint-Gall, some *indienne* cottons from the American islands, and she also spied a few *costumes à la Creole,* styled after the New Orleans fashions of America.

But tradition was well served by the splendid silk gowns with their great *paniers* and low-swept necklines. Catherine had chosen to wear a deep red gown *à la Polonaise,* Marina saw, with panels of varying lengths down the front, *sabot* sleeves, and edged neck collar of white silk. She was dancing furiously with everyone who asked and was thoroughly enjoying herself,

Marina observed. For herself, Marina had chosen a redingote with soft lines, of lemon and cerise stripes and *marinière* sleeves. A band around the neckline emphasized the creamy contours of her breasts.

Her gaze next found Aldo Gamborelli talking to people of wealthy banking interests. She saw his eyes nervously glancing at the tall clock in one corner of the room. Her own lips formed a smile she could not repress. The guest of honor had not arrived. In fact, the Duke d'Albatore was almost an hour late. Already some of the guests had mentioned this and Giacomo had twice come to tell her that dinner was being overcooked.

Marina saw her guardian beckoning to her and she began threading her way across the crowded salon, forced to stop and talk every few steps. The Ambrosinas from Turin wanted to inquire about her health. Carla Tocqueville wanted to gossip. Lady and Baron Summani wanted to tell her how beautiful she looked. The La Broccas from Sicily, in a small circle of Sicilians, wanted to shower her with compliments on the party. Marina put off each bid for her attention as she moved through the crowd, smiling to herself at the passing sentences that trailed her as she went:

"Where are the Cellinis of today? We need a new Renaissance."

"Did you hear about Firenza Tullio and the carriage driver?"

"Napoleon Bonaparte? A second-rate general."

"The Archbishop of Milan refused to go to the Francasi wedding."

"Give me the French designers. They know what to do with a woman's body."

The voices drifted away, and Count Gamborelli's falsely amiable face appeared before her. "I do not understand this. Something must have happened to delay his carriage." His manner exuded charm.

"Perhaps he fell from the coach and broke his neck." Marina smiled back. Her guardian returned her pleasant gaze, although she knew shock and anger were battling within him. "I am going to announce that dinner will be served," Marina said firmly. "I'll not wait any longer." Shock almost won over civility and for an instant Aldo Gamborelli's face seemed about to dissolve into rage.

"No, you cannot. You must wait for the guest of honor. Anything else would be a breach of etiquette," Aldo Gamborelli protested, grasping her arm painfully in an attempt to stay her which would be interpreted by the guests as merely affection.

"I am the hostess. I can do whatever I please." Marina laughed lightly, suddenly enjoying the ball even more than she had expected she would. She turned away and lifted her voice.

"Everyone please enter the dining hall. Dinner will be served now," she called out. A murmur of pleasure swelled as she felt Aldo Gamborelli's hand pressing hard into her flesh.

"Little bitch. What will the duke say when he arrives?" her guardian whispered savagely into her ear as he smiled. "This is an insult."

Marina pulled her arm away and faced the count with her dark blue eyes afire and her voice hardly audible. "Don't ever touch me again, do you understand?" she told him. "I don't care about your duke or about you."

"You will care, you high-class little slut. You will care," the count answered through lips that hardly moved. Marina spun around and strode away from him, following the others into the long, gold-and-cream dining hall where dinner was laid out upon the long tables spaced in parallel rows. No seating arrangements had been planned and the guests chose their own places. She saw Catherine beside Rudolfo Consigna, the young consul from Naples, and the empty chair on her other side. Marina circled the table and sat down at Catherine's side.

"Marvelous, Marina," Catherine whispered. "Everything's been going just beautifully. But everyone's been asking where the guest of honor is."

"I don't know and I only hope he never shows up at all," Marina murmured. She leaned back as one of the waiters set a small tureen of *bisque de homard* before her. She toyed with it, suddenly not hungry, her stomach knotted with hope. Perhaps something had indeed happened to the Duke d'Albatore. Perhaps a last-minute reprieve had been given her. She glanced at the next table where her guardian sat. He was not having his soup either, she noted. The noise of conversation had subsided to a low hum as other dishes were brought in, the wine served, and the artichoke hearts set on each table in large bowls. The main course was next and the guests attacked it hungrily, though, due to the delay, it was indeed overdone.

But she was able to take only a few bites when she saw one of the outside attendants hurry into the room, search out the count, and rush to his table. She read the man's lips as he leaned forward. "The sound of a coach approaching," he announced. Count Gamborelli leaped to his feet, started for the doorway, then paused and beckoned to her. She made no move and saw his eyes grow almost colorless as he came around to where she sat.

"You will greet our guest with me," he informed her politely. She could feel other eyes turning and focusing on her. It was the proper thing to do, of course, and she rose tight-lipped, unwilling to be accused of bad manners. She followed the count outside where two more carriage attendants peered up the road and she heard the sound of galloping hooves close at hand.

"You see, he was simply delayed." Aldo Gamborelli insisted. "You can explain going ahead with dinner without him. It was your doing." Marina said nothing but the knot in her stomach had become a leaden, dispirited weight. There was to be no reprieve. The sound of the hoofbeats were close, and suddenly, from around the slight curve of the road just beyond the villa, the coach appeared, pulled by four horses galloping at top speed. The ornate, top-heavy vehicle bounced and swayed and the shape of a figure was visible at the driver's seat, but no one seemed to slow the racing steeds.

"Catch them, fools," Marina heard the count shout, and the attendants ran out, flinging themselves at the horses' heads, seizing bridles, and clinging to them as they were dragged. The count caught hold of a loose rein, dug his heels into the ground, and sent up twin geysers of dirt as he, too, was dragged forward. Marina watched the horses slow down and saw great clouds of steam rising into the night air from their dilated nostrils. Finally they halted, snorted, backed, and stood still. Marina looked up at the driver. He lay bent over on the seat as though ill but she saw that his wrists and legs were bound. Only then did she see the figure of the footman atop the roof of the carriage, also bound hand and foot. Her eyes dropped to where the count was yanking the door of the coach open.

A figure rolled out and fell to the ground, half against the bottom step of the carriage. He was stark naked and his wrists were bound behind his back. Marina recognized the round, mustached face of the Duke d'Albatore, his eyes wide with embarrassed fury. Her eyes roved down the round, soft-fleshed, porcine little shape, the folds of his Buddha-like jiggling belly, down to the tiny little organ below. He looked, she could not help thinking, like a dissipated Botticelli cherub. He was making angry sounds with his lips—words that would not come out as words—and his eyes fastened on her as she stared at him. The laughter had bubbled to her lips uncontrollably as she was both amused and repelled by the fat, doll-like littly body no longer protected by the flattery of custom-designed clothing.

"Get away from here," she heard the count scream at her as he whisked off his coat and threw it over the duke. She backed up a few paces but did not leave.

"Good God, what happened?" she heard the count ask as he began to untie the Duke d'Albatore's wrists. One of the attendants held the jacket over the guest of honor's midsection as the count worked at the wrist bonds.

"We were attacked on the way here," she heard the duke say as he finally found words. "A cutthroat—he took my money, every jeweled ring I had, and my clothes while six of his rogues stood by. He called himself the Red Camorra."

"*Bastardo!*" Marina heard her guardian swear as the wrist bonds came loose and the duke brought his arms around to clutch the jacket to himself. Marina's guardian turned again, saw her still there, and exploded in rage.

"Get inside, I told you," he screamed. "Tell the other guests that the duke will not be joining the party. Tell them they can leave whenever they wish."

"I'll tell them no such thing," Marina retorted. She cast a last glance at the duke as he was helped to his feet, clutching at the jacket as it almost dropped away from him, his face horror-stricken as he was secreted upstairs by the back steps. Marina turned away and returned to the dining salon, over which a hush had fallen as everyone waited to hear what had happened.

"The duke's carriage was attacked by the Camorrists," she announced. "He was not hurt but he will not be appearing. However, please continue to enjoy yourselves as though nothing had happened."

A murmur of shock and dismay swelled around the room like an unseen runner. In moments Catherine was at her side, her round face sober with concern. "What a terrible thing!" she exclaimed.

"Not terrible enough," Marina answered and ignored the horror in her cousin's eyes. She left Catherine to the attentions of the young consul and drifted from the room. By now the duke would be in the safety of the west-wing guest room and her guardian would be with him, clucking and sympathizing, offering apologies for what had happened. As for the others, they would finish dining and return to the main salon, but the ball would not go on for long, since a cloud had been cast over it. The guests would try to leave in groups, their carriages staying together for safety.

Marina sighed deeply. Perhaps there were no painless victories. Hers still waited for the dark of the little fisherman's hut. The pretending was not finished. She positioned herself near the tall oak-front doors to bid the guests good night. She hadn't long to wait. The Evolis from Bologna were first, followed by a small but hasty procession. Most had left when her guardian appeared, his face drawn and tight.

"You are lucky. I convinced the duke that it was but embarrassment which made you laugh at him beside the carriage," he said.

"And it is but his arrogance which makes him believe you," Marina returned.

"Mind your words, damn you," the count growled. "The duke leaves early in the morning. He wishes to see you tonight. As soon as the last guest has departed, go to the west wing."

Marina considered refusing but decided not to. Too much confidence or resistance on her part might well trigger her guardian's shrewd, distrustful mind. Smoldering anger was enough. Overconfidence was dangerous. She was glad for the interruption of more guests taking leave. Others followed quickly, all with murmurs of sympathy for the unhappy incident. Finally only the servants were left, with Catherine standing at the foot of the stairway.

"I had a wonderful time in spite of everything," Catherine declared. "Is that disgraceful?"

"No, I'm glad you did." Marina laughed. "I'll be down to see you off in the morning."

Catherine leaned forward and kissed her cheek. "Good night, dearest cousin. You'll see. Everything will turn out for the best."

Marina nodded and watched Catherine negotiate the stairway in the voluminous, paniered gown and decided that optimism, like rebellion, must be in the genes also. She turned and made her way to the guest room at the west wing of the villa. The door to the room was open and she heard her guardian's voice from inside. She reached the doorway and halted in its rectangular frame, standing as straight as she could, letting the round swell of her breasts push up over the neckline of the gown.

In a borrowed robe far too large for him, the figure of the Duke d'Albatore seemed even smaller than the caricature of a naked cherub Marina had glimpsed earlier. But, of course, all she could think of was that very scene, of his little round, jiggling belly and the immature folds of skin beneath it. But she saw his eyes, now bright as the buttons on a wax doll, examine her with darting movements. A greedy satisfaction came into the small, brown orbs—an obscene anticipation.

"More beautiful than I'd remembered," she heard him remark, his voice high and nasal. "Come closer, my dear."

Marina stepped into the room and walked to where he sat. He reached a small pudgy hand out to touch her cheek and let it run along the side of her neck, down across her shoulder to the top of her breasts. "Smooth," he murmured. "Very nice. I like a woman with smooth skin."

"I didn't think you'd disapprove," Marina stated crisply. The little man spoke to her guardian without taking his eyes from her.

"You said she had a tart tongue, my dear Aldo," he remarked. "That's of no consequence. I like spirit."

Marina felt her hands opening and her fingers stiffening as the thought of lashing out at the lecherous face before her rose in her mind. His eyes glowed with thoughts of the future and he rose, patting her arm paternally. "I am told you are full of wild notions, my dear," the duke said. He laughed, an unexpected, high-pitched sound. "You are young. I will teach you that there are many roads to romance," he assured her.

"I think you mean pleasure, not romance," Marina snapped back.

The oversized robe lifted loosely as the round form under it shrugged. "Pleasure, romance, they are all words. I concern myself with desires, not with words," the duke replied. He half-turned to her guardian. "You may announce the betrothal. I shall plan an early wedding." His quick glance at Marina flung possession at her. "Yes, an early wedding," he repeated. "Such beauty is a danger. It could be marred by those who neither deserve nor appreciate the subtleties of enjoyment."

Marina felt her cheeks grow red. She knew the duke would view it as modesty. "You may go, Marina," she heard her guardian's cold voice order and she turned at once, forcing herself not to run from the room. She halted in the corridor outside, pressed her eyes closed for a moment, and held back the scream of rage that wanted to erupt from her. She heard the Duke d'Albatore's voice from inside the room.

"I shall have the cardinal officiate, of course," he was saying.

"The cardinal," she heard her uncle echo. "Will he really do that?"

"The cardinal will do whatever I want him to do," the thin, high voice replied. Marina fled down the corridor, past the servants still clearing away things, and up to her room, slamming the door shut behind her. She stood for a moment, trembling in anger. What an arrogant, vile little man, she thought in furious silence. She couldn't imagine a cardinal having anything to do with him, much less be at his command. Yet she had heard that corruption had reached into the Church, some said almost as deeply as before the Reformation. She pushed the thought away. It made her uncomfortable. Besides, she had more than enough wrongs to occupy her thoughts.

She was still more fortunate than most young women who found themselves in the same circumstances, Marina reflected as she began to undress. They would not have their way with her. She had planned and prepared and now was grateful for that more than ever. All the misgivings and the moments of remorse and shame were in the past. Now, there was but tomorrow night. She could do nothing but carry through to the finish. For Gilbert Tosti, there would be passion, pleasure, and love. For her, there would be pretense, victory, and bitterness. A dark triumph indeed.

In the west wing of the villa, the door to the guest room had been closed. Inside, Aldo Gamborelli sat across from the Duke d'Albatore, watching the man's small, brown eyes grow sharp.

"The girl is a bonus, an expensive bonus perhaps, yet essentially that," the count said. "Your funds will not only provide the men we shall need but make you a part of our mutual venture."

"That is what interests me most, of course," the round, robed figure replied. "The news from France has convinced me to go into this thing with you, my dear Gamborelli. The talk of revolt continues to spread. I understand there have been riots in the streets of Paris and of Marseilles."

"And still Louis does nothing," the count murmured.

"Some say that Marie Antoinette runs the country. She certainly runs the King, and that is perhaps the same as running the country."

"It is bad. Revolts spread. They fill the minds of the rabble everywhere," the count said.

"Exactly," the little man agreed, his face darkening with a frown. "Now is the time to move, before trouble can grow. New power, new strength, a consolidation of authority, is the surest way to prevent wild ideas from taking root. Besides, new masters and new conflicts will keep the people's minds occupied with their own troubles."

"Of course, my dear d'Albatore, I count on you to see that Rome does not interfere," Marina's guardian added. "Rome has been frowning on any further expansion."

"Rome is divided. There may be protests, but little more," the duke told him confidently. "You may rest easily on that score."

"Then we are in full agreement. Everything is ready to go forward as soon as the additional funds are in hand," the count said.

"You will have them the morning after I bed your gorgeous little blossom," the high-pitched voice answered, taking on an instant note of anticipation. "A new flower opened, a new venture begun, a fitting combination of events."

Aldo Gamborelli nodded in agreement, a happy combination of events indeed. And only a beginning.

CHAPTER THREE

THE DUKE D' ALBATORE had left in borrowed clothes before she came downstairs and Marina was not unhappy for that. She had no wish to see his lusting, greedy eyes devouring her again.

Cousin Catherine's good-bye was, as always, tearful. Catherine reveled in passing moments, meetings, reunions, good-byes. After successive rounds of hugs and kisses, her cousin's carriage finally left for Naples. Marina watched it roll down the road till only a balloon of dust gave evidence that it had ever been there.

She went into the house and paused at the open door of the study. Her eyes spied the leather-covered ledger open on the roll-top desk. She moved around the desk to the front of it and her eyes ran down the columns of figures on the open pages. The numbers showed the income from the tenant farms, both in tithes and in profit from produce sold. Marina ran a finger down the length of the columns. She saw no losses from any of the farms and a frown dug into her brow. The ledger showed no need to supplement the villa's income properties, no losses to need the Duke d'Albatore's money. Intent upon the figures, she heard nothing until the fist slammed down onto the page before her.

"How dare you? How dare you pry into my ledger?" Count Aldo Gamborelli shouted. He tore the book away from her and Marina felt fear, but for only a moment, as anger rushed to her aid.

"Your ledger? It concern's the villa's lands, the operation of the farms. I've every right to see it," she threw back at him.

"You've no right to anything, do you hear me?" he screamed. "Little bitch." She felt more than saw the stinging slap that smashed against her cheek. "You'll mind your manners with me."

Marina's face reddened, the slap still stinging, and she reached for the ledger, caught hold of one corner of it, and tried to pull it free. She saw Aldo Gamborelli's face contort with fury. He held onto the book, then turned and flung it away where it landed in the open doorway. "Bitch," he hissed again. "Rotten little bitch." His hands reached out and closed around her breasts. She felt his fingers prying and reaching. His lips worked and small sounds came from them. Marina twisted away, beyond his grasping fingers, and reached out to find the base of the hurricane lamp on the desk. She flung it at him with all her strength. The count saw it coming too late. He tried to duck but the base of the lamp caught the edge of his temple and Marina saw the red line break out across his skin.

Her fury exploded and she reached out, grasped a marble pen-holder and flung it after the lamp. "Touch me, hit me, you stinking lecher," she screamed as her guardian fell to one knee when the marble pen-holder caught him on the shoulder. A small brass inkwell came next as Marina, turned tigress with tears of rage blinding her eyes, threw whatever she could lay her hands upon. The inkwell smashed into the wall a fraction of an inch from where Aldo Gamborelli tried to regain his footing. Marina cleared her eyes, picked up a heavy volume on architecture that lay on the table, heaved it at him, and the count fell forward as the book grazed his head. His face pale, he saw Marina pick up a small but solid carved stool. He flung himself through the doorway, into the corridor outside, scooping up the ledger as he ran.

Marina, her breasts rising and falling with each deep draught of air she gasped in, slowly lowered the stool. Her hand came up to touch her cheek, an automatic echo of pain no longer there. "You wait," she panted after the figure that had vanished from sight. "You'll see, you stinking cur." She marched from the study, kicking aside the inkwell on the floor, furious at herself for having let his slap so enrage her. She went to the garden and stayed to prune some of the bushes with Tomasino the gardener to work off her fury before finally returning to her room. The day dragged by on leaden hours but the purple-gray of dusk finally began to lower itself over the tall spears of the cypresses. Marina changed into a simple loose-necked dress with a voluminous skirt, aware of more anticipation than she'd expected.

She didn't bother with the pretense of going to dinner but lit a small lamp and stayed in her room until Felice came to once again hand her the brown cape. "Have you seen the count?" Marina asked the girl.

"I think he is in the study. The door is closed," Felice replied.

"Good," Marina said grimly and pressed the other girl's hand. "Someday I shall make all this up to you, Felice," she promised, then swirled the cape around her and hurried from the room, down the back stairway and into the night. A moon, almost full, hung low, a baleful sentinel as she left the stable on the big chestnut hunter. She hurried the horse through the cedars, down to the little seacoast hut. Gilbert Tosti was waiting in the doorway as she reached the shack, his arms encircling her neck at once and his lips seeking hers with a hunger that surprised her in its intensity.

"Marina, my Marina," Gilbert breathed as he pushed the door closed behind her and pulled her down onto the blankets on the floor. She discarded the cape and arched upward, pressing her breasts up into him. She sought his mouth almost harshly and felt his hands encircle her full breasts. Gilbert's desire was no sham, had never been, and now it reached her, sending out its own sparks. She felt his fingers upon her thighs, caressing, seeking, warm, under the folds of her gown, and suddenly she felt her body responding, his frenzied passion evoking its own answers.

Her lips clung to Gilbert's and she felt her thighs move and part, begin to unfold as a flower unfolds its petals. Desire moved within her as Gilbert's young body pressed down upon hers. She felt his hot flesh sparking her own, and she heard her own soft moan. As Gilbert moved to reach inside her, she moved to welcome him, no more holding back now, surprising herself again with her own eagerness.

He was coming to her now, almost, almost...almost, she felt herself counting the moments, waiting, wanting, burning. The sound that shattered the night was not her own scream of pleasure, not Gilbert's groan of fulfillment. It should have been, but it was something else—unreal, an imagined intrusion. She heard voices, shouts, heavy footsteps, and Gilbert's body was being pulled from hers. "No," she gasped, clinging to him, refusing to let go of the moment of moments that was about to be hers. "No," she gasped again. But he was torn away, and as she opened her eyes she saw the wavering light of torches and behind them shadowed figures. Then hands were yanking her up, the wide skirt falling down to cover her legs. The figures had faces, some of which she recognized, men whom her guardian had used from time to time, and then another face came into view, the thin-cheeked face of Aldo Gamborelli.

"Bitch," she heard him fling at her. "Stinking little slut." Marina blinked. It was some sort of horrible dream, she told herself. The slap that half-turned her head around destroyed that desperate hope. Her eyes sought Gilbert and she saw him held between two men.

"Take them outside," she heard the count order, and she was almost dragged from the shack. A circle of torches lighted the night and she saw Gilbert's frightened face, eyes seeking her, depending on her. She had told him she could handle everything, hadn't she? The count stepped before her, blotting out Gilbert.

"Carry on under my nose, will you? Make your own little arrangements to satisfy your little tramp soul?" he snarled at her, the pale eyes made of ice. He spun around, and pointed at Gilbert.

"Hold his arms out while I put a bullet through his worthless hide," he commanded.

"No," Marina heard her voice cry out. "You can't do that."

"I can do whatever I please," her guardian spat at her. Marina scanned his face to see if he were simply enjoying her fear. But she saw only bloodless stone.

"But it was all my fault," Marina said.

A sound resembling a laugh escaped the man's lips. "I'm quite sure of that," he commented acidly. "But he'll pay for his part in it."

"No, you can't," Marina cried out again. "I began it, pressed it, made it all happen. None of it was his doing. I'm responsible for it, do you understand?"

Aldo Gamborelli's eyes turned on her, round agates of ice. "The flame may attract the moth, but it is the moth who is killed," he hissed.

"Don't, oh, God, no. It wasn't his fault, none of it," Marina repeated. Her eyes met Gilbert's terror-stricken orbs. The count's hand came up and she saw the heavy-barreled pistol in it. The two men pulled Gilbert's arms out from his sides and held him between them. It couldn't be happening, she told herself. It couldn't end this way. The single explosion shattered her thoughts and she watched Gilbert Tosti's young body shudder, twist, and his chest turn red. She heard her voice as though it did not belong to her. *No. No, no, no. Please, no.*

Count Gamborelli's voice cut into her numbed mind. "He'll be an object lesson for any other fool prompted to listen to you," he snarled. Inside her, Marina felt something twist and tear, and felt a terrible sickness engulf her. Hands let her go and she fell forward to her knees, the world spinning away in grayness. Her stomach heaved, great spasms sweeping through her. The grayness parted enough for her to see the still, young body crumpled on the ground. She fell forward into the mercy of nothingness.

She woke only when she was lifted onto Orion. She managed to cling to the saddle horn, bent over and her stomach a hard knot inside her. The world did not seem to exist. There was only pain, a consuming, obliterating guilt that was physical in its impact. And a scene she would carry with her forever. As if in immediate reply the scene flashed through her mind at once, Gilbert's body twisting, shuddering as the bullets struck, then his inert form on the soft beach, all his tomorrows gone.

Marina did not sit up in the saddle till the procession reached the villa. She saw Aldo Gamborelli's straight-backed form on the horse nearest to her and watched him dismount as casually as though he'd come back from a morning canter. She'd never stop hating him, she knew, just as she'd never forget this night of horror. She slid from the horse, almost collapsing on legs that seemed made of water. She walked as in a dream across the *terrazzo* and into the house, her guardian close behind her. Once inside, she found the strength to draw herself up and turn to him, to the colorless eyes that held the smugness of satisfaction.

"I've saved you from your own stupidity," Aldo Gamborelli said. "You are too shortsighted for your own good. Had you succeeded tonight, you'd have ruined yourself beyond even your far-fetched dreams of freedom. No man, not even a peasant, would have accepted you at all. You'd have simply been used goods, soiled, a whore, and an outcast! Apparently you can't comprehend that fact."

"Maybe I'm just a whore at heart," she said. "Or perhaps I loved Gilbert Tosti passionately. You'll never know anything except one fact. You will pay for Gilbert Tosti's death, you monster."

Marina turned away and stumbled up to her room to sink down upon the big bed. She wanted to cry but felt only a terrible tightness pressing her inward, allowing no tears to give relief. Where did one find tears when the guilt was beyond tears? Aldo Gamborelli had killed Gilbert with his heavy-barreled pistol, but she had indicted the innocent boy with her deceit and selfish determination.

Still moving as if benumbed she pulled herself to her feet, unbuttoned the dress, and let it fall to the floor. Taking a pair of scissors from the dresser, she ripped and cut the garment till it lay in shreds on the floor. Gathering these, she dropped them into the gold-leafed wastebasket in the far corner of the room. Avoiding the mirror, she fell into bed and buried her face in the pillows until sleep finally came to wrap itself around her.

But, like the torn garment, sleep was a shredded thing. The night became a succession of wakings, her breath drawn in deep gasps, sounds that were half-sob and halfscream tearing from her throat. And each time the same picture seared across her mind—Gilbert Tosti's pleading, frightened eyes and then his twisting, shuddering body. Only with dawn did exhaustion come to offer deep sleep.

The room was yellow with sun when Marina woke, bathed and dressed, feeling heavy as though she wore a suit of chain armor. She sat for a long while, staring down at the orderliness of the garden. Only when the distant sound of the church bell drifted through the noon warmth did she stir. The bell was the deep one at the monastery of St. Gregory atop the first hill past Calabritto. Only when the wind blew from the east did the sound carry this far, but it carried this day and not a leaf stirred outside. Marina rose, her deep blue eyes dark with inner pain. The monastery was not for confession. St. Catherine's in San Angelita was the parish church, in the center of Gilbert's village. A far different kind of pilgrimage this time, Marina observed silently as she went downstairs, ignoring Aldo Gamborelli's tall, thin figure by the study door. At the stable, she had Buffo harness the road cart to one of the carriage horses and wheeled down the narrow side road that circled its way to the little fishing village.

Perhaps, at St. Catherine's, some small measure of comfort would wait. She had heard, not too long ago, of the young village girl who'd given herself to a passing soldier. Father Scunigi had banished her from church and village, ordering her to spend two years with the Abbess of Blessed Raphaela in Basilicata. Marina would welcome banishment, she told herself, though the count would no doubt intercede at once to prevent that. But confession, penance, a baring of guilt, those things were suddenly overwhelmingly important. It was a time when there was but one place to turn.

The narrow road led into the south end of the village, where the houses were bathed in brilliant sun, looking baked and almost new. Women with small hand-carts and men carrying nets dotted the street that edged the shore. A small, open-air market was crowded with buyers. But as Marina drove the road cart slowly down the street, she heard the silence fall upon the little village. Eyes found her, heads turned to stare with hard, accusing eyes. As she passed a trio of women she heard the epithet flung at her: "Whore!" Another followed: "Deceiver! Harlot of death." Marina did not move but kept her eyes straight ahead, catching only the glimpse of small boys when the rock flew to strike her shoulder. A heavier followed, crashing against the side of the cart. The horse started to buck and Marina pulled back on the bit and steadied the animal.

"Did you come to mourn?" she heard a woman call from behind her. "Do you seek more victims for your lies?" another voice flung out at her. "Haven't you done enough here?" The shouts faded away and a last, small stone struck her between the shoulder blades. She hurt too much inside for such outer pain to bother.

The steeple of the church rose up at the end of the village, and Marina halted the road cart outside the open door of the church and tied the horse to a hitching post. She went into the dimness of the church, halting to let her eyes grow accustomed to the change from the bright sunlight outside. The little church was cool and silent, with statues of the saints adorning every niche—a touch of the Sicilian in the architect. She heard the soft scuffle of sandals and turned to see Father Scunigi approach, hands folded in front of the black cassock, the knotted cord hanging from his waist. He was a round-faced man with fleshy lips and short hair cut in a style approaching a monk's circle. Father Scunigi nodded and smiled at her, then reached out to pat her arm.

"Marina, my dear. An unexpected pleasure," he said. Father Scunigi had a fawning quality which always bothered her, but he was the sole priest in the small parish.

"I want you to hear my confession, Father," Marina requested, unsmiling. Father Scunigi nodded, his round face calm, then waved one hand to gesture to the confessional booth. Marina stepped into the booth, waited as he went into the other side, and then seated herself before the mesh screen. As she searched for a way to begin, she heard the quiet words from the other side of the screen. "Tell me how the tragic events of last night began, my dear, Marina," the priest said. "Tell me your part."

Marina took a deep breath and let the words rush from her as they wanted, as if they had their own will. "It was my fault," she began. "I led him on, I involved him. Gilbert's death was my fault. I used him for my own purposes. His death is on my soul."

She paused, then heard Father Scunigi coax her on. "You must tell me details, everything, all about your secret meetings. You must tell me how you felt each time. Intent is very important. Forgiveness may lie in places you do not suspect," he murmured.

Marina drew in another breath and began from the first meeting she had had with Gilbert Tosti. She did not hold back, refusing to spare herself. This was no place for a parade of small omissions to soothe the conscience. Finally she came to an end. It had been a sorry litany of wrongs, the very telling turning her stomach into knots. Father Scunigi was silent for a long moment, then his voice came to her quiet and calm.

"You are to say twenty Hail Marys each day for a month and make a Novena to our Blessed Mother starting next Tuesday,"

Marina heard the priest say. She waited, but there was nothing more. The frown rippled across her forehead.

"Is that all?" she asked finally.

"You must not blame yourself too much, Marina," Father Scunigi replied. "You could not foresee such a tragic ending."

"I didn't care, don't you understand? I didn't want to think about what might happen," Marina protested. "If I hadn't led Gilbert on, he would be alive now."

"We are not here to question the strange ways in which the Lord's will is done, my dear," the priest replied. Marina felt her temper spiral.

"The Lord's will had nothing to do with this. Only my uncaring selfishness," she snapped.

"You must not be too hard on yourself, Marina. Gilbert, God rest his soul, was a young man old enough to know right from wrong," Father Scunigi intoned. Marina shot to her feet, pushed the small confessional door open, and stepped outside, her eyes dark fire as the priest followed her out.

"So did I," she bit out. "What of that girl who laid with the soldier? You banished her," she reminded the priest.

"She was not a young woman of breeding and high birth, of education and sensitivity," Father Scunigi said quietly.

"And so she is treated differently? Right isn't right and wrong isn't wrong no matter who it is?" Marina shot back. Father Scunigi shrugged and started to reply when she cut him off. "She was not the niece of Count Gamborelli," Marina declared.

She saw Father Scunigi's calm expression darken. "You are too upset to reason clearly, my child," he said.

"I reason very clearly. One cannot ignore the power of the parish's most wealthy patron. A double-standard exists in the house of the Lord. What mockery," Marina flung at him. Father Scunigi's round face seemed to take on new folds.

"Only youth can so easily ignore reality," he countered. "The Church must exist in this world."

"No," Marina shot back. "The Church must only stand for right and the word of the Lord. If that means it does not exist, so be it. The cross, not comfort, my dear Father Scunigi."

Marina whirled and almost ran from the church and into the sunlight. She had done the wrong things for the right reasons and learned the price of that. Now she had come to the right place only to hear the wrong answers. As she climbed into the little road cart she found herself remembering a quotation from Isaiah that Brother Justus was fond of repeating. She heard his voice as clearly as if he were beside her: "And judgment is turned away backward and justice standeth afar off." Marina snapped the reins and the horse broke into a gallop as she sent the little cart careening from the end of the village. There were no answers here for her, and she would not accept forgiveness for the wrong reasons. That was no better than deceit for the right reasons.

She turned the little cart onto a steep, winding path that led into the hills. The wind was clean, a good feeling against her skin, and her onyx hair blew out to trail behind her like a wild tiara. She let the horse continue to gallop, turning onto whatever little pathway that came upon his flying hooves. She was not running away. There'd be none of that, she knew. The count had too many in his power for her to find sanctuary and escape. Still, the thought clung. Perhaps there would be a night dark enough and long enough for her to outdistance the pursuit which would certainly follow. Perhaps. Another desperate hope.

She heard the horse breathing hard and pulled back on the reins to slow his headlong gallop to a trot and then a walk. Had he been racing just for the sheer pleasure of it, she wondered, or had he been running in the vain hopes of fleeing the cart and harness which made him a prisoner? To guilt, remorse, pain, and anger Marina added despondency. She let the cart crest a ridge. The cool wind had stopped and the sun beat down upon her and she felt tiny beads of perspiration coating her forehead. The little path suddenly became a crossroads bordered by tall, thick fir trees. Something moved to her right behind a curtain of branches. Marina reined the cart to a halt. A horseman moved into sight, then another from the other side. She heard a sound behind her and whirled in the seat to see a third rider. Each wore the loose-sleeved, open-necked blouse which she recognized at once. The words came from her lips in a half-whisper: "*Camorrists!*"

The horseman nearest bowed his head in agreement. He had a face as lined as tree bark and wore a curling, black mustache. "You have given us quite a ride, Signorina Valerian," he remarked.

"You were following me?" Marina gasped out.

"Not following but riding alongside you through the hills on either side. Ever since you left San Angelita," the man said.

"You were watching for me?" Marina questioned.

The horseman nodded. "Follow me," he ordered abruptly, wheeling his horse in front of the cart. Marina let the cart move behind the rider, aware that the other two horsemen had fallen in behind. The first horseman halted at a small clearing and pointed to it. "Leave the cart here," he told her.

Marina rolled the road cart into the spot, tied the horse to a low branch, and stepped from the seat. "You will go on foot from here," the horseman said. Staying in the saddle, he threaded the horse through narrow openings between large thick-trunked fir trees, finally halting to dismount himself. "We go through the back way," he commented as Marina felt the ground grow steeper, the soil shallower, giving way to rocks and the thin trunks of tamaracks. A narrow defile of rock appeared and Marina followed the man and his horse through it, turning to see that the other two men were tagging along. A soft call sounded, then echoed, and she looked up to see a sentry high atop the rocks.

The defile suddenly opened into a small, grassy knoll. The men who'd brought her there seemed to vanish and she was alone. She moved forward onto the small, grassy place and the figure appeared from one side, a ruby-red camorra first catching her eyes. She moved her glance to the man who wore it, then felt her breath drawn in sharply. Not since the statue of Apollo in Milan had she seen so riveting a man. But the statue was of marble and this man breathed, vibrated, radiated power, warmth, and something more—that indefinable quality people call presence. Thick, black curly hair fell loosely over a leonine head, a strong, straight nose, skin bronzed by the sun, eyes dark as ripe, black olives. Marina watched those black orbs take in the rose-tinted alabaster skin of her face and shoulders and then linger on the deep curve of her breasts. She thought she detected a faint spark of approval in the black eyes.

"I do not have to ask you who you are," Marina said.

"A name given to me by the people," he replied in a voice of soft steel. "It is a convenient alias."

"The Red Camorra," Marina remarked slowly, turning the name on her tongue, savoring it.

"It sounds almost beautiful from your lips," he said. Marina searched for a smile to go with his words but found none.

"You have another name, of course," she probed.

"Generoso della Passione," he said and waited, watching the surprise come into her eyes. "My mother had both a flair for the unusual and a sense of the future," he added.

"Does it fit?" Marina asked. "Are you generous of passion?"

He still did not smile. "Very much," he answered. "I am generous of passion, in love and in hate."

"And in taking what you want?" Marina asked.

"Sometimes," the strong, unsmiling face replied.

"Why did you bring me here? Your men said they'd been waiting and watching for me."

Generoso della Passione came closer, placed one finger under her chin, and lifted gently, his dark eyes examining her critically. "I was told you were most beautiful. I wanted to see for myself," he said.

"Were you told correctly?" Marina returned.

"No. Words do not do justice to your loveliness."

"Don't you ever smile?"

"When it is a time for smiling."

"Then tell me really why you brought me here," Marina pressed. She saw his deep eyes grow smaller and a tightness touch his lips.

"Because you are Gamborelli's niece," he said. "And because of Gilbert Tosti." Marina felt the fear come to stab at her. She searched the olive-black eyes and found no assurances.

"An eye for an eye?" Marina interpreted.

"Nothing so crude as that," the Red Camorra said. "The young fisherman was killed last night to assure your virginity. This is the one, single reason for your value to the count. That is what you are to him, the price you command for him, and that is what I shall destroy."

"You'd strike at him through me."

"I will take away the one thing about you he values above all else. It is the only fitting retaliation for last night," the Red Camorra told her.

"And if I refuse?"

"It will still be done," Generoso della Passione affirmed. "Indeed, I would not expect you to submit willingly to anyone but a man you loved, such as you were about to do last night."

Marina looked away, afraid he would see the thoughts mirrored in her eyes. The world had twisted and turned back upon itself. All that she had planned was to be hers in an entirely unexpected way. The only fitting answer for last night, he had said. If only he knew the real meaning that was to have been last night. But she'd not turn from this reprieve, this second chance for victory. The Genovese had a saying, *Bisogna voltar le vela secondo il vento.* You must shift your sail with the wind. She'd heed their mariners' wisdom.

Marina returned her eyes to the man who watched her. She had to shift her sails, measure up to the image he had of her.

Anything less would make him suspicious. "I will fight you," Marina declared.

"You do as you must. I will do as I must," he replied. He moved toward her. With a quick movement he flung the red camorra off and stood bare-chested before her, bronze skin glistening, shoulders and pectorals smoothly muscled. She watched his hands unbuckle the wide belt as he stepped from the leather trousers to stand before her in only a brief undergarment. Marina let her eyes feast upon his body and could think only of the description of the archangel Michael in the book of Daniel: "Clear as topaz his body was; like the play of lightning shone his face; and like burning crossets his eyes; arms and legs of him with the sheen of bronze."

He reached out and pulled the string that held her blouse at the neck. His hands began to lift the garment. Marina felt her breath growing tight. It was about to happen, all she had planned to have happen, and yet once again it would not be right. A terrible rage exploded within her, all the shattering horror of the night erupting. "No," she cried out. Her hand shot out, smashing into his face. She wanted to stop him—no charade any longer. She wanted to stop him from doing what she wanted to have done. The contradiction was real and clear. She'd no more will to deceive. One man lay dead because of her deceits. Gilbert Tosti deserved more than another deceit in his name, more than another wrong done for the same reasons. "No," she cried out again and clawed with her nails. "You don't understand."

"I understand what has to be done," he said, and she felt herself flung backward onto the grass. She kicked out with one leg but he turned to catch the blow on one muscled thigh, then caught her by the shoulders as she tried to twist away. Her blouse came open and she felt the rush of the cool air over her breasts, saw him pause to let his eyes move across the full, cream-white softness. She used the moment to pull an arm free and strike at his face. He turned, caught at her wrist, and pressed her backward.

The billowing skirt rose and she felt his steel-spring legs on hers, forcing her thighs apart. She fought back, trying to draw her knee up into his abdomen. It was ineffective as he pressed forward. She felt his hardness against her and then his lips found hers, smothering, drawing, stirring. She gasped denial, and yet something beyond her control answered his caresses. She felt her back arch upward, cry out in protest—at herself now—and then it was happening, not as it should, yet undeniable in its overwhelming reality. She felt burning inside her, hating and wanting, protesting and answering.

His hands holding her arms let go of her, found her breasts, and the small of her back. She brought her fists up to strike at his face, clasped her hands against his head, held there, tightened, and drew him to her. For all the overpowering strength he had used on her, he was strangely gentle, filling her with more pleasure than pain. She heard herself moan, answering the sweet stab of ecstasy only hinted at, the delights only sampled. The moan became a sudden, sharp cry with protest in it, as suddenly she lay alone and he ended his taking. She saw his eyes looking down at her, a frown digging into his brow.

"You are a basket of surprises, Marina Valerian," he said. "I can say only that it had to be."

She sat up and let him look for a moment longer at the full curves of her breasts before pulling the blouse closed. "Apologies?" she asked tartly.

He thought for a moment. "In a way." His eyes were suddenly touched with sadness. "You are a victim, too, in truth."

"No apologies are needed," Marina replied. "You did only what I wanted Gilbert Tosti to do. I planned for him to take me. I lied to him, made him think I loved him."

She saw the bronzed Apollo straighten, his frowning eyes probing into her. "I think I begin to understand. You also wanted to take away the one thing which made you of value to Aldo Gamborelli. But he interrupted your plans." He paused, going over his conclusions again in his mind. "But why did you fight me just now? Why didn't you just let me take you?"

"I've had too much of lies, too much of deceits. I wanted no more of the wrong thing for the right reasons." She halted, suddenly unable to stop the sob that caught at her voice. "And I wanted the first time to be the wonderful time."

She felt his hand touch her cheek, looked up into the olive-black eyes, and saw kindness there. "It seldom is, small consolation as that may be. There will be another time when it will be the wonderful time, the right time. You are as unusual as you are beautiful." He turned from her and pulled on his trousers. "And now we both have our wish." She did not miss the wry humor in his tone. "Which turned out to have a sameness to it."

"Why do you pursue Aldo Gamborelli so singularly?" Marina asked as she rose, straightening her clothing. "Because he is the cruelest of the cruel, the greediest of the greedy?"

"That's part of it," Generoso della Passione admitted.

"But not all," Marina pressed.

"Not all," he replied, his voice taking on grimness. "Once my family owned a fine piece of land in the valley. The count came to my father, convinced him it would be good to take him in as a partner, and pointed out he could invest in livestock and equipment. It was like taking an octopus in for a partner. He ended up cheating my parents of the land and everything on it. I was away at the time, but on some pretext he had my brother put in jail, where he died unexplainably and suddenly. I vowed I'd make Aldo Gamborelli pay."

Marina watched the man in the red camorra. With this man, at the right time, she could know the full taste of ecstasy, she reflected. Her loins still throbbed from his taking, and his giving. "I should like to know more about Generoso della Passione and the Camorrists," she said. "Perhaps here I can find more than I did at the village church."

Generoso della Passione smiled, the suddenness of it surprising, the sweeping warmth of it encompassing. "What did you expect to find there?" he asked.

"Justice, payment, not cowardice masked as mercy, not special favors for special people," Marina snapped.

"You still have faith, ideals. That is good," he observed. "Corruption, human greed, the thirst for power, those things have reached into the Church as they have everywhere else. The counter-reformation needs a new reformation itself."

"Hardly the words of an ordinary bandit, Generoso della Passione," Marina remarked.

The embracing smile touched his face again, a hint of rue in it this time. "I was in Florence studying to be an advocate, a lawyer, while your guardian was cheating my parents out of their land. But I found that it took money, connections. I objected to so many injustices I saw that I finally wound up in jail. When I got out, I began to see that the laws are for the wealthy and powerful. The ordinary people have no rights, and seldom, if ever, find justice."

"So you organized the Camorrists," Marina pursued.

"Not alone. There are others in other places. We help those who need help, try to help the people settle their disputes in a just way and give them hope that one day things will be better. We strike at those who torture, kill, steal, oppress, those who take everything and give nothing in return. We are not perfect, but we try." He regarded her with a sudden hint of laughter in his eyes. "You approve of those goals, Marina Valerian?" he asked.

"Yes. I would like to be part of them," she declared.

The black eyes continued to regard her speculatively. "Possibly," he said finally. "That would have to be seen."

"You mean you don't trust me," Marina flared.

"I mean I am a man of caution because many others depend on me to be that."

"What would make you trust me?" Marina questioned.

"Time, perhaps. Actions. Proof," he said. "Why is Aldo Gamborelli in need of so much money so suddenly? Why has he bartered you for the Duke d'Albatore's sizable funds?"

Marina bit her lips. "I don't know. He tells me he's had losses, that the lands are not returning a profit. Yet the ledger showed no such problem."

She saw Generoso's frown darken his eyes to little pinpoints of thought. "I've heard rumors of plots involving the Kingdom of Naples and Reggio di Calabria. There is talk that Rome has an interest in it. But there is always talk. Rumors are as thick as deer flies after a rain."

"You think my dear guardian is involved in something such as that?"

"I'd like to know. Perhaps, if you returned, you could listen, watch, and tell me what you learn," Generoso said.

Marina felt the excitement catch at her at once. "Work with you? Oh, I should like that," she replied. "But how would I get word to you?"

"In time I will show you where to find me."

"In time. After you trust me," Marina shot back, and he shrugged his answer.

"Meanwhile, I'll come to you someplace," he offered. "I know just the place. Behind the villa there is a little garden. I'm the only one who ever goes there. Not even my guardian knows it exists, a *giardino segreto*. You can find it by following the tallest cypresses, then turn south at a small brook."

"I'll find it, never fear," he assured her. "When you've something to tell me, tie a ribbon on a branch there and I'll come back in the night."

"Yes, all right," Marina cried, her eyes shining in excitement. The tall, vibrant man put his hands on her shoulders.

"There will be danger. Aldo Gamborelli will no longer need to keep you for his arrangements. You will be worth nothing to him now. He'll not hestitate to do away with you if he learns you are helping me."

"I'll be careful," Marina promised.

"Good." Generoso smiled. "There are things unfinished between us, Marina Valerian. He took her hand and turned, then led her through the defile onto the narrow path that wound back to the spot where the cart had been left. He took the reins, drove to the place where his horsemen had halted her, swung down to the ground, and lifted her from the cart. "Now you will go back and tell the count what happened to you," he said, "but he may not believe you."

Marina frowned at the remark.

"Frankly," he added, "you do not look like a woman wronged, violated, forced to do things against her will."

Marina felt herself color. "What do I look like?"

"Like a woman who has had an experience not altogether unwanted," he answered. "Like a young woman more excited over what is to come than what happened today—and that we cannot have. You must present the right picture. He must discard you, put you aside, ignore you."

Marina was about to question further when the blow with its sharp, searing pain sent her crashing into the cart. His hand shot out again in another hard slap. She cried out in pain, saw her blouse ripped down, her breasts tumble free. Still another slap sent her falling to one knee. He seized her jet hair, yanked her around, and she screamed. Her surprise disappeared in a surge of fury and she sought his thick, curly hair, clawing at it. He grunted, smashed her across the face, and she fell back. He landed atop her and his hands pressed her legs open as she tasted the trickle of blood from the corner of her mouth. He was going to do it again. "Bastard," she spit out. "Lying, rotten bastard."

She managed to bring her knee up, to sink it into his abdomen as she bit his wrist. "Oh, damn you," he gasped, falling away as Marina tried to twist from beneath him. He grasped for her, and she felt the skirt rip down one side and fell forward as his arms wrapped around her legs. Her breath seemed to vanish as he slapped her again, and through eyes filled with tears of rage, she kicked, bit, screamed. There was no trust anywhere. Everything turned to ashes. Perhaps it was only what she deserved, she thought, as she fought back, sobbing, twisting her body, refusing his attempts, hating. Then, as suddenly as he'd begun, he let her go and she fell forward, felt the damp soil against her face and rolled over, blowing dirt from her mouth. She felt herself lifted gently into the cart to lay gasping on the seat. Through the pain, she felt his hand caress her cheek and thought she heard him murmur, "A thousand pardons, but it had to be, my lovely devil!"

She shook tears from her eyes and saw Generoso della Passione step backward and bring his hand down in a sweeping blow on the horse's rump, followed with a second. The horse reared and raced off, and Marina clung to the small handrail to avoid being tossed out of the cart. The horse, running hard, sent the cart skidding around a curve, and automatically Marina groped for the reins, found them, and pulled back. But the horse was in a frightened gallop and she'd no strength to pull him to a halt. Her mouth was dry and her eyes were red with tears. Her arms hurt and her face was colored and stinging. She glanced down to see her blouse hanging in shreds, her left breast bearing a red welt.

It had all happened so quickly, but through the rage still clinging, truth filtered through her consciousness. He hadn't taken her again but he had made her fight in fury, brought real pain and tears to her, made her hate him as he hadn't done before. He had known exactly how she'd react. She was still sobbing, still aching with pain as the horse, covered with lather, raced into the driveway of the villa. Buffo saw her first and propelled his stout form out to seize the bridle. His yell alerted Felice; then Pietro and then Aldo Gamborelli ran from the house as the cart halted.

Marina saw his eyes staring at her, taking in her shredded blouse and bruised breast, her ripped skirt. Her face was streaked and the trickle of blood from one corner of her mouth was a dried red line. There was no need to act as she gasped out the words: "The Red Camorra."

"Oh, my God. No, no, he didn't," her guardian hissed.

Marina nodded. "Just look at me, damn you," she flung out. The count's eyes moved over her again as she made an unsuccessful effort to cover her breasts with the shredded blouse. She saw the belief in his eyes, horror and shock turning to towering rage, his colorless orbs turning almost blank. Two of her personal guards had come up to stand nearby.

"Get everyone onto a horse," the count cried out. "I'll have his head on my wall. I'll cut his eyes out. I want him. I want that thieving bastard."

He rushed off toward the stables, giving Marina one more glance of icy fury, and something more in it—contemptuous dismissal. Felice was reaching up to her, wide-eyed, and she let the girl help her from the cart. She winced in pain and needed no acting for that either. Felice helped her to her room, and Marina asked that she be left alone. Felice nodded in understanding, and drew a hot bath for her. Letting the shreds of her clothes fall away, Marina paused before the mirror. She saw her hair matted with brown mud, her face streaked with soil, her mouth trickled with blood, her breasts bruised and reddened. She hurt all over.

Acting would not be enough, he had said. Her mouth turned down and her anger rose. He'd done his task too well. He could have warned her of what he'd planned, surely. She understood now, of course, and yet he seemed to have gone at it with too much zest. He could have done with a little less, she told herself angrily. She'd not forget that. Deep inside her small stirrings questioned, disagreed, wondered if less would have convinced Aldo Gamborelli as thoroughly and instantly as he'd been convinced.

One had but to look at her to know she'd been assaulted. Still, Marina's fiery temper clung, urged by the pain of her bruised body. He could have done with less, she muttered again, disregarding inner voices that reminded her of the last caress and the softly murmured apology.

Her ribs ached as she stepped into the tub, sank down in the hot water, and gasped. She lay there, letting warmth filter through the pores of her skin. Finally, stepping from the bath, she dried herself gingerly and lay across the bed. Her hand moved to touch the red marks on her right breast, the tiny signature of teeth, and her lips refused to deny the slow smile that formed itself. Generoso della Passione, she murmured silently, a man well named. Never had she met a man such as he, deep pools of eyes and deep pools of the spirit, a throbbing vibrancy that could, in an instant, become quiet strength. Her eyes closed and she did not fight sleep.

The dusk had darkened the garden when she woke and heard the sound of the horses galloping to a halt. She rose, winced, put on a full-length dressing gown of deep yellow silk, and went downstairs. Aldo Gamborelli was in the hallway, knocking mud from his boots. He straightened as Marina came down the stairs, took in the onyx hair against the deep yellow of the robe, the full swelling beauty of her breasts. He seemed to groan with his eyes and his thin lips muttered words. "He'll pay. I'll find him yet. He'll pay," he growled.

Marina felt the scorn inside her touch her voice. "Perhaps the Duke d'Albatore will lower his standards," she taunted.

Her guardian's eyes took on bitter horror. "Not that low," he snapped. "Not a man in his position. Even a pig farmer wants to be the first one if he can."

"I know. You are all victims of your own stupidities," Marina snapped. "Then perhaps you'd best just not tell him what happened," she suggested. The thought had not occurred to her and she felt a sudden fright as she voiced it.

"He would hear. By tomorrow, news of this will be all over. The servants saw your return. They all have tongues like chattering apes," Count Gamborelli muttered in disgust. He looked at her as though he wanted to throw her away. But as Marina held his stare, she saw his eyes change, darken, move across her body. "But you are still beautiful," he murmured. "Rotten but beautiful. Perhaps I should enjoy you myself."

Marina's eyes grew dark and pinpoints of flame blazed in them. A cold rage seized her as she answered in a voice hardly above a whisper. "Touch me and I will kill you," she hissed.

The pale eyes flickered for a moment. "We'll see," Aldo Gamborelli replied, turning from her to stride away. Marina stood quietly and let the churning inside her subside, forcing her hands to unclasp. He knew she had not thrown idle threats at him. It would be enough. Aldo Gamborelli might try to do away with her. He would not hesitate to have her killed if he felt it necessary. But he would not risk his own life just in the pursuit of pleasure. The senses did not mean enough to him for that.

Marina drew a deep breath, then went into the kitchen where Giacomo gave her a large bowl of soup, thick barley and *tubetini*. It was more than enough with a slice of bread. She felt nourished when she'd finished but so terribly tired. Returning to her room, she heard the sound of the coach, then peered through the window to see her guardian climbing in and then the carriage rolling away into the night.

Marina undressed, took off the deep yellow robe, and sank down on the bed, pulling the coverlet over herself. The night had come to cloak the land in its stygian shawl. The remorse and pain deep inside her were still very much there. It would be a silent companion for always, she knew. But now, for the first time in longer than she wanted to remember, she faced the next day with hope instead of despair. Aldo had no doubt ridden to talk to the Duke d'Albatore, perhaps to salvage what he could for himself. But she was no longer part of it. Their twisted, contradictory standards had been turned back on them. Her guardian had been right, of course. There was no way the porcine little lecher could accept her now. She would have been able to laugh had not Gilbert Tosti's face been seared into her.

But before she slept, her thoughts drifted to the Red Camorra. He was in his hideout by now, somewhere in the hills. Was he alone, she wondered, thinking of her? Or was he with a village girl? Restlessness swept over Marina at once. She had to learn patience, she told herself. Generoso della Passione had to trust her first. But there would come another time, she promised herself. He was not a man to be forgotten. And she was no longer the untouched. No, she corrected herself, she was no longer a virgin in one sense, but in the way that really counted she was still untouched, still waiting.

Yet this night she would sleep as she had not slept for a long time. The world that had seemed to spin back upon itself had set itself right. But she still had debts to pay and but one way to pay them: to help those unable to help themselves, to do the right thing for the right reasons, for Gilbert Tosti, for herself, for the spirit of justice. We grow up quickly in the crucible of pain, she reflected.

She turned on her side, her bruises promising both pain and pleasure.

CHAPTER FOUR

ALDO GAMBORELLI faced the two men in the paneled library. He felt as haggard as he looked. The visit with d'Albatore had not gone at all well, frustration and rage making the duke more insufferably mercurial than usual. But, thank God, he hadn't closed the door entirely. He'd listened to the alternatives proposed. And now this unexpected morning visit from Gracchi and Vinabruti, both demanding details which he was still unable to furnish.

The count faced the sour-looking taller man. "You'll have to tell your people they'll hear details when I have them ready," he said.

The dyspeptic-looking man's glance was a protest. "You said you had the funds ready and waiting for your use," he reminded.

"I do have them," Aldo Gamborelli answered. It was close enough to the truth. They had as much as been in his hands when that stinking Camorrist cutthroat wrecked everything.

"My sources will not wait much longer," he heard Gracchi say. The other man's acidity was even more irritating than usual. "They must have word of definite action by the end of the month or they cannot pledge support."

"They will have it, by the end of the month," the count announced firmly, relieved to see the two men rise to their feet. He escorted them to the hired carriage waiting outside, then returned to the library, all too aware that his grand plans were perilously close to disintegrating before his eyes. He had already tasted the sweetness of more power than he'd ever had, a base from which to rule and live in the manner which befitted someone of his talents. He would be glad to get away from this villa and the Valerian money which he forever had to invent ways to pilfer. And that bitch of a girl. She would doubtless cling to the villa now that she was untouchable, and make existence as miserable for him as she could. But if he could salvage his plans he would leave her and all her problems behind. She had been the stepping stone of it all—until the stone crumbled from beneath him. He slammed a fist down on the library table. Maybe all was not entirely lost, he contemplated. Maybe not entirely.

He strode from the library to change into riding clothes and make rounds of all the lands. It was time to crack down on the stupid oafs that tenanted the farms. They needed a lesson in discipline, and he was in the mood to give one.

Aldo Gamborelli had closed the library doors when his two visitors had conferred with him, but he had neglected to note the half-open windows hidden behind partially pulled drapes. So he had not seen Marina on the side terrace by the open windows, ostensibly examining the row of chamacrops planted in the wooden boxes along the wall. She had hurried away as soon as she saw the count's visitors rise to leave, and she stayed at the rear of the house till he had escorted them to their carriage and returned inside.

How important was what she had heard? Perhaps not at all, yet it might be another piece to fit into a pattern. It was worth passing on to Generoso, she decided. Still moving slowly, her pulled muscles and bruises very much with her, she walked through the garden to slip beyond the last manicured hedge and cross into the wild, wet tangled woods. Pushing her way through the denseness of vines and low branches that seemed to resent a human intruder into their domain, she stayed on the narrow pathway until magically the trees parted to reveal the little secret garden. Taking one of the small blue ribbons from her sleeve she tied it onto the low branch of a bush.

It was unlikely that Generoso would come this first day since their meeting, and even more unlikely that he'd find the little garden so quickly, but she promised herself to return that night to see if the ribbon was still there. She'd forced herself not to think about Generoso della Passione, but she had merely deceived herself, she knew, for his presence had been with her from the moment she'd wakened. As she dipped into a low spot on the ground, her thigh muscle contracted in pain and she found thoughts of Generoso instantly flavored with something like anger. She had more than one reason to want to see him again, Marina decided.

When she reached the villa, Felice was at the door. It was her first meeting with the girl since she'd returned in the little cart yesterday and she saw the concern in Felice's eyes. "I am so sorry, my signorina," the girl said. "Nothing but bad luck seems to follow your steps."

Marina pressed Felice's arm.

"Things are seldom as bad as they seem to be," she replied and saw the quick frown of uncomprehension touch Felice's young face. "Someday we will have a long talk, when the time is right," Marina added. It was as much as she dared say now. She heard the sound of galloping hooves, then turned to see the count and six of his men thundering to a halt.

"Five miles chasing a decoy, exhausting horses and men," she heard him snarl as he dismounted. "But I want a party out every day searching the hills until we pick up a trail."

He started into the house, then saw Marina. He glared at her as a man glares at something which is beyond his reach, she thought, and enjoyed the feeling. Brushing past her he stormed into the house. Marina found the servants avoiding her glances, uncertain of how to act with her and uncertain of her feelings. She was a woman who had been dishonored, and, in the tortured rules of this land, that it was not her fault made only a minor difference. So she kept the expected posture of inner hurt and quiet withdrawal, hardly speaking to anyone. Her public shame suited her purposes perfectly, allowing her to wander about and sit alone without supervision.

But that evening, when the dark turned the day cool, she knew frustration. The count was making plans with all of his men, assigning each a part in his rotating scheme to have riders scour the hills each day for the Camorrists. Marina could find no way to leave the house unseen, and by the time the men had left, it was far too late to journey to the little secret garden. Had Generoso been there by chance he would have left already. She went to sleep angry, slept poorly, and woke late. When she went downstairs, a parade of tenant farmers was bringing the count their monthly tithes. She had no chance to slip away till dusk, and she hurried when the moment came, pushing through the thick underbrush of the woods too fast. She stumbled, and felt the sharp pain of bruised rib muscles and her temper rise at once.

When she reached the little garden, the ribbon was not on the bush. She felt her breath drawn in sharply. Had he come during the night? Would he return now? As if in answer, she saw the figure step from the trees at the back of the small clearing, then move toward her. She saw the olive-black eyes scan her figure and linger for a moment on the bruise that was turning her forearm into a spot of purple redness. She thought she saw a tiny gleam of amused satisfaction in his eyes and felt her anger explode at once. Her hand swung in a wide arc, almost landing on his cheek, but he was too quick and brought his own hand up to deflect the blow.

"That was for the last time," she snapped.

His arm came up behind her waist, pulled her forward, and then his mouth was on hers, pressing her lips open in sweet harshness. He pulled back just as suddenly. "That was for now," he said. She held his eyes with hers, felt her breath in short deep draughts, anger still clinging to her. "It would not have worked any other way," he said. "You had to be more than acting. To risk less was to risk everything."

His eyes refused to let her deny the truth and she let a sigh of acceptance escape her. "You were right," Marina admitted. "But I have my own temper."

His smile embraced her. "I know."

"And I don't let go easily. That's bad, I know. I harbor hurts."

"Only hurts?" he asked.

Her eyes softened. "No, I harbor the good things, too. They balance out, I hope."

Generoso held up the blue ribbon.

"There are plans for something," she said. "Though I don't know what. But my guardian has been planning some under-cover move."

Hurrying, Marina told the tall, bronzed man of what she had heard and of the two visitors to the villa. When she finished, Generoso lost himself in thought for a moment.

"More pieces and parts," he said finally. "But nothing that can be fitted together."

"Then I will keep listening and watching," Marina assured him quickly.

Generoso took her hand in his. "I am afraid of that. If he finds you are spying on him, to say nothing of meeting me, your life will be in danger. You are worth nothing to him any longer, remember."

"I want to do it, Generoso. I don't want him to grow more powerful and control the lives of more people. Not that cold, merciless monster! I'm in the best position to find out what he's up to," Marina reminded him.

His hands, warm and strong, took her by the shoulders. His deep eyes were grave. "Then promise to be careful. Take no unnecessary risks. Think and look before you act," he cautioned.

"I promise," she agreed. "I wondered about you, Generoso. I wondered if you'd find my little *giardino segreto,* or if you'd come at all."

"Why would you wonder that?" he asked.

She shrugged. "Perhaps you had second thoughts about taking the niece of Count Gamborelli into your confidence."

"Can you meet me tomorrow?" he asked.

"I will try." She smiled.

"This is a lovely little place, but not one in which I can relax. You think only you know of it, but you may be wrong. Do you know the lake at the foot of Mount Abressa?"

Marina nodded.

"Meet me there, at this time tomorrow."

"All right." Marina waited, her lips slightly parted, her head raised up to his. But he stepped back, and as she caught the tiny pinpoints of light in his eyes, felt her anger sputter at once. "Never do what's expected, is that it?" she commented tartly.

He allowed a half-smile. "With some wine, one wants to drink deeply or not at all. A sip is not enough."

"I can see why you wanted to be an advocate," Marina returned. "Words come easily to you."

Generoso did not reply; he half-bowed and stepped backward into the line of bushes. They closed over his figure and she could not hear him vanish through the woods. You will thirst for this wine, Generoso della Passione, Marina promised silently. You will thirst and I shall satisfy and be satisfied on my own terms.

Sleep was a tossing restlessness that night. The air had grown heavy, thick with summer damp, and the covers grew too hot. She woke to cast them off a little after midnight, then heard a horse stamping outside. She rose and went to the window that looked down upon the front entrance to the villa, taking in the columned entranceway. A single horse was tied there and as she looked down the door of the house opened and yellow light pushed into the night. She watched as Aldo Gamborelli emerged with a man who wore a messenger's leather pouch slung over one shoulder. The man went to the horse and her guardian handed him a sealed envelope which he placed in the leather pouch.

"You have indeed brought good news," she heard the count say. "The letter I've given you must be delivered to Ettore Baldi personally."

"It will be done," she heard the messenger answer. Marina stepped back from the window as the man swung into the saddle, heard the villa door close as she returned to bed. *Ettore Baldi,* she repeated to herself, fixing the name in her mind. She slept, and in the morning, putting on a habit for riding, went downstairs, passing her guardian, who paid her only a disinterested glance as he sat scribbling on papers. She took Orion from the stables, went down the usual path for a morning canter, then switched and headed for the lake at the foot of Mount Abressa. She halted there, aware that other eyes observed her arrival. She dismounted, sat by the water, brushed her hair till it glistened with dark lights. She caught the glimpse of the ruby-red camorra when he finally came through the trees on the charcoal-gray charger with a black mane and a black tail. She told him quickly about the count's nighttime messenger and the name she'd heard.

"Ettore Baldi is a trafficker in whatever you want, a specialist in the unsavory. Obviously your guardian has need of his special services," Generoso observed.

"But what need?" Marina frowned.

"That answer could explain many other things. I have others trying to find out what can be learned. Baldi operates out of Rome and Palermo."

Marina looked unhappy. "It seems I bring you but useless little pieces."

Generoso's hand covered hers at once. "Every piece is important. In time we will fit them all together."

"Then I shall try to bring something for you each day," Marina exclaimed, brightening at once. He laughed as his hand caressed her hair.

"You are as unusual as you are beautiful," he mused. "You make me feel as I do when trudging through a swamp I come upon a lobelia or a milkweed—magnificent beauty in an unexpected place."

Marina did not reply, except with her eyes. "I must go," he told her, then leaned down and brushed her lips with his. Her hands tightened on his camorra instinctively, lingered, and then she drew away. She stayed until he disappeared into the trees, then she returned to the villa. No ordinary man, she repeated to herself, and inside her experienced no ordinary stirrings.

It was the next day that she heard Pietro and Carlos talking in the small room just off the kitchen. "The letter came from Cairo, I tell you," she heard Carlos say. "I saw the mark on it when the count took it from the mail tray."

"From Cairo," Pietro echoed in awe. "I've never seen a letter from Cairo."

Marina went on, adding the piece of information to her morning's tasks, and in time found her way to the stables and went out for a ride again. She paused often to look behind her to see if she were being followed. One quickly learns the ways of the hunted, she reflected. But she saw no signs of anyone and rode on. Aldo Gamborelli obviously felt secure about her inability to cause him neither good nor harm. Marina sniffed disdainfully, happy to let him believe that.

When she was with Generoso she told him of the letter and saw his frown of consternation.

"Many things come out of Cairo," he mused. "It is a place of intrigue, a fertile field for bad seeds. It has always been such a place. I'll add this to the others."

The meeting was brief, but his lips lingered on hers. Each time she came to bring him another small piece of news his lips held hers a fraction longer. One day he cupped her face in his hand.

"Next time, arrange to stay away longer. We will go to the mountains, you and I. You will see where the Camorrists live," he said.

His words implied more than that, of course, and she felt happiness leap inside her. They'd spoken of trust, an acceptance.

It was but a few days later when she arranged to leave on a "shopping trip," perhaps to Naples, she told Count Gamborelli. He appraised her as she prepared to leave.

"You've borne up quite well after your experience," he observed. "Amazingly well. Continue to take care of yourself."

Marina walked away with uneasiness dropping over her like a shawl. Good manners were unusual for Aldo Gamborelli. Interest and concern were unheard of, and she felt an undefined alarm. It was definitely out of character for him, almost as if she were still of concern to him, her well-being still of value. Yet, perhaps it had been a moment less meaningful than she thought, she decided as she hurried to the stables and took the little cart. This time she saw the red camorra through the trees as she arrived, and as Generoso emerged on the charcoal charger he reached down, lifted her from the cart with one arm, and swung her onto the saddle in front of him.

"Watch how we go. I will show you how to reach the caves. Take note of the markings," he told her. He helped her by pointing out key places—a gray-brown old cedar with a twisted branch, a stone that wore a cap of green star moss, and a circle of stunted pines. As they neared the caves the foliage grew thick, then suddenly opened, and a stone clearing lay before her, a half-circle of caves around it. The big, burly man who'd first brought her to Generoso came forward.

"This is Tonio, my right arm," Generoso announced.

Tonio's nod was acceptance. "Generoso tells me you are different," he said. "I believe him." Marina nodded at the compliment and slid to the ground as Generoso dismounted and Tonio led the horse away.

"Come, let me show you our hideaway," Generoso beckoned, and she felt the strength of the hand that encased hers. He led her through an opening, down a narrow passage of rock which suddenly opened into sunlight, and she found herself on a small ledge, looking down over the half-circle of the caves.

"They interlock," Generoso said. "We can disappear if we must, though no one has ever found us here. We can vanish with horses, equipment, everything. The hart has its harbor, the boar its couch, the marten its tree. The Camorrists have their caves."

There was indeed a feeling of safety and security. A kind of haven had been formed here. Marina looked down upon other Camorrists, in varying color blouses, some polishing gear, others gathered around an open fire where a side of pig turned on a wood spit. She glimpsed two girls, one stirring a kettle over a smaller fire, then saw a third carrying water buckets.

"From one of the mountain villages," Generoso explained, catching her thoughts with disturbing ease. "The body as well as the spirit must be nourished if the men are to be content." She cast a glance at him and saw his eyes holding glints of laughter.

"And Generoso della Passione, does he nourish the body with village girls, too?" she asked.

"Sometimes. Should a Camorrist bed only with ladies of high birth?" he asked and Marina frowned at the stab of jealousy that flared inside her. It was an entirely new feeling for her. She'd never known jealousy of any woman, to say nothing of nameless, passing girls. He took her hand and led her back into another passageway. Marina glimpsed roomlike openings and cots inside the caves, upended buckets, candles burning. He turned sharply and she fell against him, followed, and saw him halt at a doorway hung with a muslin curtain. He pushed it aside and entered. She saw a large cave area, lighted by torches and candles, which took the dampness from the stone. A flat bed rested on the ground at one side, pillows and a casual rug lying beside it. Two large trunks stood on the other side of the cave.

She saw a wooden box set in the center of the stone room with a half-wheel of *strachino* upon it. Generoso reached into an opening in the stone and brought out a bottle of red wine. "The stone crevices keep it cold," he remarked, opening the bottle and handing it to her. "There are cups but we do not need them. Drink—we are celebrating, are we not?"

She nodded, lifting the bottle to her lips. The wine felt good and warming. She sat down on the pillows, drank again, and handed him the bottle. She sat back and heard his voice softly probing. "A sadness came into your eyes, Marina. For yesterday or for tomorrow?"

"Both," she replied. "For not being able to turn back the clock, to undo what has been done."

"Ah, how many people have wanted to be able to do that?" he asked, and Marina searched the strong, vibrant face.

"I don't think you ever have," she said. "I don't think you ever look back."

"You are right. To remember is not the same as looking back," he agreed. "But I look always forward."

"To everything?" she questioned. His smile held layered wisdoms.

"To everything. Some things more than others. Especially to you. We have touched bodies. We will perhaps touch spirits as well."

"I think we already have, Generoso della Passione," she murmured, and his lips touched hers in a gentle answer.

She could not help the small light of mischievousness that crept into her eyes. "What if I told you that I long to touch bodies again with you, Generoso della Passione? Would I surprise you? Shock you?"

"No, only please me." His eyes were solemn. "But not this day. There isn't time. A shopping trip does not consume the night, and next time, I want the night, all of it, alone with you."

"I know," she said. "I'll wait for that time." It would be the right time, the wonderful time, she told herself.

"Come finish your wine and cheese before you must go. I'm sure the count is full of small suspicions always."

"Yes, he acts strangely, not at all in character," Marina replied, thinking of her guardian's concern for her.

"Tomorrow I shall be near your *giardino segreto*. We can meet there," Generoso suggested. Marina nodded, finished the wine, and stayed in his arms until the sun began to bring the dusk along in its last rays. She had clung to him, exchanged hungry kisses, felt his body against hers, and enjoyed the holding back now, for the time was near, she knew. She would not hurry what was too precious to hurry.

Later he took her back to the cart, kissed her quickly, and galloped off without another word. She smiled quietly. He knew when words were valueless sounds. She was moving down the dusty road when she saw the four horsemen galloping toward her, recognizing them as the count's men out on his constant patrol. They slowed.

"Have you seen anyone?" the lead horseman called. She shook her head and they went on. She smiled. Generoso had galloped off for a reason. He had known, or heard their presence with an alertness beyond hers. The count's heavy-footed men would never see, much less catch, the Red Camorra.

Marina slept soundly that night, and the next day, when she went to the little secret garden, she had more news to tell Generoso. "It is the time when the profits paid by the tenant farmers will be taken to Naples," she revealed and Generoso's smile became broad.

"Excellent. This time those who have been milked dry shall have what is rightfully theirs returned to them. Tomorrow we meet by the lake again." Marina answered his kiss. "You make it more and more difficult to leave you each day," he acknowledged. She did not reply but later, alone, thought: *You make it difficult to think of anything but you, Generoso.*

In the early hours of the next day, she watched the count direct his men as they put the heavy coin bags into the wooden chest and place it aboard the carriage. Two folded rugs were tied on over the chest, completely covering it.

"As usual, I will ride alone inside the carriage, traveling leisurely, bringing some rugs to be rewoven in Maddaloni," the duke told the others. "The rest of you will ride back out of sight. I shall fire a shot if there is trouble."

Marina watched from the doorway as the carriage rolled away and her fingers dug into the palms of her hands. The method apparently was one he always used to transport the money. But now he had added protection. Generoso could well be the one taken by surprise. She knew a feeling of utter helplessness as she turned away from the doorway. The minutes became thorns pricking into her as they ticked off into hours, until at last it was time for her to ride to the lake. She forced herself not to gallop the horse from the stable. Two of the count's men were there, shoeing a horse. Only after she had gone well out of sight of anyone at the villa did she turn a trot into a full gallop. Fear and apprehension rode with her and her stomach churned like a buttermill.

She halted when she reached the lake and thought about trying to find her way to the caves. She had imprinted each turn and marking in her mind. Just about to take the first pathway up into the mountain, she saw the charcoal-gray horse move into view, the straight figure sitting easily in the saddle. She closed her eyes for a moment, then opened them to make sure she had not imagined what she wanted to see there. But it had been no figment conjured up out of wanting. He noted her anxiousness at once, but then it was plain enough in the darkened concern of her eyes.

"I try to expect the unexpected," Generoso said. "The good count is nervous. He would take extra precautions."

"When he didn't return, I grew sick inside," Marina replied.

"He is walking back with three of his men who can still walk," Generoso related. "It will be dark before he arrives at the villa. We let him reach the edge of Maddaloni before we struck."

He wheeled his horse and Marina followed, again noting the marks that led to the caves. There were more women in the stone clearing when she arrived, an air of excitement swirling through those gathered there, and she saw the wooden chest with the rugs over it placed near one of the cave entrances. Tonio came to greet her, with two other men he introduced as Raoul and Fillipi. "It is Marina Valerian we must thank for our prize this day," Tonio said. A murmur of approval followed and Marina glowed as Generoso led her away.

"How quickly you have become one of us," he exclaimed, then, his glance quick, half laughingly, he asked, "Does that frighten you?"

"No," Marina said. "Not so much as other things which have happened so quickly too."

Generoso did not answer but the olive-black eyes danced. Under a wall torch inside a corridor, he halted, pressing his lips to hers. She felt herself answer, her lips parting, inviting. "Don't be frightened, Marina. Never be afraid of what is right, or wonderful."

"It is not that which frightens me. I keep being afraid that something too wonderful will be taken away," Marina said. "And I have found something wonderful here." She stepped back, gesturing to the sounds of laughter coming from outside the stone corridor. "I have lived in many fine places, the grand villa of Valerian, the fine houses of friends and relatives, but there is more real warmth here in these caves than in any of the others."

Generoso smiled. "Grand architecture, fine furniture, and expensive decorations—those things do not bring warmth.

People bring warmth if they have warmth to bring. Many fine cathedrals are but monuments of stone. The first great shrine to St. Michael was the cave on Mount Gargano. Perhaps these caves will be our shrine."

His lips pressed upon her mouth again and she answered. She stayed in his arms till it was time for her to leave. He held her close, speaking of plans for making a better world, caressing her face and her shoulders. When she had to go, her skin burned. The words she had once spoken to Gilbert Tosti found echoes, but this time they were not hollow: "Do not play games with me, Generoso. You have made me care too much too quickly."

"Why not?" he asked, a smile edging his lips at the frown that darkened her eyes instantly. "It is no more than you have done to me."

She felt the frown vanish and clung to him as he walked to where Orion waited outside. "Tomorrow," she said. "In the afternoon." He nodded, lifting her into the saddle and sending the horse cantering away.

Marina reached home before the count and his three men stumbled to the front door of the great house. She heard his voice shouting fury as he trudged to his room. The days that followed became patterns of happy waiting, each meeting a reunion, as though they had not touched for months. Each was too short, though. Her guardian had grown increasingly watchful of everything that went on in the villa. Then one morning, in the little secret garden, she had news for Generoso: "The count plans to be away through the night. He goes to Capri."

Generoso's eyes narrowed. "I have learned that Ettore Baldi, the trafficker, also travels to Capri. Perhaps we shall be able to fit in pieces soon." He frowned in thought for a moment, then let his eyes find Marina. "Will you come tonight?"

She nodded. She had learned the way on her own now. "I will be there, before the dark."

He did not smile. There was no need. Smiles were for afterward. Marina made her way back to the villa and found her guardian ready to get into the carriage which had been returned to him by local farmers. Three of his riders were on horseback ready to accompany the coach. His eyes roved over her face.

"Do you not wish me a good trip, my dear?" he asked, his lips forming a cold smile. Marina did not reply. "The results of my trip may affect your well-being," he suggested.

"Nothing you can do can affect my well-being any longer," Marina snapped. "Or have you forgotten?"

His thin face tightened at once. "Far from it," he snapped and ducked into the carriage, pulling the door shut after him. Marina went into the house and to her room. She gathered a robe and a few things, preparing a small bag. Staring at it for a moment, she emptied it on the floor and flung the bag aside. She would not go prepared, expecting. It was wrong, somehow an intrusion. She took only herself to the stable when the first hint of dusk etched the sky. She rode with the gathering twilight, watched the swallows as they dipped in great swoops to their night shelters.

It was almost dark when she poked her way through the dense wall of greenery that hid the half-circle of caves. A glow of warmth from two fires reached out to her as she walked the horse to the hitching stand. Her eyes automatically went to the entranceway of the center cave, but no tall, straight figure stood in waiting. "You know the way in, Marina Valerian," a voice said, and she saw Tonio in the shadows nearby. She moved forward, into the opening, which was damp and chilly with the night. The torch on the wall gave a fitful light that barely outlined the narrow stone passages. The caves were an eerie place after darkness fell—quieter and more secretive. She found her way to where the muslin drape formed a door, pulled it aside, and stepped into the inner room. Soft warmth enveloped her at once from a log fire that burned against one wall, confined by a circle of stone. Her eyes moved to the low, square bed. Generoso rose from it. He wore only the leather breeches and the firelight danced against his bronzed skin.

He held out a hand and she moved toward him, running, flinging herself into his arms. His lips were instant caresses, his hands parting the buttons of the dress, pushing it from her shoulders. She gasped as her breasts touched his skin. His arms lifted her up, then put her down on the bed, and she pushed herself free of garments as he did the same. She reached for him, drew him to her. There was music now, the wine was in the chalice. She heard the sounds of her soft cries, pleasure beyond the power of words, made only for gasping, murmuring, wanting sounds.

Slowly, tenderly, he moved with her, his mouth warm upon her breasts, letting trembling eagerness turn into wild abandon until she did not know the writhing, wanting, throbbing body that was hers. Too much, too much, she heard herself groan, more than she could absorb, and yet not enough. She gasped out for more, clutched him to her, clung and held, grasped, pleaded, gave. A tide of terrible sweetness rose inside her, sweeping her up as if she were atop a giant wave, carrying her higher, higher until suddenly it flung her into space, into the moment where time halted in a shimmering void, and her scream was not a scream but a paean to Priapus.

The wild wave became a gentle pool, engulfing her in quiet, a peace she had never known before, and slowly she opened her eyes to find Generoso beside her, watching her. Her eyes held his with silent words and she saw his slow smile. "It will be still better," he said.

It could not be better, her glance responded.

"You will see," he said. Later, after they ate roast pig, wine, and fresh green beans, she came to believe his words as he brought her the sweet, wild wave once more, and afterward she held his head to her breast.

"I once heard that there is always one man whom you never stop loving, who always owns a part of you," she said. "I never understood that till now."

He lifted his face to hers. "And there is always one woman to whom you cannot stop giving yourself. I am lucky that it is one so beautiful, so passionate as you."

Vows, Marina thought, of a kind, yet far stronger than many said before an altar by appointed lovers and hired priests. She slept in the strong arms until the dawn came and he woke her with his lips gentle on her breast. "Time for you to go," he told her. "We will not take risks. The count may return unexpectedly early in the day."

Marina dressed and paused to have coffee outside from a pot that simmered on the fire. "I'll be safe going back alone," she assured him. "I want to ride by myself. Till tomorrow." He brushed her lips with a soft kiss and she prodded the chestnut gelding on through the thick woods. She rode slowly, feeling born all over again, the world a new place. The early-morning light filtered through the trees overhead, not unlike the Kentish tracery of a cathedral window. She did not deserve such utter happiness, Marina mused. Yet it had been given her, a gift to be repaid out of her tomorrows, a gift of love to share with others.

She needed to know nothing more about Generoso della Passione. In his touch she had felt the sensitivity deep inside him; in his strength the compassion that was part of strength. It was its own book of revelations, this coming together, this making love. For those who could feel, who brought their own sensitivities, it said so much more than mere flesh could say.

She stabled the horse quietly as Buffo stretched out in an empty stall and snored loud enough to cover her movements. Flitting across the few yards to the garden, she hugged hedges and entered the villa, hurrying to her room. She had bathed, changed, and freshened by the time her guardian drove up in the carriage. She saw him hurry to his room, where he stayed closeted for most of the day. Marina was surprised to see the carriage made ready again that night, and she listened and watched as he ordered Pietro to have Giacomo prepare a lunch for four the next day. "I am expecting company and I shall return by dawn, in time to receive my guests," she heard him say.

Marina waited only till the sound of the carriage faded before she hurried to the stables. It was an unexpected opportunity, one she would not waste. It took a little longer to find the hideaway in the dark and she was grateful for the moon. Sentries halted her unexpected appearance, then let her pass. She wiped away the concern on Generoso's face when he saw her with a happy embrace. "Nothing has gone wrong? You have not fled?" he questioned.

"Just into your arms." She kissed him. "Unwilling to miss this chance." She told him of how the count had left, and of his expected company for lunch.

"I will tell you who it is the moment I can get away," she went on. "Maybe we will have some of the answers we want tomorrow."

"You can stay till one hour past midnight," Generoso replied sternly, then, swinging her into his arms, carried her back through the cool corridors of stone to the square bed. She let her fingers find buckles, buttons, and drawstrings, bringing his powerful body into the open for her lips to caress. She explored dark hollows and thighs of muscular sinew, places of unexpected softness and exciting hardness, and knew she was learning the many dimensions of love.

Later, naked against his warmth, she talked of idle thoughts that had often lain lazily in the mind. "When the Villa Valerian is really mine, and all the land with it, I want to make everyone a part of its riches. All those who give to its soil should share in its rewards, not have to pay tithes as well as rent." She hugged Generoso to her. "And you will help begin a new era, a new spirit across the land. We will pioneer new ways to happiness."

He let his fingers lift the jet tresses, pressed them down again. "Perhaps, my love, perhaps. If only more felt as you do. But we could make a beginning. However, first the plans of your guardian must be stopped. Whatever they are, I am sure they will not bring happiness to the ordinary people."

Her arms tightened around his neck as she reached upward, then backward to pull his head down to her. "Can you possibly be as happy as I, Generoso?" she asked, suddenly wanting reassurance, overwhelmed by her own contentment.

"Yes. Did you not say we have touched with more than lips, more than bodies?" he reminded her gently. "That is more than most people find in a lifetime of searching."

He turned, pulled her to her feet, pressed her body against his, and caressed her with his touch. "It is past midnight. I will take you back." He watched her as she dressed. "Your every movement is beautiful, my love," he said. "I think it is no whim of chance that I found you."

"No idle chance, Generoso. There are currents that sweep people together, and they have smiled on us," she replied.

She leaned back to feast her gaze on his body as he slipped into clothes, etching every graceful muscle on her mind. She understood, perhaps for the first time, why the ancient Greeks revered the male form more than the female. Finished, Generoso walked with his arm tightly around her waist as they went out to where the horses were tethered. The fire was banked, glowing fitfully, and the circle of stone caves held silence inside it. Generoso rode with her through the moonlight, side by side, his arm reaching out to touch hands with her. Finally the still night led them to the dark outlines of the villa. He leaned over and found her lips. "Be careful, my darling," he whispered. "Forever is waiting for us."

Marina held the taste of him in her mouth as she rode to the stables, then hurried up to her room. She slept with the feel of his body beside hers, the taste of him in her mouth, the strength of him in her loins.

Tired more than she had realized, she slept through the morning sun and woke to find her room flooded in yellow, the day moving toward noon. She dressed quickly in a sleeveless *basque*, a short dress fit for riding, in deep red with white trim around the collar and lapels. The air held humidity and heaviness, and the leaves did not move. She went downstairs and had coffee and fresh buns Giacomo had baked. A luncheon table had been set in the dining room, she saw, and she started to walk through the open front door of the villa. The edge of the garden would be a casual vantage point to see the arriving guest, she had decided. As she started through the door, the two figures stepped out from the sides to block her way. She recognized them as her guardian's men.

"You are to stay in the house, Signorina," the one said. "Orders from Count Gamborelli," he added apologetically.

"I will do no such thing," Marina snapped back. "I'll go wherever I wish in my own home." She started forward but the two figures closed to block her way again.

"The count has given orders that you are to stay in the house, in your room," the one insisted. Marina's dark blue eyes gathered fire as she spun on her heel, stormed back into the big foyer to find Aldo Gamborelli and saw his thin figure in the study doorway.

"What is the meaning of this?" she threw at him. "How dare you give such orders?"

The sunken-cheeked face seemed to sneer without changing expression. Marina heard the sound of a coach-and-four coming into the driveway outside. "Take her to her room and stand guard outside," the count barked at the two men. "She is to be kept there until I send for her."

The two men stepped to her side as Marina stared at her guardian. "What is this all for?" she questioned. The count ignored her and spoke to the two guards.

"Get her upstairs. Don't be afraid to use force if she tries to leave," he ordered.

Marina felt the men take her arms. "No, I demand an answer," she flung back at the colorless eyes of Aldo Gamborelli. "You've no right to do this."

The two men were pulling her to the stairway. Twisting, she tore her arms from their grasp. "Let go of me," she hissed. She started up the stairway by herself as they followed close behind. Halfway up she halted and glanced down at the figure of Aldo Gamborelli still in the foyer watching her mount the stairs. "Who is this mysterious visitor that I must be locked away from like some idiot relative?" she spit out.

"No man of mystery at all," her guardian replied with his lips turning up into the excuse of a smile. "It is the Duke d'Albatore, a man of infinite compassion. He has come to discuss business matters with me over lunch. Then, sullied though she may be, he will return home with his bride."

CHAPTER FIVE

He will return home with his bride. The words whipped into Marina through a surge of disbelief. But the two guards were pushing her into her room, closing the door behind. She heard the words again and felt her head moving in denial. It was impossible. He was not here to take home his bride. That was contrary to all their rules. It was impossible.

The high, nasal laugh drifted up through the open window, and she rushed to look down. The coach-and-four was drawn up before the entrance and the Duke d'Albatore's rotund little form was just disappearing into the house. *He will return home with his bride.* The words danced now, a tantalizing rigadoon in her brain. She sank into a chair feeling dizzy, almost numb. It just went against everything, she thought, a contradiction of contradictions. But the Duke d'Albatore was here, and she was a prisoner under guard in her room. He had come to take her back. She didn't doubt that, whatever the reason.

Marina rose, her dark blue eyes deepened with fury and fear. The duke had come to take her, but it could not be as his bride. Aldo Gamborelli must have made some other arrangement to salvage victory from his defeat. But what? Marina pressed her eyes closed, pushed away thoughts. That would only waste precious seconds. There was time only to flee.

Not through the door. Not with the two guards stationed outside. Marina ran to the window. A narrow drain for rain to run off formed a ledge that ran along the roofline just behind the window. As a little girl, she had often clambered out upon it, always to the horror of her mother. Marina pushed her head from the window, leaning out as far as she dared. The narrow drain ledge was still there, but it was older, perhaps weaker, and she was no longer a slip of a girl. Yet it was her one way from the room.

She glanced down at the coach-and-four by the entrance-way. Three horsemen had ridden up, tied their steeds to the rear of the vehicle, and were lounging nearby. If they happened to glance up, she'd easily be spotted, but it was a risk she'd have to take. She lifted herself onto the broad sill of the window, swung her long legs over, grasped hold of the uneven stones at her left, and pulled herself up. She felt her body sway out, pulled hard with one hand clutching the bottom edge of the open window, and brought herself back. Stretching one arm out, she grasped the edge of the first corbel, stretched a fraction more, and took a firmer grasp. With a silent prayer, she pushed herself upward from the sill, pulled upon the edge of the corbel, clung for a precarious second, then pulled herself up to lay with hands holding the first corbel and letting her breath return. She began to pull along the protruding stones, using each corbel to move her closer to the little drain ledge.

There had been no shouts from below. So far, no one had seen her. Her hand found the ledge and pushed on it. The stone seemed solid enough. Marina lifted herself upward onto it, slowly putting both feet down on it and beginning to edge her way along the drain. The roof rose and then dipped to a tall oak. Marina resisted a desire to hurry, for fear of falling, and inched her way along. The distance was not great, but it seemed miles. With tortuous slowness, the oak came nearer and was almost within reach. She edged another step and grasped the tree as her feet dropped from under her. She heard the sharp clatter of stones as a section of the ledge fell away and her hand flailed air, then gripped rough bark and leaves. She closed around the branch, pulled on it, swung outward, and found another branch with her other hand. She stayed there, swaying for an instant, listening to voices raised in the distance. The clatter of the falling ledge had been heard.

Marina let herself slide down the branch, wrapped her legs around part of the tree trunk, lowered herself, switched to a still sturdier branch, and dropped to the ground below. The voices were now joined by others. Marina ran, darting across the open area to the stables. She heard a shout and cursed under her breath. Racing into the darker, quieter air of the stables, she saw Buffo look up in surprise as she flung the door of Orion's stable open and threw a bridle on the horse. Buffo was starting toward her and frowning when she bolted from the stall, disdaining a saddle. Bringing her hand down on the hunter's rump, she raced from the stables at a full gallop and looked back at the villa to see the count on the terrace, the Duke beside him.

"After her," she heard him shout. "Bring my horse."

She glanced back again and saw the three horsemen who had come with the duke start to give chase. Bending low on the hunter's back, she sent the big chestnut gelding crashing through underbrush. They would hear her of course and follow at once, but it was the shortest way to the lake and to Generoso. Clinging, not daring to go at full pace without a saddle, Marina spurred Orion up a rise, turned to race along the top of it. She heard the others following too closely, driving their horses all out.

Marina glimpsed the brilliant blue of the little lake, turned down a path toward it, and glanced behind her to see that the three horsemen were gaining and had her in sight. She snapped a hand on Orion's rump again, let him have his head, and clung to his back, hands pressed against the thick neck for balance. She saw the fallen log appear and tensed every muscle. She'd often taken higher jumps during a hunt, but she sat in a saddle then. The horse leaped, flew over the log, and came down. Marina felt the smooth, unbroken back of fur send her sliding forward. She clutched at the stout neck, squeezed her thighs hard, and barely managed to avoid falling.

The lake lay in front of her and she turned up the first pathway that eventually led to Generoso's hideaway. Behind her, the three horsemen wheeled to follow, very close now. The others would have taken up the chase and were undoubtedly closing ground. Suddenly Marina felt sick. The terrible realization twisted her stomach. She could not go to Generoso. She could not find the safety of his arms. They were too close behind her and there was no way to shake them loose. To continue was to lead them, and those who were on the way, to Generoso's hideaway. Her lips moved, the wind catching at the words that sobbed from her. *"I wanted to come, my love. I tried."*

She pulled at the reins, turned Orion's head as the horse fought her, and started through thick brush that led down a steep incline to a small ravine. She glimpsed the line of horsemen just appearing in the distance, the rapier-thin figure of her guardian unmistakable among them. They saw her, swerved, and headed down the ravine to cut her off. The first three pursuers continued to come after her. The ravine flattened out and she shifted herself on Orion. But the others were cutting in to block her. She tried to double back along the ravine, and they separated into two groups. It was no use, she saw. The first knot was already cutting off flight backward.

She reined the panting horse to a halt and patted his lathered fur. She stayed atop his back, sitting straight as the count came to a halt and the others formed a circle around her. He raised his riding crop and his thin mouth twitched. Marina did not move; she refused to flinch as she watched him pull his arm down with effort.

"You bear a mark already," he said. "I'll let the duke do as he will with you."

He turned and led the others as they began to ride back, forming a box around her. Marina rode with back straight, head held high, giving no sign of the churning, spearing pain inside her. Only one thing held good in it. Generoso, in the mountain fastness behind her, was safe from prying eyes and attack. She had refused to let that happen. He would hear in time, and understand.

The procession reached the villa and she saw the rotund form of the Duke d'Albatore waiting by the coach. She slid from the back of the horse to stand in front of him and saw the snake-like deadliness in the small button eyes. "I've had all your things packed and put on the carriage," he announced. "We want you to look your most beautiful always."

"Why?" Marina asked. "Why are you taking me back with you?"

"To be a bride, of course." He laughed, a high, mirthless laugh. She heard her guardian's cold laughter join in. The duke's laughter stopped abruptly, the round-cheeked face growing dark. He slapped her across the face, a stinging, sharp blow. "Never try to run away from me again," he hissed. Turning to one of his aides, he snapped orders. "Tie her and put her in the coach. Hurry, I've wasted enough time already."

Marina felt her arms pulled behind her back, rope tying her wrists together, and then she was yanked forward into the coach and pushed into a corner of the facing seats. The duke and her guardian exchanged words for a moment longer. "You can go ahead with practical steps now," she heard the round-faced figure say. "She'll not cause any trouble, I can assure you."

"I'll tell my people at once," the count replied. The duke climbed into the coach, pulled the door closed, and sat down across from her. The vehicle began to move at once and she tried to look away from the tiny eyes that watched her with malevolent satisfaction. It was difficult, she found. She was like a bird fascinated by a snake's cold orbs.

"Why?" Marina asked again, letting the one word drop softly from her lips. The little man put his head back and she heard the high, nasal laugh resound through the coach. "I told you, my dear, to be a bride. You must learn to believe me." He reached forward, undid the top buttons of the sleeveless *basque,* then one more, letting her breasts show almost entirely. "That's better," he remarked, settling back. "It is a long trip. I may as well enjoy the scenery."

The coach traveled at top speed, the ride full of ruts and bumps, to the enjoyment of the duke, who eagerly watched each time her breasts half-fell from the opened *basque.*

But Marina watched the road signs pass, saw the words cut into the large sign between two pines: LAZIO—ROMA. She watched as the coach took the first turn. They were in Lazio but not going to Rome. The road widened, became smoother, the dusk outlining the rows of pines that frowned down on them. She saw the *palazzo* before the coach turned into the driveway and recognized it for what it was at once, all the courses in Roman and Medieval architecture she had sat through in the academy in Florence suddenly redeeming themselves.

She glanced at the evil little man across from her as the coach drew closer to the great structure. "This is yours?" she asked acidly.

He nodded and folded fat fingers contentedly over his chest. "An acquisition resulting from the bad business ventures of the De Monta family, added to the interest charges on loans they couldn't pay," he remarked. "A magnificent structure, isn't it?"

"Cockroaches can live in fine houses," she snapped, watching the round eyes grow smaller.

"You'll regret that tongue of yours," he muttered. Ignoring him, Marina let her eyes take in the *palazzo* before the last light of dusk faded. It was one of the ancient houses which had been built in twelve or thirteen hundred B.C. by the Romans, converted into castles in medieval times, then passed to Renaissance princes, and finally made into *palazzi* by their seventeenth-century owners. Her eyes noted the high string-courses and the decorative work over each arched window, the mark of the architect-designer Peruzzi, obviously the last of those who had worked over the labors of others.

The coach came to a halt, and the door was opened from outside. Marina stepped out and, almost fell from the carriage, unbalanced by her wrists bound behind her. "Untie her now," she heard the duke order, then she felt the ropes being cut. She brought her hands around quickly and rubbed her wrists. She saw the duke watching her massage her left wrist.

"If you're waiting for gratitude, don't bother," she informed him.

His fleshy lips, small mock cupid's bows, tightened. "You'll be taken to your room. My grounds are patroled by hand-picked guards. Do not even be so foolish as to try to escape." Marina agreed silently. Even if she escaped the grounds, she knew nothing of the land here, where to go, where to flee. Her visits to Lazio had been to Rome and Latina, nowhere else. Here she was truly a prisoner. She turned from the Duke d'Albatore and followed the two guards into the *palazzo*. Three other men bore her things in trunks and boxes. The duke had indeed seen to it that all her things had accompanied her.

Inside the great foyer, which was tiled in black-and-white *terrazzo*, she halted as the duke motioned to the ground-floor corridor. "The third room at the end," he told the men with the bags.

"A bride who is a prisoner," Marina added with mock sweetness. "Hardly the usual thing."

"You are hardly the usual bride, my dear." The round face smiled.

Marina followed the guard down the wide corridor. The duke insisted on maintaining she was to be a bride. Macabre humor, she wondered. Or something more? The guard opened the room and she stepped inside. It was a large and opulent room with an enormous bed in deep pink silks and matching canopy. The furniture was satinwood, inlaid, and not unlike the delicate workmanship of the Englishman, Chippendale. A row of arched windows appeared to flank a low terrace wall, each window draped in the same deep pink silk as the bed. A bride would certainly be enchanted with the room, but not this bride, Marina mused, as her things were brought to her.

When she was left alone, she noted there was no latch on the door. She began to unpack some of the things, hanging out the full dresses that would quickly wrinkle. There was no knowing what she might yet need here. There was no knowing anything. A wave of despondency swept over her as she suddenly realized she was totally alone, a prisoner, subject to a fate which she could not as yet imagine. She rose, went to a door that was closed, pulled it open, and saw a marble bathroom, white and gold. A very tall faucet hung from one wall. Marina turned it and the water flowed almost at once, not hot but pleasantly warm. The duke was a total sybarite, indulging comfort and the senses at every turn, she realized once again. A terrible chill touched her and made her skin suddenly flinch. Was she to be one more special indulgence for the duke? Was she to be a bride of pleasure, to be used and misused and then done away with to avoid complications?

It was not beyond question, yet somehow it did not hold the ring of truth. Her guardian had completed something to his great satisfaction and it revolved around her. A bargain of importance had been struck, a price of a sizable nature paid—more than she would bring as merely an indulgence. The duke, voluptuary that he was, had an Arab's eye for a trade. No, there was more, and that frightened her. Grimly she made a silent promise. While she was here, she'd listen and watch every little thing she could. If she could find the answer, perhaps she could find a way out of whatever she faced.

She shook despondency away by allowing herself to think of Generoso. He would have his ways of learning what had happened and who had taken her. But his mountain fastness was a good distance from Lazio, not to be covered in an hour. The coach had taken most of a day. He would never make the mistake of racing into a trap like a schoolboy. He would have to plan, reconnoiter, and wait his chance. It would all take time.

But perhaps that would be a blessing in disguise. Perhaps by then she would have learned important things. Gathering confidence to herself as one gathers a protective blanket, Marina pulled the *basque* from her shoulders, then stepped from the skirt. She went into the bath, let the warm water shower down upon her, and found thick, deep-gold towels to dry herself. Among her things she found a nightdress, slipped into it, and turned out the bone-china lamp atop the dresser. Darkness flooded the room, until after a moment the pale hand of the moon touched the windows and crept into the room. Marina sank into the canopied bed, the deep pink silks soft and smooth. Before her eyes closed in the sleep of exhaustion she envisioned a strong, fine-lipped face with a shock of black curly hair and deep eyes. Take courage, *cara*, the vision whispered, *coraggio.*

She nodded against the pillow. She had found a love, a completeness never found by most. It wouldn't be torn from her like this. She wouldn't let it be. Great gifts were not given for so short a time. Or were they? "No," she insisted to the darkness. "No." She slept, and dreamed of Generoso entwined in her arms.

The moon moved down over the skies of the *campagna Romana,* the vast province of land that stretched out in a semicircle from the city of St. Peter. Its rays lengthened to gild the sleeping girl in the canopied bed with silver, softly glinting from the jet-black halo of hair that lay against the pink pillow. Marina turned, suddenly restless. The night had moved into its deepest and she turned again, dimly imagining she heard voices. She felt her eyes flutter, then half open. The voices came again. It hadn't been a dream.

"Look how magnificent she is," the voice said. Marina pressed her eyes tight, then opened them. She saw heads—one, two, three. Fuzzy outlines at first, they then became clearer. The one in the center came into focus first, a round-faced man with little eyes. A low candle set atop the dresser cast a dim, flickering light that mingled with the silver of the moon.

Marina sat up and stared at the Duke d'Albatore. He wore a loose-sleeved nightgown. The two guards beside him were in shirts and wide-belted breeches. "Get out of here!" Marina shouted. "What are you doing here, spying on me while I'm asleep?"

"A beautiful woman is even more beautiful asleep," the duke replied. "And you are beautiful. Sullied but beautiful." He reached out and began to pull the nightgown from her shoulders. She slapped his hand away. "Come now, my dear. You've no honor to protect."

"It is my right to give myself to whom I choose," Marina shot back.

"How amusing," the duke commented. He turned to the two men. "Wait outside the door. I'll teach my bride about her rights." Marina watched the men leave the room and close the door. The little round man's leap was unexpected, a surprise in speed and in act. He landed atop her, knocking her backward onto the bed. "Now, my fine-born little baggage," he breathed. His face came down to find her breasts as his hands held her wrists. She felt his arm give as she pushed. Turning her head, her teeth found the lobe of his ear and bit at the same time as she pushed up and back. He screamed in pain as he fell half off the bed. She raked his shoulder with her nails, missing his face as he dived forward. He could move with surprising agility. She watched him scurry across the floor and find his feet. "Guards," he screamed, holding one hand to his ear.

The two men burst in immediately. "Hold her," he commanded. "Tear that thing from her."

Marina saw the two men come at her; she tried to leap to one side, but she slipped on the smoothness of the sheet. Arms caught her and flung her onto the bed, ripping the nightdress away. She was held, arms outstretched, naked, able only to writhe. A mere twenty-four hours earlier, she had lain much like this, writhing and twisting in passion. This was a mockery of that moment, an obscene travesty, and she felt shame for that, not for her nakedness.

The duke's button eyes were bright as he stood at the foot of the bed. He pulled the nightgown over his head and stood naked before her, as he had that night when he'd toppled from the carriage. But now he stood straight, not bound and doubled over. There was little difference, she noted. His fat belly jiggled as he came toward her. Marina knew she should have felt fear. He was an unpredictable little man. Instead, all she could think of was Generoso's bronzed beauty as he came to her, the lithe strength and breathtaking, pulsating power he offered. She stared at the fleshy, soft form that came at her now.

"I shall give you a night you'll never forget," the high, nasal voice promised.

"With that?" Marina heard herself ask, unable to hold back words. She felt her body shudder and could not halt the laughter that suddenly welled up from inside her. It fed on its own tensions, she knew, a strange release of the knots inside her, but she laughed again and then again.

"Stop that, you damned slut," she heard the duke scream, poised at her legs. "Stop it, stop it." But Marina did not, indeed could not, stop. The little figure was laughable and she could not take her eyes from him. The slap raised a red mark on her thigh and another on her abdomen as he rained blows upon her. "Stop it, stop it, damn you," he was screaming, his breath exploding in short gasps. He almost catapulted over her, his hands reaching for her throat. "Damned high-born whore," he screamed. "I'll show you."

His thumbs tightened on her neck, and Marina felt her breath constrict. The laughter hung in her throat but was slow to leave her eyes. His round face was red and his eyes were tiny points. His mouth panted curses and then he fell to one side, sliding from the bed. Slowly he pulled himself to his feet, speared her with his eyes. "You're worth too much to kill. That's all that saves you," he panted. Marina felt the two other men release her arms and watched them take a final look at her naked loveliness. Their eyes made her shudder far more than the Duke d'Albatore's pathetic attempts. She lay still until the door closed after them and she was alone.

Marina rose then and felt a wave of weakness rolling over her. She had been more than lucky this night, she realized. Her dissolute captor would have to try again, if only to salve his own bruised masculinity, undoubtedly with more planning next time. She blew out the candle, donned another nightdress, and then collapsed onto the bed. One fact had come out of it: She'd not been brought here just as a bride or as an object for his pleasures. Her instincts had proven right about that. She was being saved for something else, as part of the victorious bargain that had been struck by Aldo Gamborelli. Even "marred" she had a value to them.

But what value? Certainly in Lazio, there was no more tolerance for a woman stained. The same rules held everywhere. Rome dispensed mercy, not justice. But she was of value to them. The original bargain had been shattered and a new one made to replace it. The thought flung apprehension and fear around her like a net. She closed her eyes and forced herself to sleep. It was her only refuge now.

CHAPTER SIX

MARINA HAD WAKENED and was dressed when the door pushed open in the morning and a woman entered. She was a heavy-bodied woman in a black dress, her face seamed by the years and her eyes dulled by the world. Her hands were rough and heavy-fingered—hands that had known only hard work.

"I am Anna," she announced. "I am to stay with you whenever you leave this room."

"A chaperon," Marina bit out. "How considerate."

"I only do as I'm ordered to," the woman said. "But I have learned it is better to make the best of things, not the worst."

"And I believe in making the worst of some things," Marina returned. The woman shrugged her thick-set shoulders, disapproval in the gesture. "Just how long is this charade to go on?" Marina asked.

"I don't know. I don't concern myself with such things," the woman said. "Breakfast is being brought up to you. I will come back after."

She turned abruptly and but moments later a guard brought in the breakfast tray: buns, cut apples, and coffee. Surprised at herself, Marina ate hungrily and when she had finished the woman appeared as if my magic.

"You may go wherever you like on the grounds," the woman informed her, "if I am with you. There is a siesta between twelve and two. Then you must stay in your room."

"And the duke?" Marina questioned. "Does he not want to see me?"

"I have not been told so. He has a busy day," the woman replied.

"You are his housekeeper?" Marina persisted.

"And more. I am well paid not to talk of the things I see at the *palazzo*," the woman replied. She answered questions with a weariness that did not disguise a dogged adherence to orders.

"I think I shall spend the morning right here," Marina remarked. The woman nodded, backed away, and strode from the room. Marina saw the door closed on her and glimpsed the two guards outside. Going to the arched windows of the room, she saw that they afforded a long sweep of the palace entrance. She drew up a chair and positioned herself to command a view of the entranceway.

By noon the duke had entertained at least four separate visitors, each of whom stayed but a short while. The hours between twelve and two grew oppressively hot and Marina, finding the siesta welcome, stretched on the canopied bed and half slumbered. A try of food was brought by the woman Anna, and Marina picked at it as she continued to watch the procession of visitors.

At twilight the woman appeared again. "Do you not wish to go for a walk?" she asked gruffly. Marina declined. "I am surprised my host has not been to see his bride," she probed.

"The duke is much too busy for you," the woman growled. Good, Marina answered silently as she was left alone again. It was after dark, when most of the place seemed to sleep, that Marina heard another carriage draw up, and went to the window to see the visitor arrive. The spear of light from the doorway caught the deep red robes of a cardinal and Marina watched the churchman hurry into the *palazzo*. He stayed at least two hours, then left, a red wraith in the night. Marina went to sleep frowning. The uneasiness was with her the next morning as more visitors arrived, this time rougher men in work clothes. Once again the hard-faced woman came to her with breakfast, but this time

Marina consented to a stroll through the palace. Her eyes eagerly sought out a closed door behind which she heard the duke's high voice. It was, she noted, directly down the long, wide corridor from where she was held.

Returning to her room in time, she saw the same pattern of visitors as the day before. When night came, another carriage drew up and a cardinal emerged. Not the same churchman, she realized, for this one was much taller and more imperious.

Marina tiptoed to the closed door of the room. Holding the knob with both hands she turned it slowly, hardly moving it at all until she felt the door latch give way. Pulling the door open an inch, she could peer into the dark hallway. Only one guard was outside her door, fast asleep in a chair tilted against the wall. Marina opened the door wider and stepped halfway into the corridor. She could see down the straight line of it to the great entrance foyer where a wall lamp lighted two very awake guards armed with muskets at the door. Their presence did not concern her. She was going only as far as the thin wedge of yellow light that reached into the dark corridor from the room where the duke's voice could be heard.

Leaving her door ajar, she moved from the room on bare feet, casting another glance at the guard. His head was tilted to one side and his breathing heavy with sleep. She hurried on, the marble floor cool against the soles of her feet. Staying against one wall, she reached the sliver of light from the room and crouched down.

"As a Bourbon, the king has to be involved eventually," she heard the duke say. "His queen is Maria Caroline, daughter of Empress Maria Theresa."

"Do not give me history lessons, d'Albatore," she heard a low, impatient voice intone, a voice, she thought, which must be the Cardinal's. "What is more critical on that score is that the queen is also the sister of Marie Antoinette. If there is a revolution in France and the mob takes over, the Bourbons would inevitably be drawn into a conflict with the revolutionary government."

"That is precisely why Gamborelli has put together this venture. The Bourbons may be forced to flee. Their power base is weak to begin with, as you know, my dear Cardinal," Marina heard the duke answer. "But if Naples were to rule Reggio di Calabria, under Gamborelli and myself, we would have a new, unified, and more powerful state. In time, we might expand northward into Tuscany. With Rome's permission, of course."

"Of course," the low voice of the cardinal mocked.

"We have made arrangements for the armed militia needed for such a coup," the duke went on. "But men alone are not enough, as we know. We need money to run the new state after the conquest, funds for a treasury, a proper system of government. We'll get little from the Calabrese. They are poor as it is."

"So you look to the Church, of course," the cardinal said.

"For spiritual leadership as well, Your Eminence," Marina heard the duke add hastily.

"Spare me the piety, d'Albatore," the cardinal snapped. "I agree with your venture. So do some of my fellow churchmen. But as you know, Rome is divided. Many, in high places, are against the Church taking part in such ventures. Many do not want to see the city-states grow more powerful. They want peaceful mergers." He sighed, paused, then went on. "However I am not one of those. I understand the use of power. I can speak for those who agree with me. Cardinal Moglianeri came to visit you last night, I understand."

"Yes. He said he'd go along with whatever you decided." Marina heard the low voice pause again, then the sound of a chair being moved and footsteps as the cardinal paced back and forth in the room.

"I will tell you what I, and those churchmen who think as I, are prepared to do, my dear d'Albatore." The cardinal spoke firmly. "You tell me you've arranged for the men and arms to attack Reggio di Calabria, correct?"

"Yes. The plan is to land at Cetraro and cut off the produce and supplies from the north that the city must have. They will have to send out their forces to meet us then."

"I'm not concerned with military details. If you succeed with that part of the venture, we shall provide the funds for the treasury and the operation of the new state," the churchman replied. "Naturally, we shall expect that we who have cooperated with you shall control all the ecclesiastical aspects of the new state."

"Naturally, Your Eminence. We understand each other perfectly," Marina heard the nasal voice exult. She rose and then moved back up the corridor. The guard still slept as she returned to her room and quietly closed the door. She threw off clothes and climbed into the canopied bed. At last she had real intelligence for Generoso, now when he was out of reach. Her guardian's plans had shape and substance now, made of greed and devious arrangements, grand designs for power and wealth. Marina felt a stab of depression as she thought of the cardinal who had been in the room with the duke. The Church was indeed a house divided. Some of its princes sought power with as much zeal as the merchants and moneylenders. Some of its princes and some of its soldiers, Marina reflected sadly, thinking at once of Father Scunigi. He played the same game on a smaller scale.

Generoso, Generoso, hurry, she whispered silently. The outlines are mine now. We know what they plan. Only one thing remained shrouded. Where did she fit into these grand plans? Bargains had been made, with the duke supplying money for Aldo Gamborelli's plans for men and arms. It was clear now that she had once been the count's contribution, his part of the bargain: her body and her untouched beauty for the duke's money. But she had ended that. What new bargain had been struck? What possible place did she fit into now? Fear swept over her at once—fear that her freedom and Generoso might be lost to her forever.

What if he had not learned where she'd been taken? What if her guardian had silenced anyone who had seen her leave? What if Generoso searched vainly and furiously in the wrong places? Another day had passed and the obscene little duke had left her alone, but would he continue to do so? Was she truly fortunate for that, or did his absence really mean that something far worse waited in the shrouded reasons for her being here?

Marina pressed her face to the pillow. She pulled sleep around her again. It was the one refuge she had. In sleep she held Generoso to her breasts. In sleep she remembered ecstasy. In sleep she hoped.

Plunged into sleep, Marina did not hear the door as it opened in the deep of the night, did not see the round figure that approached her as she lay more naked than not in the heat of the summer night. Lying half on her side, she did not see the Duke d'Albatore shed his robe to stand naked at the foot of her bed and imagine himself making love to her. His whispered words did not reach her as he gyrated, twisted, heaved his short, fat body backward and forward. "You'd learn, you beautiful bitch," the whispered gasps came. "You'd learn not to laugh at me. I'd have you flogged each day and then take you right after. I'd have you on your knees to me each night. You'd never laugh again at me. If I didn't need you, if you weren't promised, if Gamborelli hadn't arranged the whole thing around you, you'd learn about laughing."

He continued his movements harder, panted whisperings faded, and then the round form almost leaped upward, a half-stifled hoarse cry bursting from the thick lips. Marina woke, pulled herself up on one elbow, her eyes misted with sleep. She rubbed her knuckles into her eyes and never saw the slap that knocked her back onto the pillows although she felt the burning, sharp pain of it. Tears automatically erupted to flood her eyes. She heard soft, running footsteps and shook her head to clear her eyes. She was alone and the door ajar.

Marina stayed motionless for a moment, listening and peering into the dark of the room, but she neither saw nor heard anything. Only the stinging pain of her cheek was proof that she hadn't been alone. Frowning, she rose, closed the door, puzzled and more than a little afraid. This was a house of perverted dangers that lay like a squid waiting for a chance to ensnare a victim. She could not wait any longer for Generoso, she concluded. In the morning, she'd look for a way to flee. She'd disregard the odds and take a chance. Once again she sought peace in slumber but she woke often through the rest of the night. However, by morning, she'd gathered enough rest in bits and pieces to feel refreshed. When the woman appeared, Marina suggested a walk outside and the woman nodded, faint surprise in her seamed face.

She followed discreetly, a mock chaperon. It fitted this *palazzo,* where everything mocked—a place of grandeur steeped in decadence, an architectural treasure owned by a grotesque. Her attention turned to the guards patrolling the grounds. There were many—too many. It was little wonder that the duke kept but a single sleepy guard outside her door at night. Obviously he felt confident that the guards outside would foil any escape. She noted the passages at the extreme ends of the outer grounds which dropped steeply into woods. Unlike her own villa, the stables, and repair areas, the carriage house and kennels were all part of the structure itself. No separate buildings dotted the grounds. There were no places to hide and pause on the way to freedom.

Discouraged, Marina returned to her room. The woman's world-weary eyes seemed to know why she had gone for the walk outside. "I'll not be going out again today," Marina told her. "There's no need for you to stay about." The woman paused at the door, glanced back, and her eyes took on a hint of pity as she went on. Marina went to the window, inexplicably disturbed. Perhaps she had imagined the expression in the woman's eyes, but it stayed with her as the day wound itself to a close and went away only as she embraced welcome sleep once more. This time the night passed without unseen visitors.

The next morning Marina had just finished her bath when the door of the room flew open to admit the duke and three of his men. She pulled a robe around herself and looked down at the small, round figure that came to a halt in front of her. "Take all her things," he barked at the men as his eyes stayed on her. Marina kept the alarm from her face.

"I thought I was to be your bride," she remarked.

"Oh, you will be a bride," he said. "But not mine."

Marina felt the dryness of her lips and let her tongue touch them. "Whose?" she asked softly.

"A man of great wealth," the duke allowed.

"One who does not care if I am, in your words, sullied?"

The round little eyes almost shone with delight. "Precisely," he snapped back. "A man who collects wives. A man for whom you will be a rare jewel to add to his collection."

"The man who is supplying the army for your ventures?" Marina dared and saw the round face darken at once.

"Where did you learn of that?" he asked.

"He is the man, isn't he?" Marina countered. "This is how my kind guardian salvaged his bargain."

The duke's face conceded surprise at her accuracy. "Aldo Gamborelli is a resourceful man. He knows who to contact," the duke acknowledged. "Together, we were like gold miners who had found gold only to have it turn into worthless metal. But what some men will not accept others eagerly embrace. Aldo went to Ettore Baldi, the trader, who quicly arranged an agreement satisfactory to everyone." He laughed for an instant. "Except for you, of course."

"But then I never counted, not from the very start." Marina was unable to keep the bitterness from her voice. The names became part of the plan, they fitted in, the secret visitors and hurried trips by her guardian all falling into place now. Except one last name: he to whom she had been promised as part of their unholy bargain.

The man had cleared from the room, leaving one box of dresses for her. "May I dress?" she asked coldly.

The duke gave a mocking bow. "Please go on," he said.

"Alone," Marina bit out.

"No," he snapped. "I would feast my eyes once more on your magnificence." She read the malicious lights in his doll's eyes. He would extract one last moment of embarrassment from her, one last indignity. He'd make her do his bidding once more, seizing a last, substitute pleasure. Marina's eyes held a dark blue flame as she turned from his leering face. It would be her own variation on a theme, the final performance she had wanted to give at the ball.

Marina opened the robe, let it slowly slide to the floor, loosened her hair so it billowed in a glinting, gleaming black background behind her rose-tinted alabaster skin. She walked slowly, undulatingly to the box of dresses, held one up, let her breasts turn to him, then away. She dropped the garment, reached for another, and toyed with that. She walked near to him, moving her hips slowly and sensuously. She made her eyes smolder with an invitation that was a dare wrapped in silent laughter. She stretched, rose on tiptoes, and pushed her breasts forward. The duke was breathing in harsh little gasps. She half turned from him and then glanced back.

"Maybe I'd rather stay here with you," she purred, turning fully to him again. She heard the short, strangled cry that tore from his throat, and then he was running, flinging himself from her, racing out the door and into the corridor. The sound of his heels echoed as they clattered down the smooth tile flooring. Marina's eyes narrowed. She made a harsh, snorting sound. The weak cannot even gain a weak victory. Aldo Gamborelli had the icy strength of real cruelty, and the duke was but his creature.

Aldo Gamborelli was the engineer of all that had happened. Her account with him was still to be settled.

Marina pulled on a green gown with sleeves trimmed in orange, picked up the rest of her things, and hurried from the room. Three men waited and one took her box while the other two fell in step on each side of her. She saw the carriage ready and waiting, the duke in one corner, his fleshy lips almost in a pout. He did not look at her as she got in and sat down opposite him. The horses started off at once and Marina saw that only two horsemen rode behind the coach. She watched as the *palazzo* disappeared behind the trees and the coach took a road marked *Formia*. Soon the seacoast came into view and the route went along the roads that bordered the shoreline. The horses were not driven and the coach stopped often for rest and water as the day grew hotter. The duke had said not a single word to her and Marina was not unhappy for that.

They were halfway to Formia, she heard one of the drivers remark as they halted at a wayside resting place. A party of farmers came along, each carrying two large wicker baskets filled with figs and dark purple plums. The duke rested outside the coach, fanning himself with a plumed hat, and Marina drank from a natural spring that bubbled up between two rocks alongside the resting area. The two horsemen who followed, the driver and his helper, lounged against a fallen log. The fruit pickers found ready and eager purchasers as they halted to offer the contents of their baskets. One man, thin with a limping left leg, came over to Marina. He picked a large, ripe plum from the basket and handed it to her.

"I have no money," Marina told him. "I am sorry."

The man's eyes, blue behind a grizzled countenance, continued to press the plum on her. "Go on. Take it, a beautiful lady like yourself," he muttered. "It's a gift. Take it." His eyes were sharp, strangely intent, boring into her. "Be careful of the pit," he warned.

He shuffled off at once and the others followed. Marina turned the plum in her hand and saw a fine slit at one side of the skin. She bit into the plum, found it ripe, sweet, and juicy. She took another bite cautiously, letting her teeth seek the hard pit. They came down on something soft where the pit should have been. Her eyes flashed to the others. No one watched her. She pulled the fruit apart in her hands and saw the small, folded piece of paper where the pit should have been. Unfolding it as she devoured the rest of the plum, she read the word penciled on the stained paper: *Soon.*

Marina dropped the little square behind a rock, her heart pounding. Generoso was near, watching from someplace, waiting for the right moment. Perhaps he'd been watching the *palazzo* for days. She tried to keep the burst of happiness from her face, forced her lips to turn down sullenly as the duke called out to go on. She climbed into the coach across from him, stared out the window, and found it was terribly hard not to look happy when one's heart sang in silent joy.

They made two more stops, in small coastal villages where the leather water bouget at the rear of the carriage was filled and where more fresh fruit was purchased. At the last village a vintner provided the duke and his party with wine, but Marina declined hers. The duke seemed so disinterested in what she did that at one point it seemed almost as though she might be able to wander away by herself. But when the driver caught sight of her she returned immediately to the coach. It didn't matter now. She had but to wait, and be ready.

It was blue-lavender dusk when the coach reached a small inn facing the sea at Formia. It was clear that arrangements had plainly been made in advance, and the innkeeper, a nervous man who seemed unable to keep his hands quiet, apologetically showed her to a room where the lone window had been nailed over by boards. "Duke d'Albatore's orders, madam," he informed her and hurried quickly away. The door of the room still ajar, she turned to see the familiar round form coming up to her, keys in hand.

"There's water and a wedge of cheese inside, the innkeeper tells me," snarled the duke. "Enough to hold you for the night."

"You're too generous," Marina answered.

"If you want to wash the road dust off, there's a place at the end of the hallway," he hissed. "I'll wait till you're done with it."

"Before locking me in for the night?" Marina queried.

"Precisely." The little man then pushed open the door of the room diagonally across from hers and was gone.

By the time Marina had finished bathing, night had descended, and through a tiny window she could see an almost full moon hanging low in the sky. A small smile of confidence touched her lips. Generoso had not yet made his move, but when he did, it would be here in the seacoast village of Formia. Probably in the dawn hours, when the others were asleep and the sentries at their least alert, she mused, slipping into her dress and strolling back down the hallway to her room. No sooner had she reached it than the duke appeared, brandishing the keys that would soon make her a prisoner. Marina swirled past into the little room as he paused in the doorway, one hand on the knob.

"By now you've heard from him, of course." It was a statement, not a question.

"What?" Marina frowned.

"By now you've heard from this Red Camorra cutthroat." Marina felt her legs tremble and she clutched the edge of a splintered, worn end-table.

"I don't know what you're talking about," she murmured, her words almost stumbling from her lips. His smile had smugness curled around it.

"We gave him plenty of opportunity to contact you during the ride here." The duke's tone was almost gleeful. "We've been expecting an attempt to rescue you and, needless to say, we've planned for it. Your guardian caught one of the Camorrists.

Under torture the man told of a black-haired beauty who had been visiting their leader. We decided that we'd kill two birds at a single blow by taking you to meet your new master while using you as the bait to hook our scarlet fish."

Marina sank down on a wooden chair, attempting to mask the horror that filled her. "As he has obviously contacted you, but has not yet struck, he is most likely planning an attack during the night or at dawn. In either case, we shall be waiting." Marina's eyes stared at the round face, too numbed to feel hate. "A sizable force is poised, staying back, awaiting only my signal. You see, you are of value in so many ways."

Marina sprang, hands stretched out to take the grinning face, a scream of pain and rage vaulting from her lips. The little man slammed the door shut as she fell against it, clawed the wood, and heard the lock turned from outside. "Sleep well, my dear," she heard the voice from the other side call out. "Look on the bright side. You will lose a lover and gain a husband."

Marina flung herself against the door, kicked on it, pounded on it, screamed oaths. It did not move. Slowly, she sank down along the rough wood to lay crumpled against the bottom of the frame. Deep, groaning sobs wracked her, finally turning into hoarse sighs as she pulled herself to her feet. She went to the single sealed window. Through small openings between the boards she could glimpse the night, the sliver of the moon, a fistful of stars. She tugged at the boards, first one, then another, finally giving up. All had been fixed with iron nails so heavy that two powerful men could not pull them free.

She flung herself upon the cot pressed against one wall and drew her knees up as pain seemed to tie knots in her stomach. Gilbert Tosti had died because of her, and now she was the lure that would lead Generoso to his death. Love was supposed to bring happiness, not tragedy. She pressed her face down upon the coarse cotton sheet and felt a great ache flooding her body as though the fever were upon her. The little barren room had become not a place of confident waiting but a dungeon for the body and an execution chamber for the spirit. Like some caged animal she rose and began to crawl along the walls, pressing, feeling, moving her feet along the baseboards, then on her hands and knees across the floor, hoping desperately for a loose board, a weak spot, any flicker of escape. But the inn was a solidly crafted place and the wood old but strong.

She halted against the cot and draped herself over the edge of it. Her eyes closed, but there was no sleep. All she could see were Generoso's olive-black eyes with love and trust and courage, full of vows. The tears that wet her face were silent pleas, anguish without word or sound. She lay with despair as the night drifted slowly toward the day. With each hour invisible bands of steel tightened around her chest. Pulling herself up, she peered through the slitted openings between the boards of the window. It was still dark. *Don't let morning come,* Marina whispered. *Stay the dawning.*

The lone candle in one corner of the room flickered and caught her eye. It had almost burned down. If only it could burn down this room, she thought bitterly. *If only . . .* the words caught in her throat. Pulling herself up, she went to the window. The moon had slipped behind the trees, on its way to bow to the day. But maybe there was a chance, Marina found herself thinking, a chance that would alert Generoso as he watched from wherever he waited. She whirled, pulled the rough cotton sheet from the cot, and tore strips from it. She stuffed them into the slits between the boards, pushed others up into crevices between boards and the window, letting the ends hang down. Not enough, she realized and pushed more strips into the window, draping them around the edges of the boards. Then, satisfied, she stepped back, brought the candle over, held it to the first of the cotton strips, watched it catch fire. She lighted each of the others, then bent over to avoid the smoke that began filling the little room.

Using part of the sheet to protect her hands, she pulled the remains of the candle from the holder and frantically wedged it into a corner between the bottom board and the window. The smoke was growing dense and, falling to her knees, she crawled to the other side of the room. The rags were burning but were giving off more smoke than flame, it seemed, as she watched from the floor, just under the layer of smoke that rose to the ceiling. She saw a sudden flash of pure flame, brief, then dying out. She held her breath, then saw another as the old wood began to catch. The cotton was sending up great smoke billows now, and the acrid gas began to move down to the floor.

Marina felt her breath tightening, her lungs growing heavy, when suddenly a great ball of flame leaped upward and she heard the sound of the window shattering outward. A trail of sparks rose upward as the boards fell away, burning furiously now, and the smoke leaped from the window into the air. It was gray outside, for the dawn had come. She saw the wall around the window blazing upward and heard the sound of shouts coming from outside. Marina gathered herself and ran, diving headlong through the flaming window. She felt the ground give as she landed on the cool, wet grass. She found her feet and ran. Behind her men were shouting. Marina did not look back but made straight toward the line of trees that rose up ahead of her.

"Marina! Here," she heard a familiar voice shout. She stumbled, searched the gray day, then saw Generoso's figure beckoning to her from a clump of brush.

"No. Run, it's a trap!" she shouted. Three shots rang out to drown her words and she saw Generoso wave her on again, then start toward her. "No, no, run!" she screamed. "They're expecting you. It's a trap. Run."

But Generoso ignored her words, raced forward, his arms reaching out, sweeping her against him. "My darling, Marina," he breathed into her ear.

She pulled back, her eyes wide with fear. "You must get away from here. They knew you'd come. They used me to bring you here. It's a trap." Beyond, she saw Tonio rising from the bushes, a heavy-barreled revolver in his hand, then more Camorrists in their distinctive blouses. Generoso's eyes narrowed, sweeping the terrain, when suddenly Marina saw one line of horsemen burst into view from the left and another from the right. A fusillade of shots rang out but not from the onrushing riders. Another line of attackers, on foot, appeared behind the treeline, firing as they came.

Generoso, his fact tight, pulled her into a small clump of scrub brush. Behind him, Marina glimpsed men throwing water on the fire which still burned, though not as fiercely. "I have failed you." Generoso groaned. "And my men. I should have foreseen the possibility of this."

"No, my love, you could not foresee it," Marina contradicted.

His eyes disagreed, grew deeper with pain. "You must run back toward the inn, then to the right. Go along the shore. You can get away in the confusion. We'll hold them off."

"No, I'll stay here with you," she protested.

He shook his head. "Save yourself. Let there be at least that out of it. If I can get away, it must be alone." He glanced up at the line of horsemen galloping closer from both sides. "Go, my darling, now."

She found in his lips a brief sweetness, terrible in its fire and anguish. "Just find me again, my darling. Find me wherever I am," she murmured. He kissed her one final time, then rose, urging her up, pushing her away almost roughly. "Run," he ordered. "Run like the meadow deer."

Marina obeyed and raced back into the smoke line that drifted to the right; then she turned to stay in it, holding her breath in long gasps. She dropped to one knee after a few moments and saw Tonio beside Generoso, a thin line of Camorrists following. They were heading for a row of thick cedars, but the duke's horsemen had converged, firing wildly after the fleeing figures, and the attackers on foot added to the deluge. Marina glanced behind her at the inn and glimpsed the duke against a corner of the building in a half-crouch, well out of the line of fire. She ran on, ducking below the smoke, turning to seek out Generoso again. She spied the shock of black, curly hair almost at the oaks, Tonio's burly figure close behind him. The line of Camorrists following had grown smaller. As she started to turn to run, Marina glimpsed the three horsemen sweeping in from the far left. They fired almost in unison and she saw Generoso rise, stiffen, seem to hang in midair, and then go down. Her scream tore at the very air and she began to run toward the cedars.

A figure rose in front of her, the Camorra stained with blood at the shoulder. "No, *signorina*, keep running." The man caught her arm and pulled her back. She recognized him as one of Generoso's men, yet still tried to wrest free of his grip.

"I must go to him," she cried. The man refused to release her and shook his head stubbornly.

"No, he told you to save yourself. It is what he wanted. Besides, you cannot help him now." Marina stared at the man, saw that his face was etched with pain, and that one arm hung limply at his side. "I have seen too many feel the bullets. You can tell by the way they fall," he said. "Run, save yourself, for him. It is why he came here."

Marina turned and ran—a stumbling, numbed movement. Dimly she saw the Camorrist who'd halted her move away in a crouch, going upward while she ran toward the shore. She ran but did not see, her flight a blind, aimless plunge into nothingness. Suddenly her feet were cool and wet and she could feel water lapping against her legs as she ran away from the shooting. She had to escape the sound. She had to meet Generoso somewhere, someplace far away from the massacre. She stumbled, fell, then pulled herself up and went on, feeling herself tiring, her breath refusing to lend support.

She slowed, halted, and sank down, surges of wetness lapping over her. Save yourself, she heard his voice say to her. For what, she asked silently as she lay on the pebbled sand, her eyes closed. Save yourself, the words repeated. For a life that had no more meaning, a dim voice inside her cried. For a lifetime of emptiness? Her hands opened, fingers digging into the soft, wet sand, pulling it up in small mounds as though she sought to dig a hole and crawl into it. Perhaps, she thought dimly, perhaps that would be the best thing left for her. Marina moved across the sand a few more feet, crawling like an *écrevisse* out of the Mediterranean. She lay still, then drew her legs up, half-curling her body on the sand as the sea lapped against her. Her world had ended here. To run farther was to deny the truth. The sea birds swooped low over her still form, curious, uncertain, then flew on. The creature was not for them. Nor for anyone.

CHAPTER SEVEN

S HAFTS OF REMEMBRANCE CAME FIRST, then sensation: light, heat, an inner pain; then forms: definition, tomorrows smashing into pieces, worlds falling, aimless running. Then the forms becoming substance: a name, Generoso, and the terrible pain again, feeling, sand, the touch of the sea. No sand now, no sea, but grass under her hands. Slowly, her eyes opened to see only blurred shadows and shapes. The shapes moved, took on outline, grew clearer, became faces: three men staring down at her. Behind them, the branches of trees. The sound of the surf rolling onto the sand drifted to her. A voice spoke from outside her line of vision, familiar, cold, and hard.

"She's all right. Get her up." Marina turned to see the hollow-cheeked face and marble agate eyes of Aldo Gamborelli. "You are surprised to see me, my dear Marina? I would not have missed this for the world." Marina forced her tongue to moisten her dried lips, wanting to find words to fling back, but there were none inside her. The round face of the Duke d'Albatore came into view beside the count as hands reached down and lifted her up to her feet. She swayed, then felt herself helped up as she steadied herself.

"Take her back to the inn," Aldo Gamborelli ordered. "Walk her. It will clear her head." Marina felt the hands moving her forward as they steadied her and she walked as if drugged, stumbling, her strength returning in small surges. As she reached the inn, with one wall smoke-blackened and a section charred away, she averted her eyes, not daring to look at the hillside beyond.

She tore from the hands holding her and fled into the inn where she halted as others caught hold of her again. Aldo Gamborelli, with the duke beside him, came up to the men restraining her.

"Get some women from the village to clean her up," the count ordered. "We promised a creature of rare beauty, not a slattern we found by a roadside."

Two men pulled at her, took her into a room at the other side of the inn, and stayed there on guard as others brought one of her trunks in. The duke paused in the doorway beside the taller, thinner figure of her guardian. "It will be good to be rid of her. She is indeed a package of trouble." Both men stepped away, and Marina sank down upon the edge of a hard, narrow bed in the room. The emptiness stayed. Nothing mattered. There was nothing left to care about, think about, or to feel, know, or want.

The minutes passed and the room was silent except for the hard breathing of the two guards. Finally, there was movement at the doorway and two women entered, one a young girl, thin and shy of manner, the other older and solemn. They carried towels and clothes and behind them the innkeeper brought in a large bucket of water. The guards filed out after him, closing the door. The younger girl came over to Marina. "Please, *signorina,* will you take off your things?" she asked. "We must do what we have been hired to do."

Marina stared at her and neither said anything nor did anything. Her eyes were dull, filled with emptiness. The girl reached out and began to pull Marina to her feet while the older woman helped from the other side. Marina felt the women slip her dress down and begin to wash away the dirt caked on her legs, arms, and face. They bathed her with the warm water of the bucket; their hands were gentle, their touch was kind. "You are most beautiful, *signorina,*" the younger girl commented, honest awe in her voice. "You will feel better now," she added, drying Marina's rose-alabaster skin with one of the towels. The other woman had began to brush the onyx hair, but the younger girl took the brush and went on with the task.

Finally she stepped back. "Your hair is lovely once again. Now, will you choose a gown from your things in the trunk?" Once again, Marina only stared at her and edged down to perch upon a hard-backed chair. The younger girl faced her, pursed her lips, began to make a remark, held back, and then tried again.

"*Signorina,* listen to me, please," the girl pleaded. Marina let her eyes meet the girl's hesitant gaze. "There was talk of what happened." Marina, hearing her, felt a sudden flood of tears mist her eyes. "You loved him very much." Marina could only nod. The girl hesitated again, then plunged ahead. "You must go on," she insisted. "You must not turn away from the world."

Marina felt her lips move; she heard the words come out whispered and hoarse: "From a world that holds nothing anymore?" she questioned.

The younger girl nodded solemnly. "Yes, even such a world. You must go on, for him. You can do no less. It is what he wanted for you, why he came to you."

The girl turned away with the awkwardness of those embarrassed by their outspokenness, but Marina was deeply moved by her words. "Thank you," she said sincerely, "thank you."

The girl gestured to the trunk. "Please?"

Marina nodded, reached out, and took the hairbrush from the girl's fingers. "Yes. I'll finish. I'm all right. Thank you again." The girl flashed one more glance of understanding, then turned and slipped from the room with the other woman. Marina stood still for a moment more in her aloneness, then, stepping to the trunk, selected a simple gown *en chemise,* pale blue, with soft, flowing lines, cut deeply at the neck. She finished brushing her hair until it glistened like a black flame. She turned as the door opened to admit Aldo Gamborelli, his cold eyes appraising and appreciating. She ignored the short figure that appeared at his side.

"That is better, much better," Gamborelli murmured. "And just in time for the bride-to-be to meet her new master." Marina noted that he had not bothered with the appellation "husband." He gestured to the doorway, then stepped back. "After you, my dear Marina."

Inside her the numbing ache remained, but Marina had drawn deeply of the unexpected strength of the girl's words. Her eyes met the count's satisfied, smug stare with dignity.

She brushed past him, head held high, into the low-ceilinged common room of the inn. The odor of charred wood and smoke still hung heavily in the air, a vaporous monument to failure and anguish. A man waited in the center of the room. A blue, long cape hung around his shoulders; beneath it was an outfit of burnished gold, and on his head was something resembling a *kiyaf-fah* but looser, flowing more freely. His dark eyes stared back at her from a heavy face with a prominent nose; it was a face lined from indulgence, not labor. His eyes devoured her and he ran a tongue over his heavy lip. Two figures stood flanking him, glistening Moors wearing only trousers and short, open vests. Each carried a curved Moorish dagger in a wide sash at the waist. Each had a bald, shaven head.

Marina saw the man in the cape let a slow smile cross his face. "Magnificent," he murmured as Aldo Gamborelli and the duke followed into the room. "You did not lie, my good friends. She is magnificent." Taking a step forward, he cupped his hand under Marina's chin.

"I am Kharoum ben Hassad," he announced.

"You stink of perfume and oils," Marina retorted.

"We warned you," she heard the duke begin, but the man cut him off with a wave of one hand, then let his smile grow tighter. His eyes did not leave her and his thick lower lip pushed forward.

"Many beautiful things are poisonous," he replied. "We shall take the venom out of you, my little pigeon. Then you will indeed be a jewel in the harem of Kharoum ben Hassad."

The last piece had fallen into place, Marina saw in silent grimness; the way Aldo Gamborelli had salvaged victory was now painfully clear. He had found her a buyer who wanted her for his own strange purposes. The finalities were easy to put together now; the duke had made a different kind of exchange. She fastened a glance on her guardian. "I see that conquerors need armies," she snapped.

He lifted his eyebrows. "You have been keeping your ears open, it seems," he returned. "Indeed, forces were recruited without any of the city-states involved and no tales carried to anyone. Kharoum ben Hassad's Arab armies will sweep out of the East as once their forefathers did, but this time they will conquer for the new rulers of Naples and Calabria, not Mohammed." He half-bowed to the large-nosed man, who returned the gesture.

"Take this beautiful jewel outside to the boat," Kharoum ben Hassad ordered. The two Moors flanked her at once and Marina felt insignificant beside the muscled, shining bodies. She cast a final glance at Aldo Gamborelli, then moved from the inn with the two huge Moors beside her. Outside, the later afternoon sun cast a glow across the shoreline behind the inn. Marina saw the rowboat pulled halfway onto the sands, four crewman in turbans standing beside it. Beyond, riding easily offshore, she saw the vessel. Countless afternoons at her father's side returned at once to her memory. He had loved the sea and ships, had always regretted he hadn't been a Genovese, and had passed on to his daughter his great knowledge of ships and sails. The vessel before her she recognized as an Algerian chebec, high-sterned with a long, sweeping slope down to the bow. Three lateen sails hung loosely in the late-afternoon calm.

Marina stepped into the small boat and the two Moors waited on the sand beside it. Kharoum ben Hassad, the duke, and Count Gamborelli halted a few feet from the boat. "The main body of my fleet sails north now. I will meet them and we shall sail for the attack at Cetraro," Marina heard the Arab say. "When we have secured the position, another force will sweep up from Sicily and we will have them trapped."

"Exactly as planned," the count agreed. Marina watched the men exchange bows, then Kharoum ben Hassad walked briskly to the small boat, swung aboard, and pulled her—not too gently—onto the stern seat beside him. The two giant Moors pushed the boat free of the sand, leaped aboard, and rowed to the ship in but minutes. The vessel was painted dark brown, Marina saw, and the sails were graying canvas, patched and shredded. She glanced at the vessel as the boat came alongside it and a ladder was lowered for her to climb aboard.

"Hardly an impressive flagship for an invasion flotilla." She sniffed.

"We are not a maritime people. We hire vessels to take us where we want to go, not to play games on the sea," the man remarked. He snapped fingers at the Moors. "Put her in my cabin and set sail at once," he commanded. Marina went with her captors as they led the way down a passage in the center of the ship and put her into a surprisingly large cabin with a huge bed of soft pillows and silk sheets stretched across the far end of the cabin. They closed the door as they backed out, and Marina immediately went to an oblong window cut in the side of the ship where she saw the water moving under the side of the vessel. They were underway quickly and the setting sun was astern. They headed south, she noted, as she pulled in her head. The cabin, she saw, had been done up in makeshift opulence, drapes hung here and there, huge pillows flung at random on the planked flooring.

Marina sank down on one of the huge cushions and felt the corroding embrace of despair sweep over her. Kharoum ben Hassad obviously intended her to be a special member of his harem. Undoubtedly, to have a beautiful Western woman as one of his wives would accord him a special status in his world. And what would it accord her? Marina shuddered. Another kind of debasement, perhaps worse than what she had known. Whatever her new life held, she would not submit quietly. She tried to tell herself that she wasn't afraid, but the lie shriveled inside her. But fear could be an ally, supplying her with a desperate courage, she decided as she closed her eyes and listened to the sound of the water rushing against the hull.

She dozed fitfully, waking each time with a half-cry, having dreamed of Generoso's tall, bronzed form running toward her, arms outstretched. The terrible depression came at once each time, and she pressed her hands to her forehead and bent low, fighting with the pain that became a physical thing, only to fall back into another half-sleep of exhaustion. It was dark when she awoke to see the door open and reveal the figure of Kharoum ben Hassad, with the two Moors close behind him. He carried a lantern, then set it on a shelf; his two black shadows lighted other lanterns in the cabin. Light stretched outward, filling the cabin.

Marina watched the two Moors. They were lithe and powerful, and a beauty of their own was carried in each effortless movement as they drew the curtain over the small window, rearranged pillows, and pulled the sheet back from the makeshift bed. Kharoum ben Hassad held a half-curled navigational chart in one hand and seemed tired.

"Wait outside," he told the Moors, and they vanished, silent, dark wraiths. His eyes roved over Marina. "Working with the charts always fatigues me. I am not made for this plotting of courses. Tonight, I shall ask only that you pleasure me gently. It will allow me to appraise how many subtleties you have yet to learn."

He tossed the chart aside, whipped off the cape, and undid his clothing, enough for Marina to see the fold of fat around his waist. "Take the gown off," he ordered. "You cannot pleasure me in all that cloth. I want to feel your skin."

"I'll not pleasure you. I'll not touch you," Marina spat.

Kharoum ben Hassad's eyes narrowed as he stepped closer. "You are not courageous. You are stupid. Has it not become clear to you that you are mine to do with exactly as I wish?" he asked.

"Obviously not," Marina returned.

"I am being kind with you now. Do not abuse my patience," he warned.

"I don't want this kind of kindness. I don't want you," Marina countered. Kharoum ben Hassad sighed deeply and seemed about to turn away when his arm lashed out in a backhanded blow. Marina felt his knuckles crash against her cheek and staggered backward, almost falling. The Arab's eyes had become fragments of fire.

"You need lessons in manners," he snarled, aiming another blow at her. Marina twisted away, shot a hand out, raked his face with her nails, and heard his surprised cry of pain. He stepped back, put a hand to his cheek, then withdrew it to stare down at the red upon it. Astonishment and rage covered his face as he backed from her and rapped on the door. It opened instantly and the two Moors sprang into the cabin.

"Take her," he ordered. The men moved in a half-circle and Marina tried to race forward between them, but she was seized at once as, quick as panthers, they leaped to pin her arms. She was flung onto one of the large, thick cushions and was held down as she saw Kharoum ben Hassad step closer. "First you, Ahmed, then you, Izmir," he indicated. His eyes flicked to Marina. "You will learn to enjoy me," he sneered. "When they finish with you, you will beg for me next time, plead for my touch. If not, we will repeat the process until you do. It will not be long."

Marina felt the one Moor release her wrist and step back as the other came down atop her and pinned one arm against her throat, allowing only enough air to permit her to breathe. She felt his other hand lifting her gown. "No," she gasped out. "No." His reply was to squeeze her thigh as she cried out in pain, her legs parting. Her hands could reach no further than his waist as she hammered at his ribs with clenched fists. She might as well have pounded against a stone wall, she realized. Again she cried out in pain as he brought his knee down hard between her thighs, forcing her legs wider apart.

He began to move upward against her as frantically her hands struck, pulled, and pushed at his waist. One hand passed over something cold, something metallic. She brought it back and felt the handle of the curved Moorish dagger. As his head came down onto her breasts she glimpsed Kharoum ben Hassad watching from a few paces away, a cold smile curling his mouth. Marina screamed in panic as her attacker pressed himself down onto her, starting to thrust forward. Her hand touched the hilt of the curved dagger again, closed around it, and pulled it free. She brought it back to her waist as the Moor rose for an instant and came down hard onto her. She felt him go deep onto the blade and heard his groaned gasp. Her hand on the hilt of the dagger shuddered, and his weight lifted from her as he turned with eyes wide, one hand clutched to his abdomen. He fell to the side as Marina pulled backward, then pushed herself up along the edge of the cushion, the half-red blade still in her hand.

The second Moor stared at the other, then started to come at her, but Marina raised the blade. He halted, one hand on his own dagger. "Stay away from me," Marina warned, taking in Kharoum ben Hassad's astonished eyes. The Moor hesitated, looking at his master. Kharoum tried to take a step toward Marina, but she made a quick, darting motion with the blade and he stepped back.

"Leave her," he ordered. "She is too beautiful to risk in a battle with daggers now." He gestured to the man on the cabin floor, shuddering his final breath. "Take him outside." He looked up at Marina. "You cannot stay awake through the night," he said. "You are most foolish."

"I don't intend to stay awake. I want a cabin, a closet, anything with a lock inside the door," she demanded.

The Arab's thick lower lip pulled down. "You think you can give orders here?" he questioned. The second Moor was dragging the first from the cabin. "I could have Izmir kill you at the price of his own life. He would obey my command."

"Then do so," Marina shot back.

"No, my little venomous adder," he retorted. "Death can be the easy way out. You will pay for this, but in my own way and my own time. Pehaps then you will wish I had ordered Izmir to take you."

"I want a place with a lock," was her only reply.

Kharoum walked to the door. "There is a small cabin with a lock, a place sometimes used for storing valuables. This way."

"You first," Marina demanded, moving to come up behind him, the curved dagger thrust at his back. Kharoum spit on the deck in disgust as he led the way from the cabin. The room was down a short passageway of the vessel, and when they reached it he halted at the door. "Move back, away from the doorway," Marina demanded. She heard the sounds of the Moor dragging the other up the companionway to the deck as well as other voices drifting down. Kharoum ben Hassad stepped away from the little cabin and Marina went to the door and saw that the lock was in place, with a large-handled key in it. Moving with darting quickness, she stepped inside the little cabin, slammed the door shut, and turned the lock. She heard Kharoum ben Hassad pause on the other side of the door.

"Tomorrow will come," she heard him say, then move off. Marina found a torn mattress at one side of the small storage cabin and torn burlap sacks strewn about. She wiped the dagger on one of the sacks. An empty barrel stood in a corner of the storage cabin, and she rolled it against the door as a further precaution. Sinking down upon the torn mattress, she could not halt the trembling that began to shake her—shuddering, quivering spasms that she could only wait to subside of themselves. Finally, they quieted and she lay still, falling asleep with the curved dagger held tightly in one hand. At every sudden sound in the night she came awake to glance fearfully toward the door.

But the lock stayed turned and the barrel in place. She awoke as daylight made its way in through a small, portholelike window high on one side of the storage cabin, much too high for her to peer through. She moved the barrel aside, then carefully lifted the door latch. With the dagger poised and ready to sweep forward, she pulled open the door and peered out onto the empty passageway.

She slipped from the little cabin, moved along the wall to a water barrel where she glanced around, then put the dagger down and washed her face. Hunger gnawed at the pit of her stomach. A stream of sun came through the hatchway opening and she saw the steep steps leading to the deck. She started cautiously up them. At the deck opening she halted, peering over the edge of the top step. Kharoum ben Hassad, his back to her, conversed with half a dozen turbaned men on the high stern deck, but it was the sight beyond the rail of the chebec that held her gaze. An armada had rendezvoused; each vessel was crowded, each deck thronged with the men of the Arab armies. And as many more were crammed below decks, she was certain. But a strange armada it was, made up of a collection of vessels hired or purchased in haste for the expedition.

Marina counted two more Algerian chebecs, a ketch, two Sicilian *veloceras* with both lateen and square-rigged sails, a scow schooner of the kind that plied the Aegean, three Turkish *caiques* with their strange, side mainsail, and four Arabian *dhows*. At the far end of the strange flotilla she spied the last craft jammed with soldiers, a flat barge rigged with three square sails. It was an armada to make the gods frown, she thought, and indeed they intended to do so. Her eyes swept the horizon to the north where the sky was growing dark, almost black, with a red line racing along the bottom edge of the clouds. As if in answer, a sudden gust of wind caught at her face as she peered over the top step. Her eyes scanned the far-off horizon again and saw that even as she watched the sky grew blacker.

The turbaned figures moved, and she ducked down, watching as all but Kharoum ben Hassad left to return to their respective ships. Another gust of wind seemed to come from nowhere, moving the lines along the ship's mast. It would come down from the north, Marina noted, gathering fury as it went. She backed down the steps, then started down the passageway, past the open door of Kharoum ben Hassad's cabin. She halted at the basket of fruit on an end-table, tightened her lips, then dashed into the cabin, scooping up a pear, two plums, and a handful of figs. They were unwieldy in the hand, and she bit into the plum, devouring it quickly, then did the same with the pear. She had just begun one of the figs when a figure appeared in the doorway. Marina dropped the rest of the figs and raised the curved dagger at once as the Arab chieftain stared at her.

"Is there no end to your insolence?" he snarled.

"Would you have given me food?" Marina shot back.

His thick lower lip pursed forward. "Perhaps," he answered slyly, his eyes raking her.

"For a price," Marina parried. The man's eyes hardened.

"You'll pay the price, never fear that," he growled. Marina moved to the doorway, keeping the sharp dagger high, slipped from the room, and scurried down the passageway to the little storage cabin which was now a place of refuge. She locked herself inside again and then sank down upon the torn mattress. The Arab was in no hurry, properly confident that time was on his side. He wanted her alive and well, fully capable of responding to whatever he was storing up in his barbarous mind. He would wait till his armies were landed, then see to her. First things first. But his armies might never land, Marina pondered, her dark blue eyes holding hope again. This vessel, no more than the others, was not built for a fierce Mediterranean storm on the open sea. Every hand on board would be busy trying to keep the ship afloat. They'd have no time to watch her. It would be a terrible risk, but it was that or wait for time to catch up to her. Marina gazed down at the torn mattress. Even water-soaked, it would float. She could drag it up onto the deck and fling herself off with it. Better the raging sea than the punishment Kharoum ben Hassad was gathering for her, she concluded again. She lay back and let the slow roll of the ship lull her to sleep, the dagger clasped firmly in one hand.

She woke when the roll had become a pitch, when the sea thudded against the wooden hull. Marina stayed on the mattress, knowing that the storm had begun to sweep down upon them. She could hear the whistling of wind through the rigging, and could feel they hadn't lowered sail yet from the way the hull pounded into the rising sea. She lay back, tension demanding more sleep from her, and closed her eyes once more. It was perhaps two hours later when she awoke, she guessed, to the sound of a mast cracking like a cannon shot. She almost rolled from the mattress as the chebec pitched far to one side.

Marina rose, pulling the mattress with her to the door. She was almost there when she suddenly flew sideways, hitting her arm against an edge of protruding beam as she slammed into the side of the cabin. She heard the scream of the wind and felt the ship shudder as it tried to right itself. Another wave, crashing onto it from the other side, helped right it. The storm was more than she'd expected, spinning the vessel as though it were a waterlogged top. Marina unlocked the cabin door, started to step into the passageway, and found herself in swirling, knee-deep water which raced into the room. She entered the passageway in time to see another cascade of water rush down the hatchway and the steps. Feeling her legs pulled out from under her, she managed to clutch at a rail along the passageway and stay on her feet. She made her way to the steps, climbed up them, clinging with all her strength as the chebec heeled over again. Straining with every muscle, she pulled herself upward and was met with a swirling deck of water that almost knocked her back down the steps.

The world was dark gray, towering walls of water on all sides, flecked with snarling white foam. The ship dipped into a trough, rose high, and Marina glimpsed the rest of the armada. Two of *the caiques* were on their sides, helpless hulks in the raging water. A *dhow* was smashing in two as she watched, spilling men like so many ants into the sea. Marina turned her head as another wave crashed down, made the vessel shudder, raced across the deck, and swept down the companionway. Only her fingers curled in a desperate grip on the rail kept her from falling. There were no masts left on the ship, she saw, and she made out the figure of Kharoum ben Hassad on the stern deck, struggling with the rudder with two other men. Faint screams of terror carried to her, and she squinted to the left. Through the deep grayness she saw another vessel turning over like a bloated pig.

There'd be no leaping into this sea with her mattress, Marina realized. Only death awaited her there. If the chebec could stay afloat till driven onto shore, she might have a chance. Her gaze searched the sea, hoping to spy the shoreline, but only mountainous waves rose up before her eyes. Perhaps they were being blown further away from shore. There was no way to tell. Marina started to move backward, her foot searching for the step below, when out of the dark grayness she saw a wall of water begin to gather astern of the ship. In horror she saw it rise higher, still higher. The wind screamed as if in triumph. Out of the corner of her eyes she saw Kharoum ben Hassad and the other two men start to run from the tiller, and then the mountain of water began to curl downward. Marina saw the white foam flecking the top of the gigantic wave. She pulled herself up out of the companionway onto the deck. This was a killer wave that would crush the vessel as though it were an egg. To be below was to be killed at once by collapsing timbers. She flung herself face down on the deck, covering the back of her head with her arms.

The towering wall of water crashed down, and Marina felt herself flung along the deck, her world obliterated by water. As she was lifted and whirled she heard the sound of wood splintering. Her eyes cleared for a moment, and she glimpsed the bow of the vessel starting to rise straight up. A giant hand of water picked her up, turned her over, and carried her past broken pieces of wood that were once a ship. She held her mouth closed and breathed through her nose as suddenly she was under water. Then wind and waves caught at her, sending her upward, and she felt air. Opening her eyes to take a deep breath she saw she was in a gray-green inferno of whirling, spinning water. Something hard crashed into her calf and she cried out in pain. Her arms caught hold of it: wood, a piece of deck planking.

It tried to race from her, but she caught at it again with both hands, clung to it, and rode with it as it lifted up onto the back of a wave. It was wide enough for her to lie on with only her legs trailing out behind. Something else struck at her, whiplike. She saw a heavy piece of rope, one end still secured to an iron ring in the piece of deck planking, the other end flapping loosely. She caught at it, pulled it around herself, making a crude lash of it, and wrapping herself tightly to the length of plank. Another wave caught at the wood, and sent it racing first downward into what seemed a bottomless trough, then up the other side. A shower of water slammed into her, choking her and filling her mouth, and she coughed and spit up enough to avoid drowning.

Marina lay her head sideways on the planking, gasping out as another wave came down to batter her. She could feel her body shuddering as though giant fists were pummeling her.

As the pounding continued, Marina felt her eyes closing; the battering was too much to stand. Only the water-soaked, wedged length of rope kept her lashed to the deck planking. Her breath seemed more water than air, and each time she tried to open her eyes and lift her head another wall of water crashed down upon her. The foaming walls of water swept over her, pulling, pounding, crashing, and tearing at her. The girl clung to consciousness until she could cling no more. The dark gray world grew black and then faded away. She did not feel the sea as it tried to tear her from the planking. Only muscles, lungs, and bones felt the terrible pounding until, with startling suddenness, as if satisfied with its total destruction, the storm whirled away. The sea had claimed complete victory.

While the wind dropped, the water continued to boil and churn. But the deck plank and the unconscious form upon it were carried over the tops of the waves, pushed toward the shore. The gray of the storm had given way to the dark of night when the pebbled beach came into view. The plank rode a wave onto it, fell back, then washed forward again to stay. The figure atop it lay motionless, unconscious, and after the storm, cool winds came to chill, blowing low across the beach. Marina did not feel them, nor the little beads that rose on her skin as the chill wind speared through her unconscious form. In time a pale, slivered moon came to look down upon the lone figure the sea had given back to the land more dead than alive.

CHAPTER EIGHT

T HE YOUNG MAN walked along the pebbled beach as he did every morning when the sun was still new to the day. He strolled slowly, barefoot, wearing a loose, brown shirt and brown trousers with frayed legs. He frowned as his eyes picked out something on the beach ahead. As the object began to take shape he quickened his pace, then broke into a run. He gasped as he reached the girl's form, dropping to one knee and unwinding the rope from around her. She wore what was once a gown but was now shredded strips of cloth.

Gently he turned her over and pressed his cheek down to her breasts. She was alive. He felt her wrist with his thumb and middle finger to find a pulse throbbing erratically. But it was the touch of her skin, burning with fever, that alarmed him most. She'd obviously lain there through the chill of the night, cast ashore from a vessel that had foundered in the terrible storm that had swept down from the north.

The young man lifted her to a sitting position, then hoisting her onto his shoulder, began to hurry back along the beach with his unconscious discovery. He turned into a small footpath that led from the shoreline; after another turn past a line of cedars the stone cottage finally came into view, neat, sturdy, hidden away in its own little glen. He carried the girl into the main room, put her down on one of two cots there, and hurried to the kitchen where an iron stove was warm with a low-burning log fire in its bowels. He heated two kettles, one large, the other small. Filling a bucket with the water from the larger kettle, he took a handful of rags from a neat pile and went into the other room. Kneeling down beside the cot he began to bathe the girl's body with the warm water, washing the sea's salt from her face and shoulders. He tore off the shredded bits of garment, tossing them aside.

The man had to pause for a moment and almost catch his breath, not able to do anything but drink in the glorious beauty of this girl from the storm. He could think only of Botticelli's *Birth of Venus*, of the magnificent beauty of the goddess rising out of the clam shell at her feet. Venus, who emerged from the same watery cradle of life, the eternal sea. He drew his breath in and bent to his task again, continuing to wash the salt of the sea from her. Finished, he changed the bucket for one of cool water, soaked more cloths in it, and began to place them over her burning skin.

The girl had not returned to consciousness, and he frowned, fearful, at her silent form. She was in the throes of fever as well as shock. The cool cloths became warm from her overheated body in minutes. He continued to press new, cool ones over her gently, taking care to avoid the places on her body where bruised marks were appearing, ugly circles of reddish purple skin. He rose, went into a small room beside the kitchen, and returned with a tightly lidded jar. Opening it, he applied some of the salvelike contents to the bruised areas of the girl's body, then returned to keeping the cool cloths on her.

He had returned to the stove and was watching the other kettle brewing when he heard her moan. Racing back into the room, he saw her struggling to rise and helped her to a sitting position. Her eyes half opened and he saw only a glazed terror in them. "It's all right," he said. "You are safe."

The girl moaned again, her eyes fell closed, and the brief moment of consciousness vanished. It returned later, as he continued to press the cooling cloths upon her, encouraged by the decrease in the fever. Half conscious, she called out and babbled names—strange cries, a mélange of things—then fell back again. But this time she was sleeping, he saw, her breath in slow, measured gasps. The fever had definitely gone down as the night returned to the little stone cottage. He made a small fire in the fireplace, ate some cheese, watched the girl, and listened to her as she continued to moan and dredge words from her subconscious.

He took a sheet and put it over her nakedness as he removed the last of the cooling cloths. Once again he shook his head in awe. Hers was a loveliness that rose above the sensuous, above the flesh and its desires, just as a beautiful sculpture or painting goes beyond the carnal. He lay down on the other cot across the room, and the firelight glowed into the deep of the night as he stole moments of sleep, waking whenever he heard the girl moan. It was nearly dawn, and when he heard her move he was at her side instantly. She was sitting up, trying to focus her eyes, and her breath came in hoarse gasps. The fever still clung, and its aftereffects had taken root. He went into the kitchen where the kettle simmered and returned in moments with a thick mug of liquid. The girl's lips were half open, her head back, and he took a small ladle and spooned the liquid from the mug.

Marina heard the voice as if it were far away, dim words filtering through to her. "Here, take this. That's it, swallow. Take some more." She felt the liquid trickle down her throat warm and strong. She shivered, then felt warmth spreading out through her from inside. The spoon was at her lips and she sipped again. It had a faintly tart yet sweet taste to it. She pressed her eyes closed, then opened them, straining through a curtain of haze. A silhouette appeared, then became more: features, then a face. She tried to focus but felt dizzy. "Have some more," the man's voice urged in gentle command, and she sipped more of the liquid and tried to focus her eyes again. She did better this time; she saw an even-featured face, a nice face with concern and caring in it. She saw wide-set eyes, gentle and softly hazel, and light brown hair that fell, tousled, over one brow.

She wanted to stay awake, but the kind face dissolved as she let her head fall back. In seconds she was deep into an exhausted sleep again. She did not see the man rise, bring a cotton sheet, and place it over her. She did not see him pause a moment to drink in her beauty again before spreading the sheet. It was during the dawn that Marina woke again, sat up, horror drawn on her face as she saw Generoso twist and fall under the bullets, then she fell back into sleep again.

It was not till the late morning that she opened her eyes again, this time to find the gentle face watching her from a chair nearby. Marina pushed herself up on one elbow, felt her lips cracked and dry, and knew that she had been brought back from the fever. The giant waves still seemed to crash down on her, trying to smash her into pieces, and she remembered losing consciousness and plunging into a void. She had obviously been washed ashore, and she focused her glance on the man in front of her. It was not just a kind, gentle face, she decided. It was quietly beautiful—strong without the arrogance of strength in it.

Marina opened her lips to speak, winced in a moment of pain, and found her voice was little more than a strained whisper. "Drink as much as you can," he insisted, and she did as she was told. The invigorating liquid imparted a taste she had never known before. "It's a bit stronger than what you had before," he commented. "It will chase away whatever is left of the fever. It is a remedy as effective as it is ancient."

Marina drank again. "It feels good," she said. "It tastes good, too."

The man's smile was warm and satisfied. "It is birch leaf, horehound, and licorice steeped in boiling water, then lemon and honey added," he explained. Marina sipped of the mug again, and found herself feeling stronger with each sip. The sheet around her slipped and she felt the air touch her breasts at once; she clutched at the cloth and pulled it up. She was naked beneath it, she realized, her eyes finding the man's face with unvoiced questions.

"The fever was bad," he told her. "You had been chilled through after the temperature dropped and you were washed ashore. For a time I did not think you would survive."

"I owe you my life," Marina said, finishing the brew, her voice growing stronger.

"You owe nothing to me. It was meant that you live," he replied simply. "What is your name?"

"Marina. Marina Valerian."

The quiet smile touched his face again. "Marina. From the sea. How appropriate."

"And you?" she asked.

"I am Paul Davore," he answered. "I live here."

"And where is here?" Marina inquired.

"A forgotten place, near nothing, near nowhere of importance. A place not far from the sea and not far from the hills. Shepherds live here, also goatherds, a few fisherman, and farmers. A cluster of houses stand together and might be called a village. Some few people are woodcutters, a few others are midwives. Some go south to Reggio di Calabria to work and return only at the week's end."

"Are we near Reggio di Calabria?"

"A day's ride, perhaps two. You were aboard a ship that foundered in the storm, of course."

"Mine and many others with it," Marina said, and saw his eyebrows lift.

"But you were the only survivor. There was no one else. Yet you say there were other ships?"

"It is not a simple story," Marina demurred.

Paul Davore's eyes were touched with sympathy. "I imagine not. You cried out often—strange things of fear, anger, and pain. I could not put any of it together."

"Let me tell you."

He leaned forward, concern in the hazel eyes at once. "Do you feel strong enough?"

Marina nodded. "I want to talk about it. I was on a ship that was part of an invasion armada bringing armies of Arab mercenaries," she began, and watched Paul Davore's frown deepen. "The plan was to attack Reggio di Calabria and establish a new city-state made up of Calabria and part of the Kingdom of Naples. My own guardian, the Count Aldo Gamborelli, and the Duke d'Albatore, were behind it, though they were not aboard the ships." As Paul Davore sat back, she hurried through the rest of the story, not sparing her role in the agreements, ending with the storm that wiped out the armada of sorry hulks. She faltered only when telling of Kharoum ben Hassad and of how she had been the prize in the unholy bargain that had formed the core of Gamborelli's plan.

She left out but one name, one chapter of the sorry story—that of Generoso della Passione. It was too private, too painful for telling. It did not bear on the main outlines of what had happened, its importance sacred to her alone, a memento of a time which, in its own way, would live inside her forever.

She fell back, exhausted by the telling of her story, realizing how very weak she really was, and her eyes closed of their own accord. "I'm sorry," she murmured. "I can't keep awake longer."

She felt the gentle pressure of his hand on her forehead. "Sleep," Paul Davore soothed. "The fever hasn't returned. It is just exhaustion." His last words had already trailed away as Marina succumbed to fatigue.

It was dark when she awoke to find a fire glowing in the fireplace. She was alone. She started to push the sheet away, then realized once more that she wore nothing under it. Gathering the top inward, she fashioned the sheet into a relatively modest gown and carefully rose from the cot. Her legs refused to support her and she fell backward at once. She tried again, this time using a small table nearby for support. On weak and tentative steps she crossed the room and found a small, cold country-crude lavatory. When she returned to the room, she paused at the doorway of another small room adjoining the kitchen and saw that it was filled with bottles, jars, urns, boxes, and baskets, as well as small sacks of dried leaves and herbs. Her legs had begun to cry out in protest, and she hurried across the room and fell onto the cot as exhausted as though she'd climbed a mountain. Where was Paul Davore, she wondered as her eyes closed and fatigue swept over her again.

Later, waking, she heard him in the room, held the sheet over her breasts, and rose up on one elbow. Paul turned from where he'd been putting wood on the fire.

"How do you feel, Marina?" he asked, smiling at her.

"Better, but very weak," she murmured. "I got up before, when you were away. It drained me completely."

"I was detained—a special trip to Valenza, over the hills," he explained. He rose and came over to her, his hazel eyes serious. "Your body as well as your spirit has been battered into exhaustion. The fever drained you, and before the fever, the sea physically assaulted you. It will be more than a matter of hours before you are well."

Marina nodded, then sat up. He turned and started for the kitchen. "I've some hearty barley soup with pork in it," he called back to her. Marina, rearranging the sheet around herself, noted for the first time the dark bruises on her body and saw the salve that had been put on them. She followed his serious eyes as he returned with two bowls of thick, fragrant soup and sat down beside her.

"My bruises look terrible, but they don't really hurt," she commented. "Your salve is very effective. Another antique remedy?"

He smiled and watched her take the soup, plainly enjoying it. "Yes," he admitted. "I find the natural substances contain all kinds of properties. To make that salve you take a cup or more of red sage leaves, a handful of celandine, and boil everything in water. Then the herbs are strained out and the liquid mixed with a large pint of honey, a cup of thyme, and a cup of rock alum. You boil the entire mixture together and then keep the result in an earthenware crock."

"Are you a healer?" Marina asked.

He looked into space for a long moment, then let a small, wry smile come to touch his lips. "I try, in whatever way I can," he said.

"Is that what is in all those bottles and jars and sacks in the little room?" Marina asked. "Your herbs and plants?"

He nodded and the rueful smile remained. "I collect all I can while the weather lets me. Cloves for clove oil when there are tooth problems; camomile, marjoram, mint, and parsley for the stomach; oil of cajeput and marigold for stings; red clover and sarsaparilla for the blood—there are so many, many gifts for healing nature gives us. You see, there are no physicians near here. None want to labor in the hills and the backwater places. There are but a few midwives who know only how to deliver a child. Yet the people have needs, inner and outer. In our hard winters the workmen are forever hurting themselves, the women overworking themselves and falling ill."

"You studied to learn this?" Marina asked.

"No, no, not study as you mean it," the young hazeleyed man replied. "When I was a boy I had a neighbor, an old man who taught me about herbs and plants and the gifts they carry for man within their roots, seeds, and leaves. It has come in handy. The people have learned to trust my collection of remedies when they are hurt or ill."

"They trust you," Marina said simply.

His smile was almost shy. "I like to think that." He was modest as well as gentle, Marina decided.

As he took away the soup bowls, Marina studied his slender, supple form. She found herself wondering what the touch of his hands had been like as they moved across her unconscious body, bathing hidden places. Suddenly she was sorry she had not been aware enough to know, and silently chastised herself for the thought. But he had unquestionably saved her life. He had succeeded where the man who loved her had failed, and lost his own life in the trying. She put her head back. It was a strange world, one that defied understanding, sometimes seeming without any reason or order in it at all. The deep sigh that escaped her came from the depths of her chest, and she closed her eyes. She opened them slightly when the hand touched her forehead, soft as a goosedown quilt.

"Do not fight sleep. It is the greatest healer of all." She heard Paul's soft words and did not open her eyes but let her hand reach up to touch his.

"Thank you, Paul, for everything," she murmured.

His finger touched her lips. "Sleep. Just sleep."

Marina obeyed and drifted into a dreamless slumber, which lasted through the night. Daylight had stroked her face for almost an hour before she woke, shook her head, focused her eyes clearly, and sat up. She felt a thousand times stronger. Swinging her legs from the cot, she stood up and almost fell, dizziness making the room spin. Strong arms caught her as she started to topple backward, then eased her back onto the edge of the cot. "When will you believe me?" she heard him say with faint annoyance. "Do not attempt too much too soon. You are still weak." She looked up, fearing a frown, but she saw only patience and she pressed his arm gratefully with her hand.

"I'll do better," she promised. "Though I've never been much for taking advice."

He laughed; it was a warm sound. "I'm sure of that." It was her turn to frown.

"What makes you sure of that?" she protested.

"Beautiful women seldom need to take advice. Their beauty brings them everything they want." He felt the pain touch her face.

"Not always," she said bitterly. "I can swear to that."

Paul's hand cupped her cheek. "I'm sorry. I did not mean to bring you pain. It was a poor witticism," he apologized.

Her hand circled his wrist and she felt a surge of warmth for this compassionate man. "No, you're not to blame. Your words were basically true. There are always exceptions. I suppose I am one."

"You must have loved him very much," Paul said, and she felt the surprise leap into her eyes. "Only love can bring that particular kind of bittersweet pain."

"Yes, I loved him very much. He will always be a part of me," Marina admitted as her eyes met Paul's. "You see where others would not see."

He shrugged. "A matter of opening oneself to others. He stepped back, pushing aside the moment that had encircled them. "I must go and do my tasks. You rest. When I return I'll bring you something to wear. No fancy gowns, I'm afraid, such as you're used to wearing, Marina Valerian."

"Whatever you bring will do." She smiled. He was at the door when she called out in unplanned words that just fell from her lips. "Paul?" He paused. "Hurry back."

"Yes," he answered and went on. Marina sat back on the cot, then got up, slowly this time, testing herself. A little dizziness pulled at her, but she waited and it passed. She went into the kitchen, heated water in the large iron kettle, poured it into the bucket, and bathed slowly, washing away the rest of the salve on her bruises. She felt drained after the effort and was happy to lie down on the cot. It was midafternoon when she woke, sat up, and found herself listening for Paul's footsteps outside. She was disappointed to hear only the singing of a nuthatch.

Letting her eyes roam the room carefully for the first time, she found a bookshelf in one corner and went over to it to see works by Comte and Molière and two volumes by Francois de Fenelon. Brother Justus had been devoted to Fenelon, unashamedly proud to have an Archbishop of Cambrai that was a poet and man of letters. She saw works by Gozzi and Goldoni, Aretino, Boccaccio, and Aquinas and a copy of *The Divine Comedy* by Dante. Two volumes by Goethe and Schiller, in the original German, caught her eye.

She straightened up, her lips pursing. Paul Davore was not unacquainted with learning. She turned, excitement prodding her as she heard his footsteps. She was almost at the door when he entered, a sack in one hand.

"I was investigating your library," she admitted. He came to her, touched her forehead, then drew his hand back, nodding in satisfaction. "A second day without fever. You are on the road to recovery." Turning, he spilled the contents of the sack on the cot. Marina saw two blouses, pale green and yellow, and two dark skirts, brown and gray. "I did not know the size," he said ruefully. "Besides, most of the young women here have hips far wider than yours."

"They'll do fine. I can take a tuck in them if necessary." She paused. "I'm glad you noticed how much slimmer my hips were," she added, and was surprised by the coquettish tone in her voice. She saw his face turn crimson, giggled, then impetuously hugged his arm.

"I'll start dinner," he said. "Chicken tonight, nothing with spices for you yet."

Marina watched him disappear into the kitchen. He was so different from any man she'd ever known. Without trying, without intent, his gentle strength curled around her, warming and lifting. She turned to the garments on the cot, let the sheet drop from around her, and slipped into the skirt; then she donned the yellow blouse. It was a little tight and the skirt a little loose. The others were the same, only in reverse. But they were wearable, and when Paul came out of the kitchen she had the yellow blouse on over the brown skirt. He halted and blinked.

"It is true," he murmured. "Real beauty is not a matter of clothes." He moved closer. "Now lay down for a while, Marina," he ordered. "Gather strength in small doses." She obeyed and was surprised at how welcome it was to stretch out on the cot. Later, at dinner, as she sat across from him at the low, wooden table he brought out, a long candle encircling them with soft light, he spoke of what had brought her aboard the vessel.

"Those who plot may well try again," he theorized. "This attempt failed, but there may be another."

"I'm sure there will be. My esteemed guardian has the scent of power and wealth in his nostrils. He will not give it up easily. Now that he thinks I am dead, he will have to find another prize to bargain with, perhaps the villa and the estate."

"We must think of a way to prevent another attempt. There are too many independent empires now. We do not need more." Marina nodded agreement. They would have to find a way to prevent another coup, she told herself. And her vow to pay back Aldo Gamborelli had not been a passion of the moment. Yet now she wanted only to rest here in the comforting warmth of the little cottage. To partake of the gentle strength that was Paul Davore's eased her grief for Generoso and diminished the anguish to a deep but bearable pain. She heard Paul's voice, his question spearing through her thoughts.

"What do you think so seriously about, Marina?"

"I'm sorry." She laughed. "I strayed down little side-roads of the mind."

"You can do better than that," he persisted quietly, and she laughed again.

"I was thinking how strange a thing fate can be," she remarked. "I could have died on the beach. Or I could have been found by a lecherous band of cutthroats and saved only for their pleasure. But those things didn't happen. You came, you saved my life. Why? It must have a meaning. Or do you think things just happen, everything by chance?"

"You seek more wisdom than I can give," he chided gently.

"If fate governs us, if we are guided and our footsteps aimed, then why does it all go so wrong, so often?" Marina wondered.

Paul Davore shrugged. "St. Thomas Aquinas said that God writes straight with crooked lines. That's the best I can do for now."

"That's good enough," Marina replied, rising to help clear away the dishes. "Your kitchen could stand some straightening, Paul," she commented. "Would you mind if I did it tomorrow?"

"I would be indebted. But only if you promise not to tire yourself."

"I promise," she agreed.

Later that evening he asked more about her background, and she happily told him of her schooling, and of life at the great villa as a little girl. "Nothing is wasted, nothing that is good," he remarked when she finished. "It will serve you one of these days." He rose and looked down at her with his soft hazel eyes. "It is time to sleep. I shall hang a sheet to divide the room."

"Why?" Marina sked. "Certainly I have nothing to hide from your eyes."

A patient smile edged his lips. "It is I who need the barrier between us." She saw a light dance in the hazel eyes, then reached out to touch his chest with her hand.

"Please, Paul, I don't want any barrier between us. It's silly, perhaps, but I don't want it. Blow out the candle, the dark will be enough. I want nothing that will make me alone."

"I understand. You've been through more than most young women experience in a lifetime," Paul soothed. Marina rested her head on his chest for a moment, drawing of his strength and understanding, which seemed to flow from him as currents flow from a magnet. He leaned over, blew the candle out, and the cottage was plunged into blackness. "Good night, Marina." His hand brushed her hair for a moment, then pulled away. She heard him undress and after she had done so herself she pulled the sheet over herself as she lay down on the cot. She wanted to think about Paul Davore but tiredness swept over her, the body asserting its own priorities.

When she woke in the morning, the other cot was empty. She saw the note atop it, swung out of bed, and hurried to read it. "Back later. Do not overdo. Paul." She crushed the slip of paper in her hand, disappointed—and surprised at that disappointment. She had wanted to see him when she woke, to have tea with him. How quickly some people can find a place to take hold, she murmured inwardly. Or was it only herself—vulnerable and needing someone? No. Paul Davore was more than a convenient rock to rest upon. He reached her, touched her with a rare compassion that helped stir the soul and held hope at its center.

Marina paused in her thoughts of Generoso's olive-black eyes and his tense fire flashing before her, and she smiled. Generoso would be a part of her forever—never to be found again and never to be matched.

His loss was a scar no more erasable than a saber wound on a cheek. But the village girl's simple words had held wisdom. Generoso, of all people, would want her to go on. He was too alive, too intense a person to want otherwise. In Paul she had found the quiet strength and understanding to go on, but he meant only warmth, friendship, and empathy, nothing more.

She heard a sound outside, walked to the door at once, saw the tail of a deer disappearing into the brush, and refused to admit the disappointment that stabbed at her. She found a jar of camomile tea in the kitchen, made herself a mug, and sipped it as she began to bring orderliness to the room. Paul was not a master housekeeper, she decided. The day passed quickly enough as she halted frequently for little catnaps, surprised at how quickly her energy gave out.

Paul returned at dusk and she was at his side instantly. Her lips brushed his cheek in another unplanned gesture that seemed totally right. He held up a bottle of white wine and a large turbot.

"A gift from Pietro the fisherman. I will cook it for you in a fine *court-bouillon*."

"I saw some turnips in your cellar storehouse. I'll fix them."

"You have been snooping." Paul laughed.

"Of course," Marina tossed back. His arm encircled her waist in a quick hug.

The evening came quickly, the turbot equal to any the finest of chefs could prepare, and she was luxuriously tired by the time the night grew late. "Good night, Marina," Paul said gently as she paused in front of him, her eyes probing his. She reached up, kissed his cheek, and his hand tightened for a moment on her arm. He blew out the candle, moved from her, and Marina slid quickly out of her clothes, lying under the sheet in happy satisfaction. Friendship, warmth, and strength—they were enough, she told herself.

In the morning, she woke to find Paul dressed and making tea in the kitchen. He was ready to leave by the time she had washed and dressed, on his way to help others. It was a nice feeling, she reflected, borrowing warmth from his work, his "tasks" as he had called it.

"Paul?" she called as he reached the door. "Hurry back." He left a quiet smile with her and went on.

The days became a pattern, a quietly happy fabric of peace and warmth. Her strength returned until she could manage an entire afternoon without pausing to rest. And each day she found herself counting the minutes until Paul's return. In the evenings they talked of books and people and the ways of the world. Marina knew a kind of happiness she had never felt before. Day by day, hour by hour, Paul became her world. Almost afraid at first, then quietly eager, she embraced the meaning of love again, with a sense of reverence, as a child embraces an unexpected gift.

Someday she'd question Paul more about his gifts as a healer, she told herself. He was too young to be a healer. Most she'd heard about were old sages and not learned in languages, arts, and letters. But it was an honorable profession, though physicians looked down upon it with their microscopes and new discoveries. Paul Davore was a most unusual man, she concluded, as though she'd not already decided that.

It was but a few nights later when his words sent a shaft of unreasonable panic through her. "I daresay you're almost your old self. Soon you will ready to leave here," he announced, and saw the darkness flood her face. His hand reached out, took hers. "I didn't mean to upset you. You are welcome to stay here as long as you wish," he added at once.

"No, I'm sorry," Marina countered. "I know I must go. It's something we have to talk about." He rose, went to her, and put his hand against her cheek.

"Not unless you are ready to talk of tomorrow." She pressed his hand tighter to her face and found his palm with her lips. He put his other hand on her shoulder, rested it there, holding her against his chest.

"Paul." She uttered his name through tight lips and felt her arms reach up to encircle his neck. Then her mouth found his hungrily, pressing, demanding. He held back, then answered with honey-sweet kisses.

As suddenly as it had happened he tore away from her, his soft eyes clouded with something she could not read. "No." The word was torn from his throat. "It would be too easy, here, staying together as we are. It would change everything. It wouldn't be right, not now."

"I know," Marina agreed. "It would change everything. You don't want that."

Paul's eyes found a burst of pain she could not mistake for anything else. "I don't know. Your loveliness can sweep away all else. I don't know, and until I know, it is not right."

When she didn't answer he reached out again and took her hand in his. "Not everything is so simple. You are wiser in these things than I," Paul said gently, a shy smile edging his lips. The smile broadened as he read her eyes. "Do not look so surprised, my Marina," he said. "We are not all men of experience in all ways."

Marina felt a strange secretly pleased warmth inside herself. Paul Davore was like a multifaceted gem, full of unexpected rays at every turn, full of refreshing discoveries each day. "Then you have never loved," she mused. Little lights came into his eyes, sparkled there.

"I did not say that," he replied. He brushed a stray strand of her black hair back from her forehead.

"You're laughing at me." She pouted.

"A little," he admitted.

"Paul." She was suddenly grave, her eyes probing again. "What if I said I loved you?"

He did not turn from her eyes but met their probing gaze. "I'd say that we must talk a lot more of this thing called love."

"And of wanting?" she pressed.

He nodded slowly. "And of wanting," he echoed. "Give me a little more time."

"Wanting is an impatient taskmaster," Marina insisted. "And you want, Paul. I can see it in your eyes when you watch me. It is the right kind of wanting, Paul, with love behind it."

He leaned over, kissed her forehead gently, then quickly blew out the candle and stepped from her. "Good night, Marina."

She went to her cot, pulled her clothes off, and smiled in the darkness. He had not agreed—but he had not denied. She would wait till they spoke of love again.

She slept at once, and for the first time woke early, before Paul. She looked across at his sleeping form, then rose and crept on silent, bare feet across the room. A sheet was thrown loosely across his hips and she took in his long, well-formed legs, his smooth-skinned chest and shoulders. It was a nice body, almost boyish, a body for holding, for awakening. She wanted to move onto the cot beside him, she wanted to touch him. There was much he didn't know. He had admitted that. Certainly he hadn't known the kind of wanting that stirred her. Loving and wanting—they went together for her. But she turned away and wondered if perhaps she was the one with much to learn.

She lay down and was watching when he stretched and sat up, his eyes finding hers. "How long have you been watching me?" he asked. There was no anger in his voice, she noticed.

"Not long," she responded, stretching her arm out and finding her blouse. He slipped into his trousers and rose, opened the door of the cottage, and let the morning's new sun rush in.

"Since you've been here, I haven't walked on the beach before breakfast," he told her. "But I shall do so today. It's usually a quiet place. The sea gives a touch of eternity to the land."

"I'll heat some bread," Marina called as Paul waved and went from the cottage. She had bathed and dressed when he returned, and had the tea and hot bread ready. He ate and seemed wrapped in his own silence. She did not intrude. Finished, he came to her and put a hand on her face. "I must dress and go tend to those who wait for me," he said. "Tonight, we shall talk of love."

"I'll be unfair," she warned.

"I know," he replied solemnly, then turned and hurried from the cottage. The moment he left, she began to count the minutes until his return. She had fallen in love with Paul Davore, Marina told herself. Not the white-hot passion she had felt for Generoso, but a soft, abiding love. It was as simple as that. She knew herself. She knew that time meant little. He would say that she hardly knew him. But what she felt was a kind of knowing that reason and logic could not touch. Even her hatred for Aldo Gamborelli and her sorrow for Generoso receded. Love can heal, she had come to learn.

Marina happily prepared dinner later in the day, lamb brought from the village the day before, artichokes, figs, and dates. Paul returned with a bottle of the local red wine and lighted the large candle as the night began to close out the day.

Marina, clearing away dishes, saw his eyes narrowed, watching her. "We needn't talk if you don't want to, Paul. Perhaps there really isn't any need to talk."

His sigh came from deep within him. "There is a need, but there may not be the right words. Words can make one a coward."

"And love? Wanting? What do they make out of one?" Marina asked. "A lion, shameless and selfish?"

"Sometimes."

"Then I am shameless and selfish, and I love you, Paul. I am blessed twice over, knowing love when I thought I would never know it again."

"You are grateful to me. Gratitude is a poor substitute for love," he murmured quietly.

She brought her mouth to his, pressed his lips open, sought with her tongue, and felt his body tremble. She drew back. "Do you think that a substitute? For anything?" she charged.

"No," he conceded hoarsely. "It is I who cannot define love as simply as you. It is I who cannot want as purely as you."

"Then I will help you know yourself." Marina unbuttoned the pale green blouse, letting it slip from her shoulders as she unclasped the skirt and felt it fall to her feet. "As you found me that first morning, Paul. But now I can return your touch."

His eyes moved to her breasts, lingered, moved down the line of the abdomen, down further, and then returned slowly to her face. "Maybe," he breathed. "Maybe you can help me know myself. But till then, till I am certain, I will not make love to you wholly, completely."

"Then take of my giving," she urged, undoing the ties of his shirt, pushing it back from his chest. She pressed her breasts against him, heard his soft groan. He moved back onto the cot and she slid down with him, pulled his head to her. "Paul, my darling, my love," she whispered. "I know you want me as I want you. I know it inside myself."

His eyes held uncertainty, a mixture of desire and anguish. "It is easy to want such loveliness. I knew that the first morning when I bathed the sea from you. I marveled at your loveliness then, spoke to you of it in my mind."

"Tell me now, Paul," Marina requested. "I can hear it now."

His eyes caressed her breasts as he stepped back and moved down her body once more. " 'Thy breasts are like twin fawns that browse along the lilies,' " he said. " 'Thy lips drop as the honeycomb. Honey and milk are under thy tongue. How much more delightful is thy love than wine.' "

"The Song of Solomon, the Canticle of Canticles," Marina recalled. Its poetry rushed back now, as she pressed hands against Paul's chest.

" 'I delight to rest in his shadow, and his fruit is sweet in my mouth,' " she murmured. " 'His eyes are as the eyes of doves by the rivers of waters, his legs are as pillars of marble set upon sockets of fine gold. I am my beloved's and my beloved is mine. He feedeth among the lilies.' "

Paul smiled down at her. "I should have known you would know the passage." She found the top of his trousers, pressed down, then opened the buttons and caressed him with her hands.

"Just stay with me, please," she pleaded. "Let me hold you." His only answer was to stay as he was, his head against her breasts. Slowly, his hands found their full roundness, traveled down along her ribcage to the soft swell of her belly. His touch made her skin glow, yet she was strangely soothed at the same time. Drawing her hard against him, he held her motionless, then slowly released her as his hand stroked her. Marina felt desire turning into sweet, soothing peacefulness. Her eyes sought his face, so youthful yet so wise. Had he ever been with a woman, she wondered, the question stirring strange excitement within her at once. He knew love. That knowledge shone in his eyes, in the gentle, compassionate tenderness that was part of him. Only one who had loved could feel with such understanding. But had he lain completely with a woman, explored fully the dimensions of ecstasy? The question stirred her again as she rested her face against his.

He moved, finally, drawing his hands from her, looking into her waiting eyes. Leaning forward, he pressed his lips upon her eyelids, first one then the other. "It is time to sleep, my Marina." He halted her protest with a finger upon her lips. His smile was touched with the hint of gentle laughter.

"There is yet another passage in that Song of Solomon you quote so well," he told her. "I would leave you with it to think upon, my lovely." She waited, watching the hint of laughter stay and a sadness join with it. " 'I charge you, daughters of Jerusalem, by the gazelles and hinds of the field, do not arouse, do not stir up love, before its own time.' "

He rose, swept the flame out on the candle with his hand, and vanished in the darkness. Marina lay quietly, his words turning slowly inside her. A reminder? A thought? A warning? Before she slept, one thing more clung to her. The quiet, inner strength had risen up, on this night, to hold fast against her beauty, against her blandishments, against his own desire for her. But there would be another time, she told herself. He was too sensitive to reject the gift of love, and she offered it with all her heart. The night had been a beginning, a wonderfully different beginning, entirely in keeping with the layered depths that were Paul Davore.

She slept soundly though her loins still thirsted, and in the morning she clung to him in the doorway. "Hurry back," she urged him, each word a sweet sound. Throughout the day, Marina cleaned the little cottage, working quickly, thinking only of Paul's return. A special dinner, she decided, for their special night together. She would go into the village—the cluster of houses Paul had told her about—and find something special. She'd not visited there yet, well aware that the people of these backwater places often viewed strangers with alarm. But today she would go, Marina decided, and brave unfriendliness if need be. Hurrying from the cottage, she took the path that led down to the shoreline, walking quickly, almost dancing along the way, thinking only of finding ways to please Paul.

The beach curved, but a road led inland and she took it, reached a low rise, and saw the dozen whitewashed houses just below. They clung to the sloping ground like so many mushrooms on a log. She continued down the path, slowed as she came to a tiny church, hardly larger than the houses nearby. Stone, the steeple was fashioned of pieces of gray slate. She watched two shawled women enter the open front door, then a young girl go in, covering her head with a bandanna.

Marina halted in the doorway, peered into the dim coolness of the little church, and glanced down the single aisle that led to the simple altar. Two women were talking to the priest at one side of the pews. His back was to her, but his long black cassock made him look very tall and slender. She wanted to go in to the altar and kneel before it in thanks for the happiness she had been given after tragedy had struck so deeply. Perhaps the priest could find her a kerchief with which to cover her head, she wondered. As she looked at him, he turned. She saw the gentle hazel eyes, the light brown hair that fell, tousled, over one brow. The young priest's eyes grew wide as he saw the transfixed figure in the doorway.

Marina stared at the cassocked priest as breath seemed to draw out of her body. She stared and stared and seemed to have turned into stone. The interior of the little church disappeared into a blank wall. She pressed her eyes closed, then forced them open. The church was back in place, the young priest was staring at her. It had not been a vision, no strange flight of the senses. It was Paul, looking at her over the white edge of the priest's collar showing above the cassock. As he took a single step toward her, she was shocked out of her trance. Marina whirled and raced out of the little church.

"Marina! Wait!" She heard Paul's voice following after her, but she was running along the dirt path, plunging away from it to race into the thick brush. There seemed to be great pieces of something falling on all sides of her—the world crumbling away—and she heard someone sobbing, great broken gasps of sound that followed along whichever way she turned. She ran wildly, heedlessly, seeing nothing, when her foot struck against the stump of a cut tree. She fell forward, pitched down onto the ground, and lay there unmoving.

She made no attempt to rise, her hands clawing into the ground, knotting pieces of grass into tiny clumps. Finally, pushing with the flat of her hands, she lifted herself up, turned, and leaned against a nearby tree. She felt as though she were a china pitcher that had shattered, made up now of only little shards and jagged bits. She wanted to disbelieve, but disbelieving was impossible. The senses are cruel, only allowing self-denial when they don't stab like a lance stabs—all the way through.

"No," she heard herself whisper. "No." But the word was empty, as empty as she. Crying out to halt the destruction of happiness had become a futile litany, it seemed. Twice she had found love, twice she had clutched at happiness, and twice it had been torn from her.

The first time happiness had been shattered by brutality, by the greedy, grasping hands of evil men, this time, by something far different. One torn from her by hate, the other by love. They were different kinds of helplessness, different kinds of anguish, but the first was better, she decided bitterly. One could hate back. Satan was easier to deal with than God; the lines were clearly marked, the forces unmistakable. Marina's eyes grew darker. At least the first heartbreak held no betrayal in it. The word shuddered inside her, tried to deny itself, but she clung to it. Why not, she asked herself. Betrayal did lie in this pain. He had lied—not directly, but by omission.

Marina's lips tightened in a rueful grimace. So many little things suddenly revealed themselves in a new light. Of course he hadn't denied being a healer, a healer of souls first and bodies second. Then there were his words to describe her from the Song of Solomon, words he knew well. And his learning, his quiet strength, the way he comforted and reached out. All these things were part of love, *his* kind of love. Even the admission of inexperience in some things was all part of the same fabric. *We must talk more of this thing called love,* he had said, and anger flared up inside her emptiness. She made a sharp sound. "No. We shall talk of this thing called betrayal," she muttered aloud. Why hadn't he told her? Why had he kept the lie of silence? She had to know. Somehow, that went deeper than anything else; it hurt more, it angered more. Why, why, why? Why had he said nothing? Why had he let her find love again? It was more than unfair. It was cruel.

Marina pulled herself to her feet and began to retrace her steps to the little cottage, using the pointed hurt to keep her from collapsing in shattered emptiness. She'd become lost, she realized, finally found the path again and went on, each step leaden. She felt the overwhelming pain again, as she had when Generoso fell before the hail of bullets and her world collapsed. The same but different. She grimaced. Happiness denied forever and happiness forbidden were not the same. One cried out in anguish, the other in denial. One cried for solace, the other for help.

When the stone cottage came into view, the door opened. Her steps quickened despite herself, but she halted in the doorway. He was there. He'd tried to find her, obviously. He was still in his cassock and looked perhaps handsomer, she saw, as she felt the pain inside herself, now stronger and somehow more comforting. Marina stepped into the room and a single word vaulted from her lips. "Why?" She could not hide the bitterness in her face. "Why didn't you tell me?"

She was glad to see the helpless pain in his eyes, felt angry satisfaction at it. "I don't know," he replied simply. "A combination of many things—hiding, perhaps."

"A kind of lying," Marina snapped.

"Yes, I suppose so," Paul conceded gravely, with no attempt to deny or to excuse himself. She hated him for that, too, even as she loved him for it. "At first, it didn't seem important," he went on. "Then, later, I never seemed to find the right moment. I knew you were growing to care deeply."

"Yet you said nothing," Marina cut in.

Once again, his eyes did not hide pain. "Don't you think I asked myself why? Don't you think I lay awake night after night about that? You see it only as a lie, a callous violation of your love. Can you not see it for what it was to me?" He put his head down, pressed his face into his hands for a long moment, then looked up at her. Haggard lines etched his face. "Finally, I had to face the truth. I did not want to tell you. Can't you understand what that meant? Can't you realize how completely that wrenched me?"

Marina did not answer, staring only at the pain that filled his eyes, but, like a small, flickering flame, realization began to sear her. "It meant that I did not want to be a priest with you. I did not want to do anything to stop your loving me. Suddenly, I did not know myself any longer. Everything that was me was no longer me. All that was sacred to me suddenly no longer held the same importance. Can you not understand what that did to me, my Marina?"

Marina felt the anguish of his words. There had been no betrayal, not as she had seen it, not as she had taken it to be. Her pain had been made of hurt and her own angry reactions, but there had been so much more. She understood that now and reached a hand out to touch his face. "We have met in pain as well as love."

He nodded solemnly. "It was wrong not to tell you. I knew it all along. But how could I tell you when I could not tell myself?

It is a stunning realization to find that you do not know who you are. It chills the soul."

"And last night? Didn't that tell you anything?" Marina asked, her arms encircling his neck.

"Nothing I did not know already. That I can want you, hold you, touch you, and that I am a ship adrift, without a star to steer by," Paul answered, sinking down onto the edge of the cot. She sat beside him, her hand in his.

"Love is a star to steer by, Paul."

"Yes, but which love? Which commitments, obligations, selflessness? I had all that. I must find out what happened to it. I must know that first."

"I sound like the serpent in the Garden of Eden. The temptress," Marina remarked.

His hands cupped her face. "I do not mean to make you that. But don't you see, my darling, I must know beyond doubting, beyond wondering. I thought I knew who had called me. I must know again. Anything less would be a lie beyond lies."

"And what if that other love holds fast?" Marina asked.

"Then my tomorrows are marked out clearly for me," Paul replied tonelessly.

"And what of my love for you, what we've found together?" Marina saw the look of helplessness touch his eyes.

"I don't know," he said.

"Would it shock you if I said I wouldn't care, that I'd still love you, that I'd still want to be with you and be yours?" Marina asked. "It's been done before, Paul. This wouldn't be the first time."

"And you'd be called what others have been called, a priest's woman. Such a woman is an outsider in the world, in the Church, in everything, perhaps in herself."

"I wouldn't care," Marina insisted. "When you really love someone, you love them no matter what. Isn't that what love means?"

"For those who can love without violating another love or another commitment. I have already violated my own commitments," Paul replied heavily.

Marina refused to accept his words. "Others violate theirs," she insisted and saw his questioning glance. "There were things I did not mention when I told you about the plan to create a new city-state. There were cardinals of the church involved, and also monsignors and priests. They wanted power and wealth as much as my guardian and d'Albatore." She saw Paul's eyes take on new sadness as she told him of Father Scunigi and his standards of convenience and cupidity.

"Yes, there is corruption everywhere. Why should the Church be entirely free of it? Men are men and their weaknesses sometimes transcend all else." His eyes found hers, speared her with allusiveness. "Do two wrongs make a right?" he asked, as much of himself as of her. "It is my own weakness I think about."

"It is happiness I think about, our happiness," Marina countered. "You know we have found something special, Paul."

He rose abruptly, the pain creasing his face again. "Yes, I know that." He stared out through the open doorway.

Marina, watching him, felt a terrible surge of love engulf her. She wanted him, needed him more than she'd realized. She wanted to be the first with him. She wanted to be the first to unfold new wonders for him, to lie with him in the garden of the senses. The desire was so strong, so real, that it shocked her. Suddenly she understood the real meaning of being first. Its spirit lay not in the gross eagerness of taking but in the joy of giving.

She reached up, pulled his lips down to hers. His mouth answered, opened, and held on hers until she pulled back. "Please, Paul, please. Don't turn your back on us. Don't deny what we feel for each other."

He looked into her dark blue pleading eyes and the slow, wry smile came again to touch his lips. "No, I can't deny that.

The question is what can I deny?" She put her head against the smoothness of the cassock and knew the truth of his words.

After a moment, he stepped back. "I must return. There are still others I must see at the church."

"Yes, of course," she said quietly. "Hurry back."

She found things to fix for dinner, not the special something she had wanted, but enough, and there was more than half a bottle of wine left. As she worked at preparing dinner, she thought of Paul listening to those who came to him in the little church, comforting, compassionate, healing with the spiritual strength that had been given him to give to others. The pain in his eyes as she had accused him of betrayal returned to her. She was the fortunate one, she now realized. She had nothing to deny—she had only to accept, to embrace love without questions.

That was what she'd do, she decided. She'd live for now, wanting him, helping to show him love. There was no other way. Right or wrong, she'd stay with Paul, to be as much a part of his life as the world would permit. Tomorrow would come in its own time and its own way. Till then she'd put aside all deep thoughts that could rend the heart with questions of right and wrong. Till then she'd live to embrace each moment. To do otherwise would be untrue to herself, and to Paul.

She had dinner ready when Paul returned in his cassock, and when he had changed into the brown, frayed trousers and brown shirt so familiar to her, they sat down at the table. "Tell me about the little church," she asked as they sipped the wine.

"The people had neither the time nor money to build more than the church. I told them I did not need a rectory. This cottage once belonged to a woodcutter. It has served perfectly well," Paul said. "But these poor people here come to me for more than I can give. They deserve a better life, a human dignity that other men deny them. They ask me to intercede for them, as though help and happiness could be given for the asking."

"Who better to ask than you, Paul?"

He shrugged. "I give hope when they need practical help. I feel as though I've failed them so often."

"You don't fail them," she insisted. "Hope has to come first, before help, before anything else. The dream before the act." She hesitated. "It's the same with everything." She moved to him, pressed her lips to his face, found his mouth, and held there. Her hands moved along his body, and, in a moment, almost trembling, he pulled back. His eyes searched hers.

"Did you think I wouldn't?" she asked. "I do not step aside easily, Paul. I fight back for what I want." He nodded, understanding. Her mouth sought his again, demanding, refusing to be denied. The candle burned out, the night grew deep, and he answered her caresses, aching with the pleasures she brought. But once again he merely soothed, stroked, and made her content to lie beside him, skin against skin, touching, drawing in warmth, finding new joys.

Later, in the cradle of his shoulder, she heard him whisper his thoughts aloud to her. "The senses make emotional orphans of reason and principle."

She caught the sudden bitterness in his words and tightened her arm around his chest. She fought down a tremble that coursed through her. It wasn't wrong to be there in his arms, she told herself. How else could he know what to deny? How else could she fight for happiness? She let her eyes close, let sleep turn away the questions that gnawed.

Live for each moment, she told herself again and again in the weeks that followed. The little cottage became a place of happiness, yet an incomplete happiness, and she discovered a patience she never knew was hers. But patience was not enough. The nights of warmth and sweet togetherness were not enough. The anguish came more and more often in Paul's eyes. When the senses should have soared into full wing, they were held back, shadowed by a rival she could not reach.

"It's not helping, is it?" she asked one night when she woke to find Paul sitting up, his eyes clouded with thought. "I'm not making you see anything clearly. Maybe that's a kind of answer."

His hand found her face. "No, it's no answer to anything. Indecision is never an answer. It is weakness, my weakness."

"Then don't choose. I told you, I only want to be with you, no matter what."

His glance held patience and love. "Don't choose? Be unfaithful to both loves?" he chided gently. "No, my darling. That would be compounding wrong. You have taught me more than you know about myself. I've been content with pleasure instead of answers."

"And I want to help, to make you see, to give," Marina returned.

"Sometimes, to hold back is to give."

Marina knew that disappointment showed in her face. "It's not in me to hold back, Paul."

"I know. That's why there must be more space and more time between us. I need to know what I cannot live without," he replied.

"Yes, I know," Marina murmured. "But the idea of leaving here, of going away and just waiting—it terrifies me. I haven't your strength. Or your selflessness."

"You are needed elsewhere, Marina." Paul's voice was firm with conviction.

"I am needed?" She frowned. "No, not I, not even by you, not yet, not completely."

He cupped her face with his hands. "You are needed, and being needed gives us strength. I've been thinking about those who planned a new city-state of power and despotism. You said princes of the Church were part of it. It was no wildfire scheme, then. It will be put into action again."

"Yes, I'm certain of that. I don't doubt that they are preparing new forces this very minute," Marina agreed.

"Then they must be stopped—and only you can do that."

"I cannot stop them," Marina protested. "They think I died with the others in the storm. If they knew I lived, they'd kill me. I know too much."

"Yes, only you know the faces of the cardinals, monsignors, and priests. They are the real strength of any plan. Armies can only conquer. Without the power of the cardinals—their influence, backing, and wealth—a new city-state could not operate. They are the ones who must be exposed and named. Then the rest of the plot will fall apart."

Marina nodded, her lips tightening in memory. "Yes, I know their faces. I printed each one in my mind."

"Then you must see them again," Paul insisted.

"How? By luck? By recognizing one in a passing procession in a tiny village?"

"No, but there is a way. I will take you to a most unusual man who lives near here, at Spezzano. He is most eager to hear what you have told me. He will find a way to stop this despotism."

"Who is this man, Paul? How do you know him?"

"We met when I was a seminarian. He lectured to us and we became friends. He is a nobleman in the true sense of the word, a baron by birth but a believer in the dignity of all men. For that he is despised by most of his peers. His life has been threatened in the past because of those he has helped."

"Indeed, a most unusual man," Marina echoed.

"His name is Baron Vittorio Amati. He is no longer young, except in spirit, but he has influence and friends in high places, in governments and in the Church. He knew Rousseau and Voltaire and corresponds now with the Englishman, John Locke. He will know where to turn."

"All right, I'll go to see him," Marina consented, unable to contain her sadness. "I'm sorry," she murmured at once, her arms encircling Paul. "I know it is the right thing to do, for you, for us."

His kiss was one of sweet sorrow that stayed with her through the night. In the morning, as he left, he paused at the doorway. "I'll borrow a donkey wagon and be back before noon." Marina nodded, wanted to say "Hurry back" as she did every morning, but the words stuck in her throat and her eyes blurred. She turned away, waited till she could no longer hear her footsteps, then flung herself on the cot to succumb to tears that refused to be held back. Finally she rose, angry at herself for giving way to them.

She was waiting outside when Paul returned in the noonday sun, driving the wooden cart, a small but sturdy donkey hitched to its shafts. She carried a small net bag with some fruit and the other skirt and blouse Paul had brought her. "We will not reach his home till dark, I'm afraid," Paul apologized.

"I'm in no hurry," Marina answered softly. They rode in silence for a good part of the way, the kind of silence only those who love can know, talking without words, touching without hands. The path wound into the hills, past rows of lemon trees and tall pines, then down into hollows filled with olive groves. The darkness drifted down like unseen and unfelt raindrops, blanketing the land, just as the donkey cart turned into the driveway of a great villa and Marina glimpsed a baroque fountain surrounded by cultivated avocado trees, swamp cypresses, and ginkgo trees.

"You will feel more at home here than in the cottage, from what you've told me about your own lovely villa," Paul remarked.

"I will feel at home no place ever without you." Marina's hand stole over his. "When will I see you again? How will I hear from you?"

"I will find time," Paul assured her. The cart rolled to a halt before a fine house columned in a semicircular portico. Servants helped her from the cart and Paul showed her into a sumptuous yellow foyer trimmed with red moldings. A spritely figure, not as tall as she, clothed in a pearl-gray collared frock coat without cuffs and with matching trousers, entered the room. His eyes, brown and bright, held her at once, full of life and quick wisdom. His face wore the lines of age with grace, and his smile welcomed her as he embraced Paul.

"What a wonderful surprise," the man said and Paul introduced her at once.

"Baron Amati, this is a special friend, a special person, Marina Valerian." Baron Amati's eyes took in Marina at one quick glance, and she felt he knew more about her than many who'd known her for years. "Marina has a most important, and disturbing, tale to tell," Paul informed him.

"Over dinner," the baron said. "And perhaps in a fresh gown, one that Marina is more accustomed to wearing than skirts and blouses." His smile was disarming as he met the question in her eyes. "Forgive an old man, my dear, but experience teaches you to tell immediately a young woman of taste and schooling. The best of schools leaves a stamp that shows through everything."

Marina nodded at the compliment. "And do you keep gowns on hand for young ladies who wander in from the road?" she wondered.

The baron's laugh was quick and full of honesty. "Bravo. Well taken, young woman." He turned to Paul, his eyes sharp, probing each expression. "And where did you find this charming, quickminded beauty, my dear Paul?"

"On the beach. That is part of the story she has to tell." Paul smiled.

"All right, I shall wait till dinner," the baron agreed, then turned back to Marina. "I do indeed have a closet full of gowns, though the ladies who avail themselves of them do not usually wander in from the road. They are mostly nieces and cousins who come to visit and stay longer than they planned. I am sure there is something to fit you. I'll have one of the maids show you to your room. You are staying the night, of course?"

"Not I," Paul said. "I will leave later and be back for my tasks by morning."

The baron's glance held unasked questions but he did not voice them then. He ushered Marina and Paul into a large living room whose walls were painted sea-green and turquoise with yellow accents to represent a leafy arbor with a Chinese landscape replete with pagodas. "I see you've a taste for chinoiserie," Marina remarked.

"An indulgence," the Baron replied. "I like the airy lightness. It's a relief from the overworked baroque of our Neapolitan craftsmen." A young girl appeared and the baron instructed her to take Marina upstairs. Marina followed her, executing a quick curtsy to her host, and found herself in a room of delicate blues with stucco so fine it almost resembled lace. The girl opened sliding doors of a large closet and Marina saw the array of gowns there. The girl indicated a bath with a sunken tub surrounded by marble tile. Without asking, the girl turned gold faucets and began to fill the tub. Marina waited a moment, then spoke. "I'll finish," she told her and the girl bowed and hurried from the room.

Marina pulled her blouse and skirt off and felt the dust of the roads all over her as she stepped into the bath. At other times she would have thoroughly enjoyed the luxuriousness of the lovely house. Now she thought only of Paul's departure.

Bathing quickly, she dried herself, brushed her hair, and found a simple sheath dress with a brilliant blue sash ribbon tied at the waist. It fit almost perfectly, and she hurried down the stairway adjacent to the room that had been given her. A servant showed her to a small dining room, where Paul and the baron were already seated.

Paul's eyes grew round as she entered. "How truly beautiful you are," he murmured.

"Indeed," the baron echoed. He rose and pulled a chair out for her opposite Paul and next to his own. "Paul has told me some of the story. I can't wait to hear the rest from you."

While she was served bouillon with curved crusts of bread lightly touched with parmesan, then a rich, red filet of beef, Marina recounted all that had brought her there. Baron Amati insisted she start again at the beginning and she complied. But once more she left out Generoso and her private pain. When she finished, the quick brown eyes grew surprisingly reflective. Espresso was served, but the baron took only a few sips of his.

"This is not something for quick decisions," he contemplated aloud. "It will require careful thought and examination. Paul tells me you have consented to be my guest and to brighten an old man's home until I think of how best to handle this most serious matter."

Marina nodded, meeting his eyes, which were now grave. "Good. I shall sleep on this, and in the morning you and I will go over each detail again."

"Paul said you would fight against another empire of tyranny. Any city-state run by my guardian and the Duke d'Albatore would have to be a tyrant's paradise."

"Then we shall find a way to stop that," the baron assured her.

Paul turned to Marina. "It's time I started on my way."

Marina felt bands of pain suddenly tighten around her. She rose, groping for words. "I'll go outside with you," she almost whispered, suddenly terribly conscious of the older man's eyes on her.

"Yes, please do that, my dear," the baron urged. "Night air is hard on old joints." Marina cast a grateful glance at him, and walked quickly beside Paul. At the cart outside, her arms tightened around him and she murmured, "Paul? Hurry back." Her lips clung for a long moment and then she forced herself to step back and turn away from the little cart. She hastened into the house, not daring to look after Paul. The door closed behind her, shutting out the terrible sound of the little cart rolling away. She became aware of the figure watching her after a moment, met Baron Amati's eyes, lifted her chin high, and tried to smile.

The older man did not destroy her effort with questions. He nodded gravely. "I'll look forward to seeing you at breakfast, Marina."

Marina agreed with a glance, started past him, halted, then probed him with her eyes. While she had been dressing upstairs, he and Paul had talked alone. The question had to be asked.

"Did Paul tell you anything else about me?" she inquired.

Vittorio Amati returned her gaze solemnly. "No. Did he have to?"

The answer had been given her with a graciousness that bore an edge. There was little missed of what came before Vittorio Amati's bright, quick eyes, she decided. He had given no sign of approval or disapproval, and she was grateful to him for that. She liked this spry little man. He could be a friend, certainly someone to listen to and to heed. And of course, Paul had known as much before bringing her here.

Marina turned away and started for the stairs, suddenly frightened of tomorrow. *Hurry back, Paul,* she breathed silently. *Please, please let me be yours.*

CHAPTER NINE

BREAKFAST WAS TAKEN in a bright, sunlit anteroom with white, wrought-iron chairs and a square table to match, the walls adorned with sprays of jonquils and snapdragons painted onto whitewashed stucco. It was a room designed to send the day off to as good a start as possible. Baron Amati, in a deep blue-jacket with gold-edged lapels, had been waiting for her, and as she entered he put aside a small stack of letters and papers.

"You brighten a day that brings dark news," he remarked. He extracted a letter from the pile, holding it up between thumb and forefinger. "The morning post brought it from a friend in Paris, André Boldino."

"What kind of dark news?" Marina asked as she sat down to a bowl of sliced orange and mint ice.

"Storm clouds are gathering fast, I fear." The baron held the letter in front of him. "Paul told me you studied in Paris and know French." Marina nodded. "The assembly has defied the king. They have refused to be dismissed. Les États Généraux has stood up to Louis. That is monumentally significant."

"It will provoke a direct confrontation."

"Exactly. Even Louis, spineless nincompoop that he is, cannot ignore that challenge. His response, of course, will be the only one he knows; more repression, more jailings, more hangings—another display of royal insensitivity."

"Which will serve as more fuel for the revolutionaries," Marina interjected.

"Exactly," Baron Amati concurred, his fist clenching. "André writes that there are plans to storm the Bastille as a signal for revolution throughout France."

"But surely there must be some who see the storm clouds building, others of his court." Marina frowned.

The baron leaned forward, his brows, too, coming together in a frown. "Of course. In Louis's court there are those who encourage both sides for their own ends. They support the revolutionaries secretly, but only because they see an opportunity to seize power for themselves, to step into chaos and become the new tyrants. They are indeed wolves in sheep's clothing."

"You have someone specific in mind," Marina ventured.

"One above all the others, Robespierre. He is clever, two-faced, immoral. He covets power as a miser covets gold. He will find a scapegoat besides the king in which to cloak his own ambitions, most likely the Church. Not that the Church hasn't done enough on its own. When the masses turn to pillage its cathedrals and pillory its cardinals, the Church can only look to its own actions and inactions. So many of the Church's princes are involved with the excesses and sins of the royal court that they, too, will pay the price."

Sorrow moved into his quick, bright eyes and he sighed deeply. "One extreme replaces another. Revolutions of this kind, filled with fever and mob anger, bring their own excesses. I daresay that if it comes, it will be a revolt not just against an immoral and decadent monarchy but also against the entire past. The bones will be thrown out with the soup. When they substitute a new government for the monarchy, they will try to substitute a new religion for Christianity."

Marina leaned back in the chair. "Your information has alarmed you that much. You really believe there will be a revolution in France."

"Inescapably. The little signs are there now. They mean the time grows near. Before a kettle boils over, it simmers, lets off steam, and rattles the lid. It is the same with people when they grow close to exploding." Baron Amati took up the letter again and read from it. "André writes, 'They have taken to openly calling themselves the Carmagnoles, and the *carmagnole* is worn all over now.'"

"The *carmagnole*? The short jacket?" Marina frowned.

"The same, introduced to France from our own carmagnola in the Piedmont, where it is the workmen's garb. They have adopted it and wear it now as a badge of the revolutionaries."

Marina's eyes grew soft for an instant. She had known another garment worn as a badge, had held herself close to it. The camorra would always hold a special place in her heart, not merely a memory but a part of her that would stay forever. She heard the baron's voice going on and quickly brought her attention back to him. "You know, they call the Queen 'Madame Veto.'"

"Madame Veto?" Marina echoed.

"Yes, that is the people's name for Marie Antoinette because they know it is she who vetoes everything that would benefit them. They have come to know that it is she who dominates Louis." The baron's brows furrowed again. "The spirit of revolutions, if not their armies, spreads. Your guardian and the others knew that. I do not want to see the Church here as deeply involved in power and politics. I do not want the people of the Italian states to see their church in the same light as the revolutionaries in France see their clergy. Rome is a house fighting itself. It needs all the help it can get. That is why it is vital that the cardinals you saw, and the others, be exposed, stripped of their positions and their power. They defy the express orders of the Pope and the very spirit of the Church by this hunger for power, this playing in wealth and greed. They want not to serve but to rule. They wear the robes of Christianity but not its principles."

Marina shrugged. "But how can they be exposed? How can I even find them again before a new version of the plan goes into action? By then it will be too late."

Vittorio Amati's quick eyes darted to her, then looked down at the backs of his knuckles as he folded his hands together. "That is the question I have yet to resolve. I think I must visit a few friends I can trust to hear their thoughts." He rose abruptly and gestured with a sweep of his hand. "I shall be back sometime in the night. Treat this house as if it were your own villa. There are stables if you wish to ride, and my gardens are unique in all of the kingdom. Enjoy it as you wish."

"You are most gracious." Marina rested her hand on his arm.

His quick eyes danced. "Were I but ten years younger I would woo you with all the guile of experience."

"Were I but ten years older, I might well listen," Marina retorted, joining in his infectious laughter.

"Only a most unusual man could keep up with both your beauty and your mind," the baron lectured her gently. "Never settle for less, my dear."

"Never," Marina promised, watching him hurry off with a rapid stride that belied his years. She went back to her room, changed into the skirt and blouse Paul had brought her, then explored the gardens, wandering beyond their ordered beauty which carried the *chinoiserie* motif of the interior of the house into the outdoors. Small benches with pagodalike roofs dotted the landscaping with ginkgo trees and little wooden bridges forded small streamlets. When she returned to the house it seemed empty, disturbingly so, and she realized that without the presence of Vittorio Amati the great house was but a magnificent museum, beautiful but lifeless. Much like herself, Marina reflected. Without Paul's warm, loving presence, she was only a shell, empty of passion.

She found the library and closeted herself with its riches. Volume after volume on shelves upon shelves of playwrights of all countries met her eye, many translated into Italian but many in their original languages. Giambattista Vico, Bruno Giordano, Boccaccio and Alfieri, Campanella and Belli lined one shelf. Above them, Jean de la Bruyère, Molière and Montaigne, Marivaux and Mme. de Sevigny, Shakespeare, Goldsmith and Spenser filled the next. The ancient Greek tragedians came next— Sophocles, Euripedes, Aeschylus. There were more playwrights, some minor ones she'd never heard of, and on another wall were volumes of political leaders and statesmen—Frontenac, Marat, Mirabeau, Tallyrand, Grenville, Burke, Walpole, Malpighi, Borgia, Machiavelli, and Torrecelli.

More and more she was coming to respect the spry little man with the bright, quick eyes. Perhaps he would indeed find a way to stop Aldo Gamborelli and his sorry cohorts. But could he help her with Paul? Would he if he could? There was respect and friendship between the older man and the younger. She would talk to Vittorio Amati about Paul and herself. She would make him understand.

One of the servants knocked discreetly on the library door to tell her that dinner was ready. She followed him to a small table set for one, replete with a wine glass and small carafe of white wine. She dined in solitary splendor and wondered how soon one grew cold with loneliness dining alone.

Baron Amati had not returned when she went upstairs to bed. "Good night, Paul, my love," she whispered as she lay on the wide bed and closed her eyes. Dimly, as she fell off to sleep, she heard the sound of a carriage arriving below.

In the morning she woke early to a buffet breakfast arranged in the small anteroom. She took fruit, croissants, and coffee and sat by one of the windows, breakfasting and continuing to stare out at the driveway, watching workmen—including a gardener with only a large pruning shears—arrive in small road carts and old wagons.

"Waiting for someone?" she heard a voice ask. She turned to see Baron Amati there, watching her intently. Almost embarrassedly, she realized she had been doing exactly that.

"Did it show that much?"

"Only in your eyes, shadowed with hope and anxiety as each figure appeared down the roadway." He smiled. He sat down along the edge of the window seat, almost offhandedly sliding words at her. "You know, I've known Paul since he was a seminarian. I was a financial adviser for the seminary then."

"Yes, Paul told me," Marina responded.

"He combined compassion and intellect to an extraordinary extent even then. Paul was one of those everyone agreed had all the God-given qualities for the priesthood," the older man recalled. "Of course, it is always difficult to know if one is really meant for the priesthood. It takes a slow looking into oneself, and there are often doubts."

Marina lifted her eyes to meet Vittorio Amati's gaze. "What are you trying to say, Baron?" she asked tensely.

"Do not be angry with me, my dear," he cajoled her. "I understand your love and I feel deeply for it."

"It is not a passing thing. I do not give love lightly," Marina snapped. She saw only empathy and patience in the quick brown eyes.

"I did not think otherwise. Yours would not be an ordinary love, for Paul is not an ordinary man. I do not know that you fully understand the total meaning of that. Most of us can love one person, some of us more deeply than others. Sometimes we can love two people at the same time for different reasons. That is our nature, what has been given us to do. But only a few among us have the capacity, the special ability, to bring a different kind of love to the world—a love not confined to one person, not dedicated to a single individual, but to all people everywhere. That is why the priesthood is called a charismatic gift—given to one to share with many. And it is given to but a few."

"You're asking me to turn my back on Paul, on the happiness I've found with him," Marina pressed.

"No. I am asking you to match the gift given to Paul, that you help him be faithful to that special calling that is his," the baron replied. "Do not wait and watch for him. Do not call to him in spirit. I believe we receive such messages in ways we do not understand. Let time answer you. If Paul is to come to you, it will happen. Meanwhile, you must put him out of your mind."

"You ask the impossible."

"Perhaps. Then devote all your thoughts to what I have to propose to you," Baron Amati countered. "I have consulted with confidants who think as we do about the rights of man. I have formed a plan. Only you can make it work."

"Go on."

"Only you know the churchmen involved in the plans hatched by your guardian and the Duke d'Albatore," the baron began. "And as you now know only faces and not names, you must go to Rome and find them."

"To Rome?" Marina frowned. "I could spend a decade looking through Rome and not find them."

"Yes, but not on this visit. You will be going to Rome at a time of special festivities. All Rome will be celebrating the one hundred and seventy-fifth anniversary of the installation of the first Bernini columns in St. Peter's. There will be parties all over, at certain places in particular. Those whom we seek will most surely be there," the baron assured her.

"And how will I attend these parties?" Marina wondered.

"I have a house in Rome. It once belonged to an aunt who married an Orsini. My sister, the baroness, lives there now. She will have invitations to every important fete."

Marina saw his lips purse and heard a half-annoyed grunt escape him.

"And she'll go to every one of them, I'll wager," he continued. "You will go with her. We'll have to provide you with a new name and lineage. Let's see, what shall we call you?"

He paused a moment as if to contemplate, then his eyes twinkled. "For one with the beauty of an angel, the only possible name is, I think, Angelica. Yes, Angelica is perfect. Now, for the family name."

Again he paused. "You are an angel, but an angel in the service of justice. You will become a distant relation of that most famous Venetian family, the Giustiniani. So, my dear, bid farewell for a while to Marina Valerian and meet the angel of justice, Angelica Giustiniani. You'll be a beautiful creature of mystery and intrigue, a woman of adventure. That will insure tongues wagging and everyone wanting to meet you."

"Including those whom I saw at d'Albatore's place," Marina finished.

"Without a doubt. You'll learn their names and give them to me when you have them all in hand. But you must try to find out if the new plans are underway and what they are. I'd imagine it would be difficult to duplicate the first venture exactly."

The baron paused, his eyes narrowing at the tiny lines of thought that touched the girl's smooth brow as she looked down at her lap. "None of these men have ever seen you, have they?" he asked.

"No," Marina said. His face relaxed with a measure of relief. "Then you'll not be in any danger on that score. But there *will* be danger, I'm afraid. Does that trouble you?"

"No," Marina answered, not looking up.

"Many of those you'll meet are steeped in intrigue. They are always on guard, so to speak. They are dangerous if they feel their worlds threatened. You must be curious, but frivolously so, your interest in those who may provide rewards and *divertissement* a transparent thing."

"I understand," Marina said, still keeping her eyes averted, the small furrows still digging into her brow.

"Then what is troubling you, my dear?" she heard Vittorio Amati ask. She lifted her eyes to meet his and tried not to sound childish, but knew she wasn't succeeding.

"I want to see Paul before I go," she said, not looking away this time, her lips pressed together in a thin line. "I can't devote all my thoughts to this without seeing him again. You ask that I match the gift given Paul, that I help him be faithful to the special calling that is his. I don't know if I can be that selfless. I have to find out for myself."

"Is that all of it, Marina?" the older man asked gently.

"I don't know," she replied abruptly. "Maybe there's more, but that's part of it, and that's enough."

Vittorio Amati nodded. "Yes, that is enough. Of course you may see Paul. You are no prisoner here."

Marina held his grave eyes with hers. "I know that. But I want to see Paul with your approval."

"You have my understanding, but not my approval," Vittorio Amati said not unkindly.

"I'll have to be content with that," Marina retorted. The baron rose, the quick brightness returning to his eyes.

"Then it is settled, an exchange of sorts. But first we must outfit you with a wardrobe befitting a woman of the world, a beautiful creature of pleasure. It will be no effort for you to wear such clothes, of course. You have spent your life wearing them. But we must find a place to have them made for you. We cannot go to any of the major fashion centers. Gossip travels like the wind, especially where many other fine ladies will be having gowns made. We cannot have anyone telling of the beautiful young girl being outfitted at the shops of Rostelli or Signora Baldi."

"When my mother wanted something very special, she would journey to a little-known designer and dressmaker, a man by the name of Duran. He worked with the great fabric houses of France and studied with Rose Bertain. He takes but a few clients, but I'm sure he would take me."

"Where is this *marchand des modes*?"

"In Taranto. It will be a journey, I'm afraid," Marina said.

"Anywhere we go would be a journey. We will leave in the morning. You must prepare to spend as many days as necessary for him to fit a complete wardrobe for you," the baron said. His eyes showed a hint of a twinkle. "I shall enjoy the visit. It has been many years since I've taken a young woman to fit a wardrobe. It will make me feel young again."

Marina found herself laughing again with Vittorio Amati and realized how little she had laughed since leaving the little cottage. "And when we return?" she asked, growing sober at once.

"You shall see Paul. One of my men will take you to him," the baron promised. "Now, I've many things to do, my dear. Till dinner, enjoy the day."

Marina returned to the guest room and let the day slip away into night. When she went down to dinner, there was no further talk of Paul, as though both kept away from the subject out of respect for the other. "I wonder if I will be able to carry the banner of concern about others, of justice, as long and graciously as you have," Marina asked the older man.

"I'm sure you will, my dear," replied the baron. "You carry concern from the heart. Mine has more often been an intellectual position. I would change with your approach any time. It is less apt to fail one. The wisdom of the heart is more solid than logic."

The baron sat back, losing himself for a moment in private recollections. But later Marina took his words to sleep with her, words well worth holding close, she knew. She fell asleep quickly despite her anxious thoughts about the trip that would bring her closer to returning to Paul.

The coach-and-four waited outside the house when she went downstairs in the morning, Marina saw. As she finished breakfast, the baron appeared and hurried out to the coach with her at once. In moments they were flying down the roadway. "It will be a long enough journey," he remarked. "We will spend the night in a small inn and be in Taranto by morning. You will be able to find this Duran, I trust."

"I went with my mother only twice, but I was impressed. I think I'll remember. His house was near the shoreline of the gulf of Taranto."

"That should help to find it," the baron replied. Marina sat back and enjoyed the warm, lush, fertile land. In the early dark they arrived at an inn hospitable and full of country charm. Marina slept well and rose early, and before noon they had arrived in the sun-kissed, bright shorefront community of Taranto. She directed the coachman out of memory, frowning and pressing her eyes shut to bring back almost lost years. The house came into view and memory flooded back. Signore Duran had become plumper and more excitable than she remembered him but then she had been largely on the periphery of the visits. He remembered her mother at once and surveyed Marina as though he were a buyer appraising an *objet d'art*.

"Yes, yes, I can see your mother in you." He clucked. "But, meaning no disrespect, you are more beautiful."

"I want you to provide a wardrobe for this most beautiful young lady," Baron Amati told the dressmaker-designer. "I will pay the extra costs for added help to have it finished as quickly as possible and kept as quiet as possible. The lady will be at you disposal for fittings every day if need be."

The dressmaker inclined his head in thought. "Be assured, the lady's name will never be mentioned. And I happen to have extra help available. It can all be done as you wish. It will be a pleasure to design gowns for a body such as this instead of the overfed hens that ask me to make them into nightingales." He strode to a huge wooden chest as tall as he was, pulled open wide drawers, and revealed bolts of fabric neatly set inside.

"First we choose the material—taffeta, velvet, satin, silks, gold and silver metal threads, brocade, paillettes, and chenille. I love embroidered work on the gold-threaded silks and I love moiré effects," he said, growing excited quickly. "Then the style of gown is matched to the material. Only then do we begin to take measurements."

"Get on with it, whatever it is," the baron urged. "I shall be doing other things while you're here. The coach will pick you up later in the day." Marina nodded and the spry figure hurried out. The tailor began work at once, sending out for two assistants who came at once—one a thin, olive-skinned girl who handled fabric with love, and the other a tall, lanky young man. He quickly showed his expertise with scissors and pins.

By the day's end, material and styles had been chosen, initial fittings already begun. "I never realized one could grow so tired being dressed and fussed with," Marina said to the baron, who had returned.

"Fashion is work." He chuckled quietly. "Signore Duran is a man of sophistication. He has not questioned this old roué's purchasing fine gowns for a beautiful young woman. I daresay he is not as hidden away as you think."

"I only hope he continues at this pace." Marina sighed. The wish was fulfilled. The tailor was a man of energy as well as talent. The days fell into a pattern of fittings, corrections, and more fittings. Frequently, he would intersperse his directions and remarks to his assistants with murmured comments meant more for himself than anyone else. "What a waist to circle," he'd say and, a little later. "Such breasts to mold with fabric. *Magnifico.*" When he asked if Marina would come for final fittings at night, she consented eagerly. By the week's end, Baron Amati had acquired a new tan on the beaches of Taranto and Marina a new and elegant wardrobe. In the trunks the baron purchased, she saw to the packing of pierrots, pleated dresses, redingotes, chemises gowns *à la levité, à la circassienne, à la polonaise,* dresses of cloth *indienne,* casaquins, and a brilliantly sashed gown, *à la creole.*

Trunks secured to the back and top of the coach, the long trip to the baron's house began. "You will be the talk of Rome,

Marina," he assured her. "Certainly that section of Rome which will attend the parties. It will be worth it if you can uncover the names and the plans we must know."

Marina nodded. At another time, the wealth of gorgeous gowns to wear would have excited her. Now she could think but of one thing: soon she would be with Paul again. The baron's villa was reached at night, but by the next morning Marina was up early, trying to hide a sudden nervousness that had swept over her. Vittorio Amati was not a man of small cruelties, and he had a covered rig and driver waiting when she came downstairs. Marina had put on the yellow blouse and brown skirt Paul had brought her, and she saw the Baron's eyes smile in understanding.

"I still think it would be better not to go," he said with a shrug.

"I know. But I must go," Marina declared.

He helped her into the rig. "Toward Amantea. She will find the way from there, I'm sure," he told the driver. Then he waved to Marina as she sat back and the rig rolled away. She was soon grateful that Vittorio Amati had chosen a covered rig for the sun became intense, flooding the countryside with heat. He was a man of wisdom and experience, Marina reflected, wondering if she were making a mistake in not listening to his advice. A surge of misgivings rushed around her but she quickly pushed them away. She had to see Paul, whatever the hidden reasons of the soul.

The heat of the day sapped her strength and she drowsed part of the time. The man did not drive inordinately slowly. It only seemed so. Each mile was like ten. As they neared the narrow part of the land, her misgivings gave way to eagerness. She had the driver halt at a farmhouse where she bought vegetables, a piece of pork, and a goatskin of the local wine. It was midafternoon when her uncertain directions finally brought the rig to the little cottage.

"The baron gave me instructions to return for you in the morning," the driver told her. How had Vittorio Amati presumed to know that she'd stay the night? He knew her—she sighed—perhaps better than she knew herself.

"Yes, in the morning," she ordered the driver and hurried into the cottage. The quiet, cool peacefulness caught at her at once. She had lived here such a short while, yet it was as though she had never really lived anywhere else. She immediately set out preparing dinner, peeling and paring vegetables, keeping one ear alert for the sound of Paul's footsteps coming up the path outside. It was nearly dusk when she heard him. She went quickly into the front room and was standing there as he pushed the door open. His eyes grew wide with astonishment as he saw her. She flew into his arms, felt him draw her tightly against him, and then her lips were seeking his in desperate eagerness.

He held her very close after a moment, his lips against her ear, touching the very tip of her ear lobe. "Marina, my Marina," he murmured.

"I had to come, Paul."

"I've no answers, not this soon," he told her softly.

"I did not come for that. I came because I had to see you before leaving for Rome." The words tumbled from her lips as she told of her impending mission.

When she finished, he held her close. "I wish there were another way, but plainly there isn't. You'll carry it off, I'm sure."

"It shouldn't be too long a time there, but there's no telling really. I had to see you once more before going," Marina repeated. "You're not angry with me for coming, are you?"

"No, no. I only wish I had answers to give you. The only thing I can tell you is that I've longed for you." Paul's voice caressed her like his touch.

"That's all I need to hear, my darling," Marina murmured. "Let's not talk of tomorrows or of yesterdays. Let us just have tonight."

His arms around her was his answer. It would not be complete, no more than any of the other times had been. She knew Paul's inner strength too well to think differently. But she would give of herself and be content. Much later, when the cottage had been plunged into darkness, the moon silently stole into the room to bathe her full, soft beauty in hesitant light and to let her eyes move across Paul's supple, smooth body. Of all the extra dimensions of love, she'd learned still one more with Paul. With each gasp of newly discovered pleasure, his awakening became hers, his ecstasy transformed hers. As he lay half asleep, his chest touching her breasts, she felt a warm contentment, a special kind of satisfaction. She had come here, this was where she wanted to be. Despite the incompleteness the moment was all her wishes come true; she would lay sorrows to rest and dangers to the morrow. She turned on her side, pressed herself tight against Paul's chest, and let sleep erase all straying thoughts.

The moon had slipped behind the trees when she woke, startled, almost sitting up. Fear bathed her in a moment of ice. Fear that had no face, no name, just a sudden burst of fright. Paul awakened as she moved. "What is it, Marina, my lovely? You are trembling."

"Nothing. I don't know. A bad dream, maybe." She lay back and let his arms enclose her. It had been no dream. It had been real terror. She lay quietly until she had stopped trembling. "Kiss me, Paul," she whispered. "Let me love you till the night is finished. I don't want to sleep again."

Her lips opened for his mouth and her hands sought him with desperate eagerness. The fear had turned from sudden fright into a strange urgency. Dawn came soon enough, perhaps as a reprieve, for she lay back in quivering exhaustion. The terrible, desperate urgency still echoed, as though the night had been seized because it would not be hers again ever. She shuddered, swung from the bed, hurried into the other room, where she braved the cold water from the bucket and washed the night from her body. Washing it from her mind was beyond possibility or desire. She dried herself with a cloth and donned the blouse and skirt.

Paul, in trousers, stood by the opened cottage door as she came out and leaned against him. The sun stretched its warm fingers across the ground. "The rig will be here soon," Marina murmured. "I'll be going then."

She wanted no reply and received none. The sound of the wagon wheels scattering pebbles intruded on their silence. Paul cupped her face with his hand, kissed her gently. *"God writes straight with crooked lines,"* he murmured, repeating St. Thomas Aquinas's words. "Remember."

"I'll try," she told him passionately. "Oh, I will try."

The rig came into view as the sun peered over the line of trees. She hurried out to meet it, both brokenhearted and content, but with the strange fear still raging deep inside her.

CHAPTER TEN

ROME, ALWAYS AN EXCITING CITY, was festooned with flowers and hung with banners. The Tiber was lined with multicolored flags on both banks and the bridges were draped in bunting. Marina had thought the baron was going to accompany her to the Eternal City but he arranged a handsome coach to take her alone.

"It's best this way. My presence could scare away some of the wolves," he'd told her. "I sent my sister, the baroness, a letter telling her you will arrive and the reason for your visit. You'll need no better guide to parties than Rosalie."

So, with the coach laden with trunks and boxes of new clothes, she'd set off on her journey. Upon reaching Rome, she gazed from the coach window, like any tourist, at the great dome of St. Peter's sparkling in the afternoon sun. The baron's townhouse, gray stone with newly painted white window frames, nestled on a curved, cobbled street just off the Piazza Colonnia. She was admitted by an elderly butler who introduced himself. "I am Puli," he said. "The baroness will be right down."

As her things were brought in, Marina was shown to a pleasant room with walls of intarsio paneling and richly brocaded couches. It was but a few moments until the Baroness Amati entered, or rather swept into the room, Marina thought, as behind the baroness trailed yards of turquoise taffeta. Marina failed to keep the surprise from her eyes when she saw a woman at least twenty-five years younger than the baron. She waited as the Baroness Amati halted in front of her, appraising her with direct openness.

"Marina, my dear child. Oh, I must remember to call you Angelica! I thought Vittorio had one of his poetic attacks when he wrote me about you, but I see he was only being honest. You are strikingly beautiful," the baroness said. "Are you tired from the trip?"

"A little. A good nap will cure me," Marina admitted.

"Good, because the very first ball of the week is tonight, the Contessa Garramondi. She's always first, though seldom best." The baroness was pleasant-looking rather than pretty, with youthful, smooth skin, a roundcheeked face, and the same sparkling eyes as her brother's. She exuded an infectious enthusiasm that made it easy to see why she loved parties and people.

"The contessa's affair will be a good introduction for you. She seldom has the best people in Roman society but there will be plenty to carry tales about the beautiful newcomer. And you can practice your verbal fencing."

"I hope I can carry it off." Marina ventured.

"You'll do splendidly," the baroness replied. "Come, I'll show you to your rooms."

"This is most gracious of you, Baroness." Marina smiled.

"Rosalie, my dear. If you call me Baroness they'll think you don't know me. All my friends call me Rosalie," the woman informed her.

It was impossible not to like the Baroness Amati at once, Marina decided. Though she usually disliked women who made a career of parties, Marina saw that Rosalie Amati's open enthusiasm about them disarmed her critics. Marina was shown to a suite of two rooms and a chamber room on the main floor of the house, the main room featuring landscaped scenes of elysian fields with a carved stone fireplace and drapes of deep red trimmed in a salmon color. All her trunks and boxes had been put against one wall of the room.

"We'll leave at eight for the contessa's affair," the baroness informed her. "That will give you ample time to rest. I know you'll be the sensation of the week."

She swept from the room like a turquoise cloud and Marina closed the lacquered door. She unpacked, put her things into a huge walk-in closet in the adjoining bedroom, then shed her clothes and lay across the queen-size bed. She fell asleep, and when she woke the day was slipping away. But she was refreshed, and anxious. The more parties, the better chance of finishing her purpose here and returning. They also filled the hours, allowing less time to think about Paul and about the emptiness which even his love had not quite sealed off. As she chose a dress for the evening, a touch of grimness settled onto her lips. It seemed her destiny to wear a mask. Angelica Giustiniani. Once again she was playing a role. One day she'd be finished with masquerades forever, she vowed.

She undressed further, stood nude in the room, and went into the chamber room where a marbled bath was set in a floor of rose-colored quartz. She turned on the two carved faucets, each made to resemble a porpoise, and watched the water flow into the tub. Jars of bath preparations lined a low shelf, the contents of each written on labels hung from each lid. She chose one marked "Sunset." It held, she read as the water slowly filled the tub, strawberry leaves, mint leaves, orange leaves, ten drops of rose geranium oil and ten of lemon oil, a palmful of camomile leaves, and the same of geranium leaves. She poured a little into the bath water, the fragrance rising up to her nostrils almost instantly. She luxuriated in the scented water and then finally rose and dried herself on thick towels.

Because of what the baroness had said about the Contessa Garramondi's affair, Marina chose a simple chemise gown of delicate buttercup yellow, cut with a deep V at the neck. Her black, lustrous hair fell low behind it in striking contrast. She was outside, in the foyer, as the baroness came downstairs and halted in front of her. "How magnificent," the older woman breathed. "I do not believe in jealousy," the baroness went on. "I like to stand in the shadow of truly beautiful women. The rejects are always anxious for anyone who will assuage their crushed egos."

Marina laughed as gaily as the baroness at the unabashed candor exhibited. The baroness could make one feel comfortable, a rare and wonderful quality in itself, Marina concluded. But she wondered if the Baroness Amati ever had a serious thought. Only when she reached the house of the Contessa Garramondi did she learn otherwise. "I'll not play shepherd, Angelica, but if you need me, I'll be near," the baroness told her.

"Thank you," Marina answered gratefully.

"And remember, it's Rosalie, not Baroness," the woman reminded, and Marina nodded, following her up the steps and into the house where a brightly colored room, brilliantly chandeliered, greeted them. In minutes, she was introduced to more names than she could remember and whisked onto the dance floor for a quadrille by a handsome but weak-faced young man in a pearl-gray frock coat. Others followed him in quick succession and Marina let the evening float by. She found herself enjoying the glances, the whispered comments, and the curiosity that followed her. She spied only a few clerics, undistinguished-looking men, none of whom she had ever seen. By the party's end she was weary, while Rosalie Amati seemed as fresh as when they'd arrived.

"How do you do it?" Marina asked in the carriage on the way home.

"It takes practice, and a talent for the superficial." The older woman yawned.

"I'm afraid tonight was not at all successful." Marina sighed. "I saw no one I knew."

"On the contrary. By tomorrow night at the consul's affair, everyone will be waiting to meet you. The spirit of Machiavelli still presides in Rome. Everyone plays at intrigue here." The baroness smiled. "You have burst upon the scene. Everyone wants to know from where."

Marina, alone in her rooms, undressed and fell upon the bed exhausted. A strong face that was somehow both Paul's and Generoso's flashed before her for a moment, and then she slept.

The morning sun had long flooded the room when she stirred and stretched. She rose, donning a robe at a knock on the door. It was a breakfast tray pushed by a maid and followed by Rosalie Amati in a plumed lounging robe. "I'm going to be at the dressmaker all afternoon, and I thought a moment's instruction about tonight might be in order."

"Yes, I'd like that," Marina answered.

"The Consul of Verona always gives a lavish ball at the Palazzo Farina," the baroness began. "The gentlemen will be somewhat older than last night, more charming, and also a great deal cleverer. You'd do well to prepare a dozen replies. I've found it best not to count on brilliant *bon mots* on the spot. They never seem to materialize, at least not for me."

"I'll try," Marina replied, "though I find a direct challenge stimulating enough to trigger thoughts."

The baroness shrugged. "In any case, be prepared for more clever assaults," she concluded as she swept from the room. But her words of caution proved correct as, that night, Marina found herself surrounded with suave and handsome gentlemen. Their questions and subtle probes had indeed more finesse than those of the previous night, and to each she gave an answer intended to intrigue more than satisfy. Soon she found an amusement in the game, as though she were a puppeteer making his puppets move as he wished. But once again the affair ended without her having seen anyone she knew.

The nights that followed were a succession of gay parties, of dancing and drinking wine until she was anxiously grateful for the rest each day afforded. The beautiful Angelica Giustiniani had become a celebrity, a woman of mystery and intrigue. Some rumors had it that she was really a courtesan from Florence, others that she was a wealthy young woman from Paris, and still others that she was indeed a lovely Venetian from an impoverished branch of a powerful family, looking for a new paramour to keep her in the manner to which she was accustomed. But all agreed that she was most beautiful.

The week was nearing an end when she went with Rosalie Amati to an opulent affair held at a house overlooking the Tiber. She had chosen to wear a gown *à la creole,* deep maroon with a cream inset at the bodice. One man, tall and suave, introduced to her as a wealthy importer of spices, Carlos Don Santis, was particularly inquisitive. "You sound as though you want a catalogue of my lovers," Marina snapped, and then enjoyed his attempt at apologies. She turned them aside, found an older man waiting to fill her wine glass. The baroness came by to introduce him as Mario Della Conte. "Be careful, my dear," she announced in front of the man. "Mario is the nosiest fop in all Rome."

Signore Della Conte did not seem the least offended by her words and, alone with Marina, quickly proved the accuracy of the comment. "I cannot help it. I am fascinated by people, and especially beautiful and mysterious people," he confessed. "Seeing that you are staying with the baroness, I find myself wondering if perhaps Vittorio Amati has not been your secret benefactor. I've never believed the old fox to be as proper as he pretends."

Marina allowed a tingling laugh to escape her. "My dear sir, you surprise me. Do you really think I'd tell you if it were so?" She turned away, leaving him happy that he'd confirmed his suspicions. She had taken a moment's rest beside the baroness, who was busily chattering with two portly merchants from Bergamo, when she saw the figure enter the room and hand his red robe to a servant. Beneath it she saw the black cassock with the tiny red square at the neck. The face above it was etched in her memory— imperious, sharp-nosed, striking in the way a falcon's intense face is striking. She pulled at Rosalie Amati's sleeve, and the older woman broke off her conversation with the two men and leaned toward her.

"That's him," Marina whispered. As she spoke, another man, smaller, puffy-eyed, his figure not as trim in his cassock, came to stand beside the other. "And there's the first one who visited the duke beside him."

"The tall one is Cardinal Scarti, the other Cardinal Moglianeri," the baroness said.

"Scarti was the main one. He seemed the key figure."

"I am not surprised," the baroness remarked. "Cardinal Scarti is a powerful and avaricious man. He controls a small but influential following within the Church and a greedy cabal without."

Marina watched the cardinal's brilliant, piercing blue eyes slowly scan the room and come to halt upon her. He detached himself from the shorter man and moved toward her. "Cardinal Scarti wants to meet you," the baroness murmured. "I would expect that. It is reputed that he has an eye for beautiful women."

The cardinal threaded his way through the crowds. When he finally reached her the baroness said, "Good evening, Your Eminence. I venture to say that you are on a pilgrimage of sorts." She smiled.

The piercing blue eyes narrowed for an instant, the shadow of a smile acknowledging the thrust. "The most pleasurable kind of pilgrimage, my dear Baroness," Cardinal Scarti replied, turning to Marina. "I had heard of the beautiful young woman attending the various affairs with you. I had to see for myself," he remarked.

"I trust you aren't disappointed," Marina offered.

"On the contrary. It is seldom that gossip is as accurate as it is about you, my dear," the churchman cooed. In the piercing eyes Marina saw something more than avuncular interest.

"What else has brought you here to Rome during this time of celebration, my dear?" he asked.

"Angelica, please, Your Eminence," she corrected gracefully.

"Angelica, then. A perfect name for an angel of beauty."

"What has brought me here to Rome?" Marina echoed in mock consternation. "New horizons, new adventures, perhaps. Something different." Her manner was flirtatious.

"You can find all those things in Rome." The cardinal was definitely enticed. "Sometime you must tell me more about what you seek."

"I should love to," Marina answered.

"Until then, enjoy the Eternal City." He turned and strode away.

At her elbow the baroness caught the fleeting stab of disappointment that touched Marina's face. "You expected more."

"He hardly said anything," Marina complained. "I didn't get a chance to seduce him at all."

"That's already been done. In some things you've a lot to learn, Marina. The cardinal is a cautious man. He made his opening move. He will seek you out again, never fear. Your answers were the right ones."

Marina accepted the older woman's knowledge in these matters, but Cardinal Scarti did not approach her again all evening. However, his eyes hardly left her, and she exchanged glances with him a dozen times. He left before midnight, and for Marina, the remainder of the evening became totally boring. But Rosalie Amati's words were proven true the next evening at the official Vatican ball. Cardinal Scarti was there when Marina arrived with the baroness, and so was another of the duke's clandestine visitors, a monsignor who Marina pointed out at once. "The good Monsignor Gracche, one of the cardinal's inner clique," the baroness informed her. "Now we have three names."

"And two more yet to come," Marina countered. The baroness moved from her to answer the greeting of a very regal-looking woman and Marina was left alone. The moment did not last long as a young consular official from Piedmont and Cardinal Scarti converged upon her. After a moment, the younger man left with a bow.

"I've been thinking about our brief conversation last night, those new horizons and new adventures you seek," the cardinal began. "Perhaps I could help in those pursuits."

"Could you?" Marina allowed him a sly glance.

"I presume you are interested in making new acquaintances who can help you enjoy life to the fullest," the cardinal suggested seductively.

"Exactly." Marina smiled.

"And you attach no restrictions upon such acquaintances?" he pressed.

"None," she replied, lowering her lashes. "Except that young men with hopes do not interest me terribly. I prefer a man who has achieved a certain station in the world."

"Most wise," the churchman agreed.

Marina pursed her lips in indecision. "But that doesn't always mean anything, either," she mused aloud. "There are merchants content to sit on grubby little businesses, artists willing to settle for their cold garrets, generals happy to command at dusty outposts somewhere."

"And cardinals content with a handful of quiet parishes to tend," the churchman murmured wryly.

"Exactly. I'm interested in those who wish to do bigger and better things in the world." Marina challenged.

"You seem to set little value on affection, my dear," Cardinal Scarti remarked dryly.

"On the contrary. I set great value on it," Marina countered and laughed lightly.

"*Touché.*" A smile touched his lips.

"I merely feel that affection should come after the fact, not before it. With the proper inspiration I can be very affectionate," Marina added, the tip of her tongue touching her upper lip for a moment.

The cardinal's face remained expressionless, but the sharp eyes took on tiny pinpoints of light at their centers. "These large parties bore me. One can't really have an intimate conversation," he remarked. "I prefer more select gatherings. I'm having such an affair at my residence the day after tomorrow. Could you come?"

"At your residence?" Marina echoed, her eyebrows lifting.

He smiled gently. "My unofficial residence," he corrected. "After all, everyone must have a place to relax fully, don't you think?"

"Definitely." Marina's glance held unsaid words. "How do I find this place of relaxation?"

"I'll have a carriage sent for you, at three," the cardinal replied.

"I'll be waiting." Marina smiled. The piercing blue eyes seemed to soften a fraction and with a nod, Cardinal Scarti left her. Marina drew a deep breath, fended off an immediate onslaught of other admirers, and found the baroness. Taking her aside, she told the older woman of the cardinal's invitation.

"I don't think you should go." The baroness frowned. "But we'll talk more of this tomorrow."

Marina returned to the party with her hostess, disappointed at the other woman's reactions. The invitation had been a major triumph, she felt. Putting aside further thoughts of it, she enjoyed the rest of the affair, went to sleep thoroughly exhausted, and woke late the next morning. When she entered the drawing room for coffee, she found the baroness waiting.

"I want to talk about your invitation," the older woman insisted sternly. "You're excited about going, aren't you?"

Marina shrugged, pressed her lips together as if to deny it, and then shrugged again. "All right, I am excited about it," she admitted. "I think I brought it about very smoothly."

"I've no doubt of that. You're beginning to enjoy the role. It's fun, a kind of game, but at a private party you might find yourself in another situation. You may find that others want more than flirting and bright repartee."

Marina frowned slightly. "I'll have to meet that if and when the time comes, but I must go. He will know what new plans have been put into action by now. I want to learn what they are."

"And you think you can loosen his tongue," the baroness mused, her eyes narrowing. "Perhaps," she remarked after a moment, "perhaps you just might." She rose abruptly. "All right, I've said my piece. Just be careful, that's all."

"I feel quite safe, really. Cardinal Scarti will do nothing to upset or anger me too much. After all, scandal is the last thing he wants, I'm sure," Marina attempted to reassure her.

"There are many ways to avoid scandal, my dear," the baroness responded. Her face grew grave for an instant, then shaking away the moment, returned to its usual open affability. "Remember, we've the Bartelli ball to attend this evening," she announced breezily.

"If it weren't for the other two I still want to identify, I'd not go at all." Marina sighed. "Now that I've established myself with the cardinal."

"And that would be a serious mistake. You can't drop your role in the middle of the play," Rosalie Amati lectured her. "It would be out of character. The gay, mysterious young woman who received an invitation from Cardinal Scarti would not stop attending parties just because of that."

Marina hugged Rosalie Amati. "I don't know how I'd have gone this far without you."

"Just tell that fussy old brother of mine. He thinks I don't have a mind for anything but fun." The woman patted Marina's cheek and hurried off. Her words proved more true than Marina expected as, that night, she saw the tall, straight figure and falcon's visage of Cardinal Scarti at the ball. He nodded to her and only near the evening's end came over to where she sipped champagne near an ornate silver punch bowl.

"Have any new horizons materialized tonight, my dear?" he asked.

"No, but one must keep searching," Marina parried. "Did you think I'd stop because of our conversation last night?"

"I'd have been disappointed in my own judgment if you had," the churchman answered, and once again Marina offered a silent word of gratitude to Rosalie Amati. "I look forward to tomorrow," the cardinal whispered as he moved on. Marina drew a deep breath, finished her champagne, and was happy to see the baroness signal that it was time to leave.

Once again she slept soundly, exhausted, and when she woke the next morning, a gray rain fell over Rome, its sound a soft *berceuse* that made her want to stay in bed. She could look out through the window onto the streets of Rome, glistening now, the old, stone buildings taking on a soft patina. She rose and went to the window. Rome, she murmured, city of Castor and Pollux, Caesar and Marc Antony, citadel of Christianity. Spiritual home to Paul. And to the Cardinal Scarti. The Eternal City embraced very different children. But was that not the role of a mother, Marina reflected.

She turned from the window. Her mission would soon be over. She'd rush back then with the details that would put an end to whatever new plans were underway. Soon she'd be with Paul once again. No matter what he had chosen, she'd find a way to be near him. Loving from afar was better than not loving at all, she told herself. She pressed her eyes closed and shook her head, her luxurious, onyx hair cascading around her shoulders. No—no lies, no self-deceits, Marina corrected herself angrily. She could not love from afar. That kind of love was not in her. She could only pray that Paul would find a place for her in his life somewhere, somehow.

She dressed and three o'clock came quickly. Rosalie Amati had left for the afternoon, one of the maids told her, gone to purchase a new *casque*. The cardinal's carriage arrived promptly, a closed, two-wheel surrey. The driver held the door open for her to climb in, and she paused to return the man's stare. He was tall, with extremely long arms, dressed in a black jacket. His eyes burned with a strange intensity, moving up and down her body as she paused. "I am Bruno," he said and Marina nodded in acknowledgment. His brows came together at the center of his face so that he seemed to be perpetually frowning, she noted. They were thick, bushy black brows that did not fit the rest of his hairless, somewhat fleshy face. From inside the rig, she watched him swing up to the driver's perch with one bound, using one long arm as a lever.

She sat back as the surrey began to roll along the cobbled streets, turned right, and proceeded along the edge of the Tiber. The rain continued to fall, a fine, almost invisible rain. To her right she saw the Janiculum Hill rise. The surrey crossed the Tiber at one of the curved sections before it reached the Palatine. She saw the driver open a small trapdoor to peer down at her, his glance long, staring, and uncomfortable. He closed the door and she was grateful for that. The horse turned into a narrow street to halt before a square gray building, two wings stretching from its sides with windows sealed in wood. It had a dungeonlike feel about it, Marina thought, as Bruno swung from the carriage to open an iron gate. He led the horse into a small court, closed the gate, and opened the carriage door for her. She stepped down, his hand helping her, closing around her arm and holding onto her for a moment longer than needed. She saw two small rigs lined up against one wall of the court and then the driver was pushing a door open for her, ushering her into a cramped, dim foyer. He led her to where a shaft of light fell onto the floor from another room, then he halted. She saw the door open wider and Cardinal Scarti appear. Bruno backed away at once and disappeared.

The cardinal wore a ruffled shirt and black breeches, and his welcoming smile was quietly satisfied. His arm found hers and he led her into the first of a series of rooms opening onto one another, all richly furnished with pillowed couches and velvet drapes that belied the grim exterior of the house. "It's a pleasure to see you here in my little hideaway." Cardinal Scarti smiled unctiously.

"Your Eminence is too kind." Marina returned the smile.

"No, no, none of that here, my dear Angelica. This is a place of relaxation and informality. All the usual rules and regulations are put aside here. Here I am Francesco."

"I'll try to remember, Francesco." Marina laughed.

He led her into the last of the rooms where four men, informally clothed, sat on sofas with four elegantly clothed young women. One, even in the loose coverlet shirt he wore, was instantly recognizable as a man who had visited the Duke d'Albatore in priestly robes. His name, she learned later, was Carducci, and he was a monsignor from Foggia. A low table held brandy and cheese. The cardinal introduced her to everyone, and she saw the glint of jealous curiosity in the eyes of the other women. He led her to one of the sofas, sat down with her, holding her arm in his.

"We were just discussing the need for leadership," he told her. "Strong men make strong nations."

"Do they?" Marina questioned with humor in her voice.

The cardinal turned raised eyebrows toward her. "You don't agree, my dear?"

"I'm not sure." She shrugged. "Loving men do not always make the best lovers." She had come prepared to play her role to the fullest and enjoyed the laughter that ran through the room.

"What kind of men make the best lovers?" someone asked.

"Wealthy ones who grow wealthier," she snapped at once. The answer began a new turn to the conversation and she let it flow around her, injecting comments as they seemed in order. The men were all priests, she was certain. Their remarks indicated learning and a certain stamp. Only sincerity was missing. But the elegantly gowned young women, each attractive, each smartly groomed, lacked another kind of honesty. They chattered, made bright comments, and almost seemed young ladies of taste and background. But their eyes were too full of street wisdom, their speech too careful. The feathers did not hide the sparrows underneath.

After a time the others began to drift away in twos and she was left alone with the cardinal, sipping her brandy slowly. He rose, pulled her to her feet. "Your beauty deserves beauty. Let me show you some of the other things I admire in my private home."

His hand closed around hers and he led her into a larger room, without windows and draped in dark blue velvet, like a gallery, which in actuality it was. Marina's glance went to a large portrait of a woman on the nearest wall, glowing and magnificently painted.

"Rubens," the cardinal told her proudly. He turned her to another painting, a nude with small children in a garden. "Botticelli. A rare piece."

"These must be priceless." Marina's awe was genuine.

Francesco Scarti nodded, pointing out a highly polished satinwood desk, delicate yet filled with graceful strength. "From sixteenth-century Veronese craftsmen."

Turning to a glass case, he showed Marina three Greek vases with black-painted figures, the earliest examples of such useful art. She saw a *kantharos*, a *skyphos* and a double-handled *kalpis*. "From Corinth and Iona. A major acquisition."

As he spoke, his hand moved up and down her back, softly rubbing, and she did not move away. "These are but a few of my things. I've a rather fine collection of Etruscan pieces in another room." He turned her toward him. "These should satisfy you as to my ability to acquire priceless objects."

"They are indeed magnificent," Marina responded. "But they are yesterday. I'm interested in tomorrow, the future, not the past."

He smiled. "Yes, you would be looking to tomorrow. Great plans are underway. I shall control the spiritual and temporal resources of a new city-state, a new empire."

Marina felt her pulse quicken but she assumed a mask of mild cynicism over her eyes. "A new empire?" she echoed. "Some plans are too big to become reality. In fact, I have heard there was such an attempt that failed not too long ago."

The cardinal's eyes narrowed at once. "Where did you hear about that?"

She laughed, choosing answers cautiously. "Even the woods have ears." She quoted an old Sicilian proverb she knew he'd know: " 'Wine and the bedchamber make for loose tongues.' " The reply seemed to satisfy him and his frown faded.

"This time there shall be no failure." The silkiness was gone from his voice. "You can be certain of that." Marina turned away and whirled across the room, halting.

"The house has grown so still. Has everyone left?" she asked.

"Hardly," the cardinal answered. As if to add to his words, the unmistakable sound drifted through a corridor—harsh breathing and then the half-gasped cries of pleasure. She met the cardinal's eyes as he moved toward her, suddenly glowing with an inner light. His lips found her neck and took a small bite, then moved across the tops of her breasts. She skittered away, feigned surprise.

"My dear Francesco, you shock me," she gasped.

The intense, piercing eyes held her. "Do I really?" he asked. "A young woman of your sophistication? I cannot believe that."

She shrugged. "There is always a first time for everything. Are there not vows that bind you?"

"You touch on questions far too weighty for you to concern yourself with, Angelica. It is a matter of flexibility and acceptances, a personal thing." He reached out, drew her to him, and pressed his mouth to her shoulder. Marina kept her lips from tightening. Not flexibility, not acceptances, she wanted to cry out—remembering Paul's words all too clearly—but denials and promises. The irony pulled at her. What Paul saw so clearly this prince of the Church ignored completely. Denials and promises made, commitments of the soul and integrity of the spirit.

Paul had denied completeness of their love and held to the strength of promises made to the Church. This man of the cloth in the highest of roles should certainly do no less. Yet there was no denying his hands or his lips nuzzling her neck, and she felt his fingers move into the top of her gown. Wrong, she cried out silently, all wrong. But, perversely she asked herself, had it been less wrong with Paul when it was she who had wanted, aroused, insisted? Yes, she answered. Love had been a part of that—love that was real, honest, a burning light that brought its own integrity. But the questions continued. Did love transform wrong into right? Was love enough? Suddenly she knew all the things she had only seen in Paul's troubled eyes as he fought with wanting and wondering, and now she knew she had no answers, either.

Now she knew only the hands of Cardinal Francesco Scarti finding her breasts, and a crystallization of inner anger. Paul had spoken of commitment, of sacrifices for a higher goal. She had come here for a purpose. She'd not fail in that. This was no moment for unanswerable questions that twisted the heart, but for matching wrongs. She twisted away from his hands.

His eyes stayed on her. "Come now, my angel. You disappoint me with such schoolgirl behavior," he chided. Marina stared back, heard a soft cry of ecstasy from a distant room in the house. She turned to face him fully, then unsnapped a catch at the back of the gown. As the bodice loosened, she wriggled free of it, let it fall to her waist, and stood proudly bare-breasted in front of him, enjoying his sharp gasp of admiration.

"Do I disappoint you, Your Eminence?" she asked acidly.

"Oh, my God, what beauty," he exclaimed hoarsely and reached out to cup a hand under her left breast.

Marina let him touch her for a moment, then stepped back. "Do you want what I can give you?" she shot at him. "Do you want me to be one of your possessions? Then I want more than words, more than talk about vague plans. I told you, I've no patience with hopes and ambitions and no time for failures."

The man drew his breath in deeply, his eyes still fastened on the beauty of her breasts. "And if you were given more, told details, enough to convince you that soon I will be in a position to give you anything you want?" he asked.

"Then I will give you anything you want," Marina declared boldly. Moving quickly, she stepped forward, crushed her breasts against his face as he bent to her, then pulled away as his lips opened and sought. "But not yet, my dear Francesco Cardinal Scarti." She slipped the gown back on in one quick sweep. "I have been disappointed too often, given too much for empty words."

The man straightened, gathered himself, fastened his eyes on her bold stare. "Tomorrow night is the last of the week's parties, the grand ball at the Legate from Florence. You will attend, I presume."

"Of course," Marina tossed back.

"Leave early. Bruno will be waiting outside with the carriage," he told her. "Come here directly. You will have the details of everything you want to hear. A courier is arriving tomorrow with the latest information of how things are proceeding."

"All right, I'll come," Marina consented. His arm caught her, pulled her against him, and then his mouth was hard on hers. She forced response from her lips, finally pushing him away. "If I am not disappointed, you will be satisfied," she whispered.

It was no more a lie than his promises to her, Marina told herself. He'd give her details, all she wanted to hear, to have her in his bedchamber, fully and eagerly offering herself for a piece of tomorrow. But there'd be no tomorrow. When the time came for him to assume his new role in the new kingdom, he'd not risk the scandal of taking a woman along. He'd be rid of her then.

There had been others before her, she was certain. No doubt they were satisfied with a handsome sum, perhaps some persuaded with a few threats. He'd no reason to think she'd be different. "Tomorrow night," she told him. "Now I'd like to leave."

He nodded, walking with her to the door. Bruno stood with his long arms folded, waiting. The cardinal needed to give him no instructions, she saw, as the man opened the door and took her to the covered rig. She heard the door close behind her, watched Bruno open the iron gate and return to the carriage. His intense eyes found hers again for a long moment, and she looked away first. He did not move, and when finally she returned her glance to him his eyes were still burning into her.

"Bruno, may we go, please?" Marina requested. The man blinked and seemed to emerge from almost a private, trancelike intenseness.

"You are different than the others," he said slowly, turned at once, and with his long arms pulled himself up into the driver's seat. Marina frowned at the remark. He seemed hardly a vessel of sensitivity and insight. Probably it had been an attempt at a compliment, she decided, dismissing it. The building still seemed dungeonlike from outside, she observed as the rig pulled away. She sat back and decided that the wearing of masks was an enervating business, especially when one wrong word meant failure, one out-of-character act tore away the careful facade.

When she reached the townhouse, Bruno swung down to help her from the rig. His eyes burned into her again. "Thank you," Marina offered.

"More beautiful," he muttered and started to turn away.

"Is that how I'm different from the others?" she asked.

"No."

The single word was uttered in something like a growl and he was into the driver's seat, sending the rig rolling away. Marina shook her head as she went into the house. A strange servant employed by a strange master, she thought. In her rooms she drew a bath, sinking into it eagerly. She felt unclean. She wanted to feel deep anger at Francesco Cardinal Scarti, but she could manage only contempt. He was not simply weak. That she could accept. He was not simply arrogant. She could understand arrogance. He did not merely fail all that he stood for. She could grasp failure. He was human, and humans failed their own best intentions all too often. No, the eminent cardinal did not fail, he betrayed, and for that difference she could feel only contempt for him.

Marina crawled into the large bed to let sleep wash away the day. Tomorrow night would come all too soon. She'd go, listen, absorb, make mental notes, and continue to play the role. She'd put him off, find some pretext. That would not be too difficult. Perhaps she'd have to give him another taste of her riches to hold him for another day. If so, she'd do it, quietly enjoying a triumph he neither suspected nor imagined. And then she would flee this Rome, this city of intrigues, back to a little stone cottage. She turned on her stomach, cradled herself with her arms, and slept.

In the morning, she excitedly told the baroness all that had happened. The women combined compliments with misgivings. "Can't you find some other way than going to his place tomorrow night?" she asked.

"Impossible. He expects me. He wants to tell me everything to impress me. This is the one moment that'll make everything else worth while," Marina replied.

"I'll wait up for you." The baroness looked worried. Marina hugged the woman.

"I'll be quite safe, believe me. I've become quite good at this coquette business." Marina's lips moved into a thoughtful smile. "Perhaps I've a natural talent for it," she suggested, not entirely facetiously.

"No," the baroness snapped back. "You have the natural talent, but you could never become hard enough inside. A successful courtesan must have more *cocotte* than partridge in her."

Marina laughed. This would be the last night of charades. It was enough.

For the party of the Florentine Legate, Marina wore a gown *à la circassienne*, cream-white with deep blue bands running down the length of the bottom panels. The ball was more desperately gay than any of the others as the merrymakers seemed intent on making the most of the week's end. When it was but a little after nine o'clock she caught Rosalie Amati's eyes for a moment and blew the woman a kiss. The baroness understood with a nod, and Marina slipped from the ball, hurrying down the stone steps outside. The night was moonless, and as she stood at the edge of the sidewalk she heard the sound of the surrey moving toward her. It loomed up, a black bulk, closed and somehow ominous in the night. Bruno swung down and helped her in. A dim light at one corner of the surrey cast a pale glow for a moment, enough for her to see the man's intense eyes boring into her. His face vanished as he climbed up to the seat and drove the surrey away.

Marina sat in the almost pitch blackness, felt her hands trembling in excitement, then forced them to stop. The ball had been more crowded and more hectic than any of the others, taking in three huge adjoining rooms. She'd seen some of the faces she had come to know from the other parties, but for the most part it seemed filled with new merrymakers. People were appearing at the doorways and returning to one or another of the other rooms, unable to brave the crowd. Marina smiled. Even the cardinal would be a relief from the noise and milling throngs. The gown *à la circassienne* had not been a good choice, far too large and sweeping. But the cardinal would appreciate it, she knew. The neckline almost dipped down to the rose aureole around her nipples.

The surrey halted, the door opened, and Bruno's hand helped her out. The house was a darker black bulk in the moonless night, and Bruno guided her through the iron gate. He brought her to the door, pushing it open for her. Yellow light from a wall lamp sent a weak ray out, and Bruno's frowning brows gathered together as he peered intensely at her. She saw him shake his head slowly, almost sadly. "I was right," he muttered and turned away.

She heard footsteps and the cardinal appeared, clothed in a red robe not unlike his churchly robes of crimson. "Come in, my dear," he said, extending his hand. She took it and he drew her into one of the rooms where two lamps burned brightly in brass holders. He halted in the center of the room and his eyes roamed across her face, down to the swell of her breasts over the line of the gown. "Such beauty," he commented. "Such absolute beauty. It is almost unforgivable."

His hand caressed her neck, then moved to press the softness of the rose-tinted alabaster skin that rose in twin invitations. His eyes lifted and found hers. "Do you know what a Venus's fly-trap is, my dear Marina?" he asked. She shook her head. "It is a rare and exotic plant," he went on. "It devours insects. It lures them with its beauty, deceives them into thinking it is but a simple resting place, then closes around its prey." He drew a deep sigh, let it leave his chest slowly. "As a boy, I used to wonder what the unfortunate insect felt upon being so thoroughly deceived before being consumed. I think I know, now."

His eyes held hers and a sudden chill seized her, sweeping up through her body as though an icy wind had somehow found its way inside her. "I presume there's a reason for this unpleasant little piece of information." She summoned up brashness, wondering if only *she* heard the pounding of her heart. Something was wrong. It was in the coldness of his eyes.

"Indeed there is a reason," he replied, then lifted his hand and snapped his fingers twice. Marina saw the figure step into view from the adjoining room, turned her eyes on the short, porcine little shape and dissipated cherub face, and felt her legs turn to water. She clutched at the arm of a chair, then steadied herself as her eyes blurred for an instant. She shook them clear, watched the Duke d'Albatore step into the room, his button eyes blazing.

"Ah, Marina Valerian, your surprise can be no greater than mine was a few hours ago," he snarled. "I arrived at the ball with the crowd halted in the doorway. I did not believe my eyes."

Marina met the hatred in his gaze and decided silence was best. He stared at her and there was still disbelief in his eyes. "Three sailors were found. They said everyone else perished. When the cardinal told me of this beautiful discovery, I never dreamed it was you. Never," he reiterated. "Had I not gone to the ball tonight, you would have been successful."

"On such things the world turns," Marina heard the cardinal interject. The Duke d'Albatore's round frame quivered in fury as he stared at the girl.

"Somehow, you cheated death once. This time you will not be so lucky," he growled. Marina felt the coldness grow more frigid inside her, then turned to the red-robed figure at her left.

"You would not dare try anything so foolish," she defied him. "The Baroness Amati knows I was to come here."

"Yes, I assumed as much. By now one of my men has been at her home, asking why you did not appear as scheduled and expressing my concern," Cardinal Scarti replied. "A little later, he will pay another visit to inquire if the lady Angelica has returned safely, and again informing her that you never arrived here."

Marina's tongue wet her lips, which had suddenly gone dry. "The baroness will suspect something," she countered, but failed to sound properly confident. The cardinal's falcon imperiousness allowed a chiding smile.

"Nonsense. She will suspect nothing. Even if she did, she would have no evidence of any kind. She would not dare accuse a cardinal of a crime, or even imply as much without absolute evidence. Unfortunately, young women who wander the streets late at night disappear every week. I'm afraid you shall be one of them. Except that your body will be found and identified, one more victim of the night."

Marina glanced at the pouchy little figure. The duke nodded in satisfaction. The cardinal had indeed moved quickly, Marina realized, positioned everything with neatness. A knot gathered in the pit of her stomach as his words circled inside her. The baroness disliked and distrusted the cardinal, but even she would not suspect him of the ultimate sin of murder. His logic was like a whiplash, stinging and beyond refute. And even if the baroness were to harbor suspicion she could not move without concrete evidence, and there'd be no such evidence pointing at him. He'd see to that.

The knot in Marina's stomach became a rock. She fastened her gaze on the imperious face. Francesco Cardinal Scarti did more than betray his existence; he served Satan in the house of the Lord. He walked in evil. It had been an error to hold this man in contempt. His monstrousness went far beyond that. Fear would have been more correct. But she had not feared. Everything had gone so well she had become almost smug. And now it had all exploded—now, in one sweeping moment, the clock had been turned back and yesterdays thought forgotten rose up to seize her again.

Marina held her eyes on the tall, red-robed figure. "You won't get away with this." Her voice held steel.

He laughed—an abrupt, unexpected sound. "We both know better. It truly disturbs me to destroy beauty, but I've no choice." He called out and Bruno appeared on silent feet. "Take her away, Bruno. You know what to do and when to do it. The important thing is caution—no mistakes."

Marina saw the man nod. His intense, frowning gaze rested on her for a moment and then a long arm reached out, grasping her wrist, then pulling firmly, but not roughly. "Come," he urged. "Please."

His politeness was strangely not incongruous and Marina went without struggle. There'd be no use in that, she realized. The grip on her wrist, though not painful, might as well have been a steel band. She glanced back at the two figures in the room, then her eyes passed over the round shape to rest on the falcon's visage of Francesco Cardinal Scarti.

"You are damned," she said quietly. "And even you cannot escape knowing that."

His mouth became a thin line. "Take her out of here," he rasped, and she felt the tug at her wrist. She followed Bruno into a dim corridor, then a flight of stone steps into almost pitch-black darkness. A flickering light appeared, and she saw the outlines of a stone corridor. The light grew brighter as they neared it; it became a wall lamp that lighted still another stone passageway. Droplets of dampness stood out on the stones and the air was dank and stale. She passed a barred door, a cell behind it, then another and still another. On one wall she saw iron shackles.

She'd not been wrong in thinking the house seemed a dungeon from the outside. Another wall lamp illuminated the great stone slabs of the corridor. There were no windows anywhere, and she saw a huge rat scurry along. She halted and involuntarily shrank back. Bruno stopped, looked at her, pulled not ungently at her, and she went on. At another barred doorway he took the heavy key hanging from the stones and opened the door. Releasing her wrist, he gestured to the cell and Marina entered it. She saw a half-burned candle, two burlap sacks on the floor, and a shelf with a basin of water. A heavy three-legged stool occupied one corner and an open slit trench ran along one wall as a crude sewage outlet. She heard the barred door close and turned, unable to hide the panic that burst into her eyes. The small click sounded like the thunderclap of doom.

Bruno's eyes peered at her in that intense manner of his. "Different. I knew it right away," he muttered, beginning to leave. Marina flew at the bars, pressed herself against them.

"Wait," she cried. "Bruno. What will happen now?"

He looked back but did not answer for a moment. He was not an imbecile—not with those eyes, Marina thought—yet his mind was slow and his thoughts halting. "You will stay here until it's time," he replied after a moment.

"Time for what?" Marina asked, yet knowing the answer.

"Time for me to get rid of you," he told her. She watched him slowly turn and walk back along the corridor, his long arms hanging loosely. In minutes he was beyond her line of vision and she turned away from the bars. The cell seemed to shrink, constricting her. How fitting, she thought; a crypt should be tight and this was indeed a crypt. She sank down onto one of the burlap sacks, staring at the edge of her gown. This cell had surely never seen so elegant a prisoner, she wagered. And possibly none so completely doomed. The cardinal would have no misgivings, no second thoughts, she knew. For the moment, fear and despondency became something else—a terrible sadness.

Perhaps it had been destined to end this way from the start; there were just too many wrongs piled one atop the other. *Straight with crooked lines.* Paul's words returned to her and the small sound that escaped her lips was wrapped in bitterness.

CHAPTER ELEVEN

B RUNO DID NOT LOOK BACK. He wanted to turn, to see her again, but he kept walking until he reached the end of the passageway. His long arm pulled the door open and closed it after him, then he climbed the curving, narrow stone steps that led to his room in the far end of the building. He never liked going into the dungeons. Many years ago it had been a torture chamber, when the house had been owned by a wealthy nobleman. That was a long time ago, before the cardinal bought it. The old dungeons held a different kind of prisoner after that.

Bruno LaFacci reached his room, a dreary, stone place, and slumped down into a corner beside an iron bedstand with a mattress on it. The girl stuck in his mind, as she had from the first day he'd seen her. Different, she was not like the others who came to the house with the cardinal's friends, the wealthy merchants and his priests. Those others pretended to be ladies, putting on airs, when they were really nothing but fancy *cortigiane*. His glance went to the dark, damp, and forbidding wall; the only small warmth to touch the room came from the heavy candle. He stared at the walls, and soon they faded away in the streaked stones, becoming grassy fields with girls running barefoot, fine Roman baths with naked goddesses strolling about, all for his eyes to enjoy. When he lowered his eyes, finally, the pictures went away. But the girl in the dungeon would fit his picture, he knew. Her beauty was real. Bruno LaFacci moved his legs and felt himself grow hard just thinking about her.

He shook his head slowly. The cardinal was wrong to have
her killed. The cardinal only thought about himself. There'd
been that farm girl, small and plump. She'd threatened to cause
a scandal, and the cardinal ordered him to get rid of her. Bruno
remembered how he'd wanted to keep the girl himself and how
angry the cardinal had been, refusing the request at once. The
cardinal never seemed to think about *his* needs. Bruno glowered
and glowed at once as he thought about how he had to listen to the
things that sometimes went on in the house, the groanings and
the pantings—and the screaming, too. But he was never allowed
to share in it. That wasn't right, wasn't fair. He had wants, too, but
the cardinal never seemed to pay any attention to that.

Bruno LaFacci shifted his legs and leaned back against the
corner. He owed the cardinal his life. They were going to behead
him when the cardinal stepped in and saved him. They'd accused
him of attacking the farmer's wife just outside the city, but she
had invited him in, sat on her bed, and showed him her legs.
She'd started screaming only when she saw her husband coming
back unexpectedly. But no one had believed him, Bruno LaFacci
remembered. He'd thought once that the cardinal had and that
was why he'd saved him. It took a long time before he came to
think differently. The cardinal only saved him because he needed
someone here, someone to do all the things that had to be done.
Bruno uttered a harsh sound. He had done the cardinal's bidding
and done it well. And why not? He had a roof over his head here,
a place to sleep, and food enough. He didn't need more. Where
could he, someone who could neither read nor write, find more?

But he still had his needs. A woman of his own, if only for a
little while. But even the street girls turned away from him and
those that came to the house wouldn't go near him. His eyes,
one of them said once, frightened her. The cardinal didn't seem
to understand that he needed a woman of his own. Sometimes,
Bruno recalled, he'd creep upstairs and watch the others. Other
times he'd close his ears to the moans, the laughing, the screams

of pleasure. But the cardinal just seemed to expect him to hear and see and not want. The cardinal was not at all understanding about some things.

Bruno LaFacci took off his shirt and breeches, lay down on the cot, and dreamed about the girl in the cell below, finally groaning his way to sleep. When he woke, the house was still, the morning hardly arrived. He didn't hear the steady trickle of water running down the stone walls, nor the sound of the rats scurrying about in the deserted wing of the building where his room was the only part lived in. Those sounds were part of his world, beyond notice. The girl occupied his thoughts at once, and he slowly put together the things he had to do. Nothing could be done about her for at least another night, probably not until Sunday night. The midnight streets would be least crowded then. The cardinal and the little fat one had been very upset about her. Take absolutely no risks, they'd ordered. But Sunday night was best for still another reason. There were always more killings during the weekend nights, more potential victims out late returning from parties. The constable's wagons were always busiest Monday mornings, collecting the unfortunates who had paid for their stupidity, rashness, or too much wine.

Bruno put on breeches and shirt, went into the main part of the house, stopped in the kitchen, and then made his way down the stone steps to the dungeons. The frowning brows pressed down on a troubled face as he neared the girl's cell. He wished he could think fast, the way the cardinal did, snapping out decisions. Sometimes—Bruno LaFacci frowned, he wondered if he ever really made a decision. Thoughts just seemed to form of themselves in his mind and suddenly they were there and he was acting upon them. He found himself quickening his pace now as he neared the cell, halting at the barred door in surprise.

The girl was awake. Maybe she'd heard him approach, standing in that fancy gown as though she were still at the ball. God, what hair she had. And what breasts that rose up over the top of the gown as though they wanted to burst free. Her eyes watched him as he pushed first the piece of brown bread, then a cup of barley, through the bars.

"Thank you," she said, stepping nearer, taking his offering. Her eyes did not darken in distaste when she looked at him, he saw. She held them steady, unwavering. He watched her bite into the bread and sip the barley. "Something of a waste, isn't it?" she remarked as she ate.

Bruno LaFacci frowned, "A waste? To eat?" he echoed.

"To feed someone who's going to die," she clarified. He shrugged, watching her finish the cup of barley. Her waist was small and tight. He imagined what her hips would be like—full and wide, like one of the Greek goddesses he dreamed about so often.

He came to the bars again and she handed the cup out to him. "Thank you," she repeated. More beautiful, Bruno grunted silently, more beautiful than anyone he'd ever seen, even in his dreams.

"Will it be today?" she asked, her eyes wide, like those of a child in the streets.

"No."

"I'm glad. I don't want to be killed."

He watched her eyes stay on him. They were round, serious. There was no cruel laughter in them.

"Do you do everything the cardinal says to do?" she asked. "Even when it's wrong?"

"Yes," Bruno replied.

"You care about pleasing him, about his needs, don't you?" she probed. Bruno nodded solemnly. "Does he care about you?" she asked. "Does he care about pleasing you, about your needs?"

Bruno LaFacci shrugged again. He didn't want to tell her the truth, that the cardinal never paid any attention to his needs. Just thinking about it made him grow angry inside.

"Sometimes," Bruno grunted.

"That's good." Her eyes held steady. "Sometimes people are selfish and don't care about others. You do a lot of things for the cardinal, I'll wager."

Bruno nodded. She understood, he felt. She was different than the others. "I have to go," he said. "The cardinal will want me to drive him to his other house, the one near St. Peter's."

"Come down and talk to me more when you come back," she pleaded. "It's lonely down here. You know about being lonely, don't you, Bruno?"

He turned, not wanting to go. But the cardinal would want the carriage ready. He wanted to touch her, to stay. Maybe when he came back. He hurried down the stone passageway, not looking back.

Marina sank down on the heavy three-legged stool she had brought out from the corner of the cell, then let her breath out in a slow shudder. She'd slept some, surprising herself, wakened, and made decisions. Desperation had replaced almost every other emotion in her. To survive had become her only thought— for herself, for life, for tomorrow. But not that alone, she realized. There was a monstrous evil here. It had to be exposed. Everything which Paul stood for had been warped and turned back upon itself here. She'd not been the first young woman to see these dungeons, she was certain. There'd been others who'd found them to be their last stop on the way to death.

Her thoughts had been born out of that conviction, the desperate determination to survive for more than her own self. Decisions had really been simple, but only one avenue was open to her, only one single, remaining chance was left: Bruno, the cardinal's lackey. The covetousness was in his eyes every time he looked at her; it wasn't the sharp, clever covetousness of most men but rather a kind of simpleminded wanting and all the stronger for it. But she had to move with care. Subtlety, in the usual sense, was unnecessary, but he possessed an animal awareness and was not without a self-serving bond with his master. She decided to move by stages, lead him not into the paths of righteousness but into the paths of his own suppressed wantings.

It had gone well and now she felt drained. She'd reached the right places, seen it in his uncomfortableness. She readied herself for his return. There was no way of knowing how much time was left and she couldn't afford to waste even a single moment.

Marina freshened herself with the water in the basin, which was cool and at least clean. She took off her gown, dropped it atop the burlap sacks, and waited in her petticoat and the small, laced bodice which almost fully revealed her breasts. Finally she heard his footsteps, stood up, and waited, keeping the icy determination out of her face.

Bruno LaFacci felt a kind of pounding inside himself he'd never felt before as he reached the cell door and saw the girl there, clothed only in her petticoat. She came to the bars and looked up at him with her eyes wide and childlike again. "The gown was uncomfortable, too heavy," she explained. "Are you angry that I took it off?"

Bruno swallowed and shook his head. His long right arm reached out as if by itself, moved through the opening between the bars, and felt her skin, her shoulder, down along her arm, and finally across the tops of her breasts. Smoother than silk, warm and wonderful. She didn't flinch the way others had. Different, she was. He'd known it from the very first. She stood very still as he let his fingers fondle her breasts, except for the small tremble that shook her for a moment. He could hardly keep his own body from trembling.

"You don't want to kill me, do you, Bruno?" she asked.

"No," he whispered. "But I must."

"Because the cardinal said so?"

He shrugged.

"You don't have to do everything he says," she went on. "You could keep me here. For a while, anyway."

He stared at her. The idea made him feel warm all over. Keeping her there, all for himself, with no one knowing. He felt his body begin to tremble again.

She put his thoughts into words. "You could have me, Bruno, touch me all over, do whatever you want with me. It would be our own bargain. You give me my life. I'll give you all of me."

Bruno LaFacci's mouth opened and shut, his lips working to form words that refused to come out of his throat. Finally, with a groan, he tore the words from his being. "I can't. I can't."

"Of course you can," she argued.

He shook his head. "No. They want to see the body. The cardinal insisted. He and the little fat one want to see the body," Bruno gasped out.

"The cardinal doesn't trust you?" the girl asked with surprise.

Bruno lifted his shoulders in a shrug. "There was another girl once. I wanted to keep her. He became angry with me. He made me show him the body then. He's insisted on it ever since."

"How many others have there been?" Shock joined surprise in the way she stared at him.

"A few. Only those who wanted to cause trouble. The last one tried to make trouble for Monsignor Gracche. I had to take care of her, too." He heard the small cry from the girl.

"And no one else in the Church knows of this?" she asked.

"Only the cardinal's friends," Bruno answered. His frowning brows grew closer together as he stared at the girl. "There would be great trouble if anyone else knew. It's wrong, you know. The cardinal tells me I don't understand, that it's too much for me to understand, but it's wrong, I know that."

"Then don't do what he says," the girl snapped back.

He shook his head slowly. "I have to do it. He'll want to see the body. I'll have to show him the body." He turned away, but not before he saw something go out of her eyes, a strange emptiness come over her face. He hurried from the barred door, loped down the passageway. He was wet, sweating like a plow horse. Being near her did that. The idea of having her for his own. He kept hurrying, took the stone steps two at a time, but the idea refused to leave him. All that beauty his, to touch, to use, to have. He groaned and cursed silently, and hated the world.

Marina sank to the floor, atop one of the burlap sacks. She rested her arm on the heavy three-legged stool. The last chance had been exploded in her face. She had not thought the cardinal would distrust his lackey. But she should have known as much. Cardinal Scarti was not a man to trust anyone very far. She lay her forehead against her arm on the stool. It hadn't worked. She'd thought she was winning, reaching and finding the right places. Perhaps she had, but Bruno had a rat's instinct for self-preservation. He knew where the source of his tomorrows lay.

By now, the baroness would be frantic, would have been to the constable, would have had him send his men out searching. And by now the cardinal would have expressed his own concern at Angelica Giustiniani's failure to reach his residence. All the pieces had been put into place. All that was still missing was the finding of Angelica Giustiniani's body, another victim of the streets. The cardinal would probably attend services at the appropriate moment, Marina realized with grim despair.

She closed her eyes and sat wrapped in a blanket of hopelessness. There was nothing to do now but wait in this place where time did not exist, where there was not even a window to help count off the minutes to finality. Sleep was impossible but she stayed in a strange half-awake world, almost a dream world where time stood still. The candle in the cell burned low, near its end. She heard a sound, raised her head, and opened her eyes to see a rat watching her from a corner. She rose, lifted the stool, heavy as it was, and the rat scurried through the open trench along one wall and disappeared. It had been an automatic reaction on her part, Marina realized. It didn't matter. Nothing mattered. She returned to her half-sleep, letting time move on. Another sound came after a while, and she raised her head again, recognizing the loping shuffle. How quickly we learn to respond to the sounds that become part of existence, she mused.

She looked at the barred door and saw the figure there. She rose, not in obedience to the long-armed jailer, but to the hour that had come, sooner than she'd expected. Sooner, later, she thought bitterly. Did it matter now? Had it all been foreordained? She went to the bars. Bruno's hand reached through and touched her breasts, and she saw his eyes burning into her.

"There is a way, maybe," she heard him mutter.

"How? You said they would want to see for themselves."

"My business," he replied. She decided not to press further.

"What will I do?" she asked. "Just wait?"

"Give me the dress," he grunted. Marina's eyes darkened. She refused to wonder, suspect, or toy with dark thoughts. She picked up the long gown from the floor and began pushing it through the bars. He pulled it from the other side until he had all of it.

"I'll come back when it's done," he told her.

"How soon will that be?" Marina prodded.

"Tomorrow night maybe," he answered. He turned and went off with the gown dragging from under one long arm. Marina felt herself trembling. If his plan succeeded, whatever it was, he'd return to claim his prize. If it failed, he'd return to do what he'd been ordered to do. Perhaps the choice was not so different for her. She'd bought another twenty-four hours of survival. She'd have but one chance to get more, she knew. She curled herself down upon the burlap sacks, lay back, and hoped the nauseous pain in the pit of her stomach would go away.

Bruno LaFacci held the gown in his hands when he reached his room. It felt smooth, almost as smooth as her skin. He'd thought about her offer—kept thinking about it until it was the only thing that filled his head. He wanted her so very much. It wasn't as though he were taking something from the cardinal. The cardinal was through with her, was throwing her away. It was a terrible waste and there was no reason why he shouldn't have her, Bruno thought again. He'd thought and thought to try to find a way to keep her for himself, and suddenly it had come to him. He knew the back streets of Rome better than almost anyone. He knew where the night people waited, struck and prowled. And he knew where the street girls who caused trouble for their madams and procurers were taken and done away with. He knew every back alley and dark court in Rome. He had walked or slept in all of them at one time or another.

As he thought more about it, he knew that with a little luck he'd certainly find what he needed. And then came the careful part—the part he'd have to do right or he'd be in trouble. But Bruno LaFacci had made up his mind. He'd go ahead with it. He had to. Never in his life would the chance come again to have a girl such as that one for his own. He lay back, the gown in his arms, closed his eyes, and slept. The cardinal was away until tomorrow night; he had only to rest until it was time. He slept past the midnight hour, into the deep morning blackness, then woke, rose, and went downstairs to the storeroom. He took a thick, burlap sack, folded it into a compact square, stuffed it under his shirt, and went out into the night.

He took the covered, closed rig and drove it to the edge of a rundown, crumbling district and tied the horse to a post. Moving silently on foot, he entered a narrow alleyway and scurried down it like one of the rats that ran along the cobblestones, moving a few paces at a time and halting to peer into crevices, into broken doorways, and behind crumbled walls. He halted at one wall, saw the black bulk behind it, and pulled it out. It was a man—his throat was slashed. Bruno dropped him and went on. His path became a pattern, up one alley and down another, halting at every form he found. The street people had had a busy weekend, he noted. But most of those he came upon were men, the victims of robbers.

In a dark courtyard he found a woman, but she was fat and would not fool even a blind man. He had reached the dark edges of the Tiber where a lumberyard stretched alongside the banks when he found the girl. She lay half hidden under a woodpile. She had been badly beaten—her face bloody and battered—and slain by a knife thrust into the breast, not many hours ago, as she still bled. But she was young, slender, and she had black hair—not as long and luxurious as the other girl's but enough for his needs. She still wore one red shoe of a street girl.

He took the burlap sack from under his jacket, opened it, and stuffed the girl inside the big bag. Slinging his grisly burden over one shoulder, he trekked back to where he'd left the rig, moving only through narrow back alleyways and hurrying before the dawn came to touch the streets. Reaching the closed rig, he put the sack inside, climbed onto the driver's seat, and returned to the house.

Bruno LaFacci was not nervous. He breathed no sigh of relief as he deposited the sack in an empty room. He only smiled in anticipation as he thought about the girl in the cell below. Working methodically, he pulled the sack from the girl's body, stripped off her torn and stained dress, paused to look at her thin body and shallow breasts, then clothed her in the elegant ball gown. Once he'd finished, he carefully stuffed the girl's body back into the big sack, head first. The voluminous gown took up much of the sack but her black hair was easily visible. Her head, face down, could only be glimpsed as a bloody mass. In truth, the girl had been so badly beaten that it was difficult to see her face at all.

Bruno LaFacci sat back and waited, half dozing, until he heard sounds from the other part of the house. Picking up his sack, he trudged to the main room where the little fat one was having coffee with the cardinal. Bruno LaFacci dropped the sack on the floor, his stolid face more impassive than usual. He had taken great care, arranged the contents carefully, and now he pulled the top of the sack open. The girl's body in the crumpled yet still elegant party gown came into view, and the cardinal rose to look quickly into the sack, long enough to see the gown, the body itself, and, at the bottom, the black hair pressed against the burlap, caked from the bloody head. The Duke d'Albatore looked once, gagged, and turned away. "Get it out of here," he choked.

The cardinal nodded to Bruno, and the man pulled the top of the sack closed. It had gone exactly as he'd planned it, and now he felt a warm feeling inside himself. He'd never known triumph before. It was a good feeling. He hefted the grim burden onto his back, and the cardinal took away some of his warm, excited anticipation. "Do it quickly and hurry back," he ordered. "I must leave for Bologna at once. Get the coach hitched when you come back."

Bologna, Bruno echoed silently as he nodded and left with the sack. To Bologna and back would no doubt consume three days. He scowled. Three more days before he could enjoy the beautiful creature waiting in the cell. Bruno LaFacci shrugged off the delay. He could wait three more days to have her. She'd be there when he got back. He didn't have to worry about that. He hurried with his grisly sack, and the next hour became a busy one for Bruno LaFacci. In the first dawn light, he dumped the sack and its contents at a deserted spot at the edge of the Tiber, then hurried back to the house and into the kitchen. He took a wheel of cheese and a loaf of black bread and made his way down into the dungeon. He wanted her fed and healthy when he returned.

Marina sat up at the unexpected sound of the footsteps approaching. He had come back much sooner than she'd expected. She stood up, fighting down panic. She wasn't ready, and there he was, almost at the door. She'd have to put him off, find some excuse, she told herself tensely. But the long-armed figure halted at the cell door and merely looked in at her.

"I can't stay now," he said hoarsely. "I must drive the cardinal to Bologna. It will be three days. Then I will be back for you." He pushed the food in at her and she stepped forward and took it from him. "This will keep you till then." Marina nodded, then he reached a long arm into the cell, cupped her breasts with his hand, emitted a soft groaning sound, and almost ran down the passageway.

Marina turned from the door and put the food on the stool. Three days, she echoed. Three days of reprieve, but three days more in this place. She didn't need three days to make plans, not even three minutes. They were all formed, the only possible plans that could be formed. But this time she'd be certain to be ready for him. Three days. She needed something to tell time in this windowless, airless tomb, something to help her mark the passage of three days. Time stood still here with no point of reference whatever. She could not even tell how long she slept when she dozed. But she had to find a way to know, to be ready. She heard the noise of scurrying claws on stone from the other side of the stone wall of the cell. She frowned. The rats on the other side of the wall. They came into the cell through the open sewage trench late at night, on their own cycle yet regular as any clock. They came in but once and then left, not returning until the next cycle. Probably a full day's turn, Marina calculated, and felt herself grow excited. She'd watched them enter through the drain opening and move along the side of the cell wall, then cross the cell to the far corner. It was a pattern deviating only in minor ways.

Marina took a small, loose piece of stone and drew a thick line across the floor of the far corner of the cell, forming a clear path through the dust and dirt. She set aside the stone, curled up on the burlap sacks at the other end of the cell with the bread and the cheese, then ate some of it to keep up her strength more than because of hunger. Her stomach was still knotted, and hunger had been but an occasional pang since she'd been imprisoned. The stillness became deafening and Marina found herself humming, talking out loud, anything to break the tomblike silence. Finally, she slept in spite of herself.

When she woke—how many hours later she could only guess—she rose at once and approached the thick line she'd marked across the floor by the corner of the sewage opening. She saw the footprints that had crossed it, carrying dust and dirt with them. They had come while she slept, as was their pattern. Their trail marked one visit, one cycle, one day. She smoothed the tiny footprints away, returning to the other corner and the burlap sacks. The rodents had marked one day's turning for her, and she let time trail on as she alternated talking aloud, silently hoping, dozing, eating some of the food left her, and thinking about the outside world.

By now, a girl must have been found wearing her dress and no doubt battered beyond recognition. Bruno's plan had been easy enough to discern. She closed her eyes and prayed that he had not made a replacement for her with his own hands. By now, the constable's men would have found the girl and would have reported the fact to the baroness. Rosalie Amati would have gone to the morgue with them, seen the one-of-a-kind, custom-made gown on the body, and cried out in horror. It would have been all she needed to see. For all intents and purposes, Marina Valerian was dead, probably slain by someone on the night streets, but in any case dead.

Marina's lips tightened against each other. Not yet, she vowed darkly. Perhaps appearances would still become a fact, but the moment wasn't at hand yet. That was why it was so important she be ready when Bruno returned. He would want her at once, and in his wanting would be a gargantuan lust too long denied. It was not inconceivable that he could kill her without intending to do so, Marina pondered. Or make it so that she could do no more than crawl and await his next visit. She pressed her eyes shut to blot out the scene. She had to be ready, she reminded herself silently.

But waiting might sap her strength and the silent gnawing tension corrode and drain her spirit and body. She forced herself to stay awake as long as she could and tried to estimate the number of hours she'd been awake, aware that the body made its cycles according to previous routines. Finally sleep came again, refusing to be denied any longer, and when she woke countless hours later, she again rushed to the opposite corner of the cell. Once again the parade of tiny footprints had crossed the line she'd cleared. A second cycle had passed, a second day marked. She waited again with a patience she never knew she'd possessed, and finally, uncounted hours later, she woke to see that a third day's footprints had been tracked across the line.

Marina's jaw set with a new grimness. It had been an uncertain kind of calendar, yet better than none. She had to observe its passage. She rose, lifted the heavy three-legged wooden stool, and carried it to the wall alongside the cell door. Drawing a deep breath, she went to the candle and blew it out, plunging the cell into total blackness. If her crude calendar had been wrong, she'd remain in the stygian void for uncounted hours, which sent a spiral of panic through her. The cell was oppressive enough—she couldn't stand it for very long in total darkness. In the passageway outside, a dim light from the distant wall lamp flickered fitfully. She leaned herself against the bars and waited.

Time seemed to stand still. Nothing moved; not even the rats broke the silence with their scurrying claws. Only an occasional drop of water rolled from the stones to strike the floor, improperly loud in the vacuum of darkness. She waited, gripped the bars with her hands, then opened and closed her fingers to stop them from stiffening altogether. The sound, when it came, almost frightened her: a door opening in the distance, then the soft, half-shuffling footsteps. Her calendar had not been in error.

Marina moved back from the bars, felt her way along the wall, and found the heavy stool. Bruno LaFacci reached the cell, halted at the door, his shape a black-gray bulk in the dim light of the distant lamp as he peered into the blackness.

"The candle went out," Marina called. She heard him unlocking the cell door. "Wait," she said. "I want to take off my things." But he didn't wait; he hurried as she knew he would. He rushed into the blackness of the cell and halted, hardly visible. Marina swung the heavy stool with all her might, felt it strike and heard the gasp of surprised pain. Bruno LaFacci fell back heavily against the open cell door. It had not been a full blow. Marina, the stool still clasped in her hands, swung again, and this time the blow caught the man full on the forehead. He fell backward, half out the doorway, and collapsed on the floor. Acting out of near panic, Marina brought the stool down again and landed another blow across his temple. Bruno LaFacci uttered a groan and lay still.

Her breath coming in harsh gasps, Marina dropped the stool, raced from the cell, and leaped across the still form. She did not look back as she ran down the passageway, halting only when she reached the stairway door at the far end. There she forced herself to rest, gathering a desperate kind of calmness. She began to climb the stone steps to the door at the top, then carefully eased it open. She saw the rooms where she'd first visited the house. She heard the sounds of voices and recognized both at once—the cardinal's controlled round tones and the nasal whine of the Duke d'Albatore. A hallway beckoned to her and she pressed herself to its walls. The door leading outside was but a few yards away, but she was not dressed to go wandering through the streets, clad only in her chemise and low-bodiced waistband. A coat rack stood near the door, and on it she spied the long, black cape. She reached out and pulled it around herself.

"Damn it, where is that slow-witted numbskull?" Marina heard the cardinal explode in anger. He called for Bruno again, muttering an oath when the man did not appear.

"He may be a faithful servant, but he's hardly attentive," Marina heard the duke whine.

"This is not like Bruno," the cardinal replied. "Perhaps I'd best look for him. This is an old barn of a place. Stones fall, stairways collapse. I'll have a look about."

Marina moved toward the front door. Bruno would be found soon enough once the search got underway in earnest. She had to be out of the house before that moment. She pressed both hands over the door-latch handle, began to push it down, slowly, ever so slowly. Behind her, she heard the sounds of doors being opened and the cardinal calling, going on. She continued her slow, steady pressure upon the handle, felt it click open, the sound still louder to her ears. She opened the door an inch and suddenly felt a shock. It was daylight spearing in at her. Disoriented, surrounded by dim darkness, she'd been certain the outside was also enclosed in darkness. She pushed the door a fraction wider and drew a sharp breath of dismay. A guard stood at the iron gate.

She bit her lower lip with her teeth. She should have known that the cardinal had more than Bruno in his employ. The guard stood with his back to her, and she let her eyes dart around the courtyard. The iron gate was the only way out. Marina's thoughts clicked off a calculated guess. The cardinal no doubt had many in his employ, and many knew of the visitors that came here regularly. But they'd not know more than that. The evil that was part of this place was too monstrous to share with more than a select few. Most likely, Bruno had been the only servant part of that inner circle. Gathering the cape around herself, and uttering a silent prayer that her guess was right, she stepped boldly outside. The guard turned as she crossed the court to him. There was no other way, she realized grimly.

"His Eminence wants to see you right away," she announced to the man, fixing a cool stare on him. He started to move from her. "Please open the gate for me, first," she uttered with a trace of imperiousness. The man quickly lifted the latch and Marina strode out of the courtyard and into the street. The gesture had delayed his going back to the house an extra few moments. Every second counted. She walked quickly, forcing herself not to run. Once the guard saw the cardinal, the truth of what had happened would explode. The churchman would put facts together instantly. He'd halt his search for Bruno, if he hadn't yet found the inert form of his man, and rush to mobilize everyone he commanded to find her.

Did he have the constable of Rome in his debt, she wondered. It was a possibility, for Cardinal Scarti, would try to have people in key places under his thumb. Thus, seeking help from the police was a risk she dared not take. Moving through the streets of Rome by day was another risk she dared not take. The good cardinal would have his people fanning out in every direction to find her.

She searched the buildings she hurried past, turning down into a narrow, twisting alleyway. The sky was growing gray. It would be but a few hours before dark. She halted before a cavernous structure—it had once obviously been a theater with tall columns and arched windows. As she peered through a door hanging half off its hinges she saw rows of seats inside. It was dark in the dusty interior of the place; she hurried inside making her way along the rows of seats, crude wooden benches for the most part. At the far end, almost invisible in the gloom of the interior of the abandoned structure, she saw the stage, with bits and pieces of tattered scenery and screens. She climbed onto the stone stage, moved behind one of the tattered screens, found a wooden box, and sat down on it. She was free. Now she had to stay free. Night would become an ally now, and she waited for its arrival.

In the unofficial residence of Cardinal Francesco Scarti, the churchman stared at the guard who had come in to see him. He knew the color drained from his face at the man's words, but he kept his face impassive, revealing nothing to the guard.

"The lady said you wanted me, Your Eminence," the man had said, The cardinal glimpsed the Duke d'Albatore's jaw drop down, his lips moving soundlessly.

"I changed my mind. Return to the gate," the cardinal ordered, managing to keep his voice down. The man retreated and Cardinal Scarti's lips pulled back in a grimace of frustrated rage. The bitch. The high-bred, scheming little bitch, he swore silently. And that stupid cretin, Bruno. He was probably in the dungeon with his head bashed in. If he wasn't dead he would be later. But there was no time to think about that idiot now. There were more important things to do.

"She could hide anywhere in Rome," he heard the duke whine.

"That's why I won't waste time trying to scour every crevice in Rome," the cardinal snapped. "She won't go to the constabulary. She's too smart to risk that. There is but one place here where she'd go, and I'll have that covered in fifteen minutes."

"What if she doesn't show there?" the duke asked.

"Then she'll try to get out of Rome to make her way south, back to Calabria, no doubt. We'll seize her on one of the roads from Rome. We can cover them much more easily." Cardinal Scarti moved toward the door at once. "I must go and see to that immediately."

"And I'll return to my place. There's work to be done yet, you know. Our new allies insist on more careful planning than the Arabs," the duke observed.

"Go. I'll find our little troublemaker. The trip to Calabria is a long and difficult one. She will never finish it alive." The cardinal strode away, his face rigid with fury. Cardinal Scarti was too egotistical a man to feel fear. This little piece of baggage had proven unexpectedly ingenious, and now she knew more than enough to hang him. But he had not come this far without knowing how to outwit and outmaneuver those who stood in his way. Certainly this scheming little wench could not do what far more powerful men had been unable to do. And this time he'd see to her finish himself.

He flung himself out into the courtyard. "My carriage," he called to the guard at the gate. "At once."

CHAPTER TWELVE

MARINA COULD GLIMPSE a corner of the sky through one of the upper windows from where she sat behind the screen. She watched it turn blue-purple, darken, and grow into the blackness of night before she rose, groping her way through the abandoned theater and out to the street. Holding the cape around her neck, she moved from the alleyway onto a wider street, paused, peered at street signs, and took her bearings. The town house lay north of where she was, and she turned, hurrying along the streets, staying close to the buildings. She halted at every corner to glance around. Every knot of men made her shrink into a doorway until they passed. Horsemen riding in pairs made her flee up side streets.

The trek became one of small dartings from place to place. What should have taken a little more than an hour took most of the night. But finally she reached the cobbled street where the townhouse occupied the middle of the block. She paused at the corner, realized that her legs were trembling, and waited until the wave of weakness passed over her. But she had made it, and she started to move down the street. A tiny glow of light almost opposite the town house entrance caught her eye. She froze. The tiny glow came again. Someone was smoking, standing across from the baroness's home. Marina peered down the street, squinting. The tiny glow of the cigar came again, but she had shifted her eyes to the other side of the street. A dark form took shape a yard or so beyond the front steps of the town house—a second man in the shadows.

Marina backed around the corner, leaned against the wall of the house there, and let a deep breath escape her. She had been stupid, she told herself angrily. She should have expected the cardinal would anticipate her goal. He was not one to panic. She did not trouble herself to try the back of the house. They would be there, too, she knew. But she had to get to the baroness some way, and knew the sharp stab of frustration. She was so close and yet so far. There was no way to get into the house. They'd be upon her the moment she moved toward it. She'd been lucky they hadn't glimpsed her as she rounded the corner, she realized.

Marina moved away from the wall, started to retreat, and moved down a narrow street, wracking her mind for a plan but finding none. The street opened onto a broad avenue and she halted, biting her lips. A woman in a black shawl sat on the corner selling flowers, mostly violets and peonies from a basket. Marina saw no one halt to buy anything; the basket was still full. Suddenly her brow furrowed. Sometimes the flower vendors went from door to door. In a few long strides she was at the woman's side; she saw a lined, weary face look up, a brief instant of hope flare in the tired eyes. Marina shook her head, and was sorry she could not buy a bouquet.

"I have no money," she said quickly. "But I need help. You can do something for me and perhaps sell your entire basket."

The woman's eyes held wary curiosity. "Sell my whole basket?" she echoed.

"Do you know where the Baroness Amati lives?" Marina asked. The woman nodded. "All you have to do is deliver a message," Marina went on.

"What message?"

Marina looked past the woman for a moment, saw one of Rome's innumerable fountains a few streets beyond. "Go to the house and ask for the baroness. Tell her that Marina lives. Tell her to take her carriage and go to the fountain down there."

The woman glanced down the avenue. "The Lovers' Fountain," she replied.

"Deliver that message, and the baroness will give you more than your basket will bring," Marina told her.

The woman studied her for a moment, shrugged, then rose. "I can lose nothing but a few minutes of time." She sighed. "Nobody is buying anyway tonight."

"Thank you." Marina smiled, pressing the woman's arm. "But give the message only to the baroness, no one else," she cautioned.

The woman nodded and began to shuffle away. Marina followed in a moment, halted down the street at a spot where she could see the town house entrance, and watched the black-shawled figure slowly move down to the doorway and pull the bell ringer.

The door opened after a few moments, and Marina recognized Puli's figure as he stepped onto the front step, spoke to the woman, then turned and closed the door. The old woman slowly descended the front steps, basket in hand. Marina glimpsed the man as he moved into the street to peer at the woman, then retreated to take up his post again. Grimly, she waited as the woman returned and halted in front of her.

"The baroness is not there," the woman explained. "The butler told me she was in mourning, that she'd gone to visit her brother." Marina closed her eyes for a moment, forcing herself not to sink back against the wall. The baroness had gone to tell Vittorio the terrible news. And, of course, Paul would hear it then, too. Marina opened her eyes. She had to find a way to Spezzano, somehow, some way.

"I'm sorry," she said to the old woman. "I've nothing to give you, nothing at all, except thank you." The woman shrugged and walked on. Marina stayed for a moment and fought down the trembling that seized her body. Spezzano. Calabria. It might as well have been the end of the world—but she had to go there.

First, though, she had to get out of Rome. Danger was everywhere here. Before day returned, she had to be away from it.

Marina straightened herself and drew a deep breath. She could see a string of lights marking one of the bridges across the Tiber. She began to walk toward it, once again keeping to the shadows, watching each corner as she crossed, moving with caution. If she were caught, there would be no second chance to escape. The good cardinal would see to that.

The bridge was a narrow one, only a few others crossing it, and she hurried over to the other side. The Palatine Hill rose up on her left as she turned south along a wide dirt road. Trees lined one side, and a moon had come up to help light the way. In the black cape, with the hood up to cover her onyx tresses, she could well have been a man trudging along the edge of the road. A few slow-moving carts laden with barrels passed her, and she was forced to step into a roadside ditch by a thundering carriage that flew by. Mostly, though, the road was still, with few travelers. Marina kept a steady pace that she hoped would keep fatigue from overtaking her too quickly.

The hope had been a hollow one, she realized, as her leg muscles began to scream in protest and the soles of her feet began to burn. She looked back down the road, realized she had come farther than she'd hoped, and knew that the body set its own limitations. She felt weakness beginning to pull at her and hunger stabbing its own demands. A field opened up on her right, and she saw the moon etch a farmhouse, two barns, and a trio of haystacks. She turned from the road and made for the darkened structures. The haystacks beckoned, and she glanced up at the moon. It had traveled quickly across the sky. The new day was not too many hours away. Sleep demanded attention before anything else. She crawled onto the largest of the haystacks, forming a resting place for herself at its wide base. With the cape over her as a blanket and the hay softer than any bed she had known since her last night at the townhouse, she fell asleep at once.

The heat woke her. She opened her eyes and her skin felt wet with perspiration. The morning sun had turned her den of hay into a yellow steam bath, and she pushed the cape back, letting the air rush over her skin. She peered out through the curtain of hay, saw the bright green fields and the farmhouse, now clearer and larger than it had seemed in the night. As she peered out, feeling not unlike a rabbit hiding from view in the bushes, she saw a farmer emerge from the house with baskets of onions and turnips in his hands. He put them in a heavy-wheeled, open-topped road cart with high sides. He made two trips from the barn with more vegetables for the cart, then clambered into the driver's seat and went off, turning down the road. Marina waited and watched, and saw a woman come from the house, a pail of chicken feed in each hand. She circled around out of sight behind the barn, but the cackle of hens rose to fill the air. Only when the woman went back into the house with the pails empty did Marina crawl from her straw hiding place, dragging the cape with her.

She darted to the next haystack, then the next, and finally raced to the barn door, slipping inside the big structure. It was cool in the barn and she saw stalls for half a dozen cows, which were empty, and four horse stalls. One was full with a big, powerful draft horse. Marina approached the stall, excitement stirring in her at once. This was no saddle horse, but it would take her farther and faster than her still-tired legs could carry her. Apologizing silently to the farmer, she opened the stall gate, found a bridle, and slipped it on the huge horse, leading him from the stall. He was tractable and steady, as were most of his kind and, grasping hold of his mane, she pulled and swung herself onto his back. He started for a moment, not used to riders, but she kicked her heels into his sides and he went forward, pushing the barn door open with one lunge of his powerful head.

She let him gallop across the fields, heard the shouts of the farmer's wife behind her, turned him down the road, and let him continue to gallop on. He slowed soon enough, his heavy legs not made for distance running, and she let him pick his pace. Even without a saddle his broad back made for easy-chair riding, and she loosened the cape around her neck as the sun grew warmer. She would have to find a skirt and blouse—a garment to wear— she realized. She'd never be able to make the long trip with the cape over her chemise. The road began a slow incline, then leveled off, and as she rode around a turn she reined the big horse to a halt. Two donkey carts, a heavy flatbed wagon, and three carriages were halted ahead of her. She peered forward and saw men on horseback across the road at the head of the line.

Marina edged the horse up to the last of the donkey carts. A young man stood at the head of the donkey while an older man held the reins from the driver's seat. "What's the trouble?" Marina asked, looking down from her high perch atop the draft horse. The young man cocked an eye up at her.

"They are searching the carriages," he replied, gesturing with his head. "They are looking for someone, it seems."

Marina nodded, kept her face expressionless as her pulse soared and she felt the blood pounding inside her. She had heard more than enough. She knew who was being sought and who was doing the seeking. The cardinal had his people set up roadblocks, anticipating her flight southward. The roadblocks would not be on this road alone, of course. He'd have every road out of Rome under watch. Marina backed the big horse, wheeled him around, and walked him into the line of trees at the side of the road. She cut through the trees, emerged in a field choked with brush, and spurred him through it. His heavy legs and hooves trod the brush underfoot as he forged through places that would have dismayed the ordinary riding horse. The terrain remained heavy with rugged brush as well as trees dotting the landscape, and she wove in and out of leafy arbors. She'd gone perhaps a mile when she heard distant shouts behind her.

Murmuring an oath, she slapped the big farm horse's rump and he broke into a heavy-footed trot. The youth with the donkey cart had told them of the girl who had taken off through the fields. They'd have it easy following the trail of the big work horse through the trampled brush. She had perhaps another fifteen minutes before they'd catch sight of her, she guessed. She gave the horse another hard slap and he quickened the trot. A ravine, deep and heavily wooded, took shape on her left as the horse moved along a ridge of brush and trees. Marina swung her legs over his back to the other side and gauged the distance to the thick brush below. She raised her hand, held it poised, saw a heavy clump of brush coming up in the ravine, and brought the slap down hard on the horse's rump. Unused to being handled this way, he'd keep running for another ten minutes, she knew. She leaped from his back, sailed through the air, and tucked her arms tightly around herself.

She struck the thick brush feet first, plummeted through it, and felt sharp pieces of branches tearing at her, but she kept her neck pulled in. Her cape caught and slowed her down, then ripped; finally she lay at the bottom of the brush, a few yards into the ravine. She felt a trickle of blood from her arm, another from the side of her neck—small cuts from the edges of broken branches. She wiped them with the inside of the torn cape and began to make her way carefully down the side of the ravine. The brush was an ally again, preventing her from slipping down too fast. The ravine was deeper than she'd thought, she saw, as she reached the bottom. It was cool, only small slivers of sunlight penetrating the thick cover of trees and brush. A small stream traced its way through the bottom of the ravine. She paused to wash the cuts and clean the dust and dirt from herself, taking the cape off and dragging it along behind her as she made her way alongside the stream.

Inside the ravine she was hidden from view. Those on the high ground above would find the farm horse soon enough, but they'd have no way of knowing where she'd left his back. The thick brush she'd fallen through would close up at once, leaving no traces except at close-hand inspection. She'd no idea where the ravine would take her, or how long it would afford her safe cover. She could only follow it and hope for the best. The stream turned off after a while and disappeared into a rocky defile. Marina drank from its clear, refreshing water before it did, and continued along the ravine bottom. She traveled perhaps two miles more when the sides of the ravine began to flatten out.

The natural haven was at an end, and Marina sank down to rest before going on. Her leg muscles ached, and she rubbed her calves with both hands. The knot in the pit of her stomach kept her from feeling hunger, she realized. She'd eluded the cardinal's pursuers, but for how long, she pondered. They knew she was in the area and had no doubt called in help. They'd have every road blockaded while others swarmed through the region like hounds after a hare. Marina stretched her aching legs and lay back on the ground as the sun filtered soothing warmth through the trees. Once again she knew the smothering feeling of despondency. Once again all her efforts seemed destined to fail, her struggles foundering again in the face of fate. She lay still, terribly tired, and yet a gathering anger, a slow spiral of rage, rose up inside her.

"No," she heard herself say aloud. "No, damn them." The spiral of anger grew, ballooned inside her; it was more than simple courage, more than inner strength. The fury was part of her, the spirit which had made her rebel against Aldo Gamborelli selling her off like a piece of merchandise, the same spirit which made her rebel against mindless, warped callousness. In all that had happened she had begun to understand the meaning of that inner spirit, the quality which gave it life. It was not simply a shout of protest but a cry of hope.

Out of pain and despair she had learned that to rebel against wrong is to be a seeker of dreams, to want to make the world a better place. Marina uttered a bitter sound. A chaser of moonbeams was more truthful, a wanderer destined to cry more than laugh.

But she'd learned more than that truth alone. In the lustful avariciousness of the cardinal she had learned the meaning of Paul—his conscience, the purity of his strength—and now her lips were touched with an edge of bitterness. In her caring, had there been too much arrogance? Had she asked when there should have only been giving? Had she seen nothing but her own wanting? Had she destroyed Generoso through her own self-seeking? Was that why happiness continued to be a thing of moments instead of forever?

She pushed aside the questions. It was not time now. She knew only that she had to find a way back, to return to Paul—to tell him she was alive, of course, but to say so much more than that. No retractions. She wanted his love no less and would not deny that. But now she understood another definition of commitment—integrity, principles—all such big words for a particular kind of love. Out of evil, we learn the meaning of good. Out of pain, we learn to understand.

She had to find a way back. To return was to keep faith with Paul, with all that he stood for. To keep fighting was to keep faith with Generoso and all that he had held high. Time stopped for a moment as she thought of Generoso, with his olive-black eyes; that fire and flame would never go out inside her, would forever be a part of her. She rose to her feet. What better reasons could anyone have to go on? The abstract faded away. Survival came first now. The hare still had to elude the hounds.

She moved on as the ravine came to an abrupt end and rose up to a line of heavy brush. She dropped to her knees and crawled through the foliage that scratched and tore at her. A road ran by the other side and beyond it the land dipped; there she saw the rooftops of perhaps a dozen houses, but beyond the rooftops a blue line—the blue of the sea. The ravine wandered its way to the edge of the coast.

The sound of horsemen broke the still air, and Marina drew back into the bushes. She saw the two riders appear, one at each side of the road, their eyes peering across the terrain, but she stayed unmoving, watching them go past and recede down the road—and only then did she peer from her hiding place again. A tiny smile crept into her eyes as she looked out at the line of the sea beyond. The searchers would guard their roadblocks through the night and continue their crisscrossing of the area, certain that sooner or later she'd have to try to move south. But she'd not use their roads. Marina's eyes narrowed. Their quarry would not try to run their gauntlet. She backed from the bushes and crept down to the end of the ravine again. The sun was already lowering behind the hills. A few more hours would not matter now. Her road south would be one without markings. It was quite appropriate, and she smiled. She had come to Paul out of the sea and she would return to him by the sea. An omen, a good sign, she told herself as she settled down to rest.

The coolness of the night wind stirring woke her, and she sat up at once. She rose, hurried out of the ravine. A moon hung high in the sky, and she paused at the road on the other side of the bushes. In the distance, beyond the dip of the road, she caught the flicker of firelight. They had their roadblock set up there, Marina noted grimly, torches on hand to search every coach and cart that passed. She hurried across the road, over the rise and down to the darkened houses of the little coastal village. She paused at a house where a line of clothes stretched from the rear wall to a tree. A woman's blouse flapped in the soft breeze, two black skirts beside it. She crept to the clothesline and felt the garments. They were almost dry. Taking the blouse and one of the skirts, she disappeared into the darkness, moving silently past the few houses and down to the small quay that lined the shore. A dozen sailing vessels were moored, most gaff-rigged fishing ketches. She chose the smallest, stepped into it, and put the skirt and blouse inside the tiny cabin in the forward part of the ketch.

Moving carefully and quietly, Marina slipped the rope from the mooring and let the boat drift away from the quay, not daring to touch the sails. Hoisting the gaff would bring a clatter and rattling that would surely wake the village. The boat moved sideways from the quay, drifting into open water. Marina let the sea carry her further down from the houses and continued to drift until she saw the shoreline curving out, the tide carrying her toward the protruding land. She hoisted the sail then, felt the wind catch at it at once, secured the sheets, and grasped hold of the tiller. The little craft responded well, sensitive enough for a rough fishing ketch. Marina settled back, steered the boat around the outward bend of the land, and headed south. She need only follow the shoreline, she knew, letting herself enjoy the feeling of victory. She was on her way back to Paul.

Later, as the wind held a soft but steady breeze, she secured the tiller and went down into the tiny cabin. She found a jar of olives and devoured them hungrily. She also found a tin of biscuits and ate a few, putting the rest away. She stayed at the tiller, dozing off a few times as the gentle rocking of the boat proved irresistible. With dawn, the soft but steady wind died away. The shore lay within easy sight, but the sail hung limply. The sun rose to burn away the dawn mist and she saw that the sea, in its capriciousness, had decided not to aid her any further for the moment. Marina took off the streaked and torn chemise and waist bodice, let the sun warm her nakedness, then got the skirt and blouse from the cabin. The skirt was loose but had a pin which she used to tighten it. The blouse was too large but not beyond wearing. In any case, they were better than the undergarments and the torn cape. She glanced at the shore, saw that the currents were carrying her away from land, and grimaced in dismay. When she found no oar, she returned to stretch out on the floorboards by the tiller. By noon she was unable to see the shore and felt the nervousness sweeping over her.

The sun blazed now and little whorls of heat rose from the deck. She shed the blouse and skirt, lying naked in the shade of the cabin. The sea had become as glass and the boat drifted slowly with the current as the sail hung loosely, a useless appendage now. She was in the doldrums, she concluded grimly. Sometimes they lasted for days. By midafternoon she had to leave the little cabin. It had turned into a wooden oven. She slipped over the side of the boat, lowering her body into the sea, letting the coolness of the water soothe her nakedness. Finally, she pulled herself back aboard the ketch, a dripping sea nymph in solitary magnificence.

Night finally came to scatter the merciless sun, but the wind remained unmoving. The sky filled with stars and became a glittering upside-down blanket. Marina put the skirt on—the night air was cooling even though it was windless. She ate a few of the biscuits and put away the others. A half-filled jar of water let her wet her throat and stave off the pain of thirst but she kept most for the morrow. The broiling sun and its enervating rays had pulled strength from her, and she had no trouble falling asleep on the deck. She woke when she was rolled sideways and crashed against the gunwale. The dawn and the wind had come up together.

Scrambling across the deck, she grabbed hold of the tiller as the boat plunged through the sea like a riderless steed. She pulled the bow around, saw the sail bellied out full, and sailed the boat in a slow circle as she watched the sun begin to rise in the east. Unsure any longer which way land lay, she headed the boat into the morning sun, the wind behind her. She spent the morning anxiously peering ahead for any sign of land, aware that the sea currents might have carried her much farther out than she had any way of knowing. At each momentary dip in the breeze, Marina felt her heart turn over, and her eyes darted to the sail. But the wind, though lessening, held enough to maintain a nice, steady headway. Marina finished the crackers and the water and began to grow despondent, aware that she could simply be sailing deeper into the sea.

She was sitting on the deck, one hand lightly guiding the tiller, when the outline traced itself on the horizon, unmistakably the undulating silhouette of land. She gave a little cry of delight, pointed the ketch higher into the wind, and the sail filled more. It was deep into the afternoon when she turned the little boat south once again, following the shoreline and hugging the land this time. Night came quickly, and she sailed for as long as her energy would allow until she spied a small cove outlined in the trail of the moon across the water. She steered into it, dropped the small mushroom anchor at the bow of the ketch, and felt it hold. She lay down on the deckboards and slept at once, completely fatigued.

The new sun woke her, and she was up at once, shedding the blouse to lean over and freshen up with the salt water. She went to the bow, tugged at the anchor, dragged it from the depths and onto the deck, then fell back to catch her breath. The boat began to drift to shore at once, and she hoisted sail, swung the tiller, and headed out of the cove. The sea held a good breeze as she emerged from the cove, and she sat down to devote all her attention to sailing, slipping into the loose blouse again. As she neared Naples, the water traffic began to thicken and she sailed out, giving the port a wide berth and returning to the shoreline only when it was safely behind her.

Marina tried to count back but realized the days had melted together, each delay, each waiting and hiding time adding another fortnight. Time had stretched out to weeks, perhaps more than a month, since she'd first been plunged into the cardinal's private dungeon, she realized with difficulty, then with dismay. Certainly it had been at least that long since the battered girl in the distinctive ball gown had been reported found. She had lost track of time and realized that each day lost had given the plotters one more day nearer their goal. Marina pulled on the tiller angrily, coaxing a fraction more speed from the boat as she pointed higher into the wind.

She knew that by now Cardinal Scarti awaited each day with increasing anxiety and frustration. He'd be unwilling to believe she could have slipped through his network. He'd maintain his watch on the roads from Rome while drawing the search toward the city, wondering if she might just still be hiding in the city of Romulus and Remus. Marina felt a bitter pleasure at the thought, returning her gaze to the passing shoreline. A church spire caught her eye—much too high and imposing for the little village of Paul's parishioners, so she sailed on. Anxiously, her eyes sought some mark that would help her recognize her goal, but the curving, white-pebbled beaches all seemed alike and the rows of brush and trees behind them all wore the same mask.

Frowning, she saw the sun begin to arc down across the sky, moving with seeming undue haste. She wanted to make the little boat go faster but the sail refused to do more than the wind permitted. She scowled. A flat, almost treeless stretch of curving pebbled beach came into view, not unlike any of the others she had passed. The sun had lowered itself till its rays slanted across the water. As she reached the beach, she felt her hand tighten on the tiller and she turned the prow of the boat to the beach as though another hand had guided her. Whether it was the seeds of memory or a premonition of the future, she could not tell. Didn't the soothsayers speak gravely of strange wisdom given us to know, yet not know?

She sailed the boat straight forward, letting its prow dig onto the beach beyond the grip of tides. She leaped down to the pebbled sand and began to run across the softness of it into the line of brush, bursting through the other side to see the few houses before her and, then, to the right, the small church. Her eyes swept upward to the steep stones of gray slate and her breath sucked inward in a half gasp, half cry. She stood absolutely still for a moment, touched with happiness, anxiety, and a sense of wonder. Pushing her blouse into the top of the skirt and otherwise straightening her clothes, she hurried forward as the day began to turn gray-blue. The door of the little church was open and Marina stepped inside. A boy stood just inside the doorway.

"Is Father in?" Marina asked, hearing the quiver in her voice. The boy nodded, and Marina stepped into the confessional, pulled the little bell cord, and closed the door. It seemed an eternity, but it was not more than a few moments till she heard the figure move into the other side, behind the fine mesh screen. She'd hoped desperately to find the right words but as her lips opened the words tumbled forth in their own way.

"I'm here, my darling," she whispered. "You're not imagining things. I'm alive and I've come back and I love you more than ever, but I understand so much more now."

She heard the door of the confessional fling open, the figure step outside at once, and she pushed herself from the booth, her arms reaching out. She halted as if struck in the face. The priest, a wide-eyed man wearing the brown robes of a Franciscan and with a friar's haircut, stared at her. Marina swallowed, felt the world spin away, and clutched the edge of the confessional for support. She fought away dizziness, knew her face had grown scarlet, and felt her lips move as she searched for words. She dared not ask for Paul, she realized—not now, not after the things she had murmured inside the booth. She tried to retrieve the words but stammered nothing instead. The priest came to her rescue.

"You expected Father Paul, didn't you, my dear?" he remarked pleasantly. Marina's lips tightened and she felt her hands clenching into tight fists. Her first impulse was to deny his words, but she saw the gentle patience in the Franciscan's eyes.

"Yes," she replied, the word almost inaudible.

"Do not be so upset, my dear," he answered. "You would not be the first young woman to fall in love with her priest."

Marina met the patience in his eyes, lifted her chin into the air, not defiantly but with a kind of dogged honesty. "It was not as simple as that," she murmured.

His eyes studied her for a long moment. "Are you Marina?" he asked softly. She felt surprise and nodded.

"I am Father Caprano," the Franciscan said. "Please wait here for a moment. I shall be right back."

As Marina watched him hurry down the side of the church, she sank onto the edge of one of the long wooden benches. He knew her name. Paul must have told him. Perhaps Paul was nearby. Perhaps he'd gone to fetch him. Hope was a clutching emotion, reaching out to grasp at anything, she reflected. She waited, then heard the soft, sandaled footsteps of the Franciscan as he returned. He had an envelope in his hand and he held it out to her.

"This was left by Father Paul. Take it. Read it. Though it was not left for you, it is perhaps more for you than anyone else, and I am glad that you have the opportunity to read it. Take your time. Read it well. I shall return in a few minutes."

Marina pulled the letter from the envelope, looked down at the neat, evenly spaced script. Her hand trembled as she began to read in a shaft of light from the open door:

Father Dominic—

It is with a torn and heavy heart that I write this. By the time you read it, I shall be gone. You will be making your yearly visit soon, and so the good people of this humble place will not be without a spiritual shepherd until someone is sent to replace me.

There was a time when I thought I knew who I was. I felt certain who had called me to serve and I knew that particular kind of love not given to most men to know. I do not know, yet, if I was wrong. I only know that I am unsure of anything now. It was perhaps meant to be. I cannot say that for certain, but it began when Marina entered my life.

To say that she was beautiful, intelligent, and warm is only to evade the issue. I have met other beautiful, intelligent, and warm women. To say that she tempted is but half a truth. Others have tempted. Even as a seminarian I met others who attracted, others who tempted. But only Marina reached deeply to places never reached before. Her existence touched the questions of why we respond to one thing and not another, why we are pulled in one direction and not another, why we do what we do and love what we love.

I thought I knew the face of love once and found that I knew nothing. In Matthew, it saith, "No man can serve two masters." And, surely, no man can have two loves. One can want, desire, hunger for two persons at one time. One can care deeply for two people at one time, even love different things in each one. But one cannot have two loves at the same time, not in the full, real, and only complete meaning of love, because love, in its only true meaning, is to serve, to give of one's total self. To love is to dedicate, to give everything to someone or something beyond the self.

To serve two masters, is to fail each a little. To have two loves is to deny each a little. This I could not do. I had to find answers again, to look deeper into myself, to find where truth lay.

I did not send Marina away, not in the usual sense. You cannot send away a part of yourself. But she, too, knew that tomorrow depended upon answers I had to find. She left on a mission of danger, to find the names of those who betrayed the church and mankind. I have learned that she gave her life in that quest. I must share in that guilt as I now share in that pain. She paid the price for my weakness.

I could stay and carry that cross, but I cannot stay without knowing what I am, who I am, where I must follow. Marina is still with me in every way but one. The questions she brought to me are still unanswered. I am still unfaithful to the Church, to myself, to the spirit of love.

And so I leave here. I cannot comfort others when there is no comfort inside me. Strength can only be given by the strong. I cannot ask faith of others when I have failed to find it in myself. I go alone, to see whatever strengths are mine, to find again what I thought I once knew. In Matthew it saith: "Many are called, but few are chosen." I must find out if those words still speak to me. I must learn what price I must pay.

I ask your forgiveness and wish God be with you.

Paul Davore

Marina read the last of the letter again, after brushing the mist from her eyes. She was sitting with the letter folded in her lap, staring into space, when the brown-robed priest returned.

"Would you like to keep the letter?" he asked gently. "It is yours, really."

Marina nodded and lifted her eyes to him. "No one knows where he is?" She was unable to keep hope from her voice.

"No one. He has not gone to any of the retreats. I would have had word of that."

"Do you think he's alive?"

"I think so. I hope so. But this is not a time for false comfort. A man such as Father Paul, with his sensitivity, his conscience, and his compassion, may find the world too much for him. Guilt, deserved or undeserved, is a terrible master. Some men turn to the world to atone for their wrongs. Others turn away from it. Only time and his own inner self will determine that."

Marina rose. "The little cottage, is anyone living there?"

The priest frowned.

"The one Father Paul used." *Father Paul.* She had never called him that. Now somehow it sounded right.

"No, no one is using it," the priest answered.

Marina pushed the letter into the pocket of the skirt and walked from the little church, only dimly aware of objects around her, seeing yet not seeing. Her steps turned up the path, through the brush and the trees. She didn't hurry, and it was almost dark when the stone cottage loomed up before her. She pushed the door open, went in, and found the candle quickly and a taper with which to light it. Her eyes traversed the room as the light sent a flickering illumination across the walls. He had left with only his personal things; everything else remained the same. She looked into the small room and saw all the jars and bottles, the sacks and bags of herbs and leaves and ointments. Her eyes filled with tears. He had labored so humbly to heal in every way.

The letter lay in her pocket, its words written in her mind. Paul was somewhere, someplace, and she had to find him and let him know that he deserved to take no guilt upon himself, that she lived and still waited for his decisions. She felt her brow crease. Perhaps he needed her now as she had once needed him. Perhaps she could heal as he had once healed her. She had to find him, she told herself. She had to know if happiness was still there for her and for him.

Marina blew the candle out, undressed, and lay down on the cot as she had done so many nights across from Paul. His words drifted back to her—you couldn't send away a part of yourself—and Paul was here, in the cottage. She closed her eyes and found sleep, a fitful, restless sleep that saw her wake, cry out his name, and fall back to sleep.

When morning came, she woke to plans that somehow had taken shape during the night. The baron first. She had to get to him and tell him all she'd learned. Too much time had passed to delay that any further. Then she must find a way to Paul. If happiness was to be denied her again she had to know it was not because of a tragic flight from undeserved guilt and pain.

She dressed, walked from the cottage into the grass still wet with morning dew, and hurried to where the slate steeple rose up through the trees. Father Caprano was outside the church, a trowel and mortar in his hands as he filled crevices and cracks in the outside wall. He looked up as she neared, setting the mortar and trowel down. "The Lord expects his servants to be handy as well as godly," he observed. "Did you sleep well?"

"Not really," Marina replied. "I must go to Spezzano. Baron Amati lives near there. There are important things I must tell him."

"No problem. I can arrange for a cart to take you there." He paused, his eyes growing smaller. "And after you tell your story?" he asked.

"I want to find Paul." She spoke firmly. "He may need help."

"There are others he can turn to if he wishes," the priest pointed out wryly.

"Of course. You probably think I want to find him for myself. It's not that." She saw the gentle question in the man's eyes. "How can he make the right decision for himself this way?" Marina protested.

"The questions you brought are with him, whether you are there or not. He will find his answers out of what you mean, not what you are." Marina accepted his answer, understood, and knew it was not enough for her. She held back replying and followed him across the road, past the houses to the last one, where a makeshift barn leaned upon the back wall of the stucco house. He went inside while she waited, then reappeared soon with an old man, an old cart and an old mare.

"Baldi will take you," he indicated.

Marina thanked him. "I'll pay him when we reach there, Father."

"I shall pray for you as I do for Paul," the priest replied. She clambered onto the rear of the cart, and the old man sent the mare on the way at once. The few houses faded into the distance and Marina sat back against the side of the cart, trying to hold down impatience but finding it was an impossible task. The trip seemed longer than ever before, the old mare steady but unhurried. They halted once at a clear spring to water the mare, then went on. The old man did not talk, and Marina was glad for that. The sun passed high in the midday sky and began its downward trek before Marina recognized the roads that led to the baron's villa. She directed the old man, and finally the gracious lines of Baron Amati's great house came into sight. The cart moved up the driveway and Marina peered into the oriental gardens and told the old man to halt. Under one of the ginkgo trees the lean, spry figure rested on a bench, his glance turning toward her as she swung down from the cart. The quick brown eyes seemed almost dull, she saw as she hurried forward, and the spritely figure was hunched over. She saw Vittorio Amati look up as the girl in the loose blouse and too-long black skirt came toward him.

She was almost to him when his eyes widened. He rose and the color drained from his face. She spoke quickly, alarmed at his shocked face. "You are not seeing things. I'm here. I was not killed." Vittorio Amati reached out, his hand gripping her shoulder, moving to her cheek, and then pushing back her hair.

"My God, my God, it is true," he gasped hoarsely as he pulled her to him and embraced her.

"There is so much that happened, so much to tell. It's almost beyond believing."

He stepped back and the quick eyes were bright again as they peered at her sharply. "It has waited this long. It can wait a little longer while you clean up and get into something that fits. And then you must eat. You look wan and haggard; your cheeks are hollowed."

The idea of food held an unexpected appeal, and she agreed gratefully. "I'll go upstairs. Please pay the old man in the cart," she said and hurried into the house. After a quick bath, she donned a simple dress and returned downstairs. Vittorio waited by a table set with chicken, fruit, and cheese. While she ate, she recounted all that had happened. Words seemed to rob it of its horror, and yet, in his eyes, she saw that shock and disgust had left their marks. Finally she finished, and felt drained by the telling. She sat back and closed her eyes for a moment.

"I'm only sorry I could not reach Rosalie in time to tell her I was not killed."

"She will be as overjoyed as I when she learns the truth," the Baron comforted her. "It is indeed almost beyond believing, a horror tale. But we have what we need now—names, places, dates, and your testimony. I know what to do with all this. I'll have to go to Rome, to see the right people. This must be handled properly so that when the trap is sprung there will be no wriggling free for the cardinal and the others. Insofar as Rome is concerned, he is the key figure, a man of far greater evil than even his enemies suspect."

The small, spry figure reached over to a chair where a packet of letters lay. He brought them to the table, his face growing grave. "Now I've news for you. Revolution has broken out in France. The bourgeoisie have set up a new government. Louis triggered it, of course, not that it wouldn't have happened anyway in time. He dismissed Necker, who was the only minister popular with the people. On July fourteenth, the mob marched on the Invalides, fought their way in, and with twenty-eight thousand rifles attacked the Bastille. They freed the prisoners there, a symbolic gesture, and I am told hung a *carmagnole* from the flagpole. The streets of Paris ran with blood and there were riots all over France, my informants tell me."

"But Louis is still king?" Marina inquired.

"Now he is the puppet of the revolutionaries. I understand they had him kiss their new tricolor cockade at a ceremony at the Place Grève. Louis is not without a rodent's nose for self-preservation. He will go along with anything for now and hope for a time to recoup power."

"A time you do not think will come," Marina observed.

"Correct. This but a beginning. It is Robespierre who holds the real power now. The revolutionaries will not be satisfied until they have the heads of Louis and Marie Antoinette, and Robespierre will encourage Madame Veto to do all the things that will bring that day about."

"What does this mean for us?" Marina wondered.

"Ferdinand and Maria are already uneasy. If the revolution is imported here by force of arms as well as in spirit, they will certainly flee. Those who seek power for self-protection will hurry their plans, which means I must leave for Rome tonight. The things I have to do there will not be accomplished in a day. Cardinal Scarti is not without power. You will stay here, I trust, until I return."

"No." Marina spoke sharply, her deep anger focused. "Everything that has happened, all the pain and the killing, all the terrible things, can be laid at the doorstep of one man, Aldo Gamborelli. His greed, his ambition, his total selfishness began it all when he set about to sell me off for money from that little pig, d'Albatore. He is no better than the count, but it is Aldo Gamborelli who began it all. It is he who still sits on my land, holds forth in my home. You said the revolution began on July fourteenth. That means I had a birthday at the end of June, when I knew neither time nor days in the cardinal's cell. I am going back to claim what is mine."

Vittorio Amati's smile was patient. "It would be fitting to have Gamborelli sent fleeing while I am in Rome seeing to the cardinal and the others. But you dream impossible dreams, my dear. I'm sure that your uncle has the villa and himself well guarded, especially since he knows the farmers will be aroused by news of the revolution in France. You can't seriously think he would give up everything simply because you appear on the scene and demand it."

"I know better than that. I will need enough men to force him to flee, to add might to right. If you will lend me the funds I shall pay you back as soon as I have my home once again," Marina replied.

"The money is no problem, my child," Vittorio Amati told her. "But a man would have trouble to recruit such a force. We are poor of men in this land. All the best ones have fled to Tuscany and Venice for a living or are already in the king's forces. You cannot have farmers and milkmaids go against trained guards, and an army, even a small one, needs a leader. You, of all people, know how men feel in this land, how the twisted traditions hold fast. Do you think they would follow you, a girl? Come now, Marina, you would have to be Joan of Arc."

Marina saw the truth of his words, but she had formed her plans, had made her decisions. "I think it can be done," she insisted. "I will try, win or lose."

The baron shook his head. "The practical problems will be too many," he predicted. "But I know you will not be dissuaded. You have risked your life. You have known the face of pain. You deserve your chance as Aldo Gamborelli deserves punishment. All the funds you need are yours. I can have the money for you before I leave tonight."

Marina kissed the thin cheek tenderly. "I will not fail. But there is something else. I would borrow a set of pistols and your finest horse, your best hunter." She saw the frown come over the baron's face. "My father taught me to shoot when I was but a young girl, and I am an excellent shot. I learned to ride with the finest of instructors as I grew up."

"Pistols and my finest hunter. You shall have them." He shook his head in wonder. "Though I confess monumental curiosity."

"Tools for recruitment," was all she would say. He pressed her arm, but did not probe further. Marina spent the remainder of the day finding breeches that fit her, a shirt to go with them, and an extra pair of both. By evening the bags of gold coins and the pistols were ready for her. She saw Vittorio Amati off as he left in his carriage.

"Godspeed, good friend," she called.

"And to you, my child." His eyes were solemn.

She watched the carriage go out of sight, then went to the stables where a groom had a handsome gray hunter with a white blaze saddled and ready. She put the gold coins in the saddlebags, strapped the pistol belt on, and swung atop the horse. Night was lowering itself and that was as she wanted. She'd travel by night and rest by day. She wanted no unexpected meetings with anyone who might carry word to Aldo Gamborelli. She followed her plan, staying at small roadside inns, making her way north along the edge of the Apennines, the roads becoming more familiar as she neared her home. She halted on a ridge that looked down across the land-to where the villa nestled amid the pines and cypresses and waited for dark to come again. While she waited, she used a sharp stick to dig a hole beside the gnarled oak. She buried all but two of the bags of gold coins, covered the hole, and smoothed underbrush over it.

Night had come by the time she finished, and she swung up onto the horse again, riding toward her home. The hunter covered ground quickly with a long, steady stride. Samson, the groom had called him, and it fitted. He had strong hindquarters, good, driving leg muscles, and a deep chest for good wind. She reached the edge of the villa property, halted, and slid from the saddle. Other nights came flooding back upon her, all those dark moments when she'd returned from meeting Gilbert, halting at this very same spot. And the terrible wrong flung itself at her at once like a scar she would never lose. But this night she tied the horse to a low branch and crept forward alone. Her eyes picked out two men with muskets, then, a half-dozen yards further on, two more. Aldo Gamborelli had indeed added guards. She could only hope he had made no other changes.

The stables were still isolated; the guards were protecting the front of the grounds and, undoubtedly, the back. The dogs barked in the kennels as she neared the barn and she heard one of the guards curse them into silence. She halted at the barn door and peered into the flickering lamplight that cast an uncertain glow across the stables. She could see Orion's ears up in the stall at the far end. Then Buffo's huge girth came into view. He was filling a water bucket when she stole up behind him and clapped a hand over his mouth. He turned, and she saw the shock in his voluminous folds of skin as they quivered.

Slowly, she withdrew her hand. "I've come back, Buffo," she said softly. "I think you can guess why."

His eyes stayed round in the fleshy folds of his face. "There were many stories. They said you were killed," he whispered.

"It was tried often enough," Marina answered grimly. "I need your help, Buffo. You know your way among the taverns in Fiuggi. I've heard you go there to gamble." The stableman nodded. "I want you to gather the most murderous cutthroats you can find, as many as you can. Tell them they will earn more than they deserve."

"And then?"

"Tell them to meet me at ten o'clock tomorrow morning, where the two streams cross each other south of the old Roman mill." Marina spoke with authority.

"I'll try," Buffo answered. "But these men, they will be very bad ones, men you should stay away from, *signorina.*"

"Just find them for me and you'll be glad for it one day. Soon, I hope. And, of course, you must say nothing of this to anyone else."

"I understand."

"How is my dear uncle?" Marina hissed in a low tone.

"His temper has become worse. He demands more of the tenant farmers, more of everyone," the stableman answered angrily.

"Find me the men," Marina reiterated grimly, put a finger to her lips, and slipped out of the stable. She ran in a crouch through the darkness, glimpsed the figures at the front of the villa, and disappeared into the trees. She untied the gray hunter, walked him from the area, then mounted to ride to a narrow place between two boulders where she would stay the night. There she lay down and looked up at the star-filled sky. If she succeeded in her first objective, it would be a feat that would have made Generoso proud of her, for he had been a leader of men, a righter of wrongs. He'd have understood the doing of what had to be done. And if she succeeded in her plans for afterward, Paul would be proud of her for he was a shepherd, a believer in the good in all people. But everything hinged on the morning, for Vittorio Amati's misgivings had been far from idle fears. The morning would bring her a different kind of test. She closed her eyes and slept. She'd need all her strengths in the morning.

The new sun slid its way over the boulders to touch her face, and Marina sat up instantly and washed in a little brook nearby. She went to where the big, gray hunter was tethered, lifting each hoof and cleaning it. Using her hands, wet with water from the brook, she brushed his head and neck. Normally she'd let him forage among the fresh, dew-flecked grass, but this morning she allowed him no food. She wanted him wire-sharp and impatient. She rode to where the two streams crossed each other. In the distance, the ruins of the old Roman mill rose above the low trees. She took up a position half hidden between two cedars and watched them come, singly, in pairs, and one group of three, until there were ten in all. Not enough, she observed, but a beginning. Marina spurred the horse forward and confronted the ten men who had sat on their mounts eyeing each other uneasily. Now they turned their eyes on her, and she saw the frowns of surprise and disgust. In most eyes, there was something else: contempt.

For her part, she did not mask her cold appraisal. Buffo had indeed found a thoroughly scurvy lot. One had a hook for a hand, another a nose so flattened it seemed almost not to exist and still another had but one ear—and all bore scars and slashes that had healed into ugly welts. In each pair of eyes she saw cold hatred of the world. These were outcasts, no doubt made so by their own acts. Here were no idealists who had suffered injustice. Here were no seekers of a better world, no believers in the rights of others. She thought of those who had ridden with Generoso, good men driven to desperate means. There were none such in this collection. Here there were only those who had long ago lost all contact with any decent human emotions. But these were exactly the ones she wanted, men who had nothing to lose anymore, who followed but one flag, gold.

One of them, a tall man with a shaved bald pate that glistened in the sun and eyes that were narrow glittering slits, moved his horse a step forward. "Where is the man that wanted us to come here?" he growled. A gold earring hung from each ear, Marina noted.

"*I* wanted you to come here," Marina replied. She saw his head swivel and look at the others. She saw him return his eyes to her and a slow smile curl his lips.

"You want us to take you one at a time or two at once?" he demanded and she heard the harsh murmur run through the others.

"You are as stupid as you are ugly," Marina retorted evenly. His smile vanished and his glittering eyes widened. She saw his arm muscles tense, and as he snapped the reins of his horse to rush at her, the two pistols appeared in her hands and she fired, first one, then the other. The gold earrings exploded in a shatter of yellow and his horse reared up, spilling the man onto the ground. He lay there, his mouth open, one hand touching where the earrings had been.

"I could just as easily have put the bullets into your eyes," Marina said coldly and her glance flicked to the others. In their staring frowns she saw a new respect and smiled inwardly. She reloaded the pistols, put them into her belt, and again raked the others with her eyes. The bald one climbed back onto his horse, shaken.

"Who thinks he can ride?" Marina barked. The men exchanged glances in silent agreement for a moment, then one moved forward. He had a handlebar mustache, bronze eyes, and a red scarf wrapped around a neck the size of a bull. Thick, straight black hair fell loosely around his face. He tried a smile that came out as a grimace.

"I have ridden Hussars into the ground," he shouted. Marina scanned his horse—big, powerful, but heavy-footed, his rear too thick for a good hunter. She gestured down a stretch of ground that bordered the one stream. Stone fences, a hedge, and a long water jump were only part of the terrain. At the far end a sharp turn was followed by a high log fence and more jumps. The other side of the stream was tortuous with tree stumps and rock obstacles.

"Down, turn, and back the other side," Marina challenged him, spearing the man with her eyes. "Win and I am yours." She almost laughed as the mustached cutthroat responded exactly as she'd expected he would: with no nod to fair play, he spurred his horse to a leaping start. She snapped a hand on the gray hunter's rump and he responded, breaking with a smooth, long stride. The other horse was wasting energy digging into the ground too hard, straining before it was time to strain. He was ahead of her, but by the first jump the big gray hunter was stride for stride with him. She held Samson in, watched her adversary take the jump too high, his horse wasting more strength and time. The gray jumper took the obstacle with a minimum of effort—a long, clean leap—and was back on the ground and running before the other horse.

In moments, the next hurdle was cleared and the distance widened. When the sharp turn came up, Marina let Samson take it without pushing and looked back to see the other horse straining, moving too wide, its strength already sapped. Marina returned to the starting place while the other horse still heaved his way over the last few stone hedges. She fixed the man with a cold stare as he came up to her, and she saw resentment tinged with admiration in his eyes. The lessons had made their point and that was enough. She regretted that these cutthroats would not retain the lessons for long. Their attitude toward the next scullery maid they met would be little changed. Yet even a little was a step in the right direction.

"I want you to fight for me and with me," she announced, facing the ten men. "You've seen enough now so you need not be ashamed to follow me. I will offer you more money for one night's work than most of you will see in a half-dozen years."

"What do we have to do for it?" the bald one growled.

"Help me take back my home. There are hired guardsmen there. You will have to defeat them. They will outnumber you, perhaps two or three to one."

"I've done better than that," a bull-like man yelled.

"I can get a few more men," someone else put in.

"Bring them," Marina replied at once. "You will get half your pay now, in gold coins, the rest when the job is done. When it's over, some of you may have no further use for gold. The rest of you will share the difference."

"Fair enough," the bald one grunted and a murmur of agreement ran through the others. Marina took the two sacks she'd brought and paid each man.

"Meet me tonight, an hour after sundown. Bring whatever weapons you would use. I'll tell you the rest then," Marina told them.

"What happens after?" the bald man asked.

"You go your way. I don't want to know your names or see any of you again. It will be a service hired and paid for and done with," Marina said. "You will owe me nothing and I you nothing."

"What if we decide to stay around?" asked the red-scarfed one.

"You will not stay around alive for long," Marina remarked calmly. The men shrugged, then backed their horses.

"Tonight," the bald one asserted, "we will be here." They drifted away single file down a narrow pathway and were soon out of sight. Marina took a deep breath. It had gone off well. They had no scruples, no principles, but they knew an opportunity when they found one. They would do their part. Gold was far more enticing than her thighs to these men. Gold came first. After, there might be another problem. But she had planned for that, too. She wheeled the gray hunter to a patch of good green grass and let him have his fill now. Then she rode to where she had buried the rest of the sacks, dug them up, and returned them to a closer place. She lay between the boulders then and slept until the dusk wind stirred her into waking.

She watched the sun disappear behind the mountain ridges, turned the horse to the meeting place, and was waiting when the others came, once again in groups of two and three. Three new men were brought along, just as unsavory in appearance as the others. They had been told the facts and waited with the rest for her to tell them more.

"The villa is straight down from here," she instructed them. "There will be guards at the front and at the back, perhaps more hidden elsewhere. It will be your task to take them, but if a guard throws down his weapon, he is not to be killed." Marina paused, all too certain that the order would not be obeyed. "We will need that crucial second of surprise to get inside the villa. When I fire one shot, the others outside will automatically turn to the house."

"And we will hit them then." The bald one nodded, thinking ahead. "It ought to be enough to make a difference."

"Let us go," Marina rallied them, starting down the slope of the hill. Clouds obscured most of the moon, but enough light filtered through to allow for marksmanship. At the edge of the trees Marina halted, tying the hunter to a branch. She gestured for the others to do the same. "Some of you go around and circle the property until you are at the back of the house," she ordered, and six of the men vanished into the trees. The bald one stayed with the others. "When you hear my shot," she reminded him and he nodded. Marina walked away through the brush, heading for the stables. Buffo would still be there; the hour was early enough. She hurried through the now-familiar path, staying low and moving like a silent shadow through the stables as Buffo, with eyes wide, watched her pass.

The villa loomed up at the other end of the stables, a short, clear space to cover between house and barns. She bent low, waiting for a cloud to pass over the moon, ran, and reached the side of the villa just as the moon came out from behind its cover. She pressed the door handle and it opened. She stood for a moment inside the great house, feeling almost a stranger, one who was never meant to return. A wedge of yellow light came from the library. She saw Carlos shuffle from the room with an empty tray, then waited till the man disappeared down the corridor. She crept forward then, one hand on the pistol at the right side of her belt. She pulled the gun out as she reached the library. Aldo Gamborelli sat before a map spread out on the library table and sipped coffee from a large mug as he studied the chart. He did not hear her slip into the room, did not know she was there until she spoke.

"I have come back," Marina said, her voice tight. She watched him slowly lift his eyes from the map, the cup of coffee still in his hand, turn, and stare at her. She saw his lips move, the thin-cheeked face seeming to grow thinner. Aldo Gamborelli licked his lips, reined in his astonishment. It was obvious that the cardinal had sent no word of her escape from his dungeon.

"You are as difficult to be rid of as a weed," he remarked.

"I have come back for my home and to see you pay for all you've done." Marina's voice was as cold as winter's sky. She saw the colorless eyes dip to the pistol in her hand, his calm unable to mask the nervousness inside him.

"You might kill me with that. I remember you were something of a marksman," he observed. "But you must have seen the guards outside. Or is this to be a last dramatic gesture on your part, a kind of suicide?"

"I'm not here for dramatic gestures. I'm here to see you hanged or rot in a cell," Marina flung at him. "You don't think I'd be such a fool as to come here alone, do you?"

His eyes studied her for a long moment in pale appraisal. "No, probably not. What do you want of me now?"

"Tell your guards to put down their weapons, and no one need be hurt," Marina commanded. She watched Aldo Gamborelli incline his head to one side in thought.

"Probably the best choice open to me." He raised the mug of coffee to her in a mock salute. "I underestimated you. We all did." He started to bring the mug to his lips and Marina's finger relaxed on the pistol. His move took but a snap of the wrist, too fast to follow, and the hot coffee struck her in the face, sharp, searing, and stinging her eyes. Marina's reaction was reflexive. A short gasp and her eyes snapped shut, her hand flying to her burning cheekbones. She did not see the looping blow from his fist that smashed into her temple. She fell backward, but now her finger squeezed the trigger, the shot exploding in the room as though it were a cannon. She was on the floor, forcing her burning eyes open, seeing only shadowy forms, but she fired again, this time the other pistol, aiming in the general direction of the table. But Aldo Gamborelli had not come after her. As the night exploded with gunfire, he dived through the library window, rolled out onto the terrace, regained his feet, and raced from the villa. He ran, bent over, to the stables. Behind him, the noise of a pitched battle filled the night.

Marina rubbed her eyes on her sleeve, blinking furiously, and cleared one enough to see that she was alone. The room took shape, then became fuzzy again. She shook her head, regaining vision enough to see a water pitcher. Her face and her left eye burned with sharp waves of pain. She put her head back, poured the water into her eyes, felt the cool, soothing touch of it, and rubbed her face dry. She could see, though her left eye still pained her. Shouts and curses, punctuated by pistol fire and the sound of cutlasses smashing against each other, echoed from outside. But Aldo Gamborelli had fled. He was not taking part in the battle. He had used the moment to get away, and she felt fury and dejection wrestle inside her. She stepped to the broken window, saw the bullnecked man leap onto the terrace with a long-bladed knife stained with red. Two more of the band she had assembled followed him.

A few shots echoed, but the aftermath of stillness began to take over the dark. Marina saw the inert bodies on the grass of the front lawn. The bald-headed cutthroat appeared. Three more came behind him. The moment of surprise had spelled victory. The guards had been cut down, the odds more than evened in the first few moments. Marina retreated into the library. In but a few minutes eight of the band assembled before her. She did not ask about the others. There was no need to.

"It's done," the bald one barked. "You'll need a flock of grave-diggers in the morning. Now where's the rest of the gold? We're not for hanging about here."

"Give me fifteen minutes. Then come to the stables," Marina shouted. "You'll each get your share and a part of the difference I promised you."

The man nodded for the rest, but she could see the thoughts already starting to gather behind his cold eyes. Marina ran to the stables and called Buffo out from where he was hiding in the hay bin. The other servants were no doubt still cowering in their rooms. "It's over," she told the stableman. "Wait here until I return. I'll want your help."

She ran to where the gray hunter was tied, leaped into the saddle, and galloped to where she'd hidden the remaining sacks of gold. She was back at the stable before the time was out, and entering the last stall at the right, empty except for a bridle hanging on the wood side, she ordered, "Send them in one by one as they come, Buffo. Hold their horses until they come out."

Marina heard the murmur of voices approaching, stepped to the back of the empty stall, and readied everything she'd need. The bald-headed one was first, and he stepped into the stall with arrogance. She portioned his gold out and he put it into a small leather pouch.

"Now throw your weapons down," Marina said, and she saw him glance up in surprise at the pistol pointed at him. "Everything," she said crisply. "This will insure that you do not entertain the idea of coming back later tonight."

The man glowered at her as he threw two pistols and a long-bladed machette at her feet. "The knives, too," Marina said. Tight-lipped, he reached inside his shirt and brought out two deer knives and dropped them at her feet.

"These things cost money," he protested.

"You have enough gold to buy an arsenal now. Our business is finished." He walked from the stable and she kicked the weapons behind her. The next one came in, received his payment, and also stared into the barrel of the pistol. He left a pistol, a dagger and a garrote. The scene was repeated with each until the last one walked from the barn, mounted his horse, and rode into the night. "Put these things in a sack, please," she told Buffo. "Then throw the sack in the garbage pile. We've had enough of guns here."

Marina turned and stared out at the scene of carnage. "Go to town in the morning," she ordered the stableman. "Bring back the gravedigger's wagon." The stableman nodded, his eyes still mirroring fright. Marina left him and return to the house. She found Carlos and Pietro, Anna, the chambermaid, and the young boy who worked in the kitchen all huddled in the foyer. Their eyes grew round as she entered.

"The villa is mine now, at last," Marina comforted them. "All the things you heard were wrong, as you can see. Go back to bed, all of you. I will explain more in the morning." She saw something beyond confusion and fright in their eyes. She saw the fear of tomorrow forming there, and she summoned a tired smile of reassurance. "Everything will be all right," she told them. "This will be a good place to live and to work in again, I promise you." She turned, began to climb the stairs to her room. Her face still burned and her left eye stung, but her vision was unimpaired. She'd been lucky. She opened the door to her room, halting in shock. The moon let in enough light through the open window for her to see that the room had been stripped bare of her things. Only the bed remained, one sheet piled atop it. Her glance went to the walls. The portrait of her father and mother still hung there, and Marina stepped into the room, a feeling of having been violated sweeping over her. Aldo Gamborelli had been confident he'd not see her again.

Marina stood before the portrait, seeing it as if it were in bright day. "I am home." She spoke softly. "I have kept yesterday's promises. Now I must keep tomorrow's." She turned to the bed, exhaustion pulling at her, and undressed quickly. Repayment and fulfillment, she echoed silently. The first was easier than the second. She lay down and slept at once.

CHAPTER THIRTEEN

M ARINA TURNED FROM THE WINDOW. The high-sided, closed, black wagon waited for the last of its silent passengers and the men who were finishing their sorry task. She felt sick, fought away a wave of nausea. Aldo Gamborelli could have saved all those lives by simply ordering a surrender, but other people's lives had never been a concern to him. He would keep running, she felt certain. He undoubtedly had funds hidden away in the banks of Naples and he would know that things had gone awry. He'd not bother to pursue details now. Flight and self-preservation would come first. But she made a tight-lipped promise to herself. When it was finally done with, when all the others were imprisoned, she'd see that Aldo Gamborelli stayed a wanted fugitive in the Kingdom of Naples and Lazio, and perhaps one day others would accord him the punishment he deserved.

Marina dressed, went downstairs, and assembled everyone in the household, mostly men and women she had known from childhood. The tension disappeared in the joys of reunion—a reunion of sorts, however. She was no longer a child, no longer a ward of Aldo Gamborelli. Now she was a young woman, mistress of Villa Valerian and all its lands. The distinction did not dilute welcome nor intrude on joy and fond memories; yet it was a quiet presence of its own, recognized by everyone. The winds of change were shifting over the world. They would come slowly, she knew, but here, where Gamborelli had held sway, they would come faster, Marina vowed.

She addressed all who gathered before her, particularly Carlos and Pietro. "I want you to take word to each of the tenant farmers and to each man who has land that the count holds a lien upon. Ask them to come here to the villa in the morning. Tell them they may bring their families if they like, for what I have to say will bear on everyone." She paused, letting her glance take in all the others, most of whom had been here when her parents lived. "The rest of you will go on with your work as always. If you are dissatisfied with something, come to me. I can't promise miracles, not even the ability to change things terribly much. But I can promise to try."

She ended the gathering then, saw that the joy at her return was genuine, and felt warm inside for it. With the help of Anna, the housekeeper, and one of the part-time hands, she found all the things that had been in her room in the cellar, had everything returned, spent the day and into the night polishing her dresser, then finally fell into bed to sleep.

The tenant farmers gathered in front of the house with the early day. Many brought their wives and children. She had known them only as faces, a few a little better, and some, who had worked land held by the count, not at all. By now all had heard that Aldo Gamborelli had fled.

"To those of you who work on lands he held title to, I cannot say what stand the law will take," she began when everyone had arrived. "But I will do everything to see that his holdings are taken from him and the lands become yours free and clear." She heard the murmur of surprise and listened to it turn to hope. "Bravo," someone said.

"Now, those who farm the lands owned by the Villa Valerian have paid a levy each month. The count has increased it with regularity, demanding more and more. I have not had time to go over the ledgers, but I know he used the monies for himself. From now on, the profits of the produce you raise and is sold in the market will not go just to the villa. You will share in those profits. This will be a place of sharing instead of taking, of justice instead of oppression."

There was so much more she wanted to say but did not. The time was not ready for those things. Her eyes moved across the faces of the women who stood before her, the younger girls with their tomorrows still waiting, the older women who were living out their yesterdays. It was the young eyes that held her. Their lives would still be arranged for them, their feelings still ignored more than respected. But a start had been made. A chance at savoring self-respect was being given their men, a chance to enjoy personal dignity. In time, it would touch them, Marina told herself.

She saw a man with a browned, sun-dried face and a weathered, wide-brimmed hat held in his hands step forward. "It is good, *signorina*. Your words make us happy. We were about to go to the Camorrists for help."

"The Camorrists?" Marina frowned. "But they were destroyed." She felt the words catch in her throat but she forced them out. "The Red Camorra is no more."

"Yes, we know that, too. But they ride again, north of here, in the Abruzzi. There is one who calls himself the Red Camorra again, we are told. We were going to send someone to them and ask them to come here to help us," the farmer told her. "It is said they are stronger than ever now."

Someone called himself the Red Camorra. She felt fury at once. The imposter, she bit out silently. He would be like a child trying to fill a giant's shoes. It was a kind of blasphemy. She heard the farmer's voice again.

"We have no need for that now, thanks to your words, *signorina*. God bless you." She heard the murmur of agreement. She acknowledged the appreciation with a quick nod and turned away as the men began to leave for their lands. The resentment in her held with a viselike grip. There always had been other bands of Camorrists, she'd known, but in Sicily—one in

Emilia and as far north as the Piedmont. But a new band here in Lazio—it was a kind of travesty, a soiling of something that had been rare. The Red Camorra she had known in every way had been no ordinary leader, no ordinary man. Imposter, she repeated again, and hated him for his presumptuous arrogance, whoever he was.

She went into the kitchen where the coffee kettle was boiling and drank two cups of the black brew as strong as she could stand it. The farmer's words about the Camorrists had brought yesterday crashing back upon her. Damn him, why hadn't he kept silent about it? It was not a thing of forgetting. Generoso della Passione was a part of her for always. It was a thing of fire made to burn again. She pressed her eyes closed. She had to find Paul. There was still a hope for happiness alive someplace. She had to find it, to know, and most of all, to stand before him and tell him she had learned more of those inner pains he had held to himself. With hope and work she might arrive at some sanity and peace of mind.

The ledgers of Villa Valerian were a masterpiece of double entries and figures used to deceive. Marina plunged herself into unraveling their lies and to establishing a fair share of profits for the tenant farmers. Word of her return had spread in the bordering regions, and Marina instructed everyone in the villa to ask about Paul Davore when they went to the neighboring villages. She had them inquire of travelers passing through, to listen, look, and pursue every hopeful bit of information.

But there was no word. Paul had vanished as though the earth had swallowed him up. Of course, her inquiries covered only the regions nearby, such a small part of the many provinces that stretched from Sicily to the Alps. It was a futile task and a depressing prospect. But each night as she let her eyes close, having made certain that by the day's end she'd be exhausted, she murmured three words into the dark, sweet echoes of other times: "Hurry back, Paul."

Aldo Gamborelli had been going to flee to Tuscany, when he halted. Cold anger seethed inside him, but something more had made him halt. Self-preservation could not be bought if he were a man with a price on his head. The authorities had ways of cooperating with each other. A few thousand coins bought anyone's head anywhere, and that high-born bitch would gladly spend the money for his head. No, there was no flight. There was only the preservation of his peace of mind, his life, and his future. He turned from the roads to Tuscany and appeared at the *palazzo* of the Duke d'Albatore.

The duke, his fat little face sagging like a punctured balloon, had been astonished to see him. "It pleases me to see that you are as surprised as I," the count had said as he told what had happened. The round body of the duke found a chair and collapsed into it.

"The cardinal was certain he'd find her after she escaped," he said. "He never sent – word to me that he hadn't. I saw no reason to tell you anything."

Aldo Gamborelli's thin lips became a slit across his face. "Perhaps the good cardinal still thinks his pigeon is hiding in the caves of Rome. If so, he is a fool. More likely, he knows full well that she has outfoxed him and gotten away, and he does not know what can be done about it. Perhaps he is waiting to hear of her somewhere."

"He should have sent word to me." The little man glowered.

Aldo Gamborelli looked disgusted. "He is not thinking about you, nor of me. He is thinking of how to mend his own fences in case she turns up," he said. "The cardinal is thinking of himself. That is why we must do the same." The duke's glower changed to sharp-eyed interest. "She must be silenced. I know where she is.

No doubt she has already sent others to Rome with indictments against the good cardinal. The Church has its own trials, its ways of moving against its own. But if she is dead once and for all she'll have no more words to use against us. No accuser, no crimes."

He saw the duke's eyes take on agreement but the questions remained. "And our plans? All we have paid for and put into motion?"

"A shift of objectives," Aldo Gamborelli replied. "We will not attack Calabria—not now at least. We will use our forces to level the Villa Valerian first—kill her and everyone there so no one will be left to tell tales. It is the only way."

The little man nodded agreement. "Yes, she must be finished once and for all," he said in his nasal whine.

"The first of our forces have landed, have they not?" the count asked. "According to the timetable they should be on their way to Campobasso."

"Yes. They landed at Vasta. We are to meet them at Campobasso next week. They are moving inland in sections by wagon, as was planned, to avoid alarm and curiosity," the duke informed him.

Aldo Gamborelli mentally reviewed the arrangements that had been made up to this time. Troops, mercenaries from across the Adriatic—Croatians, Serbs, Slavs, Bosnians—had been recruited and paid. But the revolution in France had been an unexpected snag. The French general, Napoleon, had close ties with the Yugoslavs and the arrangements for mercenaries had met a sudden reluctance on the part of the Yugoslav officials. They wanted to wait to see what direction the revolution would take. Certainly they wished to do nothing to alienate Napoleon, whose star was rising like a rocket. But the first contingent of mercenaries had been commited and were on their way across the Adriatic. They would be more than enough to seize the villa, level it, and establish a new regime in the region.

"We'll be at Campobasso next week," he said to the duke. "There we'll sit down with their field commanders and map out an attack upon the villa. This time there must be no one left alive, no one fleeing."

"Has she a force there?" the duke inquired.

"She had a band of cutthroats. She may acquire more." He snorted a hard, angry sound. "They will be no match for our force. And this time the surprise will be mine. She will be sure that I've fled as far away as possible."

"Agreed. It is the only way," the little man whined. "While she lives, we are doomed." He looked out at the countryside. "It should not be hard to do. I only hope I can have a chance at her myself."

"After me," Aldo Gamborelli responded quietly.

Marina Valerian ate slowly, not really hungry. She was never really hungry anymore. She ate because it was necessary to keep up one's strength. She was never really anything but lonely, filled with wanting. She wondered if she ought to go away for a while. Affairs had been put into order at the villa and the new arrangements set up. It was as good a time as any, before the fall harvest time came. Her full and proper title to the land and the villa had been cleared by the land office in Naples. Perhaps she would search in other places for Paul. Each day she found herself wondering more and more if he were well, what he was doing, how he was meeting the world. Did he sit alone somewhere, disconsolate, eaten with a guilt he did not deserve? Was he laboring in a mine in Lombardy, trying to exhaust memory—the body exhausting the soul?

She took the letter from the folds of the long skirt she wore as she dined alone. It had come that day, from Vittorio Amati in Rome. He had met with high officials in the church and certain select people in the government. They believed him but they felt even more than her testimony was needed. She read his lines again:

New and concrete moves have been made by the plotters. Those here feel it would be best to wait until those new plans are translated into action. Then the evidence would be absolute—your testimony and the very acts themselves. We have heard that arrangements for foreign mercenaries have been made. Their appearance will be the final nail in the coffin. Those I've spoken to here in the highest of offices want no chance for the cardinal and the others to wriggle free. So we wait, just a little longer. Do not lose hope, my dear. The trap will close soon enough. Scarti is busy trying to position himself for a defense. He senses danger. We must move carefully, have everything we can in our hands. Payment will be coming soon, never fear.

Marina put the letter away. Payment would come soon enough, she repeated silently. And fulfillment? A promise for tomorrow—would that come too? She closed her eyes, fought away another of the waves of despair that came more and more often. She heard Carlos enter the room, and she looked up.

"Someone to see you, *signorina*," he announced. "One of the farmers who works a piece of land the count owns."

Marina looked past Carlos and saw the man, a small, wiry figure in thick boots and work clothes, waiting. "Please come in," she said. The man approached slowly, then more confidently as her smile welcomed him.

"There is talk," he began. "I thought I should tell you."

"What kind of talk?" Marina asked.

"There is talk that the Duke d'Albatore is going to come with an army. There is even talk that Count Gamborelli is with him."

Marina rose, frowning. "Where does this talk come from?" she asked.

"A man who worked for the duke stopped at the village. He was on his way somewhere. Too much wine loosened his tongue," the farmer replied. "My friend, Genovese, he heard it, too, from someone else, but he paid no mind to it."

Marina's lips grew tight. Small half-truths easily became wild exaggerations. Yet this man was no backyard gossip monger, no fishwife. He was afraid of what he had heard and suddenly she felt fear digging into her. It was all too possible. Aldo Gamborelli could well have fled to his fellow conspirator.

"This army," she asked. "Do you know more about it?"

"Only what the man said over his wine cup," the farmer answered.

"Did he use the word 'army'?" Marina questioned. The farmer shrugged. "I do not remember. He said there would be many."

The letter blazed in her pocket. "Arrangements for foreign mercenaries have been made." It fitted all too well. Aldo Gamborelli would be happy to use his mercenaries to destroy her first. "What is your name?" she asked the farmer.

"Luigi Maldano."

"Thank you, Luigi. I am most grateful to you. I must think more about this."

The wiry figure bowed low, the gesture not at all incongruous despite the heavy work boots, and as he left Marina turned to the window to stare out at the night. If there was indeed a sizable force of trained mercenaries, they would be on their way. Not even the band of cutthroats she'd once raised could stand against such a force. She would need not ten men but fifty or a hundred. She would do as well to try to move the mountains to protect her. There was no way she could raise such a force. She did not even know how much time was left her. She heard a sound behind her, turned to see Carlos by the table. He had started to clear away the dishes but now stood with his eyes on her.

"I could not help overhearing, *signorina*." He hesitated, words held back, obviously aware of what she'd been thinking.

"Go on," Marina prodded.

He tightened his lips, then blurted out the two words: "The Camorrists."

"No." Marina heard herself almost shout the word. No, she repeated silently and angrily. How much was she expected to stand? Was she to twist a sword inside herself? Was she to drench herself in the pain of memories, resurrect anguish? No, it was too much. She looked angrily at Carlos.

"If it is true, it will mean all our lives," he said simply. It was a statement of fact, a gentle reminder, and its quiet truth speared through her, telling her that she was not alone. If she fled, she would leave everyone at the mercy of Aldo Gamborelli, a man without mercy of any kind. And if she stayed, her fate would be shared by everyone else. They'd not flee and leave her. They had too much strength for that. The Camorrists—whoever they now were, they held the only hope.

"Go after the farmer. Fetch him back," she called to Carlos. "He can't be far." The butler put down the dish and ran from the room. Marina closed her eyes and gripped the back of the chair. The pain was already flooding back over her, past moments rushing forward to offer themselves as gifts she did not want. She would see this Camorrist leader and see only Generoso's face before her. She would see this follower in a giant's footsteps and see only herself in Generoso's arms. Pain upon pain, everything a reminder of happiness torn from her, by hate, by love, by men, by ideals.

She heard Carlos return, and the farmer was with him. "I'll change and go with you," she told the man, her eyes staring past him. She could do nothing else. Too many others were touched by the shadows that followed her. Marina hurried to her room, changed into riding clothes, and put a fresh outfit into a pack roll to take with her. If these Camorrists held any hope, she might well have to stay to make plans with them. In the stable she chose the gray hunter Vittorio Amati had given her. She could not bring herself to take Orion, on whom she'd so often gone to meet Generoso. The farmer had a plow horse he'd ridden, and the trip back to his land was slow.

"I do not know the way to the Camorrists," he told her. "They are in the foothills north of here. I will get the man who knows the way, a mountain shepherd." Marina waited, staying outside the farmer's house, gathering hold of her turbulent emotions. When the man returned, the mountain shepherd turned out to be a young boy, quiet and shy. He rode a long-maned pony and she set off with him at once, grateful for his shyness. She did not want to talk, and it was not until they were deep in the foothills, hours from where they'd left, that he spoke to her.

"It is late," he remarked. "But they will be up. They meet with others through the night, when no one can watch and follow." He led her down a narrow passageway. And as the moon touched the tops of the trees Marina saw crumbled walls of a building, a tall, narrow structure that had once been a bell tower. A flickering flame from open fires sent shadows up the stones and Marina gave a sigh of relief. At least there were no caves here, which meant at least one memory would be avoided. The young boy entered a clearing, and as she followed him in she saw men with muskets in hand watching.

"I have brought someone who comes to ask help," he explained. "Luigi Maldano had spoken for her."

A burly man with a cartridge belt turned away as Marina swung down from the saddle, then he disappeared into the ruins of the old bell tower. He appeared a moment later, another figure emerging behind him. She watched the second man come toward her and then suddenly halt, almost as though he'd been struck. She saw a black camorra, a boyish face, light brown hair that fell carelessly over his forehead, and soft hazel eyes that held shock in their depths. She saw the face before her lose color, stare at her with parted lips, and she heard the cry tear from her throat. *"Paul!"*

She flung herself at the slender figure as the cry still hung in the air. "Oh, Paul, Paul, my darling. It's me. The word they sent out was wrong. They'd thought they killed me."

His hand lifted her face to his and his eyes stared down at her in disbelief. "My God, Oh, my Marina," he breathed, his voice no more than a whisper. She raised up on her toes, pressed her mouth over his, and held there until finally he pulled back, his eyes still shadowed with disbelief.

"When I came back, I was given the letter you'd left. I tried to find you, to tell you that I understood so much more than when I'd left. I wanted to find you so desperately, my darling. I was so afraid you'd do something terrible."

A wry smile came to his lips. "Perhaps I have. I'm not sure of that, yet." He stepped back, and Marina became aware of the others watching. "Send the boy back." Marina did so and then Paul took her hand and led her into the ruins of the old bell tower where a small fire glowed inside a circle of stones and a blanket lay nearby. He gestured to the tower walls. "This was once a monastery. Appropriate for my hideaway, isn't it?" She caught the hint of bitterness in his voice.

"Paul, my darling. I'm the one who carries guilt." Her hands pressed against his chest. "If your faith weakened, if you broke vows, I am to blame. I cared about nothing but my own wanting you, and that was wrong. You left the priesthood because of me and that is my guilt."

His hands cupped her face. "No, Marina. I left because of what I found out about myself. Had I been truly called, I would have been strong enough to deny you. But I did not. I was too weak."

She put her hand to his lips. "No, don't say that. You held back. Your strength was real."

"No, my denial was forced. It was of the body and that is unimportant. It was not of the spirit. When I learned you were dead, I knew I lacked the strength to go on. I ran, to wrestle with myself, but I found that all I wanted to do was to strike back for you. Don't you see, my darling? Had I been strong enough, had I been truly chosen, I would have found the strength to go on. Only the very strong can fight evil with love. Only the strong do not break vows. Only the strong do not deny one love for another."

She put her head against his chest. "Paul, Paul, my darling. I almost did not come here. I almost refused to come here for help." He frowned down at her. "Things have happened too recently to talk about them," she explained. She hugged him to her. "But I am glad I came. Oh, my darling, how glad, how very glad."

He sat down and pulled her near the fire as the night wind blew. "How did you come here to the Camorrists?" she asked.

"I wandered, seeking, questioning myself, and I heard of those who struck back for others, who tried to keep the scales of justice from being entirely unbalanced. I wanted to strike back for you, and I asked to join these who fight for others," Paul replied. "But what brought you seeking the Camorrists, Marina?"

She told him quickly, only the important things that pressed toward a final hour, and as he listened, his face grew grave. The black camorra, buttoned close to the top, looked almost like an open cassock in the half-light, Marina noted musingly. When she finished, his face had set in a tight line.

"This demands answers I cannot give," he responded. "This is a field command. I lead one of our bands, but I fight under a real leader. His headquarters are north, deeper into the mountains. It is too long and difficult by night. We will go in the morning."

Marina pressed herself against the slender body. "How unexpectedly we find pain and how unexpectedly we find happiness." She glowed. He rose, pulling the blanket to one side and arranging it for her as she watched. Conscious of the question in her eyes, he looked down at her finally.

"It is too open here. Others would know, others would see. I do not want that. I do not want you to be another girl who wanders in here. Tomorrow night, at the headquarters in the mountains, we can be alone."

She kissed him quickly. His sensitivity was a gift, and wrong to deny. It was part of what made him what he was. But she could not prevent the question that arose of itself. "Have there been many girls who wandered in?" she asked. She tried to sound casual but knew she failed.

"None, my Marina, none." He touched his lips to her forehead. "None that have come into my arms." He pressed her backward gently; and she lay upon the blanket, loosened her clothes, and wrapped the blanket around herself. Paul curled up against the other wall. Small echoes of the little cottage, and she smiled to herself. For the first night in countless nights she did not call softly into the dark. She did not say, "Hurry back, Paul." There was no need anymore. He was there, across from her, a different kind of Father Paul, a Camorrist Father Paul. Indeed, there were many kinds of healers.

CHAPTER FOURTEEN

THE MOUNTAINS WERE STEEP, rugged, and heavy with scraggly brush and mountain pines. Paul rode behind her through the narrow passages, and beside her whenever the trail widened and the others followed. In the daylight it became obvious why Paul journeyed to the Camorrist headquarters. His band numbered not more than twenty, and those who came for Aldo Gamborelli would be many times that. As the trail rose up sharply along a narrow path, Paul called to her. "Only a little further." He came up beside her as the path widened and began to level. Marina saw the mountain passage draw apart and glimpsed low-roofed houses gleaming in the sun and set against the rocks behind them.

"A group of mystics once tried to build a community here in the mountains," Paul told her. "They failed, but they left these few houses. Behind the houses there are caves for horses and equipment, food, and supplies. It is a protected place. Bands can be supplied and sent in all directions from it."

He reined up, swung from the saddle, and helped Marina down. He took her arm and moved toward the center house, a boxlike dwelling with narrow windows. Behind it the mouth of a huge cave opened as if to swallow it. Marina caught her breath for an instant as she remembered other caves, other hidden-away places. She forced away thoughts that tried to take hold of her and hurried into the house with Paul. A large room greeted her; there was a rug on the floor, cushions and pillows in careless profusion atop it, and sacks of grain in one corner. A man bent over a table in the center of the room, partly obscured by Paul's figure in front of her.

"I have brought someone who needs our help," Paul announced. He stepped aside and Marina saw the man straighten and look at her. She saw the red camorra first, felt resentment flare at once, then lifted her eyes to his face. The world burst apart, spun crazily. Yesterday had leaped out of its place. She stood transfixed, unable to look away from the olive-black eyes, the thick, curly black hair, and the sun-bronzed skin—the intense, vibrant face she could not be seeing and yet was there before her. She felt herself move forward and saw the strong, broad-chested figure come from behind the table, the olive-black eyes burning with dark fire.

"I am dreaming," she heard herself gasp. "Dreaming."

"And I, too, then," she heard the voice answer. It was not a voice out of dreams but right there in front of her.

"My God. Oh, God. *Generoso!*" She felt the powerful arms gather her in, the voice call her name.

"Marina!" Lips found her mouth, lips she had never thought to know again, taste again, cling to again. Her hands pressed into the sides of his face, up into the thick, curly black hair. The impossible had become real. She had been born again. She was in the arms of her Generoso, and his voice whispered into her ear. "Marina, my Marina. It is you, really you."

She was afraid to move, afraid to think, wanting to do nothing that would shatter the moment, perhaps send it spinning away to leave but a wild dream. But his face against hers was no dream, his lips touching her ear was a delicious remembrance, and the vibrant electricity that was Generoso della Passione coursed through her. It was as if she had never left those arms that held her tight, as though nothing had happened since last she had pressed herself against him. Born again, she repeated silently, born again. It was as always, yet the world renewed; there was too much to sort out, her questions were too enveloping. Not now, not yet. It was, it existed, and that was enough, rising above explanations, reasons, reality, consuming all else. *Consuming all else.* The words repeated inside her and suddenly they were ice showering down upon her. Suddenly she was cold, seized with a terrible dawning. She pulled from the arms that held her and spun around.

"Paul?" she cried out. She cast her eyes about wildly, as a frightened fawn casts its eyes in sudden panic. But her cry echoed in the stillness of the room. Paul was not there. She returned her glance to Generoso and saw that his face had grown still with that throbbing quiet she remembered so well. He had seen everything in the moment of wild panic in her eyes.

"So you were the one," he said softly. She looked at him in helplessness and with unuttered questions in her eyes.

"He told me about himself when he came here," Generoso went on quietly, his intense, strong face solemn. "But he mentioned no names."

"I must go to him," Marina murmured, looking to the door, yet not moving. Generoso's hand closed around her arm, turned her to face him.

"You loved him once. You told him so," Generoso probed.

"Yes. I did."

"And do you love him now?"

Marina felt the wild panic sweep over her again. "Yes. That is, I thought I did. I don't know now. I don't know anything now." Her words were as confused as her feelings. "Why didn't you ever come to find me?" she demanded, falling back on unreasoning accusation. "What happened?"

"I, too, heard you had been killed," Generoso related. "That afternoon, Tonio managed to drag me to a ravine. We fell down it together, into a hidden river. I was more dead than alive. The water helped to cleanse my wounds and keep infection away. I was found, kept alive, and finally nursed back to health. It was months before I could walk alone." He put his hand under her chin and raised her face to his. "When I recovered, I could not go back to the mountains where I met you. The pain was too great, so I came here, far enough away to be able to live with only the shadow of pain. I've never really learned to walk alone. You have always been there."

"Do you think I have forgotten?" Marina asked. "Before Paul there was only emptiness and pain. With Paul, I found the strength to go on, to live again. Don't you remember your words to me that last moment?"

His hand touched her face, gently yet with vibrant strength. "Yes, I remember. I remember well." His olive-black eyes narrowed and grew almost stern. "And now, Marina? What of now?"

Panic engulfed her. "I don't know. I don't know anything. Except that I've got to go to Paul now."

"Yes." Generoso nodded solemnly. "Go. Find him." She fled this time, half running from the house. In the sunlight outside she halted, blinked, and glanced around the area. A log fire heated a kettle, and she smelled strong coffee. One of the men she'd ridden behind caught her eye, and he nodded to a pathway between two pines. Marina hurried into it and followed it until it ended at a thicket where Paul sat upon a fallen log, turning as she came up to him. He smiled, a rueful, slow smile.

"Are you all right?" he asked and she pulled him to her breasts and held him tight, feeling the wetness stain her cheeks.

"Only you would ask that." she murmured. "Only you."

He lifted his head, pulled back from her, and his eyes were soft, the rueful smile in their compassion. "That love you said would always be a part of you," he reflected aloud. "It is easy to understand now."

"I did not lie to you, Paul."

"I know," he answered. He looked away, speaking aloud but more to himself than to her. "You know, when I first came, when I first rode with him, he saved my life twice. Others here can tell you much the same thing. He gives strength. He can make others do more than they realize they can do. That is a special gift. You are not the only one here who loves him—not in your way, but in another way."

"I know," Marina answered, holding her eyes on Paul's boyish face, on his eyes so filled with patience. She did love him—his kindness, his compassion, his inner wisdom, his caring heart. She did love him, but instantly, almost in mockery, the olive-black eyes danced before her, the intense electricity of Generoso spearing into her, and she knew nothing else. She heard the cry that tore from her lips as she leaped to her feet, half running, half stumbling along the narrow path, halting only when she reached the center of the mountain retreat.

A man approached her. "Generoso asked me to take you to where you will stay." She followed him in silence. The house was smaller than the others, at the far end of the semicircle of the boxlike houses. A mattress lay against one wall, neatly covered with a white sheet. Pillows, cushions, and a blanket lay nearby, and two unlighted candles rested atop the fireplace mantel. Marina sank down onto one of the cushions and felt terribly tired. No, not simply tired but buffeted by events too much for her to accommodate. Twice within twenty-four hours she had known happiness she never thought to know again. Twice the world had exploded all around, showering total joy upon her, and all she could feel was a hollow, helpless anguish. Twice blessed, and twice condemned?

Marina lay back upon the cushions. You cannot have two loves. The words returned to stab her, yet surely that was precisely what she had. The letter rose up before her again. To serve two masters is to fail each a little. To have two loves is to deny each a little. Marina felt the sharp pain in the pit of her stomach. She would not deny anything to either. And she would not bring pain to either, but she had already done that. She wanted to tell herself it was not so, but the lie would not hold. She'd seen that pain already. In the understanding in Paul's eyes there was a terrible sadness and in the explosion of Generoso's joy a searing wisdom.

Marina turned on her side, pressing her face against the cushion. One thing was suddenly crystal clear, cutting through all else as lightning cuts through the night sky. It was not a decision, not something reasoned out and concluded. It came from inside her, a knowing that was more than wisdom. She would not bring pain to both. She would not be a destroyer. She would have to find what to deny, as Paul had once faced that choice. She cut off the thought that intruded, refused to listen to it, yet she could do nothing less. To choose, to deny, to know yourself—those took strength. Did she have that kind of strength? Now that she held happiness in front of her, did she have the strength to deny any part of it? Marina felt fear inside her, closed her eyes, and forced herself to nap, her body still tired from the few hours of sleep during the night. No more questions, she told herself, not now, not so soon.

When she woke, the sun had passed the noon hour and she went outside. Two young men by a fire tended small pieces of lamb. They put some on a stick and offered it to her. She ate gratefully, hungrier than she'd realized. She'd finished when she saw the slender figure come toward her, take her hand, and draw her inside the little house. Paul's fingers touched her face delicately, his sensitivity a tactile thing. His lips found hers in sweet tenderness, and she clung to him as a leaf clings to a stone. She did love him, she murmured silently. With Paul she was content and warm. He moved back finally, his lips reluctant to part.

"I know the terrible pain you will have inside you," he said. "I've no wisdom to give you, my darling. I would say but one thing. I know no finer man than Generoso della Passione."

Marina felt the warmth rush from her to encompass him. "How can I not love you?" she breathed, pulling his head down to hers and standing with him in quietness. When he stepped back finally, her question was mirrored in his eyes, but his small, wry smile held its own wisdom.

"Generoso waits to see you," he told her, then hurried from the house. He was nowhere in sight when she stepped outside and a moment later she crossed to the center building and entered the big room that was most of the structure. She gasped and a shudder shook her body as Generoso, with the ruby-red camorra hanging open, turned to greet her. She felt herself almost run to him. His arms caught her and held her, as his black eyes probed into her. His lips on hers did not linger, but she was aflame in that brief instant, and it was he who finally pulled back. She pressed herself against him and clung to him as a pin clings to a magnet. She heard her words, wanted to halt them, yet could no more do so than she could halt the passage of the sun.

She was born again in his arms—the truth undeniable—and all yesterday came alive again. In Generoso's arms she knew nothing else. Her own weakness, she told herself bitterly as he stepped back and she heard his words, watching his dark-fire eyes glow with intenseness.

"I know your question. But only you can answer it," he said. "Paul is a special person, a rare person. He understands the meaning of life. He seeks *why* where others only seek *how.* Such people are well acquainted with pain."

"And I should add no more, is that it?" Marina asked. Generoso smiled as he shrugged. "And what of your pain?" she pressed. His hand encircled the back of her neck and drew her against his bronzed smoothness.

"Different," he murmured. "Different." She held herself against him, not bothering to halt the trembling of her body and feeling the wanting, demanding, thirsting, crawl over her. But he stepped away.

"One thing has been decided," he said crisply. "Paul told me why you came to the Camorrists. We will act at once on that. The world does not stop for inner anguish. Evil keeps on, calls no holidays, leaves no time for meditation." Generoso frowned. "I have sent dispatch riders out to the three separate bands of Camorrists. They will come back with all the men we can muster. Then we shall plan how to put an end to Aldo Gamborelli and his friends once and for all."

"From word that came to me, they must be ready to march on the villa by now. How long will it take your men to get here with the others?" Marina asked.

"Two days," Generoso estimated. "But we will not be late for your friends. I promise you." He touched her hair, pressing his hand over it. "Now go, ask one of the men outside, they will find tasks for you," he ordered gruffly. She reached up, kissed his cheek, and hurried out.

She was put to storing grain in wooden buckets from the sacks. She felt a figure staring at her and turned to see the burly form and mustached face out of yesterday.

"Tonio! How wonderful to see you. How much better than our last meeting."

The man smiled. "Indeed, *signorina*," he agreed. "I kept the spirit of the Camorrists together while Generoso grew well again. I came to appreciate what it takes to be a leader of men."

He strode away and she returned to her work. The sun grew hot and a siesta was called. Paul came to sit with her in the shade of the storeroom. His eyes were quietly caring and her hand reached out to his and her head leaned against his shoulder. He could make the world a peaceful place just by being there. Her eyes lifted to take in the boyish face and hazel eyes that held so much understanding. A rare person indeed, a person to love. *Oh, God,* she cried silently, unable to keep the anguish out of her eyes. Paul picked it up at once, as he had so often caught her thoughts.

"In time, my darling, all in time," he soothed gently. He rose and left her, and she stared at the walls. In time, her thoughts echoed bitterly. There wasn't enough time in the world. She loved Paul, felt the wondrous, sweet longing for him whenever she saw him. She loved his caring, his understanding, his wise tenderness. She loved his quiet humor, the gentle wryness he used with people to make a point, to brighten a moment. An understanding man. What more could anyone ask? She could list all the reasons for love, and he fulfilled each in his own way.

Marina pressed her eyes closed. There was no list for Generoso. She had only to think of him and there was nothing else. It was not just the sweetness of things lost or the patina of remembrance. It was real, vivid, undeniable. In his throbbing vibrancy she came alive as with no one else. His quiet strength was far different from Paul's, yet no less gentle. When she was with Generoso the world was no wider than the circle of his arms.

She opened her eyes and her lips grew tight, not in anger but in a bitter realization. Choose, decide, know what to deny—how could she merely by thinking about it? She had an abundance of reasons for love, each and every one of them real, each beyond questioning. She had to take another way—was it a coward's way, she asked herself. Perhaps, and yet perhaps it was the only way. She would let the body give its answers where the mind refused. She would let the senses give their own wisdom where reason faltered. There was more than one way to knowing. Paul would be a completion of things unfinished, Generoso a renewal. The senses held the answers hidden in their locked vaults, mocking reason and laughing at her attempts to assign love by the mind. She pulled herself to her feet and returned to her task. It was the only way.

When the darkness came and when the camp grew still, she sought out Paul, creeping past the light that glowed from the candle in Generoso's building. She had seen Paul go into a doorway at the far end of the semicircle of houses. He spoke out of the darkness as she stepped to the doorway.

"Marina," she heard him say. "I've been waiting for you." She sank down beside him, her hand reaching out, touching bare skin, his chest.

"How did you know I would come?" she asked, feeling him move as his shoulders lifted.

"I knew," he replied simply. "Or perhaps I hoped so much that it was the same as knowing." She let her hand run down his chest, down to his abdomen. The bareness did not stop. She reached further, heard her small gasp at his nakedness, and then his mouth was upon her, seeking her breasts, finding them. Tenderness, sweet fire, soft caresses, and she responded, giving again as she had given to him in the little stone cottage. But this time he did not hold back and she felt the new eagerness, the thirsting wonder burst from him, his body arching and his lips groaning a paean of ecstasy. She was an explorer discovering a new land, and a breathtaking warmth encompassed her as his touch, so gentle yet so strong, turned the night into an endless sigh. When the moment came again, it was again new, again wondrous, and she felt him tremble against her and finally lay quiet, his head on her breast.

"Another face of love," he murmured softly. "A reason unto itself." Marina felt warm, the darkness a soft and welcome place. Another face of love indeed, she echoed silently. He turned and sat up on one elbow as the night drew long. "Go now, my darling. Go as you came, silent in the night, before the dawn and other eyes intrude on what was ours."

She rose, resting on both knees, and put on clothes quickly. His hand reached up and touched her face. "We teach when we least know we teach. Go, my darling." Marina rose and slipped from the house, then hurried along the dark structures to her room. She heard a horse sputter and paw the ground as she lay down to sleep till morning sounds came to wake her.

She washed and brushed her hair until it gleamed black light and then went outside. She saw at least twenty-five horses, the new band of Camorrists crowded into the main building. "Two more groups will come," she heard a voice at her elbow say as Tonio leaned toward her. "One later today. The other, from Lombardy, not till the morning."

Good, Marina thought. She wanted one more night. She had risen feeling warm all over, a deep happiness surrounding her like a shawl. But she needed the night. She was not failing each a little, she told herself. She was gathering commitment. Knowing had to come before giving. She put away her thoughts and watched the new arrivals as they came from the briefing Generoso had given them. She was sent to rub down their horses, along with some of the younger men in the camp. She heard their talk of campaigns, rights returned, injustices amended. These men did not boast. There was no vainglory in their talks, only hope and a kind of sadness. Each, in his own way, had learned the price of being a rebel, of chasing a dream.

It was nearly dark when Generoso called to her as she finished a piece of chicken by the fire. He brought her into his quarters, to a map spread on the table. "We are here," he explained. "There is a shortcut down from the mountains to the west."

"To the west?" Marina frowned. "That will bring us out behind the count's forces. He will be marching south by now. How can you reach the villa before him?"

"We won't," Generoso said. "It would be a mistake to try to defend the villa even if we could reach it first. It is what he expects. Secondly, the advantages would be all theirs—numbers, methods of attack, movement. They could well pin us down until we had to try to break out for food or water, then slaughter us." Generoso's eyes narrowed, his thoughts leaping ahead as he spoke to her. "No, the options must be in our hands. We will come up behind them, spread out, strike from both sides and behind. There is a perfect spot, a valley they will pass through. We can catch up to them before they enter it, I'm sure."

"*Are* you sure?" Marina asked.

He laughed. "No, not really. But I think so. It is sometimes bad to be too sure," he replied. His black eyes found hers and grew sober. "We will leave first thing in the morning when the others get here," he told her. She saw the unsaid words in the dark fires of his eyes.

"Then tonight is ours," she remarked. He said nothing and she hurried from the room, afraid that if she stayed a moment longer she'd not leave at all, but the camp was still too full of movement. She went back to the hut she had been given, and her glance roved over the camp, then the fires, three of them now, lighting the area. The second of the bands had arrived and settled in; many of the new men were dragging sleeping gear into the caves. She searched for Paul, but his slender figure was not to be seen. She walked to where she had gone to him in the night, but there was no one there. It was perhaps best, she told herself, but she wondered where he was. In her hut she sat and waited until the fires burned into embers and the camp grew still. She waited, and with each moment that dragged on she hungered, feeling her body grow hot with a volcano of wanting inside her.

It was time, she told herself. The camp was sleeping. She hurried from the room, paused to glance at where Paul stayed, and, seeing no one, went on quickly. Generoso's quarters were shuttered, a wooden blind drawn down, a cloth hung across the entranceway. She pushed it aside and entered. A low candle flickered, just enough light to see him standing bare-chested. The memory of the first time rose up at once, yesterdays rushed back to her, and she felt a stab of fright, as though this moment had been waiting all the time and her destiny never something of her own.

She crossed the room, and his hands pressed her blouse back, pulling it from her, then circled her breasts. Her lips opened for his mouth, drew his tongue into hers as an offering, a promise. The world became electric and all that she had known was hers once again. Born again, she heard herself murmur, made whole again. Made to feel complete again. She felt his nakedness against her and cried out in glorious asking. Strong gentleness and vibrant, throbbing passion he bestowed on her as a supplicant brings offerings. She cried out as he gave, asked, drew from her, and returned. No wanting alone, no body hungers alone resulted in the total ecstasy that was hers. Only that extra measure of love gave passion meaning and turned wanting into rapture.

The night was not long enough, she groaned to herself as she pressed herself to him again and again, finally lying in the cradle of his shoulder exhausted, wanting to stay there forever. "You made love as if there would never be another time," she heard him say softly. She rose on one elbow, returned the half smile that edged his lips.

"It was always that way, or have you forgotten?" she murmured.

He laughed. "You know better." He rose and pulled back the shutter on the window. "The dawn comes," he announced. She pulled on her clothes. His eyes followed her to the door, and now they held a new depth in them, a kind of awareness. She turned away, frowning as she hurried outside and saw the first tint of gray over the mountains. She went to her hut and sank down upon the cushions. She put her head back and softly pounded her fist against the ground. The senses have no wisdom, she cried out in silent bitterness. They have no right to mock reason. They had failed her just as badly, perhaps with more pain. She knew no more than she did before, only that she could respond and give to both. But the mind had told her that much. The nights had only been a confirmation, not an answer.

In Paul's arms, his slender body against hers, his wonderfully tender touch exploring, finding, giving, she knew a sweetness almost too much to bear. Paul was warmth, understanding, comfort, a special kind of peacefulness, a special kind of love. Paul was the world made good.

And Generoso was the world set on fire. Generoso was fulfillment, all wanting satisfied. He was courage and strength: an oak for shelter. In his laughter there was an embrace. In his very presence he fulfilled and encompassed. Generoso demanded and the demand was a gift.

It wasn't fair, Marina cried out silently. You *can* have two loves. You *can* take from each, want from each. She sat up, her angry words turning back on her. She was crying out about not denying herself. Taking and wanting were not love. Giving, that was the key word, and Paul's letter flashed again as a stabbing reminder. She could not give to both, she realized again, unable to look away from truth. It was not a piecemeal thing, this giving. To love was not to apportion, to reserve a part of yourself. And the senses were liars. They promised but did not fulfill. They said trust us, and betrayed that trust. She closed her eyes and gathered the few hours till morning to herself.

CHAPTER FIFTEEN

THE LAST OF THE CAMORRIST bands had arrived when she woke and went outside. She should have felt happiness, excitement at joys refound. But only a leaden pain filled her. She saw Generoso, his red camorra brilliant in the sun, astride his horse as the others mounted up. She found the gray hunter, saddled him, and waited. Paul appeared on his horse, then came to a halt in front of her for a moment. She saw the slow smile that came to touch his lips, only patient understanding in it.

"Did you really think you would find the answer that way?" he asked quietly. She felt her cheeks color, wanted to sputter denials, but saw the uselessness of it in his eyes. She could only shrug and look away. His hand brushed her face as he rode on. She watched him steer his mount to where Generoso waited on a black stallion, then she saw the two men reach out, touch each other's shoulders, and turn to ride slowly from the encampment, side by side.

Marina's eyes pressed shut for a moment and she could not help but think what a strange, mocking happiness was hers. Perhaps one couldn't really have two loves at once, but one could be both blessed and cursed at one time. Certainly she was that. She saw Generoso raise an arm, bring it down again, and the men began to follow. There were perhaps a hundred, now, she estimated. She spurred the gray hunter on, finding a spot near the head of the column where she could see Generoso and Paul as they rode together at the head of the march.

Paul's question, a silent companion, rode with her, and the first moment the column halted she sought him out, knowing that she sounded almost accusing and hating herself for it. He had been only gently knowing and yet the remark had prodded, probed, and finally upset her.

"How does one find answers?" she asked.

It was his turn to shrug, but the gentle smile came again. "One waits," he responded.

"For what?" she pressed.

"For a sign." He turned away to walk to where the others waited. Marina swung into the saddle, her lips drawn down, the answer no answer to her. But thoughts of her dilemma had to be pushed aside as she found she needed all her mental and physical energies to negotiate the mountain shortcut Generoso had told her they would take. It soon became a series of short drops, almost beyond the ability of horse or rider, but these Camorrists were no ordinary horsemen, and she refused to be outdone. The rest of the day went quickly as she concentrated on staying upright. She realized that the precipitous route down through the mountains would take at least two days, perhaps three, from the route southward. It was near dusk when they reached the foot of the mountains and Generoso called a halt to rest. She slid from the saddle, weary and drained. She was near Generoso as he came over to Tonio, squatting down to study the ground.

"Tracks here," she heard him say as he was gesturing along the ground. "They're using wagons as well as marching. These aren't more than a day old."

"Not more," Tonio agreed. "They'll camp for the night, probably. The valley is only a dozen miles on."

Generoso nodded. "How many do you make?" he asked.

Tonio studied the tracks again. "Three wagons, probably mostly supply wagons. I think two hundred men," he replied.

Generoso stood up, his face solemn. "You know how we'll do it, Tonio." The other mart nodded. "We'll go in and out, the shears through the bush."

Tonio nodded again. "I'll instruct those who'll go with me." He strode away.

She saw Generoso turn as his eyes found her. He came over to her. "We'll go on during the night," he said. "They'll be camped about ten miles ahead of where we are now. We will move up closer, then separate into three groups and circle around them. We'll reach the valley and take up positions. By morning, we'll be there waiting. Look after yourself in the dawn," he admonished. "Keep back and out of danger."

Marina went to him, resting her hand against his chest. "I would not have come to the Camorrists for this if I'd known you would face death again for me. I don't want this now. I don't want to see anyone here killed. I don't want to lose the world again."

"There's no other way," Generoso replied.

"There must be. I'll think of one," Marina countered.

He shook his head firmly. "It's too late to turn back now. It's too late and it is wrong. These paid assassins march for men of greed and ruthlessness. They must be stopped. This is the time to do it, the best chance we will have."

Marina turned away without answering, unable to find the words that would convince him differently. Or herself. She sat down with the others as they rested their horses. The time seemed short until Generoso signaled the others to mount. He put a finger to his lips and the Camorrists moved out in silence, no one uttering as much as a cough. The night grew inky as the terrain thickened, the forest closing in around the silent riders. She reined up sharply as the horse in front of her suddenly halted. She saw the rider swing down, then she dismounted as well. They went on again, each Camorrist walking his horse. A dozen yards ahead the men began to move apart to form two columns. When she reached the place, Generoso and Paul sat astride their horses and Generoso motioned for her to fall in with the men gathered behind him. On the other side she saw Tonio motion the rider behind her to his column. A third group stayed behind in a unit and she moved off with the others as Generoso led the way. Soon they were alone, the other column lost in the dark night. She felt the terrain grow into a slope, which fell off to her right and increased as they proceeded. They continued on for perhaps another three miles. "Here," she heard Generoso indicate, and she slid to the ground. Figures were dark shadows in the night around her, but the moon came out for a little while, enough for her to see Generoso and Paul standing together, closer to her than she'd expected.

"Three hours till morning. The valley is in front of us," she heard Generoso remark. "Look to yourself when the dawn comes, my friend."

"And Godspeed to you. It will be good, riding by your side again. Till morning, sleep well."

The moon drifted behind clouds, the figures blended into the darkness. When this was done with, when it was over, she'd go away, she told herself. Reason had given no answers. The senses had failed her. Perhaps time would offer more—time to look for that sign Paul had said she had to wait for. She saw the two figures in her mind again. There was another kind of love that lived here. It was given other words—friendship, loyalty, respect, comradeship—but it was love of a special kind. She'd not destroy that and, if she stayed, sooner or later she'd come between them. She'd not stay to do that, she vowed. She lay back to sleep. Dawn woke her, and through the trees the valley spread out in front of her, startlingly close. On the other side, the land rose again, banked by trees. Tonio and his column were there, she knew, behind leaf-covered fortifications. As she watched, she saw the column of men appear at the end of the valley. A ragged lot, they walked more than marched. She saw three open-sided wagons, one with bales and boxes, the other two with more mercenaries. Her eyes searched, finally picking out Aldo Gamborelli. Beside him appeared the round figure of the duke. Both rode horses just behind the first of the marchers.

Her glance shifted to the left. Through the trees she glimpsed Generoso, and near him Paul, the sun touching the light brown hair that fell carelessly to one side. She saw Generoso swing up onto his horse. Almost as one, the line of Camorrists did the same. She was last into the saddle. She saw Generoso raise his arm, hold it for a moment, then bring it down. Horses flashed forward on either side of her, darting through the trees like silent wraiths. She spurred the hunter on. Generoso was the first to break into the open, Paul close behind him. Her eyes swept to the right and the left and watched the column of riders converge, some with swords unsheathed, others with pistols in hand. They barreled into the startled mercenaries, and suddenly the air resounded with shots and cries and the clash of cutlasses. From the other side of the valley, she saw Tonio racing down with his men, firing as they came, drawing together to slice through the forward line of mercenaries.

Generoso's riders, on the other side now, wheeled, came back again, and Tonio's column did the same. She understood the shears, now, for they sliced back and forth into the mercenaries. She wheeled her horse and ducked low as a shot winged past her head. The mercenaries had been badly hurt already, the ground littered with their dead and wounded, but they began to gather themselves and focused on fighting back. She saw horses being rushed up and the count's men leaping onto their backs to carry the battle in a counterattack.

Her eyes swept the scene of carnage, peering through gunpowder and over upended wagons. The mercenaries were pulling themselves together. She saw a platoon bring up long lances, mount their steeds, and charge. Her glance caught the small round dismounted figure, pressed against the side of one of the overturned wagons, crouching in terror. She searched for Aldo Gamborelli but failed to find him. A sharp sound from behind the last wagon made her swivel. A smaller group of Camorrists raced out of the trees to attack from behind. It was a final blow from the unexpected. She saw the mercenaries wheel, turn again, unsure of which way to charge. Others came to join the knot of lance-carrying horsemen, and with a shout, more of desperation than courage, they charged forward in an effort to break out of the trap.

Marina raced her horse after them and saw Generoso holding a thin figure at gunpoint, saw the flash of pale, colorless eyes in the sun. He did not see the charging mercenaries racing up behind him, lances thrust forward. Marina screamed, but she did not hear herself in the explosion of gunfire and the cries of battle. She screamed again, but Generoso was too far away to hear. She saw him turn, almost too late, to see the lances charging at him. Then Marina saw the other horseman racing from the side, his sand-colored hair flying in the wind. Generoso avoided the first lance, ducking away from it, and knocked the second aside with his arm. But the horsemen were too many. He dove from the saddle as a lance speared the air where he'd been but a second before.

Generoso hit the ground, rolled, and avoided horses' hooves. Marina saw one of the mercenaries wheel and bring his lance up to pin the figure on the ground, a second doing the same. A third figure leaped from the flying horse into the lance that flew downward, sending it harmlessly to the right. Then, as she heard herself scream, she saw the second lance hurtle into the figure, virtually splitting his back in two. Paul's slender body lay still on the ground, the lance still in his back.

Marina fell from the saddle. She lay for a moment, shaking her head, hearing her sobs gasping out, and then she was on her feet, racing forward. Generoso pulled the lance out of Paul's back and flung it into one of the other mercenaries, then picked up another fallen lance and fired that after a fleeing rider. Marina fell to her knees beside the slender form, cradled his head against her. She wanted to find words but found only sobs. His hand came up to close around her arm and his eyes opened, his lips forming a smile. He twitched, a stab of pain stiffening his body for an instant, and then he fell back against her. She saw the smile return to his lips.

"You see, my darling. You just wait for a sign," he said.

"No," Marina cried out. "Oh, no, no."

His hand tightened on her arm—a silent admonition. "A sign," he whispered again. "Perhaps I had been chosen and I turned away."

"You can't say that. You don't know, no one knows." Marina sobbed, brushing back the lock of light brown hair that still insisted on tumbling over one eye. He moved his head in gentle disagreement.

"Straight, with crooked lines," he whispered. "Straight, with crooked lines …"

His voice trailed away. A shadow passed her face and Marina glanced up and saw the hand reach down, not to her but to Paul's fingers in a bronze grip. Marina saw the hazel eyes hold hers for a moment longer, then close, only the gentle smile staying. The scream came, but it was all inside her; it found no voice, and her body shuddered in a violent spasm. She was unable to move or see. In fact, she could barely breathe. Hands pressed her shoulders, lifted her, and turned her away. The valley had grown so still, so deathly still, she thought almost idly. A horse whinnied nearby, a voice cried out in the distance, but somehow they did not break the stillness.

Generoso walked beside her to a place at the side of the valley. She sank to the ground and he knelt at her side. Hollow and numb, anguish too consuming to accept, she felt the need to ask about the commonplace, the practical. Another sign, perhaps, she thought. We must be able to escape our emotions, or be overwhelmed by them. She heard her voice as though it belonged to someone passing by.

"It's over now," she remarked.

"It's over," Generoso replied.

The stranger seemed to consider the fact for a moment, and accepted it. "Aldo Gamborelli?" she asked almost casually.

"Alive, bound hand and foot, along with the Duke d'Albatore," Generoso informed her. "They wanted visible proof of the plot. They will surely have it now."

Marina nodded solemnly, calmly, and as suddenly as she had come, the passerby vanished, the calmness tearing apart as the truth exploded again in all its singular horror.

"I don't believe it. It didn't happen," Marina cried out, feeling Generoso's hand tighten on her arm. "No, it didn't," she called out again. She searched his black eyes for support but found none. "I don't believe in signs," she said bitterly. "You don't believe in them, do you?" she flung out, as a child demands to be corrected.

"I believe there are reasons why things happen as they do," Generoso said. "I believe there are things meant for us to see and others not for us to know."

"Straight with crooked lines?" she retorted angrily.

The black eyes did not yield. "You are here beside me, and that is as it should be. After all that has happened, you are here," he said simply.

Marina felt herself nod, understanding the simple fact as not a simple fact at all but a confirmation, a victory. "I will never forget, as I could never forget you," she said.

She felt his hand close over her arm. "I would not want it otherwise," she heard him say. "He is part of our tomorrows, our happiness."

"Take me home, Generoso," Marina said softly. It had a nice sound, a right sound, the sound of something that was meant to be. A sign indeed.